SADDLING MAHMOUD

Sebastian Bell

the book publishing company

the book publishing company

Published by the Book Publishing Company Limited
Registered in England company number 5234211

www.thebookpublishingcompany.com

Set in 11/14.5pt Bembo
Designed by Justina Leitão and Mark Buckingham
Printed in Great Britain by The Bath Press

A CIP catalogue record for this book is available from the British Library

ISBN 0 9549007 0 7

SADDLING MAHMOUD

Chapter one

At some point we leave the map. It's not a matter of falling off the edge, not exactly. But still. The three of us – two grown-ups up front, Charlie strapped in in the back.

Just off the motorway, we head cross country on the back roads. True back roads, winding, deserted. If we get it right, we take the one over the top of the wooded hill and if the day is anywhere halfway decent, this is the best bit of the whole journey, especially if the sun is shining. The road twists back on itself a couple of times as it heads up the hill, the light beneath the canopy of trees a luxuriant, almost aquatic green. In springtime, there are carpets of bluebells beneath the trees and, fleetingly glimpsed through breaks in the greenery, the odd woodland clearing bathed in golden light. On the downward side, the road ahead is splashed with dappled light and on one section which seems to stretch for ever, a cathedral-like vastness opens out in front of you beneath arching trees – monumental trees, epic trees, a vastness made vaster by slanting beams of sunlight. In the distance, there's a bright O where the tunnel ends. It's all too perfect, like a painting, except a painting will never make you *feel* this space, will never give you this sense of awe, this sense of charmed perfection, this hushed and magnificent architecture of dense and dark green, these slanting sunbeams, these delicate, ephemeral streaks of golden yellow.

And on down the hill, as you emerge from the tunnel of trees, there's a brief panorama of the most perfect countryside, flattish, lightly wooded, a patchwork jumble of picturesque fields with low hills in the distance; then it's all obscured as we sink beneath the high hedgerows. We seem to swoop, the car gaining momentum, wildflowers in the hedges blurred to streaks of colour and white traceries of Queen Anne's Lace.

Beth: "There's a T junction ahead. Left or right?"

Me: "I've told you already."

Beth: "No you haven't."

Me: "I did. I did. Two minutes ago."

Beth: "No you didn't."

Me: "I'm telling you I did."

Beth: "You didn't."

This could go on forever, obviously. Sometimes it feels as if it does, even though we're both half-joking.

"Left or right?"

I tell her (not, I would argue, for the first time) to go right.

She goes left.

She goes left and she drives like a demon; but this is so obviously not the right way: the hedgerows are thinning and we're heading into a mangy flatland of featureless, dun-coloured open fields. It's a diseased landscape, scabby, fly-blown.

And we're fading. We're becoming a line drawing, clean and delicate. A pencil drawing, simple, light grey, almost transparent.

This is how it starts, I suppose. This is exactly how it starts. This hiss and this crackle.

Or no, actually... first a spring-loaded click and the stylus arm lifts delicately, trembling yet all-too-ponderously mechanical, driven by internal cogs and gears you can just about hear revolving modestly in the inner workings. There will be half a dozen or so singles stacked onto the tall spindle and held in place by a dog-leg retaining arm – and now, with the stylus arm on its way, one of the records will flop down onto the turntable. The stylus arm will then arrive with an over-fastidious precision, a precision that is also slightly jerky, like the way street mime artists do "Robot".

And now it comes. A moment of anticipation. Then the hiss and the crackle as the stylus settles.

***

Or I'm at my parent's house and mother is showing me a photograph. An old photograph. A dog-eared old monochrome of uncle Tom (I recognise him immediately: how could I not?) astride a tractor.

"Bet you don't know who that is."

She doesn't mean uncle Tom. Clearly. She means the infant on his lap. The infant he's helping to "drive" the tractor.

Actually, the truth is, this starts on a Monday. Because Monday morning I was up at the crack of dawn and at my desk, in good order, in record time. Which was just as well because I'd hardly settled myself when the phone rang and it was Robbie on the other end.

"Robbie," I said.

"What you doing?"

"Now?"

"Yes. Now."

"Oh, you know," I said. "This and that."

"Got something you might be interested in. Fancy popping in? How quickly can you get here?"

"Half and hour. An hour. You know."

"Okay, we'll nip out for some lunch."

Lunch? I thought. Are you mad? "Why, what time is it?"

"Eleven thirty."

"Wow. Jeez. Er, look Robbie, that's going to be a little difficult."

"Okay," he said. "Whatever. Do you have today's FT?"

I did. I generally do. Someone once told me that freelance journalists tend to take the FT and so I started taking it even though I'd be lying if I said I read absolutely every single word, absolutely every single day.

"Page 23."

"Got it."

"Article on e-cinema."

"Got it."

The headline reads: **Film industry cries 'cut' over e-cinema**

"What I'm looking for," says Robbie, "is a feature, a *Reports of the Death of Celluloid have been Greatly Exaggerated*, sort of a piece. You up for it?"

I make a sound like the sound of a person laughing. "That's good Robbie.

Can I use that?"

So yes, that's probably where this begins.

Two immediate thoughts. One, that Robbie is up to something. Secondly, that this is all very inconvenient. I'd have to call Jules and rearrange, which he probably wasn't going to like.

The one thing you learn early on where Robbie is concerned is that nothing is ever straightforward. There's nothing malicious in it – but mind games of some sort are usually involved. There is a subtext here and it's probably advisable to work out what it is.

Not six months ago I punted a piece to Robbie about the death of celluloid and he actually made it the cover story of one of his magazines. Digital- or e-cinema is a sophisticated form of the technology they use to project TV pictures onto big screens so whole pubfuls of people can watch football matches. In the past, the picture quality has always been a bit fuzzy and the technology was never in a million years good enough to project pin-sharp images within the warehouse immensities of big mainstream cinemas – or even, for that matter, in the cabaret-theatre intimacies that honeycomb your average multiplex.

But that is or was changing. The technology was coming on, leaps and bounds. And if projection could be achieved digitally, that would also have immense implications for distribution too. So, back in the autumn, when the new improved e-cinema technologies were first unveiled at a trade fair in the States, I'd done that first piece for Robbie. It was all about how the whole busi-

ness of cinema would change subtly when distributors no longer had to deliver cans of celluloid film to thousands of cinemas and instead just pushed a button or clicked a mouse and sent the whole thing down fibre optic cables. It was about structure and economics but it was also about how the whole business would *feel* so different. It was, I suppose, an elegy to the power and the beauty of the celluloid experience – which was especially odd because I don't actually go to the cinema very often these days.

Now, obviously, with the reports of the demise of celluloid being exaggerated and everything, Robbie wanted to rub my nose in it. Or something.

Which was fine by me.

So I called Jules.

"Jules," I said.

And I must have caught him at an awkward moment because he said nothing. Nothing coherent at any rate. I could tell he was excited about something. Because all I could hear was this panting for breath – a sort of asthmatic inability to get his words out.

"Coats," he spills eventually.

"Jules."

"Coats. Did you hear me? Coats," he insists.

"Jules," I repeat. "Are you okay?"

"Coats, for gods' sake, coats." He's almost hyperventilating with enthusiasm. So it would be pointless trying to steamroller him; and really it's best to be patient when he goes off on one. Trust me. Jules is – or will be soon – my business partner. And every now and then he thinks he has a bright idea. Like, for instance:

Coats. Yes, coats. Eventually, he is able to explain. The idea came to him while reading a short story by Chekhov or Gogol, he can't remember which, but that's not important anyway. He's just realised how BIG coats are. They have a sort of metaphysical or archetypal significance. And maybe they're a bit like noses in Tristram Shandy – they're a sort of joke, probably a rather crude joke, that you can't quite put your finger on.

Yes. And?

Well, the point is, how many coats do you ever buy in your life? Not many, he reckons. And the thing is, they all have significance for us. They're special garments, coats are.

"No, think about it, really, how many coats have you ever bought? Proper coats. Substantial coats. Not anoraks or raincoats or cagouls or heavy jackets. Coats. Overcoats. Grown-up, no-holds-barred, old-fashioned, button-up-the-front coats."

I think for a minute and he can hear me thinking so he doesn't push me. The answer, I think, is three. It seems a rather pathetic answer. The one I had as a teenager was a grey ex West German airforce greatcoat bought in an army surplus store on Leith Walk in Edinburgh. And then, when I got my first job in London, I bought a really smart navy blue overcoat with a wonderfully silky lining that was a sumptuous royal blue when you looked at it from certain angles and black when you looked at it from others. I bought it at Austin Reed and it cost what was at that time, for me, an absolute fortune. I slowly but surely trashed it over a decade, dumping it unceremoniously on the floors of grubby pubs and leaving it behind at parties. I probably still have it somewhere – but it's a miracle if I do.

Not long after I'd bought that smart coat (and obviously having decided that I had reached that time in your life when you may presume to own two coats), I acquired another one. It was a truly awful coat and I bought it off a stall in Camden market. I really liked the look of the material, which had a sort of irregular, grey and black distorted herringbone pattern with flecks of colour through it; and I really liked the feel of it too – it was sort of coarse and rugged. I realised right away when I tried it on that it was a bit lopsided, with one shoulder pad far bigger than the other, but I thought I'd get away with it and it would be a good coat to hack about in at the weekends. It was, after all, very cheap.

I only wore it half-a-dozen times because it just made people laugh.

"I don't know," I lied. "And anyway, it's no good asking me. I don't count, do I? I mean, you know how I dress. I'm hardly going to be typical am I?"

"How many?" Jules persisted.

"Half a dozen."

"You see. And I bet you can tell me this really interesting little story about each of them."

"So? What's the point here?"

"The point is, you could do a biography of someone in terms of their coats. It would just cut through all the crap."

"So you want to do a series of pieces – *Coats Of The Rich And Famous.*"

"I'm just saying that..."

"Because if you're rich and famous you've probably got hundreds of coats. You probably haven't worn half of them. And who's going to read about the coats of the poor and anonymous?"

"You're missing the point here."

Probably. I tend to do that.

I can sense he's disappointed in me – and I sometimes wish I didn't do this. Or, to be more accurate, didn't *have* to do this. I am always the first person to point out why something won't work.

"Go on then," I add, to ease us away from this impasse. "How many have you had then?"

"Four," he says flatly.

So I put the phone down without telling Jules what I needed to tell him – that we'll probably have to reschedule the big meeting we had planned. The truth is that me and Jules are on the verge of reinventing ourselves. We are about to incorporate ourselves as a limited company, which will aim to provide a wide range of services targeted upon the publishing industry.

I wanted to call it Ferret Factory in memory of the name a group of us chose at school when we were plotting a scurrilous and extremely top secret satirical magazine on school life. But Jules vetoed that idea, probably with good reason, arguing that Ferret Factory sounded adolescent and jokey. Which was rich, because his notion (stealing my factory theme and trying to appropriate it as his own) was The Features Factory.

Oh yes, says I. Does it manufacture false noses?

Actually the problem with The Features Factory is that it's too boring and generic. It aspires to do exactly what it says on the tin. And we want to push the tin. We want to take this thing outside the tin. We want to *supersede* the tin. Don't we?

But our catalogue of ideas is going well. By the end of the month, I reckon we'll have a fat "book" to tout round various magazines and newspapers. The jewel is our 100 Motels idea, which we're actually going to go ahead and produce ourselves so that someone can basically buy it off the shelf, a more or less finished article that just needs tweaking to fit different page formats.

What I haven't told Jules is that I've been touting the piece on and off for eighteen months or so. I have faith though. It was one of those ideas that, at the time, at the point of conception, you know just can't fail.

The point of conception was early one morning at Gatwick Airport. This was ages ago – pre-Charlie, obviously. Me and Beth had arrived ludicrously early (I'm a real worrier: I want to check in two *days* rather than two hours in advance of departure time) and we were having breakfast in the airside cafeteria. The whole hospitality zone was evidently run by Granada Group, the same people who bring you the last word in luxury and comfort when it comes to motorway service stations. We knew this because on our cafeteria table, slotted into a little perspex display base, there was a laminated card outlining the extent of the group's network of service station motels.

Motels? Crikey. We knew about Granada and service stations but the motel development was surely new. Up until then, service stations had surely just been fags and mags and tea and sandwiches. But now you could stay the night. All over Britain there they were, these new *travelstops*.

The idea of which we loved, naturally.

And so we began to develop the idea. And it began to snowball. It became epic. It developed in that mood of hysteria ("yes, yes, yes, and…") that can only spring from a mixture of boredom and nervous anticipation – because although Beth doesn't share my phobia about missing trains and planes, she is, on the other hand, a nervous flier. We got fits of giggles about it, giggles that lasted onto the plane, all through the flight and for days afterwards at the other end. In our heads, the 100 Motels production became a sublimely awful mock heroic road movie, a life-changing experience, a voyage of discovery into the dark heart (or was it the soft underbelly?) of the homogenised, top-down, workstation-designed, injection-moulded plastic age.

This would write itself. There was a book here, yes, but this was also, at the very least, the sort of 10,000 word article that the weekend colour review sections would jump at. It could even be a series of articles. This would fly. It would say so much about us, us as a country or a culture or whatever, in the modern world. It would be whimsical and quirky, a fascinating take on one of life's bizarre little nooks and crannies. And we loved the dry, witty, ferociously ironic Post Modern conceit at the heart of this – that you should take something banal, irredeemably flimsy, laughably beneath contempt, and discover in it something surreal yet fascinating, rich and strange. It could be like something out of Hunter S Thompson. No, okay, maybe not Hunter S Thompson. We'd never pull that off. It would be like Paul Theroux or Bill Bryson. Witty, ironic, bad tempered, scathing. And more. Insightful. The truth is – and this is no inverted snobbery – I'm actually fascinated by these sorts of places. Airports and hotel lobbies, shopping malls. Semi-public spaces. Transit zones. It's here that the façade – the stage flat – is at its thinnest.

"You and Colin could do it."

"Take two weeks off," she'd said.

"Buy a crap old car. You'd have to have problems with the car. As a running joke, I mean, in the article."

"Colin would be up for it. He really would."

Colin, you will have gathered, is an old friend. I can't really remember why it didn't happen in the end; and come to think of it, it's almost a year since we last saw Colin. The trip didn't even reach the basic planning stage though I seem to remember having great fun pretending to plan it. Colin loved the idea – but on the other hand, right from the start I realised we were both treating it as a joke. A fantasy exercise. I'm not sure that matters. It exists, that's the point. The whole production. It not only exists, it's brilliant. It exists in arguably its purest state – not just in my head or Beth's or Colin's, but somewhere in between.

Some of the editors I deal with understand this perfectly. They see me as this great spoofer – a satirist, almost, of their world. They think I come up with wacky ideas just to amuse them and we can all have a laugh about it because no-one in the right mind would actually go ahead and commission them. They never even have to say, "No, but seriously." We just have a laugh. The annoying thing (I suppose it annoys Beth the most) is that I know people who could pull it off. They could sell the 100 Motels idea. They could do it. They really could.

Ferret Features, for instance.

But the point is. The main point. The thing I want to tell Jules at our meeting, whenever it actually takes place, is that I've realised we need to include a third partner. A photographer. Probably Colin. In fact, yes, Colin. Colin needs to be in on this, he really does.

But basically Jules will be furious that I've taken on a new brief. I mean taken it on in a personal capacity rather than selling us in as Ferret Features. Or whatever.

So yes. That's how it starts. With the crackly preamble to a piece of music. The particular record player I have in mind is (or more accurately was) a flimsy piece of equipment. There were three knobs: volume, balance and tone. The

tone range went from tinny to very tinny indeed. Father's LP featuring Herb Alpert and the Tijuana Brass sometimes sounded like a swarm of wasps in pursuit of a mosquito.

The diameter of the turntable was a fraction over seven inches, so when you played an LP, it looked just plain wrong. Unnatural. There was room for it alright, the pivot for the cartridge arm was more than 12 inches away from the spindle. But as you were about to put an LP on, it didn't look as if there was going to be room. It looked like one of those classic mismatches in scale, like a grown man on a children's bicycle.

And the automatic mechanism didn't work with LPs either. You couldn't stack a handful of them up as you could with singles. The first one (though it tended to flop down in an unconvincing manner) would play alright; but not the second and especially not the third. They wouldn't grip one on top of the other and there'd be this swishing, slipping sound as the plastic surfaces slid over each other, failing to grip, and the music came out all woozy. I don't think you were really meant to use the automatic mechanism for LPs.

This record player sat on the dining room sideboard – a substantial piece of furniture from a heroic age, evidently once an altar from a Dark Ages church or an armaments chest from the captain's cabin of a Tudor man of war. Come to think of it, it was in itself almost the size of Tudor man of war.

And because this was in the dining room and it just didn't seem right sitting at the dining room table listening to records, you tended to stand up, leaning against the sideboard. It was rather like (I now realise) standing at a saloon bar, except that sometimes you'd let yourself slump over to get your head right in front of one of the speakers.

There was a biscuit barrel on top of one of these speakers. There were never any biscuits in it – its ceramic inner lining had been shattered and though there had been an attempt to reassemble the pieces and glue them together within the wooden skin of the barrel, there was a piece missing, a triangular piece shaped like a long tusklike shard. There were all sorts of odds and ends in the barrel. I can't remember what exactly. The usual

domestic detritus probably – buttons, keys, coins, pins, books of matches, broken cufflinks, one half of a pair of nail scissors. Often, the contents of the barrel would rattle and buzz in sympathetic resonance with the music. Some records were worse than others for this. Don't ask me which ones.

It's probably at this point that it comes to me. Or no, that's not quite right. It doesn't in fact *come to me* at this point because I realise that it has been around for a while already. It has already slipped by a couple of times at a tangent. And when it hasn't been slipping by it has been lurking somewhere in the periphery of my vision. What I'm doing now is just acknowledging it. And *it* is this: I know exactly what I'm going to do with this feature. Robbie's e-cinema brief. It is going to be unprecedented. It is, in fact, going to be huge.

So I call Jules. I call Jules and this time I get a word in edgeways.

"Jules. What I meant to say earlier is that we'll have to reschedule."

"Got a new brief?"

"Yeah, sort of. It's an insult, actually."

"Turn it down."

"I don't like to."

"Oh well. Just remember. Coats."

"Jules."

"Huh?"

"Be serious."

"See you."

"We'll have to talk photographers at some point too."

"Yeah, okay. See you."

"There's someone I have in mind."

"Yeah. Okay."

"Actually."

"What?"

"Actually, I've just thought."

"What? What is it?"

"Doesn't matter."

Chapter two

And then again, we come over the hill – two grown-ups in the front, Charlie in the back – through the cathedral-like tunnel of trees with slanting sunbeams, emerging to descend between high hedgerows.

To the junction.

"Left or right?"

"I've already told you."

"You didn't."

"For god's sake it was you who asked me. A couple of minutes ago."

"Well, I don't remember."

"How can you possibly forget? It was like two minutes ago. You know. One. Two. Not a big number."

This could go on forever, obviously.

"Left or right?"

I tell her, not for the first time, right.

She goes left.

Except this time, instead of driving like a demon, she drives hesitantly and then, eventually, stops.

"Should we turn round?"

And of course I fold my arms and say nothing. There's a strained silence – but not for long because, inevitably, Charlie starts crying.

"Great," says Beth.

Oh, great.

Actually, Charlie isn't exactly crying. It's more of a whimper, her lips pursed. Most of the way, she's been asleep, strapped into her car seat in the back – now I wonder how long she's been awake, listening. Does she listen? I mean obviously she hears the sound of our voices. But how much does she understand? Or is this an atmosphere thing? I don't suppose you'd have to be hugely sensitive to be upset at the sound of raised voices.

"Look," says Beth, pointedly showing restraint. "Do we want to get there or do we not?"

The big idea for the feature, the one I was going to write for Robbie, was to take a film, any film, any classic film from the far-off days. The 1930s say. A classic 1930s film. British, of course. Any classic British 1930s film – and trace its story. I mean its story as a piece of celluloid. We find someone who still owned an original print and we find out who else had owned this original print down the years and how it had changed hands and generally what had happened to it.

This came to me almost fully formed. It happens sometimes. Not the story necessarily, I'm not saying *that* came to me fully formed, but the plot, the structure. And I'm not being entirely honest when I say any classic British 1930s film. Right from the start, in fact from before the start, there was only one film in mind.

I wouldn't be able to use this, obviously, but one of the most disturbing things I just happen to know about The 39 Steps is the fact that Alfred Hitchcock plotted it in his pyjamas. They might have been specially tailored blue silk pyjamas. But still. I've never felt particularly comfortable in the company of portly men in their pyjamas. Not that I've been in the company of many men in their pyjamas; but some portly men, with the propensity to sweat, are definitely worth avoiding, even with all their clothes on.

The even-worse thing about pyjamas is that there's always a danger of your bits dangling out, no matter how vigilant you are. And just how vigilant are you going to be once you've had a couple of cocktails with your writing team?

In the mid-1930s, Hitchcock worked as much as he could from home, which at this point was a flat he was renting at 153 Cromwell Road – he liked to get on with things far away from the interference of studio executives and it also allowed him to indulge a taste for working at odd hours, in relative

comfort. And of course Hitchcock was the sort of man who loved people to come to him. By definition, film directors thrive on power games – and Hitchcock, an uncharitable puppetmaster at the best of times, was no exception. He liked to hold court and he needed things to happen on his terms.

He also liked unsettling people, which in part explains the way he behaved when people came to visit – even the people he was relying on to get this latest project off the ground and on whom his career (by no means settled at this point) depended. He offered carefully contrived chaos; and it was sometimes like the set of a Marx Brothers film up there. Pandemonium. Writers would be summoned at odd hours for important script conferences only to find that there was a cocktail party in full swing or they would be shown through to the dining room and find themselves shuffled in among the guests at a dinner party. Even on a quiet night they'd no sooner taken their coats off than they'd be given a drink (a cocktail, naturally) and they'd be ushered through to the living room where all sorts of people they'd never met before were hanging around, left-overs perhaps from the meeting that had gone before or early arrivals for the one that would follow. Who knew? People were always dropping in and out and by any normal standards most meetings would be completely unstructured and undisciplined, starting with film industry gossip, ending in general chatter, with seemingly nothing in between. Hitchcock all the while in his blue silk pyjamas. People would often leave in the wee small hours, slightly smashed, asking each other if they'd actually got anything done. Some of the writers he worked with fretted that nothing would *ever* get done in this sort of informal atmosphere.

Were they mouldy and stale? Or freshly laundered? The pyjamas, I mean. Were they sewn up?

But actually, compared to other films of that period, the dangerous blue silk period was negligible on The 39 Steps. Hitchcock and his main writer, Charles Bennett, developed an extremely detailed treatment of the story while on a skiing holiday with their wives in St Moritz over Christmas 1934. The serious pyjama work came right at the end of pre-production when, back in London, the dramatist Ian Hay was brought in to polish up the dialogue. And, for reasons we can only guess at, he didn't mess about – he got the job done to everyone's satisfaction in only a matter of days. Which was just as well, as studio time had been booked and they hadn't even got around to hiring the cast.

The 39 Steps, starring Robert Donat and Jane Baxter. Until Jane Baxter realised she couldn't get out of a commitment to join the cast of a play entitled *Drake*. At which point the film became The 39 Steps starring Robert Donat and Anna Lee. Until, following contractual wrangles of her own, and only two days before principal photography was due to begin, Lee also pulled out.

They flew by the seats of their pyjamas in those days.

The article in my head was simple and clear and linear. This was its profound beauty. The previous piece I'd done for Robbie had been full of dry speculation about the importance of celluloid as historical artefact – all sorts of dull but worthy quotes from worthy but dull industry insiders and cultural commentators. Would it matter if, in the none-too-distant future, the classic productions of the cinematic artform were stored only in digital format? Did we need to safeguard celluloid as the primarily reference source? Did that actually matter? Did anyone care?

This new piece was going to be a story, a true story. It would start in a film archive. Probably Carlton's, because they owned the film, having acquired it when they bought the whole of the Rank Films library. Carlton would also be a good place to start because they also owned Technicolor, a company that knew a thing or two about celluloid. So yes, Carlton's film archives. This is where the journey was to begin. In a dusty vault somewhere, with rack upon rack of canisters full of coiled celluloid. Or hang on, it might not be a vault, it might actually be an ultra clean room – a whole floor, maybe – of a tall building with great views out across a city. There are still racks, though. You have to have racks, whether you're in a vault or on the ultra modern floor of some tall building somewhere. So, anyway, I'm looking down a long vista between

two racks that reach right up to the ceiling. Their receding perspective frames a girl. A woman actually, a woman in her late 20s maybe, in a light summer dress and a cardigan. A slightly retro look but not unfashionable. It appears as if she's leaning out into airy nothingness but she's actually leaning with her shoulder to the glass.

Yes. Yes of course. It's one of those glass skinned buildings. We see the girl in profile. She's melancholy. She's looking out. Out and downwards. Seeing but not seeing. She's in partial silhouette.

She's taking a break. And anyway this is a quiet part of the floor, the one most likely to be inhabited by daydreamers. She's archivist of the 1918-39 section and, if I'm lucky, she's just about to give me a name and an address.

I call the main Carlton Communications switchboard number and ask to be put through to the press office. The switchboard girl seems as sceptical as she is bored. She asks me who I am and what I want and then she tells me to hold. All the press office lines are engaged. And so, yes, yes okay, I hold. And hold. And while I hold, I listen to the theme tune from Inspector Morse. Again and again and again. Round and round it goes. One of Carlton's production companies made Morse.

And actually, it's giving me another idea for a feature. It's another of those technology-meets-slightly-marginal-and-yet-utterly-familiar-content explorations. Another report back from the communications interzone. The big question will be: Who chooses the music? Obviously, where lifts and lobbies and retail environments are concerned there's the Muzak Corporation or whatever they're called, who do everything, from installing the system hardware to market research on what sort of music is going to put your clientele in the right sort of mood.

But phone systems are different aren't they? A few years ago it used to be plonky, synthesised Bach or Für Elise played on one of Rolf Harris's used Stylophones. You'd hear the same options again and again, no matter who you were calling. These days, though, it's obviously hooked up to a CD player plugged into the main company switchboard – because with companies you call regularly you hear different stuff every day.

So who chooses the music? Is it left to the guys on reception? And if so, what are the implications? How *wrong* is it possible to get this? What does the choice tend to say about the company you're calling?

Because while I'm thinking all of this, it also occurs to me that I know someone who was sacked by British Rail, as was, for playing I Hear My Train A' Coming by Jimi Hendrix over the public address system one morning during the rush hour at Virginia Water station. Stockbroker belt. Hendrix. Full blast. Just in little bursts when each train was due. He'd locked himself in the announcers' sentry box thing down there on the platform and they had to break the door down to get him out.

The operator breaks in.

"Do you still want to hold?"

Yes. Yes I do.

I always say this even if I don't really want to hold. Actually, what I say is, "Yes, I'll hold for a little while," as if hinting that they'll lose me if they don't get a move on and then they'll be sorry.

The Morse music again from the start. That fraudulently plaintive guitar. And then the music is silenced. There's an eerie absence of sound for a while. An emptiness. And then the burr of the dialling tone kicks in.

Good start. They've cut me off.

It's obvious, now, looking back, why it had to be The 39 Steps. And I don't just mean the coincidental fact that it was there, lurking on the video shelf behind the television in the living room. Because of course in some respects it is no coincidence that it was there, lurking on the shelf in the first place.

There were many reasons why it had to be The 39 Steps – it's just that, at this point, this point of departure, these reasons were all unaware of each other, just as I myself was only vaguely aware of each of them.

Because the truth (veiled though it continued to be at this stage) was that I was once mightily obsessed with The 39 Steps. Somehow, though, I had forgotten that fact. Or at the very least I had allowed it to become submerged.

It would, I hoped, work like this. The press officer would put me in touch with the archive. And I'd visit the archive and talk to the melancholy archivist with the light summer dress and the faraway eyes. And she'd point me in the direction of a private collector. The private collector will be the one who will tell me the kernel of the story, the golden nugget at its very centre. And this collector will show me a fragment of the past, which we will photograph. Colin will be the one doing the photographing. At this stage there will also be a revelation. Something that was lost shall be found. Connections that were broken shall be reforged. There shall be tears.

I call the Carlton Communications main switchboard number again and ask to be put through to the press office and the girl on the switchboard is laconic and contemptuous once more. But she puts me through. A machine kicks in and I leave a message. I can wait. Already, at this point, I know I can wait.

Because waiting is something we do very well. Us. We're world class waiters. It's something we began to learn, and then refine into something approaching an artform, in the corridors of hospitals. For months now we have been haunting them.

Waiting has become us.

It's odd to think that I used to have a horror of hospitals. As did my father, who probably still does. When we went to see uncle Billy after his big car crash (he was conscious but very poorly, in traction, drips, the works, his face dappled with bruising, scoured by cuts, stitched in places, generally mangled, clotted, marbled, like a lump of butcher's meat), me and dad both had to leave his bedside and go outside for some fresh air because we both nearly fainted. Now I go to hospitals to wait.

And to smoke cigarettes.

A smoker will learn more than a non-smoker about the labyrinth that is a hospital. Smokers understand its topography, its formal logic and the evolution of its architectures. They know its zones, sense its temperatures. They can tell you which badly lit narrow corridor will lead back through the centuries to a hardly-used door that opens onto an almost forgotten part of the complex. A courtyard, say, in front of a Georgian building, complete with blackened columns and porticos, the stoneworked inscription beneath the heavy wrought iron hands of its stopped clock letting on that this was once a fever hospital.

Smokers can tell you how to take a wrong turning down a dead end corridor so that you find yourself in an ornate chapel, extravagantly carpeted, all pristine gilt and high church plush, its lighting tastefully subdued. They know where there's a semi-derelict room in the old wing – once a Victorian doctor's common room, but now the visitors' smoking space, left (pointedly) to reek like an ashtray. Smokers know where all the fire escape stairs are, all the gantries and inner courtyards. They've found all the free spaces that riddle this decaying honeycomb.

***

I don't know to what extent Jules understands our situation. Our situation as in the business about waiting. To what extent he appreciates it, really appreciates it. Feels it. There are some (and actually, perhaps Robbie is a prime example of this) who just don't want to know. Full stop. They don't want to know anything about anybody's kids. Or their life in general if they have kids. And maybe I too was like that at one stage.

Some who know the whole story are none too comfortable with it. They perhaps fall by the wayside. But with Jules, you never really know. The issue is somehow avoided or it's never met head on. It's sort of sidled around. He acts as if he's aware but incurious and we certainly never bring it up as an subject of conversation. Neither of us.

And then, of course, there's the fact that we still don't know exactly what out situation is. We're still waiting.

For the simple fact of the matter is that Charlie was born with a number of things wrong with her. When she was born (Beth had a caesarian) they urgently paged the head paediatric consultant. When he saw Charlie, his first words to Beth, who knew something was wrong or was going wrong, were:

"Are you two related in any way?"

He looked from Beth to me and back again. This was in the recovery room just by the theatre where they'd performed the caesarian and Beth was on a trolley. She had been confused though holding it together until this point but now she howled and her hands covered her face. I fell on her, holding her. It was all pitiful. Harrowing. Nightmarish.

But then they began hinting that Charlie, our newborn daughter, was unlikely to survive. And indeed, not long afterwards, with Beth still sedated on the ward and me distraught, roaming the corridors of the hospital looking for a place to have a cigarette, I heard our consultant (Dr Broadhurst, a little club-footed man with a blue-shadowed chin) talking to another doctor (a severe-looking woman with dark hair who had once been pretty) about a child who had just been born. This child was one sick baby. It could not (should not?) survive. Its skeleton was deformed, its vital organs were damaged or mal-formed, it was brain damaged and the odds were that it didn't have much in the way of a central nervous system.

Spookily, bizarrely, it turned out, though, that they were talking about someone else's baby. Ours was going to survive. Only it had a head shaped like an anvil – the plates of the cranium had fused prematurely. That could be fixed. What was going to be more difficult to fix were the contractures in all her limbs – and indeed the general stiffness of all her joints. Each and every single moving part. There might be brain damage too.

Etcetera.

So we were waiting. Waiting to see how she would turn out. And waiting also for the profession to make its definitive pronouncement. Its prognosis. We hadn't helped, arguably, because we'd refused repeated and insistent requests to conduct an MRI scan, pointing out that the scan in Charlie's case would involve a general anaesthetic and we didn't want to subject her to more trauma given that, as we understood it, the scan wouldn't help them form a definitive diagnosis. We were holding out for a proper full day assessment at the Neurological Institute.

That was what was hanging over us now. That was it, the heart of the matter. That was why we had become so good at waiting.

So yes, I left a message for the Carlton Communications corporate press office and I waited for a reply.

***

It's a spy film. It's also a double chase film. Or rather, a complex interweaving of chases. Following a chance meeting, Hannay sets off to make contact with a spy ring (codenamed the 39 Steps) convinced that in doing so he'll help to stop some vital documents leaving the country – and he can't go to the police because *they* believe he's just committed a murder. So the police are chasing him; and when it turns out that the spy ring are baddies rather than goodies, they're after him too. And yet, in an odd sort of way, he's really after them.

But the story has zip. You can tell that, for its time, it was unusually compelling in the pacy way it barrels along. That doesn't necessarily make it a good film, but it is somehow reassuring. It has a flippant sort of a tone about it too – a jauntiness, a cockiness – that also sets it slightly ahead of its time.

And you have Robert Donat offering a strange mixture of the boyish, the whimsical and the flippant. Heavens, he's almost cynical at times. By and large, though, he's cosy. In contrast, Madeleine Carroll, who got the gig that Baxter and Lee (and maybe others that we don't know of) had turned down, is scary. Supposedly, she's an icy blonde with a fire in her heart; but to me she looks like a woman always on the shrill verge of a splitting headache.

So it's a spy film, a thriller, a film that in our eyes has all the nostalgia value and charm of being genuinely old (which is also to imply, genuinely embryonic) while still showing unmistakably recognisable signs of the modern. In fact (and this is a fact that all film historians will bore you with if you give them half a chance) it was also the first film to be plotted according to the dictates of what Hitchcock famously called the McGuffin. A McGuffin is a wheeze, a transparently thin plot device (a thing or person, for instance, that everybody is supposedly chasing after) that gives just enough narrative impetus to the project to allow the real plot (usually a romance) to unfold unmolested.

But that's not all. The 39 Steps bundles together lots of things we now consider archetypical of spy films. That's not to say it makes much sense of them, but then no-one has ever made sense of them and nobody ever will. They're just delicious nonsense. The 39 Steps has agents of a foreign power that have burrowed into the fabric of the establishment; it has shadowy figures seen conferring under street lamps; it has an international woman of mystery; while in Hannay it has the resourceful amateur (it could be you) pitched by happenstance into the middle of a rich and strange adventure in which technological secrets are a matter of life and death. (If you're interested enough to pay atten-

tion at this point, it is clear that the spies are after, wait for it, aero engine spec-
ifications.) And even at the simplest level – a train journey into the romantic
wilderness of the Scottish highlands – there's something archetypal about the
set up.

So yes, it has charm. Even if you were set dead against it, even if you were
minded to be dead picky, even if you were to insist that it's not that much of a
film, you'd probably have to admit that it has charm.

Sometimes she'll come up to my little office under the eaves while I am
holding on the phone for someone. My office is an ordered chaos smelling of
linseed oil and dust. It looks out onto the gardens and the backs of the terrace
opposite. A reggae backing band (drums, bass, sax) has been practising in one
of the flats opposite for years. They have about four tunes and the drummer is
really good at doing the echoey, reverby rim shots on the snare drum.

"I'll need you to look after Charlie for an hour this afternoon."

"What?"

"Yes."

"But I've got stuff to do."

"But I told you yesterday."

"You did not."

I told you. I told you yesterday.

Did did didn't did.

I told you, I told you yesterday. Yeah, right. And today I try to fuck with your
head.

We were liable to fuck with each other's heads. Remorselessly. Futilely. And
then, having fucked with each other's heads, we continued to conduct our joint
and several business as if nothing remarkable had passed between us. Which
indeed was the truth.

Like the nightly routine:

"What channel's the film on?"

Looking up from the TV guide, frowning: "I've just told you."

"When?"

"Not two seconds ago."

"No you didn't."

"Are you okay?"

I told you. I told you. Itoldyou.

***

Over the course of the next few days, when she calls, I'm out; and she leaves a message for me on my machine. And when I call her back she's not available (or out or on the phone) so I leave a message for her. I've dealt with her before, this Carlton press officer, and I can't help suspecting I don't rank very highly in her estimation. She's perky, her voice always rings with optimism and efficiency, but you can tell she's the sort of press officer who feels her talents are wasted on anything less than the fielding of tough, no-nonsense questions from national newspaper reporters. She doesn't much care for features oiks ferreting around for scraps. She has no time for silly questions. Which is a shame because I specialise in silly questions.

But anyway, eventually we make contact.

"I want to visit the Rank film archive," I tell her.

"Oh," she says. "Oh."

It was around this time that I made my first exploratory foray into the attic in search of the music. That damned tune. That maddening tune again.

I brought Charlie's collapsible buggy up to the top landing then carried her up and put her in it at the foot of the ladder.

She laughed when the ladder wobbled (a hollow creaking of tubular aluminium) as I climbed it. Shocked silence as I disappeared through the hole in the ceiling. Laughter as my head reappeared in the hole. Hanging down, my hair trailing, pulling a funny face.

And then gone again.

It took me ages to find them. I was pretty sure they were in the attic and I never go up there unless I really have to. Plus the fact that, obviously, nothing is ever easy to find in an attic, because in attics your junk tends to be laid down in stratified sediments.

But find them I did, right at the edge of the floorboarded area. An old wooden Schweppes crate, maybe 8 inches by 18, that at one time held a dozen little mixer bottles but had subsequently been adapted as a container for my singles. Or the ones I'd deemed worth keeping.

I now know what the music is, of course. It plays in my head. The arm comes up and across, jerky-precise. A mechanical hesitation, then the cartridge head descends. A hiss and a crackle as the stylus finds its groove.

And then I cringe.

Nilsson. Without You.

It had an orange label, I think.

I went through my old singles one by one. I went through them forwards then I went through them backwards. It wasn't there.

But of course it wasn't. Of course.

Of course. That was the point, wasn't it?

She says, "Hi."

And I say "Hi" back.

She sounds almost chirpy. It's the super-efficient but hard to impress press officer at Carlton.

"I have a name for you," she says.

"Oh yes?"

"Fiona Murdoch."

"Great."

"Can I give you her direct line? Have you got a pen?"

"Yes."

In fact, it is already poised. It has been poised since recording the legend Fiona Murdoch on my pad. She gives me the number. I take it down.

"Okay?" she says.

"Yes," I say. "Only."

"Yes?"

"Who is she?"

Fiona Murdoch is, it turns out, head of Carlton's feature film content ownership division, including the classic British material formerly owned by Rank plus titles from other acquired sources.

I call her immediately.

Another answering machine.

I listen to her voice. It's businesslike, clipped almost. It suffers no fools, this voice. I can't work out whether I'm disappointed or not. Did I really expect her to be the blonde girl with melancholy eyes and a pastel cardigan (strict temperature control means the archive's inner space is slightly chilly even on the hottest of hot summer days) over a light summer dress? She sounds as if she has an attitude problem, this Fiona Murdoch. Do I want her in my story or not? It could work. I mean, it could work in much the same way as Madeleine Carroll, plucked eyebrows and all, worked in the film. It's grist to the mill, isn't it? A bit of conflict, creative tension.

But will she want to be in my story?

Will she consent to have her photograph taken, leaning against the inner skin of her glass building, a partial silhouette, the vast, tumbling, debris-like profusion of a city beyond?

All of which was progress of a sort. Which sort of explains why I worked myself into a state of such excitement that I just had to call Jules to tell him about it. To walk him through it, this miracle of an article that had come to me pristine in all its glorious perfection. I needed to preen myself on my own cleverness, mindful that (maybe in mid sentence) I would somehow find myself switching from demanding praise to desperately seeking reassurance.

But the most bizarre thing happened. I found myself telling him this whole other story. A story whose relevance was not clear, not yet anyway, even to me. It was the story, basically, of uncle Tom, that's to say my Great Uncle Tom – though it started somewhat off-centre.

I found myself telling Jules that, back then (and that means way back then), Sundays were relatively unpredictable. Sometimes we'd go for a walk on the Braid Hills, sometimes in the winter we'd stay indoors most of the day, growing ever more fractious in our stuffy confinement, sometimes we'd go for a drive. On the other hand, sometimes we'd go visiting either to aunt Meg's or ("I think it must be our turn to have you next week") aunt Mary and uncle Tom's.

Saturday was different. Saturday's routine was observed almost religiously. On Saturdays we'd go to Nan's.

We'd arrive in time for afternoon tea and then stay for sit down tea, a meal that you couldn't really call dinner and you couldn't really call (even in hindsight) High Tea, although it leant heavily on the sorts of scones and pancakes and fruitcakes and sponge cakes that you'd also expect with afternoon tea. In summer, the main course would be cold meat and salad and in winter it would be comprised of slightly odd and unsettling combinations like sausages and beans (baked, of course, in tomato sauce) and boiled potatoes. I mean, what was she thinking of? Everyone knew that baked beans only combined with chips. And though you could have sausages without chips in certain situations, if you had them with potatoes, the third ingredient had to be greens of some sort.

Everyone knows that. Don't they?

The strangest thing of all was that often the beans would be cold and they'd be brought to the table in a serving dish.

Sometimes, we'd play football in the back garden. Football with my brother was a delicate, almost choreographed art form. If he was in goal, he'd stand between the silver-painted metal washing line poles (the line was hardly ever up on a Saturday; and even if it was, there would never be washing hung on the line, never). You'd dribble the ball back and forward a good ten yards out from this goal and then attempt to beat him with a gentle but deftly angled shot. Or you'd flick it up and attempt to pirouette and lob him from an impossible position. No hard shooting was allowed – and anyway, in the flowerbed not three yards behind the goal there were roses. The ball was invariably a lightweight plastic thing and a punctured ball meant the end of the game and probably some exasperated parental stuff that came close to scolding. So you'd sort of make things as difficult as you could for yourself – like for instance dribbling the ball round so you faced away from the goal and then attempting to pivot masterfully and score from the unlikeliest of situations, much in the same way that our national hero, Denis Law, could pivot masterfully and score from the unlikeliest of situations. We'd also recreate goals of epic beauty, like Connolly's for Celtic in the Cup Final against Rangers where he rounded the keeper in majestic fashion, never for one fraction of one instant breaking his stride.

After sit-down tea, you went with dad to get the Pink – the sporting final newspaper. You walked to the end of Nan's road, turned left and then almost immediately crossed the road onto the little patch of wasteland (ankle deep with mud in winter: rutted and dusty in summer) that led round the side of a small parade of shops where the newsagent was. Sometimes there'd be a small crowd of men loitering impatiently outside the shop and you knew that the Pink was late again. And you'd be impatient too, not because you wanted to know the scores – if you were interested in the football scores (and I was, increasingly) you'd have got them off the telly earlier. No – you'd be impatient because when dad bought his paper, he'd also buy you and your brother a comic of your choice and some sweets too.

I don't know if I watched more telly at Nan's than I did at home – probably not – but I do *remember* watching telly at Nan's. Or at least I can remember what it felt like. It was somehow more public, more of an event. You'd be aware that people were watching you watching telly; and aunt Mary might ask you if you liked the particular programme you were watching and you felt perhaps that you had to explain or justify yourself. This was on-the-record telly in other ways too, because if your attention wandered and you were no longer seen to be watching, the danger was that it would be switched off. And maybe you also knew they had a tendency to just watch you, proudly almost. As in: "Ooh, you can tell he's very bright, can't you? Look how he watches television quietly all by himself."

Unaided. Look, he can watch television unaided. UNAIDED, I tell you.

And there'd be all sorts of commentary about what was on. This didn't happen at home (or at least if it did, it could comfortably be ignored – like when mother always struggled to remember the names of actors or actresses) but here, others in the room would make comments about what was on the screen, often using this as a springboard for conversation. Every second of viewing was potentially actionable. You had to keep your wits about you. You had to react appropriately – for instance looking bored and mildly disgusted when any love interest intruded on an otherwise wholly acceptable film.

Much of the furniture in Nan's front room was unforgiving, especially the chez longue that you basically had to perch on; but there were a couple of pretty severe armchairs too. We were meant to be down on the floor anyway and there were a couple of old office diaries, from where Nan used to work, that we were given to draw in. There was a heavy tin box that contained some ancient coloured pencils (their colours were heavy, dark and dirty) and a clumsy chunk of cast iron that was a pencil sharpener. Oh, and an old rubber that had lost all of its rubbery qualities. It was like a smooth stone that had at one stage aspired to the perfections of geometry. A skipping stone almost. A skimmer.

So we'd lie on the floor and draw in the diaries. I drew aeroplanes – mostly Spitfires and Hurricanes and Messerschmitts that all looked suspiciously alike, save for their markings – and soldiers, mostly Desert Rats in their khaki shorts and their unfeasibly large boots. (Although this was the 60s, we'd been brought

 up on an unremitting diet of the Second World War. I was absolutely astounded one year when we went on holiday to a seaside village and found that the local kids hadn't even heard of the war. They looked blankly at my newly finished Airfix kit of a Lancaster bomber. It was my pride and joy, its pristine black plastic like the differently-shaped black vinyl I would cherish later in life. I wanted these

kids to be envious, I so much yearned for them to be impressed; but to my utter dismay I couldn't even begin to make them understand what a Lancaster bomber was and why it was important.)

We'd lie on the floor, propped on our elbows or lolled onto our sides, dehydrated desert explorers scribbling last notes in 1950s unused and surplus-to-requirements desk diaries from a prominent firm of New Town solicitors.

Except when the telly was on, that is. When the telly was on, we'd fight for control of the pouffe.

The pouffe lived under the telly at Nan's and even we could see that it had once been an object of great beauty, luxury even. It was round and we imagined it as a drum, a big bass drum, the giant sort of drum that drummers in pipe bands would have protruding from their tummies and would thump with big hairy-headed mallets. But it wasn't a drum, no matter how hard you thumped it. Its sides were harlequin quarters of amber and maroon leather, sensuously soft and supple; round its middle, like a belt or a waist band, ran a silk cord, knotted securely, with tassels on its two dangling ends. The cord was solely for the purpose of slipping your fingers under, getting a good hold, and yanking the pouffe out from under people smaller than you.

The maroon leather of the round top was tooled with a complex pattern of gold. The design seemed exotic, foreign, eastern. Turkish perhaps. Or Moorish Spain. But now the whole thing was falling to bits and it was our fault. The leather was abraded, the colours fading; the seams were becoming unpicked and, although the stuffing wasn't exactly coming out of it, the inner lining was beginning to protrude, hernia-like through the gaps. In short, it sagged.

I'm not sure it was all our fault. I mean, there's no way we could have done that amount of damage in a few short years. Is there? But when everyone said that it was our fault they said it with indulgent amusement, as if it was alright really. (I hardly fret about this at all now, actually.)

We'd both sit on this pouffe, not three feet from the television screen but slightly to the side so that everyone else could see too. If they wanted to see, that is – and of course they said they didn't because television was just so much nonsense, wasn't it?

At the very least we'd nudge and niggle each other, me and my brother; but more often than not one of us would be edged off onto the floor and a full scale three-way wrestling match – me, Graeme and the pouffe – would ensue.

The technique for restoring order was obvious, really: "If you can't sit nicely, the telly's going off. No arguing now."

There never was.

We needed permission to switch the television on. We needed permission to change channel. Not that you ever needed to switch over. For a start, there were only two channels. And although Nan secretly watched Coronation Street and uncle Billy (we went there rarely but always had great fun when we did) watched The Flintstones, it was well known that decent folk didn't watch STV. They watched the BBC.

On most Saturdays, permission to switch on was withheld until about half four when we were allowed to witness the latest football scores coming through on the teleprinter. Then, after the classified results, there were scary programmes like Dr Who or silly ones like Juke Box Jury or the Monkees. Then there was tea, then you went for the Pink. And then, early on a Saturday evening, there were adventure films. The Day the Earth Caught Fire, The Lost World of Professor Challenger, The Maltese Falcon. If you were lucky, you'd be able to watch the whole thing before it was time to go home.

"Jules. Jules? Are you still there?"

"Huh?"

We shared a languorous moment of awkwardness

"Anyway," I said. "This article. Just to say I've cracked it."

I told him about how the people at the film archive had these amazing stories to tell about how various bits and bobs make their way into their possession. And how you trace the stories back, how you chase them down into the byways of individual histories. For instance, take an old man, a grandfather many times over, whose father owned a cinema in the 1930s. A man who spent his childhood in the projection room at the back of a smoky Regal Picture Palace somewhere. On the south coast somewhere. Warmington-on-Sea, perhaps. But now, having retired from a minor civil service post, he'll be living somewhere on the London fringes. Metroland, as was. A semi-detached house in a prim suburban street. The thing is, he'll have a loft full of stuff; a loft full of memories. He might have some intriguing memorabilia connected with the film. Fragments. Or he might have a story, one that will have bittersweet resonances when told in the context of the story of celluloid.

"Wow," he said. "Wow. It's brilliant."

"I know."

"So where does he live?"

"Who?"

"This geezer."

"What geezer?"

"The guy you've just been talking about."

"Well, obviously I don't know yet, do I?"

"What?"

Sometimes Jules can be incredibly obtuse. "I don't know yet."

"You've only talked to him on the phone?"

"Jules. I haven't talked to him at all."

"Why not?"

"Because, Jules, first things first. When I get through to the archive…"

"What! You haven't even talked to the film archive yet?"

Sometimes, with Jules, it's like pushing water uphill.

"Jules…"

"No-one?"

"Look…"

"You haven't, have you?"

"Well no, not exactly."

Hello, she says. Fiona Murdoch here. The system is making her voice all metallic – digitised, slightly inhuman, shimmering slightly with Doppler effect. Ironically, paradoxically, when I listened to her recorded message I could picture her. Now she is talking to me live, in real time, I can't picture her at all.

Nothing. I can't even be sure any more about how old she sounds.

"Hello Fiona, thanks for getting back to me."

No response.

No small talk. No jokes here, no foreplay. Neither given nor expected. She waits. She likes to have clear sight of whatever it is that is coming at her. She computes trajectories. I can sense this. She's a ballistics expert.

"I want to come and see your archive."

"Oh," she says. "Oh."

The same "oh" that her colleague in the press office gave me.

"Is that a problem?"

"Problem?" She's still hesitant. She's still computing. "No, she adds at last. "It's just that there's nothing to see as such."

As such?

And so she eases into her power play. She's good. She's the archetypal master of administration. And yes, she's charming. Flawlessly charming. I'll bet she's studied public relations in the marketing module of her MBA. And all the way through I can hear her managing her time. Trimming her answers, closing down avenues of further enquiry. This is business. Business is business. All the time, selling. Herself, the company, the resource, the expertise, the end product. She's an operator. She's going to go far. And the truth is I often I find myself fascinated by this whole process – my pen takes down the words but I'm actually listening to the nuances, the rhetoric, the pure technique. Maybe I actually *like* being operated on in this way.

And yes, we talk a bit about celluloid and yes, she knows her stuff; but I also get the feeling that it's a superficial knowledge. She doesn't live and breathe this stuff, she's not in love with film. She's not desperate to share, to evangelise. She's not an enthusiast. She's here to manage a resource, extract maximum value from it.

And what's slowly dawning on me is that there are no films, no film labs, nothing stored or kept. From what I can gather, that's all managed by the British Film Institute. It's like the way a monetary currency operates. The gold which underpins it never actually changes hands. Carlton might buy the rights (mainly for broadcast) to the films, but the actual artefacts themselves never move. They're interred, cryogenically suspended, at the BFI.

"You mean it's basically digitised already? The currency, the format you trade in, is now a digital master? Everything's been transferred to computer disc?"

"Well, it depends how you look at it."

"There's nothing to hold? If I'm interested in The 39 Steps, say. There's nothing you can show me?"

"It's available on VHS cassette and on DVD. I can send you a catalogue."

"So where you are, there's no archive as such?"

"You're welcome to come in at any time. We can show you round our offices." There is a smile in her voice for the first time – albeit a slightly sneery smile. We both know I have probably seen an office before.

"No tall, glass-skinned building."

"No."

They're not even in central London.

"No pretty archivist, blonde, wearing a light summer dress and a pastel cardigan."

"No."

"Oh."

Chapter three

Over the hill, through the tunnel of trees, two grown-ups in the front, an infant, just past her third birthday, in the back. We reach a T-junction and we go left. Or right. Actually, maybe this time we go right. Or we go left but stop almost immediately and double back. Because we're absolutely determined to find the place that we're looking for – and this is fortunate or unfortunate depending on which way you want to look at it, for the plain fact of the matter is that we are already hugely late and further diversions will make us catastrophically late.

We often take a break about halfway to my parents, heading off the M40, usually just into Oxfordshire, in search of a pub. And often we try to rediscover one we came upon quite by accident one time and liked so much that it instantly acquired an almost legendary status.

For a start, it scored just over 20 on my system. I give marks out of ten in three categories. 1. Location, which is usually all about whether the pub is in a village that has all the right picturesque elements: ancient church with lych gate and slightly gothic but not too overgrown churchyard complete with lichen-covered, time-eaten headstones, yew tree and the odd corner shrouded in ivy; and ideally there should be a village green (pond shaded by a willow tree, optional) and plenty of thatched and/or rose trellised cottages. The odd bit of wisteria. All that sort of stuff. But sometimes a pub will score highly in this category solely by virtue of the fact that its garden offers a spectacular view. 2. Quality of food (proper roast lunch for me, imaginative vegetarian for Beth) and beer (locally brewed hoppy bitter). 3. I'll have to use the word facilities for this category, though I'm tempted to be far more pretentious. Ideally the pub should have low ceilings, beams and interesting bric-a-brac that is *genuinely* interesting (old cricket bats, for instance: don't you find it odd that some of the really old cricket bats look a bit like hockey sticks?) or is charmingly eccentric without being twee. I have horse brasses in mind when I say twee but that's by no means the only crime. And obviously it has to have a pleasant garden where you can count on getting a seat and which has adequate sunshades.

We discovered the legendary pub one day when we were trying to find another pub in the pub guide. And then every time we went looking for it (the legendary one) we failed ended up at the pub in the pub guide, which turned out to be horrible. We had almost come to the conclusion that we'd dreamed it all up, or that we had confused this elusive Brigadoon-like pub with one we'd visited one time in the West Country.

But we persevere. We drive round in circles, cutting back through hedge-rowed country lanes to find ourselves yet again at crossroads we'd left five minutes back.

And maybe on this occasion we are rewarded for our perseverance. Miracles really do happen.

The legendary pub is in a place called Nutwood. We sort of know that now. You sit in the garden of the pub, the map spread across a table, retracing your

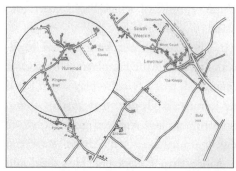

route, and it slowly dawns on you. Your problem was that you had been resisting the idea that the village was called Nutwood. Before, when you'd consulted the map, the name Nutwood hadn't rung any bells. You had relegated it to the bottom of a long list of possibilities. Somehow, you begin to realise, you didn't *want* the village to be called Nutwood – and some places do have a power like that, they have an uncanny way of hiding themselves.

It's sort of a shock, though, when you do strike lucky, to find the place absolutely heaving. (The legendary villages of your dreams are, after all, deserted villages.) There are cars parked on the verge at least a mile down the lane leading in, people walking on the roadway as if they own it. The main street (such as it is) is cordoned off and we have to reverse a good way back down the road to find a parking space. Soon you find out why. A village fete. Loads of people milling about, music and excited chatter in the air, the screams of children. A bouncy castle in the road in front of the pub, stalls everywhere, a marquee and a low stage on the green. The works: tombola, antique/junk stalls, battered cast-offs of books on trestle tables, home made cakes and fudge, the vicar in the stocks being pelted with sopping wet sponges the size of his head, kids paying to throw cricket balls at racks of old crockery. Morris dancers.

We should be charmed by all of this; but somehow our hearts sink. The pub will be heaving and we'll be lucky to get a table. The food will take ages. But no. Wrong. The pub, if anything, is quieter than usual. It's a beautiful day and yet there's hardly anyone in the garden out the back. We can relax.

They're good here. They're friendly but they don't pester you. They don't offer you a highchair that Charlie can't use. They don't look at you like you're an alien. Or some sort of oaf come to pass judgement on them, to mark them out of ten in three different categories. And although it's my father's birthday and we're expected at one and it's gone noon already, we dawdle. We take time over lunch; and when we're finished, we spend some time wondering round the village, checking out the marquee – all the usual artsy crafty stuff but a New Age edge too: ambient music, crystals, tapes of whalesong, Tarot readings – then buy a couple of books and some cakes and biscuits with faces made out of glace cherries and hundreds and thousands. A couple of gingerbread men too. Charlie can give them to her cousins later.

At one point, back out on the green, I find myself checking out the band. They've just returned from a break in their set and they're playing the sort of punchy R&B, boogie and jump blues standards that I tried to play when I first had a guitar. Route 66, Louie Louie, Johnny B Goode, that sort of thing. They're all in their paunchy 50s apart from one guy, the lead guitarist, who's clearly in his late teens. He's got all the gear – a valve-driven Marshall stack and a sunburst Les Paul – and he's good. More than competent. He's fluid and fluent when it comes to the solos; but even more impressive are all the crisp little licks and fills that give their sound depth and texture and definition. A really etched sort of a high finish. Crisp, clean, nothing too showy – he's not aiming to swamp everyone with his virtuosity – but he clearly has it, whatever it is.

I'm vaguely envious and try to imagine how he got here. Are these people friends of his dad's or did he answer an ad in the parish magazine? And where is he going with this? Does he want to be a professional musician and if so does he imagine he'll get anywhere playing village R&B? Or is this just a hobby, a talent he'll let slide when he goes off to university?

When Beth and Charlie join me I can sense Beth is vaguely irritated that I've sloped off without telling her; but despite that, there's still no sense of urgency. We wander about some more, following the village's only side street to its conclusion: a gate, a tree-defined field beyond and a couple of chestnut-coloured horses in that field. As we walk back again, we return to a familiar theme. It starts with a critique of each house we pass – and this part of the village is clearly a fairly recent addition, with newer and distinctly unpicturesque houses. No cottages here. We find much to sneer at.

"That one though. I could see us living in that one."

"Perhaps," I say. "Perhaps."

"You'd only need to go into town twice a week maybe."

"I know. I know."

"And Charlie would absolutely love it here."

The timing of this statement is immaculate, beyond dispute. Because a teenage girl is leading a horse towards us. It probably lives in the field at the bottom of the lane with the other two horses but it's not chestnut-coloured. No. There's something almost visionary about this horse. It's white. A pure, unadulterated white.

On its back is a girl of about ten, imperiously proud, wearing a riding hat. When Charlie sees the horse and the imperiously proud girl on its back she tenses in her pushchair, her arms stretching out before her. This response seems almost violent, like a seizure in its suddenness and the rigidity of the position she assumes. It's not though. It's not a seizure. This is her way of expressing of joy. Her face is lit up. The horse passes and we turn the pushchair so that Charlie can watch it mosey off down the clip clop lane.

"Goodbye horsey. Say, 'Goodbye horsey'."

She waggles the fingers of her right hand, her mouth open, silently shouting, her face still glowing with joy.

I have every right to be confused, I suppose; but this time, now that we've seemingly rediscovered this place, the inner turmoil seems particularly intense. On top of that, I'm feeling disgruntled. Not for any of the usual reasons. It's perhaps something to do with that fact that the village fete has New Age elements alongside all the Women's Institute stuff you'd expect to find. It's to do with the fact that they can field a pretty creditable R&B band. You'd probably find out that one of the fifty-year-old guys actually used to be a professional musician and was in the Rubettes or Mud or something in the 70s .

I don't know. I just feel cheated that's all.

So maybe this wasn't the place after all.

Plan B, after the calls to Carlton had got me nowhere, was that I'd go out and buy myself a copy of the film. I mean an original celluloid copy. The person I'd buy it (I don't know how many reels in their big aluminium disc canisters) from will point me in the right direction as regards its previous owners and the provenance trail will lead me back to… well to the source of my story to be.

I put some calls into the auction houses – people like Sotheby's and Christie's – who host fairly regular auctions of film memorabilia. And I also (this is something I've never done before, but you never know) take out an ad in the personal column of a national newspaper. Two days running. You know the sort of thing – you've probably seen them before and wondered in passing what they were about.

Author on forthcoming book about early British cinema seeks memorabilia, memories and anecdotes from the 1930s. Box 39.

And then of course there was the Colin question. I can't really be sure anymore as to why I had become so committed so quickly to the idea of Colin being the third musketeer. If musketeers we were. Which clearly we weren't.

Because pretty rapidly I had to admit to myself that I wasn't relishing the prospect of calling Colin – and had in fact been putting it off for days now. I often find it odd when I reflect on the fact that me and Colin used to be best mates. But I suppose it often happens this way. I had a succession of two or three (maybe more) best mates as I was growing up but I sort of assumed that when you reached a certain age you'd sort of stick with things longer or maybe even for ever. But no. It doesn't happen that way, seemingly. I took me ages to work out that grown ups – real grown ups – don't really have best mates.

We drifted apart first of all when he disappeared. I mean he genuinely went missing. No-one heard a peep from him for more than two years. It turned out he was living with a woman down in Surrey somewhere. Dorking I think. I only ever met her once. Briefly. And he completely immersed himself in her circle, to the extent that he seemed contemptuous of anything he'd previously known. It was as if he wanted to erase history and start at Year Zero.

But you can't really blame Dorking Girl. Because when that episode drew to its natural conclusion, he could quite easily have become once more the reckless, flippant, cocky Colin that he was at university, the Colin that some people didn't really like because he was a bit loud and obstreperous when he was drunk – and, as it happens, some people pointed out that maybe he got drunk too easily in the first place. But he didn't become that person again because I suppose he chose not to.

Anyway, we're not best mates these days and sometimes that is perplexing. It might even have been better if the Dorking episode had been final and I'd never heard from ever again. But no, we're in fitful contact – and it's usually me who makes the effort.

"Col. Hi."

"Huh?"

"It's me."

(Well, who else would I be?)

"Yeah?"

"How are you?"

"Yeah, all right I suppose." He says it almost resentfully, implying heartstopping undercurrents of misfortune – misfortune that you personally are responsible for. *All right, I suppose.* Implying: *No thanks to you, sunshine.* Insinuating: *What do you know about it anyway?*

On the other hand, though he's grumpy, you can sense right away that he wouldn't mind being brought out of this grumpiness. Led forth. So I chatter – and head to the inevitable point where I ask if he's seen any of the old crowd recently. We both know what the answer will be.

"Seen so and so?"

"Na."

"Seen…"

"Na."

"How about…"

"Nope."

"How about Kate?"

This time there's an awkward silence. We both know what this silence is about. I once had a huge crush on Kate, so huge it was an embarrassment to everyone, probably. And come to think of it, almost as odd as the fact that me and Colin are no longer best mates, in any widely understood definition of the term, is the fact that the whole crowd, of which we were once a part, has imploded.

For years this crowd seemed to have an incredible organic elasticity, surviving all sorts of individual defections, stroppy partners and internal tensions. Everyone assumed it had some sort of self-sustaining critical mass. Somehow, you always had this fundamental instinct that it, the group, would always reconstitute itself.

In hindsight, the focus was a flat in Kentish Town that was considered at the time to be rather cool and bohemian. Colin, more by luck than judgement, had found himself with a room in this flat. I knew Colin because I'd been to university with him. Colin shared the flat with two guys, one of whom was called Paul. Paul was really thick with a guy called Tony whose brother was John. John's girlfriend was Kate. Kate knew everybody – and in particular Kate and John knew a whole bunch of suitably Boho people who also did the stalls.

No-one would have said that Paul was the vital link in all of this. But came the time when Paul got a new job out of town, he moved away and he forgot about us within weeks. That's when the gang began to fragment. We didn't know it at the time but it's obvious now, looking back. Not that you really need to know any of this.

"Anyhow. We should meet up. What I mean to say is that we need to meet up. There's a proposition I want to put to you."

Colin is a photographer. He used to earn his living doing weddings, studio portraits, passport snaps, that sort of thing; but for one reason or another he gave that up. Now he's a serious photographer. He even has exhibitions every couple of years or so. It's proper stuff, organised by the guild he's a member of, with slightly sour red wine and lukewarm bottles of Becks; and the creative directors of ad agencies and the photo desk people of newspapers and magazines are all invited. But nothing ever comes of it – not a single sale, not a single useful contact – which tends to leave him almost clinically depressed.

I always tell him it's because he isn't giving his stuff the right chance. His photographs are almost always pictures with a story behind them. Never in them. Always behind them. The story is always obscure. His pictures never let on that they have stories to tell. They never even give hints. It's an almost superstitious, fetishistic thing – it's almost as if, if they gave up their stories too easily,

their latent power would be diminished. The power of these stories (and therefore the power of these works of art as story + picture) will gain maximum
power of the stories are discovered *after* the pictures have become acknowledged in their own right. Or something like that. And maybe it's also a proud
arrogance on Colin's part. He doesn't feel it's his role to go out and sell his own
work. He'd be quite happy to explain it if someone wants to know, but...

And actually, the tragedy is, it's usually worth asking. He does a lot of
cityscape stuff, for instance. Moody black and white shots of East End buildings. Warehouses, tenements, terraces. Near-silhouettes against cold empty skies
– pictures that you can sense were taken at around sunset on a preternaturally
still but icy winter's afternoon.

"That?" he'll say. "That's the house where X met Y."

X and Y will usually be counter culture icons from the period 1965-75 and
his photographs will chart the landscape they inhabited before they were
famous.

Or he'll say: "That's where Z was murdered."

Or: "That's the street that film director A used in the famous trippy sequence
in cult film B."

And you look at them again. You look long and hard. I keep telling him he
ought to have a crib-sheet on the wall beside each picture in his exhibitions,
basically a big caption. It could be beautifully printed on pristine white card.
But he won't have it.

He doesn't want to have to explain himself. Artists don't explain themselves.
He also does more accessible stuff, I suppose. And he also does the sorts of con-
ceptual stuff that hundreds of other people have done, like going through the
A-Z and taking a picture of every Abbey Road, say, in London. Except the
famous one. Much good all this does him. He's on the dole. Has been for years.
Not defiantly on the dole; not on the dole as an artistic lifestyle choice. Just on
the dole and intermittently very depressed about being on the dole. I keep
telling him he should call himself a freelance. Or an agent. Or, if he was really
desperate, a spy.

"Proposition?" he asks – and I can sense his eyes narrowing.

"Yeah." But instead of giving him the big picture I find myself telling him
about celluloid and Hitchcock and The 39 Steps and how I sort of see it, this
feature I'm working on, really as an archaeological project; and he loves all of
this and he starts going on about Hitchcock's London and how he was born in

Leytonstone. Before I know it, I've agreed to meet up one day soon, maybe next week even, to do a little field research and location work.

Colin is in the need-to-know category as far as our domestic situation is concerned – and as such he is, where the sum total of our acquaintances and associates are concerned, in the majority. Because on the one hand there's too much to tell; and on the other, not enough. Next to nothing is certain.

Because, as I've said before, we too were still waiting. We had been waiting since Day One.

That afternoon, the afternoon of the day on which Charlie had been born and had been taken from us and admitted to the paediatric intensive care unit where she was placed on life support... on that afternoon, Dr Broadhurst, the consultant, arrived at Beth's bedside on the ward, carrying a large buff envelope. There were x-rays in the envelope.

He was pleased to be able to show them to us. He was so happy, in fact, that there were tears in his eyes. Because it was good news. Better news. He took the x-rays one by one from their envelope and held them up to the light of the window. Come to think of it, they were celluloid too – celluloid sheets figuring the negatives of shadows, the pale ghosts of bones. I couldn't make out much and I doubt Beth saw anything at all. She was more or less immobile, propped up on pillows on a metal frame support and in any case the consultant was holding the x-rays high to the window which was behind her head.

Charlie had a skeleton. It wasn't perfect. The hips weren't aligned properly and at least one might have been dislocated. (It's not easy to tell with babies because their soft bones are basically like cartilage and don't show up entirely clearly on x-rays). The bones in her ankles and feet didn't look quite right. And of course there was her head.

Its tectonic plates, its compound hemispheres, had fused prematurely, into a flattened shape. Her head was elongated back to front, a ridge along the top, slightly pointed at the back. Like one of those go-faster, aerodynamically-designed cycle helmets. Our daughter had a wedge-shaped head.

That would need operating on.

There was something else. The multiple contractures. Every single joint was stiff. Every single moving part. It was too early to say what the implications might be.

As for internal organs, they were seemingly in working order. But it was thought best to keep her in intensive care overnight. As a precaution. For observation.

"Would you like to see her?"

"What? Now?"

"Yes."

"Can we?"

"I don't see why not," he said, glancing at a nurse who was now hovering in his vicinity. "For fifteen minutes or so."

Our hearts leapt.

He disappeared to arrange it. They were going to risk bringing her up onto the ward.

And the thing was that the longer we waited, the more apprehensive we became. I can't remember if we talked about it. I suspect that we did, tentatively. Non-committally. Talk about it, I mean. What we were feeling. I suspect that we discovered that we had both been feeling the same thing – that we'd suspected that we might never see her again. One way or another. Until the consultant, Broadhurst, had said those words, "Would you like to see her," that had been the dark thought in both our heads. Perhaps it existed somewhere in the air between us, shared by us.

But I'm pretty sure there was one thing I didn't say. I didn't say that it might not be good to see her again. To see her again, however briefly, might be... well, it might be harrowing. It might complicate things.

I didn't say that.

And so, yes, we waited.

What you begin to realise pretty quickly is that The 39 Steps has nothing to do with spies. Not really. Only very superficially. In fact, it's a fantasy. It's a trip. It starts bizarrely, irrationally, as all dreams do – a gun goes off in a theatre and as the subsequent melee spills out into the streets a stranger, a mysterious woman, asks to come home with you. Then it evolves into your worst nightmare – the girl is murdered while she's in your flat. She's murdered by a will of the wisp who ghosts in and out again in the middle of the night and there isn't a hope in hell of you proving your innocence. So now you're on the run, with all the passionate self-righteousness that burns in the hearts of all the falsely accused.

It's a nightmare; yet obviously there's something exhilarating about this. The darkness tingles with sparkles of light. It's a chase. It's hide and seek. It has the feel of a game. That's what puts the THRILL into thriller. Thrill equals fun plus a piquant hint of danger.

It's a trip. And, halfway through, it intensifies into something slightly more erotic. Circumstances throw a man and a woman together. In fact, they become locked together. The sense of inevitability is almost stifling. You identify with this too: this is your fantasy. It becomes you.

And when this erotic element is introduced, or rather, when you recognise it and acknowledge it, suddenly you see that you will reach home. It's time, in fact, to head in that direction. To look for the path. You're coming down. You can almost relax. You can anticipate what the relaxation, the letting go, will feel like. It will be good. And this is the most pleasurable part. This is when the fantasy enters Arcadia.

In the film, Arcadia is a misty country road, a hump-backed bridge, a precipitous path and a waterfall whose silver sheet of water conceals a ledge. You may hide here, behind the falling sheet of water. Man and woman. Boy and girl.

The two of you.

And when the danger has passed, it will be springtime. There is a warmth and a light in the air. Springtime, around dawn, life stirring in the thawed soil, buds budding. It will be time to head home.

In The 39 Steps, we know it's time to head home when Hannay begins whistling a tune. It's the tune we heard right at the start, in the Music Hall. It's the tune used to introduce Mr Memory.

"I wish I could get that damned tune out of my head... " frets Hannay. "I wonder where I heard it?"

In the garden, slightly drunk. When the rain stops, the clouds clear and the moon comes out, you can become disorientated. Moonlight hardens up the shadows and sometimes you find yourself stepping over them. The moon makes filigree shapes of the trees; it's as if they've been carved out of cork and maybe for a second or two you are in a paperweight scene.

It's at times like this that I become guilty. I think of the baby Dr Broadhurst and his colleague were discussing that afternoon in the hospital corridor as I passed, earwigging. I feel guilty that this child, the one they were talking about,

was close to death. And in fact was probably now dead. You have to be slightly drunk and in a moonlit garden, obviously, to be truly banal in your sentimentality.

The thing was that uncle Tom was always an important part of a vocabulary of family reference points. For instance, the time (I can't remember if this was before or after father's birthday: too many time plates have slid since then for me to adjudicate on that with any certainty) my parents came round one evening and I cooked them fish for dinner and me and father had far too much wine.

After dinner, I slipped outside to the garden to have a quiet fag on the sly. I stood down near the shed, which is just about as far away as I can get from the house without trampling into the flower beds and it's half hidden from the kitchen window by a shrub that has managed to grow to the dimensions of a small tree. It was a beautifully still summer evening. Nothing stirred apart from insects darting in the cool air in the shade of the sycamore tree.

But no, here comes father, lumbering out onto the lawn. He disapproves of me smoking of course and I know there'll be some banter about this. It's never aggressive yet it always makes me feel awkward – I'm guilty and I know I'm guilty. There's no sidestepping this. If I mock him for nagging, there will be no truth in my mockery.

And sure enough: "You still smoking those filthy things, I see."

"Yes. Now and then."

He gives one of his cod sighs. One of those eyes rolling, melodramatic sighs. "After all you put me through. Me and your poor mother."

This too is familiar territory. In my early teens I had been an anti-smoking tyrant. A bigot, an uncompromising, evangelical, puritanical zealot. We'd been shown a gruesome propaganda film at school (lots of shots of blackened lungs being dissected by post mortem scalpels) and the shock tactics had worked. I'd come home and terrorised my (occasional and moderate) smoking parents.

"There was a time when we had to hide from you."

"You didn't give up?" I'm genuinely surprised. Shocked even.

"Not entirely."

I take a couple of steps across the garden. Then I look down. I sweep my foot lightly across the grass.

"What do you reckon uncle Tom would have made of this?"

I mean the lawn. My lawn.

"It certainly looks a lot better than the last time we were here."

"And the next time you come, it will be like Highbury. Or a bowling green."

"Aye, that'll be right."

And now, once more, we are on safe ground.

Even father deferred grudgingly to Tom where matters of turf were concerned. Because Tom knew a thing or two about this. He was, after all, head groundsman at Murrayfield. And in Tom's day, Murrayfield was known throughout the rugby world as the best maintained pitch in the game. Bar none. Not, you could argue, that that's saying much. But you wouldn't want to advance that argument in my hearing. Uncle Tom's abilities are part of family legend.

It wasn't hard to slide him into the conversation. Because the thing is, I now desperately needed to know something. The question that began to rattle around my head at about this time, growing as it did from a notion the size of dried pea to something more the size of a football, boiled down to this.

What I want to know is…

Did he… was he…

How do I put this? Did he "pull people's legs"? No. That doesn't really sound right. That's not quite it.

Did he amuse himself by misleading people? Did he (and here's another expression I'm never very comfortable with) enjoy "winding people up"? Did he like testing people's credulity? Did he have a highly developed sense of irony? Did he have a mischievous sense of humour?

No, it will have to do: *Did he enjoy pulling people's legs?*

Did he? Uncle Tom. Did he? Was he?

I know what father is likely to say anyway. Father never had a very high opinion of Tom's intelligence. This was largely down to the fact that Tom would take an age thinking about a chess move and then go and do the stupidest thing possible. He'd give his queen away or break open a secure position and let you in to checkmate him next move. And when we played whist at Nan's, as we often did of a summer evening, it would drive father to distraction when Tom erroneously failed to follow suit.

Right near the end of a hand Tom would win a trick by playing trumps.

"You've still got hearts," my father would exclaim. "Twice I led hearts and both times you threw away a club. God! I thought I was imagining it. I thought I must have miscounted."

"Are you sure?" Tom would say.

"Am I sure? That was my whole strategy. I'd have cleaned up. That's the whole hand ruined."

Sometimes father could whine and whinge dreadfully. Sometimes he'd sound like a spoilt child. Even as children we could recognise that. Tom would eventually, reluctantly, apologise but by then it would be too late and father would go on and on about it, trying his best to work up some genuine, deeply felt, moral outrage. And the aunts, especially aunt Flo, would say quite rightly that he was just making a big fuss. And so he'd back off from implying that Tom had been deliberately cheating and would subside into tuts and sighs and make peevish appeals to the gods of fair play.

Father knew about Tom's failing eyesight obviously, but he basically thought Tom was stupid. I was never so sure. He was almost unbeatable at draughts, for instance. Far better than father, who I could beat now and again if only by sheer luck and the law of averages. I think I understood, even then, that gathering darkness was the main explanation for all sorts of things that Tom did.

But no. That's why I've never gotten around to asking that question. I knew what father would say: "Tom? Pull someone's leg? He was never bright enough."

It's Saturday, say. We're going out to the supermarket to do the weekly shopping. We're behind schedule because we want to do the shopping, get back home and unload it and then go out for a walk. Hampstead Heath, up by Kenwood, probably. We'll eat in the cafe at Kenwood House. And we want to get both the shopping and the walk in before Charlie gets hungry. If we're late getting back from the shops and Charlie wants her lunch then she might go to sleep after she's had her lunch and before you know it most of the day has gone and we won't have time for our walk.

So suddenly it's all a bit fraught.

Beth is upstairs getting ready. I'm sitting with Charlie on the sofa reading the newspaper.

Beth shouts down: "Are you getting Charlie ready."

Yeah, I think. As if you're not going to be another ten minutes or so getting ready. All Charlie needs are her shoes and her coat.

Minutes later she shouts down again: "Is the buggy in the car? Is Charlie ready?"

I turn to Charlie and smile. She smiles back.

And when I begin to hear Beth coming down the stairs, I slope off. I busy myself with something in the kitchen. I have a knack of looking sort of busy. Sort of about to do something really important.

So of course I hear Beth's angry voice from the living room.

I join her there. "I thought you were getting her ready."

I'm almost tempted to say: No, that's what *you* said. But I don't.

"Oh," I say, looking confused. "I thought you were still getting ready. You know how long you take."

She's putting on Charlie's shoes – soft-soled little slip-on things, obviously. Charlie's not going to be walking anywhere. Beth is putting these shoes on Charlie's feet with a ferocious efficiency. A ferocious efficiency born of long suffering and frustration.

"At least get her coat."

"Coat? Where is it?"

"Where do you think?"

I think it's probably on the long row of coat hooks ranged along the length of the hall. This is probably a pretty good guess. Charlie has hundreds of coats. We have something to cover just about any possible combination of meteorological eventualities. We can cope with climactic regions from the polar to the tropical. We are prepared for the weather of four seasons in one day. We have lots of different tog values, we have hoods, we have all-in-ones, we have waterproofs, we have lightweight summerwear.

I bring a heavy coat. A depths of winter ice and snow coat.

"Not that one!" she breathes, a hard edge of frustration in her voice.

She closes her eyes and I can imagine her uttering a silent prayer. The angry sort of prayer that may keep you from further anger.

I hadn't called Jules for days. Obviously we needed to talk but I hadn't called him because I hadn't resolved things with Colin; and I hadn't actually discussed with Colin the things that needed discussing because I'd started to fret about what had I said to him about Kate, though I struggled now to remember what it was I had actually said.

Not that it matters.

Just about everyone, to some degree or other, had a thing for Kate. (Or is this part of my fantasy world too?) All the blokes in our crowd sparkled when she was around. Any fool could see that. Paul (Colin's flatmate as was) even tried to disguise it by being really upfront about it. He'd call her gorgeous to her face and ask John (if, on one of those rare occasions, he turned up alone) where his gorgeous girlfriend was. I'm pretty sure the three of them had this running joke that if John died, he'd get Kate, like he was leaving her to him in his will.

And though she wasn't the most beautiful girl in the world, she was the one most likely to get chatted up by strangers at a party. I mean, she was beautiful, obviously she was, but not in an obvious, drop dead gorgeous, stunning, Cover Girl sort of a way. It was true that there was something vaguely Kate Moss about her – in her manner, mainly. A street urchin mischievousness about her, but a naïvety, a vulnerability too. Or maybe that was just down to the fact that her name somehow evoked Kate Moss. I don't know.

So the danger passes, it's springtime, there's now a warmth and a light in the air. A stirring in thawed soil, buds budding. Time to head home.

And we know it's time to head home because Hannay is whistling a tune, the tune we heard right at the start, in the Music Hall. It's the tune used to introduce Mr Memory.

Mister Memory? He wasn't actually called that. Hang on. Yes. Yes, actually, he was. In the film, that is. The Music Hall act in the film is Mr Memory. But it was based on a real Music Hall act called Datas. The real Datas didn't play Mr Memory in the film, though. At least I don't think so.

I've never really known what to think of memory acts. Is what they do impressive? Not that you get memory acts these days, though I'm pretty sure I did see one on telly when I was younger. You're not exactly going to make a career with that sort of act any more, though. We have too many ways to access information these days. We no longer need Mister Memory.

I, though, was about to call upon his services. Oddly enough, though I had relatively little to go on, I had actually begun to write the article. And it began, in fact, with Mr Memory. Mr Memory was going to give me what I thought was a neat way of making an evocative point about the ephemeral nature of the cinema. Or, more accurately, the ephemeral nature of film – and obviously this is central to the underlying point I want to make about celluloid. In the Mr Memory sequence, he's up on stage with his sidekick and they're encouraging the audience to ask him questions that will test his incredible talents.

A lot of the questions, as you'd probably expect, concern sporting records. One of the questions is: Who won the Derby in 1936?

There's laughter.

And Mr Memory says: Come back in 1937 and I'll tell you.

The film's official national distribution date was 25 November 1935 but there had been previews in September and there was a press and trade premier on 6 June 1935 (strangely enough, a matter of days after the 1935 Derby). The 1936 Derby was run on Wednesday 27 May 1936. So we'll be generous and say that the joke, the comic little exchange between Mr Memory and a member of his audience, had a shelf life of ten days short of a year.

It's actually a bit of a time-loop, an eddy in the seemingly smooth surface of things. The film as a work of art, or as a work as Hitchcock conceived of it in all its full richness, had a use-by date of 27 May 1936. After which, everybody knew who the 1936 Derby winner was.

Until of course they forgot. To be superseded by those who never knew.

Which might tend to suggest that Hitchcock had no conception of immortality or of his work as art. It was ultimately disposable. A consumer product. Which of course is how it should be.

"Col. Hi. It's me again. Col? Are you there?"

Sometimes he just picks up the phone and doesn't actually say anything. I've never worked out whether this is an attempt to be super cool or whether it's actually contemptuous impatience. It's like people who pick up the phone and give you this irritable *YES?*, like a schoolteacher at the end of their tether. I suppose one way or another it's a power thing. But even if it is, I can somehow forgive this in Colin. It's actually quite funny when you think about it.

"I was meaning to say. Actually it was the main reason I called in the first place. One of the main reasons."

"Mmm?" he says.

It's my turn to be silent.

"Hello?" he asks eventually.

"I've been thinking. What I wanted to say."

"Yes?"

"It's just."

"Yes."

"You know that single, I think it's by Nilsson? Without You?"

I mean obviously he knows the song. The song is more famous probably than the singer, though I have this feeling that maybe Nilsson had a couple of hits. Didn't he do the theme from Midnight Cowboy or something too? And Colin is the perfect guy to ask about this. He knows about music. He's a music buff, a music freak. One house (actually, come to think of it, it was probably his parents' house) he stayed in, he had the spare bedroom completely lined with albums. The 12-inch vinyl things in coloured cardboard sleeves. From floor to ceiling. Shelves all round, with just a gap for the door and a gap for the window. It was never a big room in the first place but with the shelving installed and filled with records it became no more than a walk-in cupboard. I wonder whatever happened to all those albums?

Anyway, he's got tons of books about music. He also used to have stacks of copies of the NME going right back to the early 70s. He is, or used to be, a monumental hoarder. Somewhere, somehow or another, he'll have some information about Nilsson.

"Mmm," he says. Meaning, *yes, obviously*.

Actually, now I think of it, this is exactly the sort of thing he might even know off the top of his head.

"I just want to find out more about it. Like if it went to number one. I think it did. And if so, when?"

Tom would often turn up, like that. While we were having dinner. I mean, he had done for years, it wasn't a new thing. Not as a ghost. Not (let's be precise) as a ghostly figure. Tom wasn't like that. He could never dominate a stage like the ghost of Hamlet's father. He was reserved. In fact, I think I learned a certain type of shyness from him. The shyness that excuses itself in wry amusement. A reticence that comes across somehow as courtesy, as noble self-effacement. For a man as hard as he was, it was almost shocking to realise that he could be almost girlishly demure. And yet he never looked weak – even when he was knocked onto his back foot he was never beaten and he had this expression on his face that you warmed to, an expression that twinkled with the knowledge that it could say more. You could imagine him, for instance, flirting when he was younger. Flirting yet not quite knowing how to take it on further.

His tweed jacket, his woollen tie, his slightly bowed legs, his hook nose, his bad eye, his neat little moustache, silver going on white. His callused hands and his incredibly powerful handshake. The paradox of his voice – deep and rumbling, as from the centre of the earth, yet glazed with whistling sibilants.

My parents were babysitting. That's why they had been round that evening. I remember because after the sun had set we, me and Beth, headed off to Stokey for a drink in a pub. And we'd only gone a couple of blocks and we were walking down a street when a Hasid attracted our attention. He'd been standing on the path by his front door but when he saw us pass he coughed, said "excuse me," stumbled forward and beckoned to us.

Could we do him a favour?

Yes, I said tentatively.

Did we live around here, he asked.

Yes, we said.

This seemed to reassure him.

He needed me to come into his house and switch off a light. It was a light in his children's bedroom and they couldn't get to sleep with it on.

"I understand," I said.

"You see," he began to explain, "It is a holiday for us and..."

"Yes," I said. "I understand."

"You do?"

He seemed more relieved than surprised.

He led into the house and we went up two flights of stairs. He pointed to a light switch on a wall just inside a door that was standing slightly ajar. I reached my hand in and switched it off. He smiled. We went downstairs again. The stair carpet was filthy. The house smelled of boiled fish.

Outside, we walked on in silence.

Then I smiled to myself and Beth asked me what I was thinking.

"It's just pathetic, that's all. Just pathetic," I said.

She frowned, yet said nothing.

Her point is that I may technically be tolerant – but I don't *respect* their culture. And she may be right but I can never work out if I should be worried that she is right. Sometimes I point out to her that my mother's family came from the Outer Hebrides and their religious observance was similarly strict. No work on the Sabbath. No working of machinery. No cooking. It all had to be prepared the day before. I tell her that if I distrust such nonsense, and I do, I am at least consistent. I'm not clannish or insular. I find it as ridiculous in my own family as I do in others.

But I suspect that isn't the point.

Early on, when osteopathy or *healing* came up for debate, I would mention the fact that an old friend of mine in Edinburgh had become a Reiki healer. She'd written to say that she could now offer healing at a distance.

We don't talk about this now – because the last time I brought it up, one of Beth's friends, Ruth, was there. Beth was explaining about the healer that Charlie was visiting and I stupidly threw in an aside about the Reiki option we now had too.

"Reiki? What's that? That sounds interesting?"

Beth remained silent.

"Yes," I said, "she's in Edinburgh. She's offered to do distance healing."

"Distance healing?"

"Yes," I said.

Another silence. Beth looked apprehensive; Ruth was frowning. Then her face brightened. "Of course," Ruth said. "I was wondering how you could do healing at a distance." She tutted, smiled to herself, shook her head. "You must think me very stupid. It's obvious though, isn't it? She uses the telephone, doesn't she?"

That, I suppose, is why osteopathy seemed like such a small concession. Because, yes, right from the start Beth believed that osteopathy might be able to help with Charlie's contractures. Beth believed generally in osteopathy. Her father had sworn by it too. He would have terrible problems, he would be bent double, hardly able to move and he'd pop round to the osteopath and he'd be straightened out in no time. Once, playing golf, he'd (Beth's father, not the osteopath) got stuck at the top of his backswing. They had to carry him there like a contorted, twisted statue, three wood still in his hands; but the osteopath sorted him out and a couple of sessions later he's back bisecting fairways once more.

This was real. This worked. No faith. No magic. No juju men. And she persisted in this, even after I'd witnessed Charlie's osteopath in action.

It happened one afternoon when Beth was forced to attend a meeting she couldn't get out of – an afternoon on which Charlie had a session scheduled. Breaking that appointment was not considered a good idea, so I took her instead.

The practice was located in a small terraced house off Stoke Newington Church Street. The set-up reminded me of a dentist's I had gone to as a child in Edinburgh – perhaps because the man who answered the door sported one of those old fashioned white tunic-coats that dentists used to wear, with buttons (or more like studs, actually) up the side rather than the middle and a severe round collar. He obviously lived here in the house because as I manoeuvred Charlie's buggy into the hall I could see into a lived-in living room off to the right. But I hadn't much time to speculate on whether this also doubled as a waiting room because we were shown right through to his consulting chamber – a rather claustrophobic back parlour. It was an austere little disinfected cube of a room with white walls and grey-green lino on the floor; and in the centre of the lino there was a bed, a massage table on a pedestal, a medical sort of contraption like the centrepiece of an operating theatre.

It made me slightly uneasy – this mixture of the domestic and the supposedly clinical. The operating table on the one hand and, on the other, the nylony net curtain on the window. The charts on the wall – diagrammatic representations of skeletal structures, tendons, ligaments, muscle formations, nerve systems – and the potted yucca plant in the corner. I was thinking dentist but there were also slightly more bizarre and outlandish resonances. Massage parlour. Brothel. Psychiatrist. Sex therapist.

More than anything, I was thinking: *Strange things have happened in this room.*

We'd been rushed through so quickly, I hadn't really had time to size this guy up. He was about my age, I thought. He was balding and slight. Delicate might be a better word. He had freckles on the backs of his hands. His skin was very pale and the hairs on his forearms were light brown, almost reddish. He seemed nervy or highly strung and I began to wonder if there was something about me that unsettled him.

He certainly had no bedside manner. He told me to put Charlie on the couch and then when I'd done that, he told me to take her clothes off.

"All of them?"

"Yes."

"Down to her nappy?"

"Yes."

I wanted to say: "But won't she be cold?" It was springtime but it wasn't exactly warm and I'd have thought twice about lying unclothed on an operating table like that – its green, slightly textured plastic surface looked shockingly cold.

I said no more.

Charlie was about a year old at this point and what with her stiff arms and everything, it could be difficult getting her out of her clothes. It wasn't any easier trying to balance her on this table thing. He made no effort to help.

I started to get the feeling that he liked unsettling people. That he wanted a weird sort of atmosphere here. It was part of his thing. Charlie wasn't fazed by this at all – and after all, I reflected, she'd been to this place before. And she'd been examined by a hundred different people in a hundred different consulting rooms by then. She was a veteran. As long as you didn't pull her about too much, as long as you didn't inflict too much pain, she would take it all with a kind of serene acceptance.

We laid her as flat as we could. The osteopath perched himself on a tall stool at the head of the couch. I sat on a plastic bucket chair at the side of the couch and held Charlie's hand. She gazed at me, a calmness and an almost sleepy warmth in her eyes. And then he began his "examination". This consisted of passing his hands all over her body. Not touching. Just passing over, about half an inch from the surface of her skin. As if he were sculpting a larger version of her in the air.

Then he turned to me, engaging with me properly for the first time since we'd arrived. I can't remember what he said. Not exactly. It was all about her energy flows and the fact that pressures were building up at certain points. The energies weren't balanced. During Charlie's last session, he'd gone some way towards improving things but the imbalances had reasserted themselves. He'd do some more work on it today but it obviously wasn't something that could be sorted just like that.

And so he began. It took me several minutes to realise that he had begun. I thought at first that he had gone into a little pre-treatment ritual, the way a musician may withdraw into a moment of deep contemplation, focusing his energies before a virtuoso performance. It was almost as if he was praying. It looked as if he had his hands spread about the top of Charlie's head – but, as before, they weren't touching. Slightly cupped, as if holding an invisible foot-ball, they hovered half an inch away from her hair. And his eyes were shut. Not tight shut. Meditation shut.

I waited for him to begin properly. The minutes ticked by. Well, they didn't actually. There was an electric clock on the wall but it its second hand moved in a silent glide around its face. The first five minutes were an agony. I was sitting in an awkward position and had been waiting for him to finish his med-itational moment before making myself more comfortable.

So I was more than a little angry when it dawned on me that this was it. I was about to say something. Then thought better of it. I slid into an easier posi-tion. I was still holding Charlie's hand. She was still looking at me. It was as if we both knew that to make even the tiniest of sounds would be inappropriate.

And so we waited.

We played a game.

I smiled.

She smiled back.

She smiled.

I smiled back.

Sometimes when she smiled I delayed before I smiled back.

But mainly we waited.

Stillness.

We were posing for a painting.

The Adoration of the Osteopath and the Gullible Father.

And waited.

And then, after 20 minutes, he broke out of the spell. Exactly that. Suddenly he unfroze. His hands drifted gently away, no longer encasing the air around her head. He opened his eyes, stretched, arched his spine and tilted his head back so that he was briefly looking at the ceiling. It was the gesture of a man who had undergone a severe physical ordeal. He seemed drained, exhausted, spent.

And then he glanced at the clock.

He must have been reading my mind – I'd half suspected that he had gone to sleep and I'd been wondering what I'd do if we began to overrun our time. Would I clear my throat noisily? Say something? Touch his arm? And if so, would he have jumped?

He turned to me. There was something dismissive, disdainful in his voice. Was he really wary of me?

The session had, he said, gone a lot better than he could have hoped for. He had almost completely removed the imbalance of pressures within her skull.

I didn't know what to do. I didn't know where to look. I was tempted to give him one hard, aggressive syllable of laughter.

"You realised she's had a major operation on her skull?"

He raised his eyebrows. He seemed to be implying that any such an operation had been quite unnecessary.

"Yes." By now I was gazing at him, more in curiosity than anger. I couldn't remember the last time I'd come across someone as cold, clipped and brittle. I could smell sweat. Ever so faintly, sweetly acrid. It made me think of school. "She requires a lot more treatment though," he added.

It's clear he means him. Treatment by him.

"I think Beth plans to bring Charlie regularly."

"But I can do no more."

"Oh?"

"We have decided to move."

"Oh." My eyes drift. The conversation having ended, I'm expecting an out. I'm expecting him to supply an exit line, I'm expecting him to wrap this whole thing up, send us on our way. But nothing comes. There's a silence, a strained silence, an unfinished business silence, and my eyes drift back to his and I add: "Where to?"

I don't know why I asked that. As if I cared. And it's the strangest thing. There's a sudden thaw – and suddenly we've thrown ourselves into the most bizarre conversation. Suddenly, it's as if we're old friends and we're used to chatting like this on a regular basis. It's as if I'm hugely disappointed that he's no longer going to be available to treat Charlie. It's as if I'm his biggest fan.

My, how we chatter. And all the time I'm struggling to get Charlie back into her clothes – which I'm failing miserably with because I can sense he wants us out of here by half past and in my haste I'm getting rather tangled up. And still he isn't doing anything to help. In fact, despite the almost genial way he's carrying the conversation, the look on his face makes me suspect he's inwardly sneering at my efforts.

They're moving to the West Country, he informs me. People are more open minded there.

And they aren't in Stoke Newington?

He makes some rather vague allusion to the fact that down there (in the West Country, I presume), the prospects are better in his line of work.

The living can be better too, I offer, helpfully. In general, that is. You're closer to the countryside. The seaside.

Yes, he says. They've (him and his boyfriend or girlfriend, I assume) come to hate cities. They've come to despise London and all it stands for.

He has become nervy again. It's almost as if he's realised he's been making some sort of a big political statement. An ill-judged, rabble-rousing sort of a speech. The sort that may provoke a storm – and, perhaps, a backlash.

Not, though, from me? Surely not.

He says he hates the traffic and the pollution.

I don't really know what to say.

But I make a stab at something, I suppose.

"The house prices are more attractive down there too."

He considers this. Then offers me an icy smile.

I didn't include any of this conversation in my report back to Beth. Before she'd left for her meeting, Beth had told me she expected an extremely detailed report on our return – predicated on the assumption that I will have participated in the right spirit. She had extracted from me a promise that I would be positive about the whole experience. She'd told me not to spoil the session for Charlie. Don't be awkward, she insisted. Try to keep an open mind. You might learn something. At the very least, *behave*.

"How did it go?" she asks.

"Oh, pretty well," I say, convincingly. But then I hesitate – and she senses my hesitation. "The thing is, though... He won't be able to see Charlie again."

"What!"

"Yes. Actually, he's decided to move to the West Country."

"What?" Her voice has become a breathless whisper. Her eyes have widened, almost in awe. "What on *earth* did you say to him?"

*****

Actually, you don't pose for a painting – you sit.

I had an avalanche of replies in response to my newspaper ad. Well over a hundred. More than a few were just plain cranky. Incoherent notes in crayon on crepe paper, from the inmates of mental hospitals. I assume the crayon stuff was all from the inmates of mental hospitals because one was actually accompanied by a little note from a ward supervisor asking me not to be alarmed and explaining that the patient in question had insisted in writing to me and it was their right to do so and in fact it was encouraged as being of therapeutic value. In the crayoned message, as far as I could decipher it, the patient seemed to be saying that he had in fact already read my book on early British cinema and had by and large enjoyed it, though with some small misgivings, reservations and caveats.

Almost all of the rest of the replies, though, were of a more directly commercial nature. There were circulars from double glazing specialists, loft insulation installers, insurance salesmen and loan sharks; there were rather pathetic begging letters from people who purported to have fallen on hard times through tragic or unfortunate circumstances that were clearly no fault of their own; and bizarrely, to my mind at least, there was marketing material from prostitutes. This may seem a somewhat harsh way of putting it and in some cases it is, given that we're talking about a broad spectrum of material here. At one end there were the sorts of cards that you'd see in phone boxes in the West End. Then there were more elegantly produced handbills and A4 sized circulars that told you all sorts of reassuring stuff about the safe and discreet nature of the services outlined. And then there were the handwritten letters.

At first glance, these seemed like the sorts of responses you could imagine someone writing in reply to a lonely hearts ad. One in particular was beautifully handwritten in violet ink on good quality stationery and was written by a woman with a distinctly elegant turn of phrase. An educated woman of some substance, perhaps in her 50s. The stationery was perfumed. Lavender maybe. But basically she was up for light sexual duties on an ad hoc but fairly regular basis in return for remuneration, terms to be arranged. It was delicately couched. In all truth it was a lovely letter and if I wasn't so much of a coward in certain respects I'd probably have tried to find out more about it and her.

I do more groundwork. Slowly it goes. It creeps forward. I've actually got enough material already to do a cheesy trade press article or one of those vacuous sorts of pieces that run in the News Review section of the Sunday Times.

"Does it matter if celluloid disappears?" I've asked people who might care, people who you'd expect to have an opinion on this. A guy at one of the big film distributors. A cultural commentator. A film critic on a listings and entertainment magazine. They all miss the point. They all answer as if I've suggested to them that cinema – the artform – is in terminal decline. Cinema has never been healthier, they tell me. Admissions have been growing for years now. Home video, DVD and digital TV aren't threatening that, they're an extension of that, ensuring that more people than ever before are experiencing high quality on-screen narrative; and what's more, all these new technologies mean that people stand a greater chance than ever before of seeing the product more or less exactly as the director intended.

But that's not what I mean.

Put it this way. How much celluloid – of classic films, say – exists in private ownership? Not the rights to the films. The actual celluloid.

Dunno, they say. Does it matter?

"But don't you see? That's the question I'm asking you."

Does anyone own films in the way that they own the first editions of books?

It wasn't a great success, that night out. That evening my parents came round to babysit and we went down to Stokey and we, or rather I, switched off a Hasid's light for him. Me and Beth didn't have much to say to each other.

But maybe it was alright, because we had just about reached the morning when the letter would arrive. It arrived unexpectedly, as we had always expected. It was addressed to Beth. It was our summons. An invitation to an assessment at the neurological institute. She read it. And then she read it again. And then she handed it to me. I can't remember if there were tears in her eyes. Or if there were, what sort of tears they were.

Chapter four

We're late, obviously. It's well after two o'clock. They kept lunch going as long as they could but in the end they brought in the birthday cake for father to blow out his candles. For some reason (maybe Graeme has to get Emma and Gregor back to their mother that evening) the cake just had to be done at lunch.

There's a mild atmosphere of disapproval about the fact we couldn't have made it here earlier, as promised. You can tell it has been discussed around the table. Emma is particularly annoyed at the way things have turned out. But then she's annoyed at a lot of things these days.

"You're late uncle Seb. You missed Grandpa's candles." It's a friendly scolding and she's trying to smile and show that she's only pretending to be annoyed; yet there's an undercurrent of sulkiness here, an undercurrent that always seems to be present these days with Emma. And you can understand why. She has already entered that emotionally confused bit that we (me and my brother) didn't enter until probably our mid teens. And what with the divorce and everything, she's got more to be confused about than we ever did.

"Gregor blew them out anyway," says mother with a smile in her voice; and then she adds, her words bobbing ever more precariously as they are swept into a purling river of laughter: "Before we'd even finished singing happy birthday."

We unload the car and load some presents onto father. There are presents for others too. Gregor and Emma show initial interest in the gingerbread men and the iced cakes with hundreds and thousands faces but they only actually nibble and leave them basically untouched on the plate. Which is understandable because they've just finished their lunch.

By now, for some reason, we're all out in the hall again, even Gregor, who's got a hold of the newel post at the bottom of the staircase and is sort using it as a pivot to sort of swing back and forwards, making the whole flight of banisters creak. He arches himself backwards, looking at us upside down.

"Did you have a good journey," asks mother, to no-one in particular. I say nothing. In fact no-one says anything. By now everyone's looking at Gregor; except mother – she doesn't give it up, she stays on the case.

"The motorway wasn't too bad? It's so busy, isn't it, even on a Saturday?"

The question's sort of aimed at Beth, we can all sense that – because after all, she does the driving; but I know she's blanking all of this, having warned me in advance that she absolutely, categorically isn't going to field any of this sort of stuff.

"Yeah. I mean, no, it was pretty quiet," I say with a calculated vagueness. "We saw some amazing birds, birds of prey I think. Hovering and circling above the road."

"Just after the turn off for Oxford?"

I glance at Beth for confirmation but none is forthcoming. "Yeah. Yeah I think so."

"Kites," says mother. "Probably kites. Whatsisname reintroduced them recently on his estate."

No-one is able to help her out with a fix on Whatsisname. Not that it actually seems important. What's important, probably, is that mother continues to hold the floor in some sort of strangely compelling manner.

"Right," I say eventually. "Kites. Okay. And we stopped for lunch obviously."

"Oh. You stopped on the way for lunch?"

"Yes. You know that pub I've told you about, the one we've been to before? Well, we found it again. We had to stop somewhere obviously, didn't we, because Charlie was desperate for something to eat. It's quite a nice little village. We, er. We took a little stroll after lunch. Maybe… it's the sort of place you could imagine moving to, actually. Charlie saw this beautiful white horse."

"Grey," says Beth tartly. All eyes switch to her, intrigued at the incisiveness of this intervention.

"What?"

"Grey," she repeats. "A grey. There's no such thing as a white horse."

Father, who has been foraging round the fringes, standing in front of the hall mirror to shape clubless golf swings, then drifting over to tousle Gregor's hair as he (Gregor) explores ways of turning his arching monkey stretch into a bat-like hang, pricks up his ears at this.

"White Horse?" he says. "Remember those ads? The magazine ads."

But for some reason, probably a mere matter of habit, everyone except Gregor seems to be ignoring him.

"Are you sure?" asks mother.

"Oh yes," says Beth.

"Really?" say I.

"Gregor!" shouts Graeme. Because father is tapping Gregor little slaps on both cheeks and Gregor's trying to dodge them like a boxer and is failing and he can't let go of the newel post or he'd just fall backwards so he's squealing not-at-all-seriously for grampa to stop it. And all the time grampa or should I say father is telling this joke, ostensibly to Gregor.

"This great big white horse goes into a bar and asks for a beer. Doesn't he Gregor?"

"Stop it grampa."

"He does, Gregor, he asks for a beer and the barman pours him one. And as the horse is leaning on the bar, taking the first sips of his beer, the barman's staring at him quizzically, isn't he Gregor?"

"Stop it grampa."

"Here, says the barman, did you know there was a drink named after you? The horse frowns, puts down his beer. What, he says, a drink called Kevin?"

"Stop it grampa."

He does.

The contrast between Gregor's manic, uncontrollable energy and Charlie's inertness couldn't be more stark. I think Beth finds the comparison distressing at times. Gregor throws himself pell mell at life and is always breaking things – sometimes, you suspect, his own head. But he just bounces off and picks himself up. Even when there's been a sickening crunch or a chilling splat or a hollow knock, there might be a dazed look of incomprehension on his face but basically he shrugs it off. He's slightly highly-strung and can scream sometimes with excitement or work himself into a real state when he's tired but I can't help thinking that we weren't half so robust – physically robust – when we were his age. We were cry babies.

But sometimes there's peace and quiet. Then the little glass-inlaid side tables are safe on their spindly legs and the big-shaded table lamps aren't about to come crashing to the floor. Silver picture frames, Lladro figurines, the brightly coloured ceramic fruit bowl from Seville, bone tea cups in their delicate saucers – all safe. There's peace and quiet when Gregor lies on his tummy in front of some cartoons on the telly, his chin in his hands, his heels languidly kicking back and forward in the air.

Late afternoon and the grown-ups have coffee and biscuits.

When the rest of the room is distracted (a point of good natured contention between father and Graeme, say) mother puts a quiet question to me. "Would you really?" she asks. "Would you really move to a place like Nutwood?"

"I don't see why not."

She nods, takes another sip of he coffee – and in the following silence you can hear the other questions lining up. Actually, not so much lining up as milling about in confusion and falling all over each other. Because yes, obviously it's hard to reach the heart of this – half the questions you might conceivably come up with are, at the moment of truth, going to prove reluctant or awkward. Some are shy, some are embarrassed and some are downright shamefaced, lurking away in the shadows at the back. Some are obviously a betrayal of hope – and I'm not sure I'd want to confront them myself. There's maybe too much pain waiting to be stepped on here.

That's the thing about living in monstrous ignorance.

Will Charlie ever talk? Will Charlie ever walk?

I don't think any of us have actually managed to pose the questions so starkly. And maybe the thing we pussyfoot around is our own cowardice.

The thing is, there has always been something in mother that makes me need to act the hurt child. To pretend I am the victim of some monstrous injustice that just can't be helped and therefore I am tragically inconsolable. And obviously it follows that if I am inconsolable I succeed therefore in loading some of this onto her because she it is who should be offering consolation. The thing is, I suppose I actually want to load some of it onto her. Not maliciously – but the whole business, this whole dialogue, can sometimes be unnecessarily fraught. I appreciate that. I can make things difficult.

Anyway, mother asks some questions. She asks some questions about child-minding and options for schools and all that sort of pertinent stuff. We're both comfortable with that.

And then she says: "You know the other day on the phone you were talking about uncle Tom?"

"No I wasn't. Was I? I can't remember that."

"Yes," she says. "Don't you remember?"

"Remember what?"

It was certainly true I'd had a haunting dream. Uncle Tom hadn't featured, exactly. It was actually about the First Aid post at Murrayfield on the day of an International.

"I meant to ask you what made you think of him."

"I'm not sure I did. Why?"

"It's just odd the way our minds work," she says, staring into the middle distance, blank yet somehow attentive – the face that used to be her knitting face when she did knitting.

"It's certainly odd the way *his* works," offers Graeme.

And at some stage, much later, we have one of those strange hissing sorts of exchanges. It's the hissing of desperate conspirators. Mother is animated and somehow incoherent and I can't help being pathetically obtuse. We're just inside the kitchen and she's trying to get something into my thick head.

"I wish you'd told me what you were planning on getting him," she hisses. "I could have told you…"

"What?"

But she's not going to answer, she can't answer, she does a double-take and she shakes her head and waves her hand like a flag, more drowning than waving, the sign language for *drop it*. Because she can hear father coming.

We move further into the kitchen, away from the half-open door. I came in here to make myself a cup of coffee (no-one else wanted one this late) and mother followed me. And, as is the way of these things, father followed mother.

Ages ago I'd put Charlie into the cot and read her a story and Gregor and Emma have been getting ready for bed for at least three hours now (they're staying, it turns out, though Graeme is leaving with them very early); Beth's turned in too, probably to read in bed and Graeme will go to bed once he's persuaded Gregor and Emma to stop mucking about. The Agatha Christie film the rest of us have been watching has just finished.

And, though I'm still drinking red wine, I want a cup of coffee too. Which is why we all end up in the cramped kitchen, sort of milling around, pretending (mother and father at least) that they're about to go up to bed after they've sort of tidied away a few odd and ends (father has carried with him a couple of side plates and a rogue mug he's managed to round up) but not really wanting the evening to end at all.

And now I want to hear what mother has to say but obviously that's not going to happen because father is dogging the footsteps of one or other of us and I suspect it's probably me actually and if I go back into the living room, he'll come through too and watch the golf highlights which I was probably going to watch anyway and the thing is I wouldn't at all mind watching with him except it means that mother will go off up to bed and I'll probably never know what she was about to say.

And though I try a couple of diversionary tactics, that is exactly what happens.

It was probably Hitchcock who put the spookiness into spying – but some of his wheezes are so stylised that you suspect they were completely tongue in cheek. They certainly come across now as High Camp. Like the bit where the

hero, his back pressed to the wall, sidles up to the window, draws the curtain aside just a fraction with his little finger and takes a sideways peek down into the street below. And of course there are two shady customers down there, their hats drawn down over their eyes, the lapels of their heavy overcoats pulled right up. They're smoking. And they're standing right under a lamppost, in its cone of light, the blobs of their shadows spilled at their feet. Maybe there are wisps of mist starting to drift about the streets.

So, anyway, there's Hannay inviting this femme fatale, this international women of mystery, back to his flat. Within seconds of Hannay closing the door, the phone begins to ring. And here's the thing. Annabella insists that Hannay doesn't answer it.

Do we wonder why? I'm not sure we ever really think it through – we just love the melodrama of it all. We don't think of enemy agents. The two shady customers smoking cigarettes beneath a lamppost in the street below. Or their equally shady colleagues who are (presumably) round the corner in a phone box making the call. We don't think about snipers in the building opposite, with a sightline into the roomspace around the telephone.

Not as such. We merely buy this metaphor of pervasive evil. We swallow it whole. Nor do we really stop to consider (and Hitchcock is definitely on thinner ice here) the ridiculousness inherent in the whole proposition. Hannay bumping into Annbella was after all the most unlikely of random events. We don't stop to remember that Hannay isn't even in the phone directory because he's just visiting from Canada and is only renting the flat on a short lease. It would be impossible to find the number for that phone. And anyway, what would happen if he did answer? What are they going to do to him down the telephone line?

Anyway.

We believe nothing.

It's more absolute than that.

We're merely turned on by the spookiness. Other than that our minds are blank. We're completely aware of the oppressiveness of that phone. We're aware of just how oppressive the ringing of a phone can be. Ringing in a bare room.

I sort of got the fact that mother was trying to tell me something about the presents we'd brought for father. Something about their appropriateness. You won't be surprised to hear that I'm useless at buying presents. Some people (and it's not just women, either) are absolutely brilliant at buying presents. For some it's almost a hobby. They stockpile in case of emergencies. They have cupboards bulging with possible gifts covering any eventuality.

Not for them the recalcitrant, graceless, *So. What do you want for your birthday, then?*

It used to be so much easier when we were small, me and my brother. Father played golf. So we each bought him a golf ball. Birthday and Christmas, a golf ball. A Dunlop 65, say, in a squeaky black cellophane wrapper that reeked of Quality. There were some exceptions, some dangerously radical departures, but mostly it was golf balls. And everyone seemed happy with the system.

Now I phone up mother and ask her: "What should I get him? Is there anything he wants?"

It's always the same. First a dreadful, dark silence down the other end of the line, as if something awful is about to pass between us. Then a sigh.

"Oh, I hadn't thought."

"No ideas?"

"Oh I don't know. It's so difficult. He's so difficult to buy presents for."

Yes, I know.

Then, after another shared silence, she ventures the information that father was looking for his good screwdriver the other day and couldn't find it. (He'd expected mother would know where it was. Words had been exchanged. Perhaps he needed a new screwdriver.) She adds that the other day in B&Q he was looking at one of those rubber-cased torches. You know, the black ones that you can bounce off the floor and never break. (I can see him now, playing with the two little nodules, one for on and one for off, and dazzling himself.)

I've always resisted the temptation to buy rubber torches.

On the other hand, I've always admired people who give inappropriate presents as a matter of policy. Colin, for instance, always gives his brother-in-law (a stuffy and slightly pompous Chartered Surveyor) Action Man type presents – like the shark repellent body creme used by Scuba divers; or a year's subscription to Soldier of Fortune magazine – and everyone pretends to be amused while not being entirely sure what they should read into this, if anything.

I don't think I can carry that sort of thing off, though. I once gave a tin of Spam to an ideologically-committed vegetarian on her birthday and she was not amused. Not at all amused. Even though I'd wrapped it up beautifully.

"Why don't you get him…" mother speculates at last. "Why don't you…"

Anyway, as far as mother is concerned, I'm pretty sure I know what's coming.

I had a girlfriend once who gave her father all sorts of foodie treats as presents. Bottles of fine wine, cognacs, Stilton cheeses bedded in straw within miniature wicker hampers. He was a generous man, filled to bursting point with bonhomie – and these gifts were always received with great roars of approval. A tasting session, in which everyone was invited to participate, would immediately begin.

My father has never been like that. There's nothing remotely epicurean or Falstaffian about him. And for my part, I don't know, maybe I instinctively feel that presents should be substantial – and that what they very definitely should-n't be is ephemeral. This is probably dreadful vanity on my part and even more probably lies right at the heart of my problems with presents. When I give a gift, I want it to stay given; I want the recipient to see it often and to think warmly of me.

"Why don't you get him... well, a bottle of whisky? You know he'd like that."

Possibly. But this has always seems to be a dismal cop out. This is the grown-up version of the golf ball. And yet it would be nice just to give in and go for this – because the thing is that this whole subject never really goes away. No matter how determinedly you put off thinking about it, people's birthdays still arrive; and even if you manage to get them something, desperately, at the last minute, there's always going to be next year to look forward to.

But this year I did something radically different. It helped that I was slightly drunk at the time. I was slightly drunk and I was passing this place called Past Times and I had this brainwave and I went in and I bought the shop.

That's not strictly true, obviously. It's a shop that, as its name suggests, does all this slickly packaged retro and nostalgia stuff, most of it dreadfully senti-mental and much of it verging on the offensively tasteless – essentially it's just one step up from a souvenir shop, the sort that sells plastic policemen's helmets.

So, no, I didn't exactly buy the whole shop. But I did leave with:

An Art Deco presentation tin of fudge

A video compilation of three episodes of Dad's Army

A framed version of one of those old "Guinness is good for you" ads with the toucan

A book, produced in vaguely 1930s style, of humorous and unlikely golfing anecdotes, complete with suitable wood-cut-style illustrations

A video of The 39 Steps, 1935, starring Robert Donat

And a whole load of other bits and pieces, including, I think, an Ovaltine mug, a Flying Scotsman key ring and a couple of travel posters reproduced from the Golden Age of Steam.

So anyway. Father went to bed at maybe 11.30 and I still sat there drinking and watching the television. Which wasn't very clever because it was my turn again on Sunday to get up and attend to Charlie in the morning (she usually wakes at seven-ish) and change her nappy and give her her milk and do her physio exercises and eventually get her dressed. And it's just crap doing all that stuff when you're sleepy and hungover.

But maybe I didn't really even notice that father had gone off up to bed.

Until mother came in.

She was wearing a dressing gown over her nightie. Her dressing gown and nightie always look as if they're made out of some horrible crackly nylon or rayon type material but they probably aren't, though for a while when we were kids we did have nylon sheets.

So anyway, she sat down and I put the television off.

She said she couldn't sleep.

And she said she wanted to tell me how heartened she was at how well Charlie was looking.

There's a deep vein of skirling sentimentality running through mother and she goes all moist-eyed when she talks of Charlie as *such a bonnie wee soul.* Which she is, obviously. It just makes you slightly nervous to hear it said in such tremulously apocalyptic tones. And although mother has this amazing knack of still, after all these years, seeming innocent, almost girlish, she also has the spirit of the Hebrides in her veins – which obviously can be twinkling and fey but it can also be dreadfully doom-laden and sorry for itself.

Anyway, she said, she just thought I'd be interested in seeing this. She'd looked it out ages ago and she'd been meaning to show me all day. At this point I become aware that there's a photograph in her hand. An old photograph, a dog-eared old black and white print.

She hands it to me. "Bet you can't tell me who that is," she says.

So that's when it happened. There and then. And as always with these things, there's a certain inevitability about the whole business.

An old photograph. A crinkle old monochrome photograph of uncle Tom, obviously, astride a tractor.

"Bet you can't tell me who that is?"

She didn't mean uncle Tom, obviously she didn't. She meant the infant on his lap. Tom is trying to hold the child in such a way that it (I still can't get into the habit of tying an infant down to a he or a she) can at least get its hands near if not onto the steering wheel of the tractor. The infant looks a little bit excited and a little bit scared but mainly put upon.

"It's me, isn't it?"

I was cheating slightly. I had a vague memory of having seen this picture before. And anyway, when mothers ask you that sort of pointed question in that sort of a way, there can only really be one answer.

Be that as it may, she seemed almost tearful that I'd hit on the right answer.

It was turning out to be a pretty mixed up summer, bleak and wintry one day, stupidly hot the next. Sometimes I'd come down in the late afternoon and Charlie would be in her buggy and Beth would be sitting with her outside at the patio table under the sun shade. Beth will be spoon-feeding her and Charlie will be eating slowly, dazed and dozy with the heat.

And the day itself will seem to be drowsing.

I'll sit down. And Beth will ask, out of nowhere: "Are you happy here?"

"Yes," I'll say immediately, nodding as I scan the question for hidden traps, snagging ambiguities, layers of meaning.

"Do you remember when we first moved in?"

She sounds almost wistful, which surprises me. So I say nothing. The world is breathlessly still.

It's almost three years since we moved here – and it's true that this day is very like the day we moved in. Hot, a dry heat, a thin heat; and eerily still. As if all the noisy people in the world were sleeping through the long afternoon.

The truth is, however, that our first summer here was not a good one – largely, I think because we brought the gloom of Northfield Road with us. There was something sinister and brooding about that house (our previous house, obviously) in Northfield Road. Actually it was only the ground floor flat of one of those huge old Victorian houses at the top of the hill; solid and weighty and ponderous, with its thick walls and its huge rooms with faraway ceilings and its huge, sturdy windows with whole forests of wood build into the casements. The building's angles were sturdy and heroic and it had clearly been built for a departed race of large boned people.

It was the house we had brought Charlie back to when we finally escaped hospital. A stiff little scrap of humanity with a naso-gastric feeding tube taped to her cheek. And maybe the intensity of those days, when the house was a laying up place between hospitals, fixed it forever. But on the other hand I suspect it had always existed on the borderland of somewhere mildly apocalyptic and that it had always oozed a sullen, indefinable sense of menace or foreboding. It had a huge living room (as big in itself as whole flats I've lived in) dominated by a black fireplace with Egyptian influences in its pillars and

decorative effects. Above the fireplace, a painting – a ruins-and-landscape gothic affair in a weighty black lacquer frame. The living room was always cool, even at the height of summer, even in a heatwave. The damp cool of a cellar or a crypt.

There was an evergreen gothic about the back garden too. Towering fir trees, merging in places to form a screen, ivy, dark vegetation shading into black. A thin garden but long, stupidly long, stretching back into forever; a patchy grassland, mossy and marshy in winter, a hay field in summer. Near the bottom there was a pear tree that produced huge fruit.

One day in the autumn of the year before Charlie was born, I gathered some windfalls. They were a pretty sorry sight – all pulped and bruised and pecked by birds – but I managed to cut away the badness and retrieve a bowlful of good bits. They tasted golden.

An even bigger pear tree, with even bigger fruit, stood in a bit of waste ground beyond that no-one had access to. You'd look enviously at this inaccessible fruit as it ripened heavily. So, yes, the fruit was the happiest aspect of Northfield. Mostly the place was apocalyptic and gloomy – and it wasn't anything to do with the fact that while we were living there, someone was murdered in the house almost directly over the road from us. Or it was very little to do with that.

Or the family arguing upstairs.

And we felt generally pretty exposed because our kitchen was overlooked by a block of flats. One day, weeks after we had moved, a woman came up to Beth in the street and, smiling sort of sweetly but madly, asked, without any pre-amble: "How is your child?"

This was odd because Charlie was at the child-minder's and Beth had never met this woman before in her life.

"I'm sorry?" Beth said. Sorry as in: explain yourself.

She did. She lived in the flats. The fourth floor. She used to watch Beth feeding Charlie. She often wondered about Charlie's condition and even worried about her.

So, yes, it should have felt magic to move here, even though we're only three streets away from Northfield. Even the house – a classic London terrace – is on a more human scale. It's right in all sorts of ways. The street is a throwback, a time warp, a zone that got stuck in the 1950s. Children even play in the street – there's no through-traffic because the top end has a metal no-go swing gate across it. And there's an old-fashioned shopping parade just round the corner with a hardware shop, a fishmonger and a fruiterer.

It's almost too gentle to be London – for which I blame the Hasids. In many of the streets round here, people paint their doors and window frames. They clip their hedges. And when they're out there, clipping their hedges, they say hello to each other. Not in every street, obviously – but even in the run-down streets, the raggedness isn't predatory. The Hasids ride black-framed sit-up-and-beg bicycles, machines that creak when they stand up in the pedals. They wear Homburg hats and have shiny shoes. And cycle clips where appropriate, obviously. And they stretch the day way into the night – they visit their synagogues and meeting rooms at all hours, it seems, and there are people out and about the whole time. Doors are open, people visiting, people chatting on doorsteps or out on the pavements.

But the truth is, we managed to bring the oppressiveness with us. I'm amazed she has forgotten this. We had a huge row over whether we should have a housewarming party, for instance. I was all for having everyone round the evening we moved in, cracking open a few bottles of wine among the packing cases and not being bothered about the mess we would make because we were going to have to start from scratch anyway. But Beth was having none of it. In the end we didn't have a housewarming party at all. And we didn't tend to have many visitors. They'd come round once in the weeks after we moved and then perhaps you'd feel they were reluctant to come again. Maybe they'd feel we hadn't quite sorted ourselves out.

It's no simple matter this, anyway. The whole area is criss-crossed by fault lines, inconsistencies, discontinuities. Stamford Hill is that strange childhood memory you're not sure is a dream or not. That ungainly, odd, unlovely, slightly-disconcerting-though-bland area you visited one day with your mother; or perhaps with an aunt because your mother had something unforeseen to attend to that day and you couldn't go with her, wherever it was, leaving you confused and slightly anxious, aware for perhaps the first time ever of possible calamity and the frailty of human wishes. There's something odd (something slightly discordant) lurking beneath the surface here, something alien and unsettling and yet so nearly familiar (a dilapidation of the familiar, perhaps), as if it were a memory belonging to someone else.

Time slips here, creating unfinished business.

That's where we are.

So we waited. It was one of those instances where time plays tricks on you. It was one of those instances where everything seems brightly-lit, etched, super-real. It was one of those instances where nothing, not even the dropping of a petal from a bunch of wilting roses in a jar across the ward, or the twitching of an eyelid of a sleeping woman in the bed opposite, will escape you. Every breath, every scraping of a chair leg, every tinkling of a spoon in a mug of tea, every dropped biro, every swish of the swing doors. You're capturing it all in pin sharp resolution, the big stuff – the chattery noise and the comings and goings clustered around the nurses' station – and the small. The music of the spheres and the itching of microbes. Nothing escapes. And yet you know you will carry nothing of it. If you want to set it down, you will have to recreate it. Imagine it. Make it up.

We waited to see the daughter we knew we might never see again. In our imagination she had become hideously ugly, a mutant, and at the same time infinitely pitiable, beautifully tragic.

I knew that someone would come and we'd know they had come to tell us something because they would glance over at us as they passed by on their way down the length of the ward to the nurses' station. And then there'd be a hushed little conversation between one of the nurses and the someone who had come to tell us something. There would be more glances in our direction.

And then the two of them, the nurse and the someone who had come to tell us something, the two of them would head towards us, Beth propped up on pillows on the pillow frame and me sitting by the bedside in one of those low slung wooden box-framed easy chairs beloved of common rooms.

So anyway, Beth would be in bed and I'd be in my chair and the nurse would arrive and would drawn the curtains round, screening us in completely.

That's what would happen if we waited.

Yes.

We waited. Maybe we talked or maybe we were silent but we waited.

And the air swarmed.

It swarmed as it does in the notorious Garden of Forking Paths, a garden where an infinite series of times exists, a growing, dizzying net of divergent, convergent and parallel times. Because here it is discovered that time forks perpetually towards innumerable futures in which all things are possible. In that garden you perceive (all around you and within your own dark body) an intangible swarming, an infinite saturation of invisible persons, secretly busy and multiform in other dimensions of time.

I didn't think of in quite that way as I sat there, waiting. But yes, the air swarmed. It swarmed all right. It swarmed with ifs and buts. It swarmed with *it would* dancing attendance upon *it were*. It swarmed with all the sorts of stuff that may make your scalp crawl.

That was what the waiting was like.

Anyway, the phone rings and Annabella in a voice of doom tells Hannay not to answer it and it rings forever. Then it stops. So now Annabella and Hannay are creeping around this spartan flat and they're somehow, naked, exposed, because there are no curtains on the windows (the flat is being redecorated) and the light from the streetlights streams in. It's all stark and echoey.

Hang on. No. It happens like this.

They're about to go into the main room.

Wait till I find the switch, says Hannay.

Not yet, says Annabella, breathlessly, enigmatically.

And then she asks him to turn the mirror (the one above the fireplace, I think) to the wall. It's another little touch we fall for. It's probably something to do with the tradecraft of assassins and spooks and spies; but also, somehow, it's charged with a meaning far deeper and more powerful than that.

(Now he can turn the light on. But does he? I can't remember.)

And then, of course, there's the bit of business with the map.

At some point during the night, Annabella bursts into the room where Hannay (who, although almost irresistible to women, is ever the gentleman) has been sleeping. The assassins have forced a window, gained entry to the flat and have planted a knife between Annabella shoulder blades – presumably as she ran from them to seek Hannay's protection.

She falls. Dead.

She lies sprawled over Hannay's bed, her dead hand flung out before her. And in this hand there is a map. And of course the camera focuses in on this map. It becomes almost like a caption shot in a silent film – the closing of one chapter, the opening of another.

It is a map of the area around Killin in what used to be Stirlingshire.

Ringed is a hamlet called **Alt na Shellach**.

Charlie is, as she usually is at teatime, strapped securely into her TripTrap high chair. And I come in and Beth immediately hits me with:

"Daddy looks tired." Mock-serious in tone. It's hard to tell if Charlie responds to this but you suspect she does, she knows there's some tomfoolery afoot. "Perhaps daddy needs a rest," Beth continues. "Or a change. That's what they say Charlie. That a change is as good as a rest."

And Beth is laughing now, laughing to herself, maybe at the thought she's obviously just had. "How about… air traffic controller. Do you think daddy would make a good air traffic controller?" Beth laughs even louder now and Charlie's smiling too – incredulously, cautiously, but clearly warming to what-ever's happening here.

And I'm smiling too. Not because I think this air traffic controller thing is funny as such, though maybe it is. No. I'm smiling because I'm thinking about the time I absolutely convinced the people I was working with, in a job long ago, that I was about to resign so I could retrain as an ice hockey referee.

To my surprise but immense pleasure, no-one ever laughed.

"Will you have to wear one of those black and white striped shirts?" they asked.

I'm smiling but actually, underneath, I'm in no mood, because I've just had the strangest conversation with Jules. Totally bizarre, actually, because I'd have sworn that Jules had little or no interest in early British cinema… or early any-thing, come to that. But it turns out that just about everything to do with moving pictures will now strike a chord with Jules. Because, you see, it turns out that his brother is a video editor in Soho (I didn't even know he had a brother until this point) and he's is about to go back to film school. So in short, Jules currently sees this as very much his sort of territory.

And then he says: "You know they're knocking down Gainsborough Studios, don't you?"

"What?"

And here's a thing. When it comes to early British cinema, Jules, he reveals, has started leaning towards cynicism – especially as regards the industry's appar-ent contempt for its own heritage. He's had a couple of conversations with his brother about this – and he has discovered that the whole scandalous point about the film business is that tons of immensely valuable material is dumped each year. The tragedy is, it's always been happening. For donkey's years now. It's a ferocious erasure of history on a Stalinist scale. Now and then, a Soho dis-tributor or facilities house will change hands and the new owner will find all sorts of archive stuff down in the cellar and they'll just hire a skip and fill it as quickly as they can. Even the BBC, which ought to know better, junks hun-dreds of hours of irreplaceable footage each year. Classic works of art. Okay, maybe not works of art, but you know what I mean. Near enough. The long and the short of it is that for decades we've been burning the house down.

"So you can forget it," he states, just a little too enthusiastically for my liking. "Nobody gives a stuff about film history."

"What do you mean? I mean, how do you know?"

"Because, er, um, ah… "

He's started doing that a lot recently. *Er, um, ah…* I can't work out if it's some sort of affectation that he's cultivating or whether it's genuine and he really is becoming more absent minded because his brain is shot to pieces. On the other hand, it might just be a bad habit he's fallen into, a form of audible punctuation, a verbal tic or a means of buying himself a bit of thinking space. Er, um, ah... The last syllable, the *ah*, is hardly voiced at all, it really falls off – in fact, so soft is it that it might actually be another *er*. "... er, um, ah... because it's just like I'm trying to tell you about Gainsborough Studios. It's absolutely bloody typical, isn't it?"

The thing is, I had vaguely heard about the demise of Gainsborough Studios. I'd read something about the possibility that they were going to redevelop the site as flats; but that was ages ago. Years ago. And then when nothing actually happened (you suspected the usual stories: local government corruption, planning permission shenanigans, dodgy finance, bankruptcies, bad blood and worse debts), they started using the derelict shell of the building as a rough and ready theatre and it was in vogue for a while as a bleak post-industrial backdrop for, you know, cutting edge, uncompromising creativity. If I thought anything about it at all, I assumed it would be like the Roundhouse – forever in limbo, condemned in theory but in practice absolutely refusing to go away.

"I mean they really are doing it for real this time," Jules says. "I get the bus past it nearly every day. This morning they'd demolished one of the main walls. You can see right in under the roof. It's a weird sort of structure actually. Funny you never notice that sort of thing before. But it really is weird being able to look in under the roof structure and see all these beams and spars and things."

"What were they made of?"

"What?"

"The roof structure?

"How do you mean?"

"Wood or iron or steel or... or aluminium, say."

Jules almost explodes. "I don't know, do I?"

My first reaction is that he's right – that this is an inane and stupid and meaningless speculation to pursue. But almost immediately I realise that maybe also he's wrong. But anyway, by now he's off on a slightly different tack.

"Me and my brother wanted to break into the site and steal something. A memento."

"Like what?"

"I don't know." This time, the *I don't know* is slightly less vehement. Sometimes Jules can sound quite sane. "I mean, even just a brick. It's not the actual object that counts, it's the fact that you've done it."

"I'd be up for that."

"Yes?"

"Yes. Absolutely."

And then, as if he hasn't heard me properly or doesn't want to have heard me properly, he doesn't pursue it – not directly at any rate. "Two nights ago me and my brother were drinking just off Essex Road and he suggested it. So that's what we did. After closing time. We went down there. But there were dogs barking, I think from inside the site. Guard dogs, you know? So we hung about a bit and went away again."

"So you want to give it another go?"

"Definitely. How about tonight?" he says.

I'm already looking at my diary. I'm actually looking at the wrong page but the thing is, it's fascinating. There's an "on this day" feature that I've never noticed before. For instance, at the bottom of the space for 7 June, it says: "1905: Norway declared its independence from Sweden." And then for 8 June, it says: "632: the prophet Muhammad, founder of Islam, died." And so on.

"No, I can't tonight. It's impossible."

"How about tomorrow then?" says Jules.

"Did you know, that on the seventh of June, 1905, Norway declared its independence from Sweden?"

"Yeah, yeah. Tomorrow?"

"No really. Did you know that?"

"No of course I didn't know that."

"I mean, did you even know that Norway was once ruled by Sweden?"

There's no reply, though I'm pretty sure he feeds me the hint of a sigh. The ricepaper-thin pages of my diary rustle and crackle as I turn them.

"Tomorrow? I'd like to say yes but I'm meeting up with Colin earlier and I can't promise. How about the day after?"

Jules tuts. "I don't know…"

"You could come round here, have something to eat, pasta or something, and we'll have a couple of glasses of wine and go down and check it out."

"What kind of pasta?"

"I don't know. Penne? Is that what it's called? The tubular type cut at an angle."

"I meant the sauce."

"Oh, em, puttanesca probably. You know – the Loyd Grossman jars."

"Oh... okay." At this he sounds bright. Almost cheerful.

"See you."

"Take care."

"Oh, Jules... " I manage to catch him before he puts the phone down. "Sorry about the other day." I hesitate. He hesitates. There's a silence. "The coats thing. It's actually a good idea."

"No, maybe you're right," he says. There's a pause, a beat in time, which concludes with him saying , "Anyway," in a sort of conclusive manner.

And that was that. I put the phone down as quickly as I could.

Actually, I had a brief twinge of elation. This might just be perfect. I had an ending. The story would end here. Or rather there. Gainsborough Studios. Whatever else was to happen, my article about early British cinema would have an ending involving me and Jules, slightly drunk maybe, scrambling about on the rubble of a demolition site.

Things don't often go this well, I can tell you.

On the other hand, between this (rather neat, I thought) way to end the piece and the article's beginning (Mr Memory, remember, then a lead, as yet undis-covered, that would open a door into a dusty and almost forgotten twilight world of celluloid) I knew there would be a long journey. If this thing had any beauty at all, and I suspected that it had, its beauty was going to turn out to be of a wild and uncanny sort.

Thus it was inevitable I'd buy a map of Killin (and surrounding area) sooner rather than later. And in fact that very day I took a trip down to Stanford's in Long Acre and I bought Ordnance Survey Landranger sheet 51.

There is no mention of Alt na Shellach on or by the River Lochay as there is in the map clutched by the dying Annabella.

That pleased me but did not satisfy me.

Beth's mum never really understood that we'd literally only moved two or three blocks. It's unusual for people to do that in London, I suppose. The city is so vast that you never expect even the smallest amount of continuity.

So, with Beth's mum, it didn't really sink in until she took Charlie for a walk in her buggy one afternoon and got a little bit lost. By sheer coincidence, when she was beginning to panic (she didn't have a note of our address or phone number or anything) she ended up in front of the old house in Northfield Road.

That really messed with her head. Something scary was happening here. Something more than time had slipped. Or she was dreaming or hallucinating. She had to work very hard indeed to convince herself that me and Beth were not inside the house there, waiting for her and Charlie to return from their walk. What made it worse was the fact that although she was really absolutely lost, she also sort of knew where she was, except that she didn't. That knowledge was useless to her – and she desperately *wanted* us to be their behind that door, waiting for her. She wanted to cling to the place. So she stood there for what seemed for ever, staring at it. Like some lost soul.

And it took her hours to find her way back to the new house, though it was literally a couple of blocks away. We were beginning to get worried.

When she got back, she was almost tearful.

We had it all planned out. We'd meet in the pub down the hill from Colin's and have an early lunch before crossing over the river (he'd got the loan of his sister's beat-up old Ford Escort for the week while she was in the Canaries with the kids and her new man) and then check out a couple of things on Colin's list before heading up to Leytonstone and 517 The High Road, where Alfred Hitchcock was born in the flat above the family shop. A greengrocer's, I think I remember reading somewhere.

But it was a really crap day, cold and grey and overcast and oppressive. It felt like March and I just had a tee shirt on under a thin cotton jacket. I had a headache too.

I got to the pub in Maze Hill some time after Noon. And of course Colin wasn't there and he didn't arrive as agreed at half past and though he lived just up the hill, hardly more than five minutes away, I certainly wasn't going looking for him. I had a drink. And then I had another one. It was hard to say whether I was angry or not because you always sort of expect Colin to be late. But I was cold right through and I suppose I was more depressed than angry.

The notion was that Colin was going to show me the real Itchycoo Park and then take a few pictures at a couple of nearby locations and there'd be plenty of time to get up to Leytonstone. And from Leytonstone I could easily get a

bus back along Lea Bridge Road and another one round the top of Clapton.

He was an hour late, sullen and red faced and definitely unapologetic. He looked a bit odd, to be honest. I'd never seen him so red-faced before – and in fact the whole effect was rather unsettling, the way his flushed face was set off against the yellowish brown of his hair. I didn't say anything though – and anyway, by and large he was distracted and fidgety and not up for discussing anything. We were both monosyllabic, pretty much.

Our food took ages to come and by then I'd had yet another drink on an empty stomach and felt fractious and disgruntled and when we'd eaten, Colin revealed that as a matter of fact he hadn't brought the car to the pub anyway and we had to climb back up the hill and I knew he'd done this because he had something he wanted to show me back at his flat, some old piece of photographic equipment he'd picked up for next to nothing at Greenwich market because it doesn't actually work but he's sure he can fix it eventually.

So we go back up the hill and it's only when we get back to Colin's flat that he reveals the whole truth – he was lying about the car or rather he wasn't exactly lying, he *could* have borrowed it because his sister genuinely is away but the fact is that it (the car) hasn't been running too well and he decided not to risk it. So we have a cup of coffee and a cigarette and I'm barely speaking to him by them. I'm cold to my marrow and sulky and evasively monosyllabic and kind of just resigned to the fuck up waste of time that this whole idea has been. It's gone half three by the time we eventually head off for Itchycoo Park (which is miles away over the other side of the river at Manor Park), on foot via the Greenwich tunnel.

A couple of times I shape to put our proposition to him. It is, after all, the main reason, perhaps the only reason, I'm here; but somehow, though we're walking in silence, each opportunity just seems to slip away. We're actually in the tunnel itself, deep below the Thames, when he breaks the silence.

"This Hitchcock thing," he says.

That and no more; so I wait a beat, a step and a half, and I say: "It's not a Hitchcock thing as such."

"Whatever."

We walk on in silence for a while. And then Colin does this very bizarre bad acting thing. He acts being struck suddenly by this amazing idea. Amazing, yet so simple, it's incredible no-one has ever thought of it before. He tuts and shakes his head and only just refrains from smacking the heel of his hand off his forehead. Then somehow he's in front of me yet facing me, back-pedalling. He looks sort of possessed.

"You know who you should talk to about this?" he says. It's not really a question. "John. John's bound to be able to help you with this sort of thing."

"John?"

"Yes. Why not?"

He's half skipping, half scuttling backwards, still facing me as he's saying this. He's still deadly serious. It's really incongruous, this intense seriousness when he's basically skipping backwards, but I don't say anything.

"John Toby?"

He melts out of skipping mode; and, elastically almost, eases himself back into the fluid rhythms of walking, falling back into step beside me. "Yeah," he says. "John Toby."

We walk in silence for a while and I suppose I'm frowning. At first I'm just plain confused but as my head clears I suspect that what I'm feeling deep down is a sense of betrayal.

"John Toby?" I say it again, as if I didn't believe my ears the first time around.

"I thought you said you hadn't been in touch with any of that lot."

"Think about it. John comes across all sorts of things on the stalls. And he could even put the word out for you. Put some feelers out. He probably knows the right people to go to and even if he doesn't he'll certainly know someone who does."

There's a certain logic here. I can see that.

"But what made you think about John Toby?"

"Well it's obvious, isn't it?"

"Is it?"

"Don't you think so?"

"Have you seen him recently?"

"Maybe." He shrugs. "Yes."

"Why didn't you say anything? The other day."

"It must have slipped my mind."

"But how? What happened? Did you just bump into him or something?"

"Look, it's just an idea, right."

I can't remember if Colin knows that John Toby sort of makes me nervous. John Toby has always made me nervous, irrespective of whether or not I once had a huge crush on his girlfriend. He made me nervous primarily because he was and presumably still is a hard little bastard who was always likely to give you a hard time, especially when he was drunk – and John was a huge drinker. An accomplished and proficient drinker. Basically he could be aggressive and he was aggressive because he was chippy. Here was a whole crowd of us who were basically spoiled and middle class and precious (he was contemptuous of the fact that we all wanted to do jobs that were, like, you know, creative) while in contrast he (or so he'd have you believe) had come up through the school of hard knocks. His skills were ultimately street skills. He liked to be feted as the king of the hussle and he maintained that the only human skill that counted for anything in this world was the art of selling. He was a guru and self-appointed expert in *the sell*. All of which was fine, even though some of us knew he wasn't quite the working class hero he pretended to be and that his dad had made good in the 1980s and now drove a Bentley.

But the thing was, first and foremost, that John was older than all of us in that crowd and he patronised us (mostly me, actually, it seemed at the time) hugely on that account. Anyway, though he aspired to be a professional Cockney he just wasn't, in the end, stupid enough. He somehow wasn't big enough. There was always something petty and mean minded about him. Professional Cockneys, I've always thought, look as if they might have big hearts. But anyway, John's real mates weren't poncey like us, they were the people like him who did the stalls (not market traders as such, not fruit and veg, more counterculture, antiques, arts and crafts) and the people he drank with down his local in Dalston. And maybe that was the only really genuine part of the act. Because John was a huge drinker. An epic drinker, a prodigious drinker, a drinker of mythological status.

Kate didn't drink very much, but when she did, she got hilariously drunk.

She was never aggressive. Sweet, perhaps a little shy. And Kate was always bright, bright in the sort of way that irritated John when he saw it in other people. Bright as in always being one step ahead of you the whole time, bright as in seeing the point of the joke long before you did. But bright in other ways too. When she smiled she could light up a room. Her eyes twinkled. I know that sounds a cliché but it really happened that way.

She was tall, slightly willowy. Almost pre-Raphaelite. Or like the girls in the paintings by that Italian artist, Modigliani. Long, elegant, sad in some respects, almost fragile. Melancholy and soulful. John, in comparison, was not very soulful. And he was squat. Not very tall at any rate. You could guess that at one time he'd been a little dynamo, muscly and light footed. As I said, in some ways a tough little bastard. But now of course he was filling out. He wasn't exactly stout yet but he'd acquired an impressive little pot belly.

What could such an elegant and graceful woman be doing with this aggressive, bittersweet, less-than-elegant character? Apart from the obvious, obviously. The thing they had in common was the stalls, because Kate ran one too in partnership with this slightly older woman called Sam. They were part of the same travelling circus that descended one day a week on various locations – Covent Garden, Greenwich, Camden Passage. The sorts of markets that specialise in the artsy craftsy with a bit of antique and bric-a-brac thrown in. Kate had a jewellery stall. John had a stall that sold macho stuff, from sports to military. It looked like a load of old tat but in actual fact, according to the man himself, he was really in the business of selling legends.

Memorabilia of a sort. Curios with stories attached. His most successful line was Zippo lighters with battle scars, purporting to have been the result of skirmishes with the enemy in Normandy or Korea or Vietnam. Nothing too ambitious – nothing that could easily be investigated for veracity or that would seem incredibly far fetched without corroborating authentication. He wasn't selling a piece of General Patton or anything – merely the vague memories of shadily outlined unknown soldiers. It worked. It was a business. So John had a stall and Kate had a stall too. That was their common ground, their meeting point. Some days they'd be set up at the same market, right next to each other.

So, yes, John Toby. Yeah, maybe he could help. But it would probably come at a price. Because (and maybe I was the only person ever to see it) there was something monstrous about John. Even though he could be the life and soul of the party. On an average evening (I've been there) he has a couple of pints after the market's wound down and then he heads home. Then over dinner he'll drink a bottle of wine and then there might be an hour when he takes it easy. But just after nine he'll leave Kate in front of the TV and slip out to the local where he'll have three or four pints of strong lager (minimum) and then after closing time it will be back to the flat with half of the pub for brandy and cigars. He'll be in bed by about 2am if he's lucky.

He's one of those people with a miracle constitution – because, come what may, he'll be up, raring to go at 6.30, showered and shaved. He looks a bit odd most mornings, it has to be admitted – his skin has a waxy quality, a slightly buffed-up look, and his face will be expressionless, moulded like a mask. It's like he's been left in front of a three bar electric fire and some of him has melted slightly in the process. But he'll be ready. Ready as he'll ever be.

"Colin, can I ask you something?"

He doesn't even think about replying to that.

So I add: "What do you think of John Toby? Really think of him?"

I can sense him smiling at that one. "Oh, you know," he says.

The thing is that no-one has ever seen him (John) staggering-around drunk. Not violently aggressive drunk. They might acknowledge he has a problem, probably, but because it's not their problem, because it's not giving them grief (quite the reverse) it's not really a problem at all. Just about every night they can see John outrageously drunk. Drunk and outrageous. This, though, is why they love him – because John, when he's on form, can be wickedly funny. And he's on form more often than not. He's a showman, a stand-up comic, a racon- teur. But the thing is, he has to have centre stage. Don't you ever dare turn your back on him when he's talking and don't you even think about walking away. And if you even think about trying to interrupt him or take the spotlight off him, he'll do something to make you instantly regret it. One way or another, he'll invade your space and make you back off or shut up. He'll tear a strip of you if it comes to that. If you get on the wrong side of him he'll manage to embarrass you very publicly. He'll create a scene that you won't like.

There's something childish, almost hysterical about this need to be the centre of attention. And in fact, I reckon he's generally a lot more volatile and emotionally unstable than people realise. He's hard, yes, he's savvy, he's uncom- promising but maybe some of the front is there because he's got an inferiority complex about all sorts of stuff. He used to take the piss out of the way that some of us read books and then talked about them, for instance, but sometimes it just wasn't convincing. You could just sense that if you'd turned on him and started mocking him back he'd really struggle. And you could sort of sense that there are all sorts of things that he's sensitive about and that actually he's surprisingly foolish and sentimental.

It often irks me that people like Colin never see that. Actually, that's not true. It doesn't often irk me at all. I very rarely think about John Toby these days. I've very little to say about him either way.

I suppose I must have changed the subject. "Did you find time in the end?"

"Eh?"

"That single I asked you about. The Nilsson one. Did you find out any more about it?"

"Oh," he says. "No. Haven't had time. Sorry. What one was it again?"

Needless to say we didn't make it to 517 The High Road, Leytonstone that day. Or any other day, come to that.

We're walking in the park (not Itchycoo Park or Manor Park, another park, miles from there), me and Beth and Charlie, and we're with another couple, Dave and Jane, say, and we'll come across this really raggedy bit of the park, all muddy and rutted and bare of any grass to speak of where it isn't muddy and rutted and Beth will say, "Oh look, Charlie, this is even worse than Daddy's lawn at home." And everyone will laugh, even me.

The heat comes down again. In the early afternoon, with the day only halfway burned down to the stub, only half turned to dust, Charlie is lying on a rug on the lawn in the shade of that shrub that's somehow managed to grow to the size of a small tree. She doesn't move much and if you didn't know differently, you might think she's asleep. But if you watch for long enough you can see her fingers moving slightly and her arm seeming to stretch imperceptibly towards the hem of the rug. It's as if she's been badly wounded on a battlefield and maybe the heat tends to do that to us all.

On the Tuesday I returned to Stanford's and bought a larger scale map: Pathfinder sheet 334, the 1:25,000, 2½ inches to 1 mile sheet of the Killin area.

Chapter five

So anyway, this is it. Here it is. This is what is important.

One Saturday afternoon or early evening (it was still light, I can remember that much) I saw The 39 Steps for the first time. It was on television, at Nan's house. Smell of stale baking, dried flowers, linoleum. Antimacassars on the chairs, a night storage heater nestling under the front windowsill.

Saturday evening. Uncle Tom was watching too. He was in an armchair drawn near to the TV; I was sitting on the pouffe to his right. He loved this film – you could tell that from the way it made him laugh and the way it made him want to be seen to be laughing. Chuckling. Chuckling is closer to it. It made him chuckle more than laugh out loud. And at one stage, he leant forward, nudged me, and said privately, confidentially, for my ears only:

"You know what the 39 steps are, don't you?"

"No."

"It's the exact number of steps from Princes Street down into Waverley Station."

I'll bet I didn't say anything. I'll bet I didn't even turn to look up at him with eyes wide in awe and astonishment. But even though I sat there unmoved, eyes still on the screen, I know that I felt awestruck and astonished. I could hardly begin to comprehend the significance of Tom's words. This was nothing more nor less than a revelation. A revelation and a secret. A revelation *of* a secret. A secret that Tom had known. Now Tom had told me.

***

Fairly early on I tried to explain the article to Beth. She was sitting up in bed, giving Charlie her bottle. I'd just woken up and was staring at the ceiling. Dawn sun was starting to soak into the curtains.

At first, I didn't think she was paying attention. She was probably listening to something on the radio. It's usually The Today Programme. When she's giving Charlie her milk, first thing in the morning, sometimes she manages to read a book at the same time but other times she goes into this sort of trance state, maybe just staring into nothingness with half an ear to the radio

It was an elaborate explanation. Perhaps too elaborate. Because, when eventually she turned to me, she said: "But you father wasn't a projectionist." She hesitated, frowned again, seemed uncertain of her ground. "Was he?"

Wait till I find the switch, says Hannay.

"Not yet," says Annabella, breathlessly enigmatic.

That's when she asks for the mirror to be turned to the wall. And in it, as it's turning, we catch an image of her.

And that's when the phone rings. It rings and rings and rings and that's when I realise that the answering machine isn't switched on.

So I pick up.

"Hi," he says.

"Jules," I reply.

"Shoes," he says. He says it portentously, like it's the codeword I've been waiting on for days. The codeword I've been sweating on, fretting on. A codeword that contains an instruction that may change lives. A signal. The Go signal. The green light. Shoes. Or it's the solution to some sort of puzzle we've both been working on. So he says it portentously but also, perhaps, triumphantly.

"Jules," I reply again. "Be serious."

No, my father wasn't a projectionist. That much is true.

"And Scotland?"

"Yes Scotland."

"Where did you say?"

"Killin."

"Killin?"

"Killin."

***

And the phone rings again seconds later and you know somehow it isn't Jules calling straight back so you let it ring for a while and the answering machine is still switched off and you're not going to switch it on now because you don't want to have the responsibility of deciding whether or not to respond to the message that will be left but in end you don't have the nerve to let it continue ringing so you pick up. And so, inevitably, it comes to this. You pick up the phone and it's John. John Toby.

I've never been able to place John's spiel. There's something in it of the professional Cockney, of course there is. The East Enders stuff. The lovable knockabout market-stall-type-geezer as beloved of the Music Hall and now reinvented for a modern television audience. There's a little bit of gangland culture in there too, especially when he lets his voice drop to a whisper. Mr Snide. Whispering Grass.

There's something infinitely more sophisticated and *knowing* about it though. Something that regards the professional Cockney with heavy irony, that realises it's all pastiche, all raw material for the process of self invention. But in the end, the thing that makes dealing with John difficult is his temperature range. He's volatile; he can change faster than any weather I've ever known. He can be in the middle of a bit of banter, all jolly despite the fact you feel he hasn't earned the right to be jolly with you and then he'll slip straight into Whispering Grass mode and then within fractions of a second seemingly he'll be Mr Angry, except you know he's probably only pretending to be Mr Angry and he's just playing it big for effect. The long and the short of it is that with John, you're always slightly wary.

He doesn't introduce himself. You just answer the phone and in reply he says: "I've been hearing a lot of things about you lately."

Cheeky banter but with a bit of an edge to it. And you want to pretend you don't know who this is. But you know you'll never pull it off so you say something lame like: "That's John Toby, isn't it?"

"A lot of things," he repeats.

And you suspect he's giving you the chance to say something like, "Oh? Nothing good, I hope," but somehow you don't want to give him that satisfaction so you stay silent and wait for him to make the running.

"How've you been keeping anyway?" he says.

"Oh you know. How are you? How's Kate?" And there you go again. You hadn't meant to draw Kate into things this early, but you couldn't help your-self. So there's already a frisson here because you wonder whether there will be any heat or spin on this when he returns it.

"Kate's fine. I'm fine. We're all fine. You're fine aren't you?"

"Yes."

"Well. There you go then. What you been up to?"

"Oh, you know. This and that. I'm doing a piece just now on the cultural significance of coats." I pause for a laugh that doesn't come. "How are things anyway? You still doing the markets?"

The thing I resent most, perhaps, is the way that he makes me slip into a mild form of Mockney too.

"Coats. Coats, eh?" He gives out a little noise like a titter at this point, breathy and spasmodic. He's trying to feel his way towards some sort of a wit-ticism. I feel almost generous enough to let him turn this into a running gag, like I'd do with Colin or whoever. "What?" he adds at last. "The dirty mac brigade?"

Which is almost embarrassing. That's it? That's his joke?

"Yeah," you tell him. "Something like that."

So it's something of a relief when he changes gear again. "Here. Listen. Colin tells me you want to ask me a favour and I thought if it's left down to you, it'll take you all year to get round to it."

"Colin? Really? You keep in touch?"

"Yeah. Well. We're in contact."

"Great. You'll have to tell me how you do it. It takes me six months to per-suade him to come out."

That just sounded wet. Somehow I can't help it.

"He tells me you want me to track down some stuff about Hitchcock."

"Does he. I mean, did he?"

"Something about The 39 Steps."

"Yeah, well, I don't know. Just some ideas we talked about. I'm not sure that..."

"Because I could very well be in a position to help you there."

"What? Really?"

"You sound surprised?"

"No. Well. What sort of thing are we talking about?"

"Never you mind. It'll cost you, naturally."

"Yeah, well. Yeah, thanks. Yeah. I'll think about it. The thing is, actually, I've got these film archive people who've been helping me out."

"Have you indeed?"

"Yes, I…"

"Well-well. You can count on *this* though."

"What?"

"That I'll be in touch. And here's a thought."

"Yes?"

"Mind how you go."

And he was gone.

And I'm sweating. While I've been talking to John Toby, I've been sweating profusely. The reason is this. Just before he called I'd fetched out the map (Ordnance Survey Landranger 51: Loch Tay & Glen Dochart) and as we were talking I was absent-mindedly scanning the area around Killin.

When I noticed something.

The railway no longer goes to Killin. The map merely shows its fading scar on the landscape. The route of the dismantled railway (or, as the map has it, *dismtd rly*) stretches back to the south through Lochearnhead and Balquhidaer Station (is this a misprint for Balquhidder?) towards Callander, which is ten miles away off the edge of the sheet.

I'm flabbergasted. I hadn't thought this through in any structured, formal manner – but somehow I'd sort of assumed that, if and when the time was right for me to make the journey, I'd be taking the train to Killin. Not directly, of course. The journey would probably be broken at Edinburgh.

But the whole point would be. Well that was it. I wasn't entirely sure any more what the whole point would be.

No, my father wasn't a projectionist. I'm not sure I can begin to explain this. The simple fact is that sometimes I have to have a legend; the slightly less simple fact is that I sometimes sort of begin to believe in the legend myself. Legend as in a cover story. Obviously having a cover story simplifies things. It's the sort of story that you tell to people just to save time – to make it easier for them to understand what you are about. Which makes it easier for them to want help you. If you tell them the truth (which is that you want them to help you with the research on an article you're writing) they tend not to be so keen on pushing the boat out for you. People are naturally suspicious of chancers like journalists. But if you give them an extra sort of emotional hook...

I don't know how many times I watched it in total but I'm pretty much aware that at one stage, over the course of a couple of days or so, I watched it over and over again. It, the film, The 39 Steps.

And I was also aware, pretty early on, that some kind of Through the Looking Glass thing was happening – or beginning to happen. I was being sucked in; my light was travelling, was being pulled through. Not into the film as such (or not *just* into the film) but beyond. And maybe also some kind of a swap was taking place. Something of that world was being given in return.

I'm still sitting at my desk, the phone rings, I answer, he says it again.

"Shoes." This time he's more insistent.

"Jules..."

Jules has been in a spiky sort of mood since we last met. Because of course we never made it to Gainsborough Studios. He came round, we had some pasta and red wine and then when Beth had gone through to the living room to watch television we sat where we were at the kitchen table, staring out through the window watching a light drizzle falling.

We opened another bottle of wine.

By then, the idea of risking life and limb to retrieve a brick had begun to pale. It somehow didn't seem so clever any more. I mean, a brick is a brick, isn't it? Whatever you tell people about it, they aren't going to be impressed.

"So what. It's a brick. Big deal."

"But it's from…"

"Gainsborough Studios? Still a brick, mate."

Then, the very next day, I discover that, actually, The 39 Steps was made at Gaumont Studios, Shepherd's Bush, the building that was later to become the BBC's Lime Grove studios.

"Did you hear me?" he insists. "Shoes."

"Jules."

"No, really. Listen."

I find myself listening.

What's the oldest pair of shoes you own? Everyone has an oldest pair of shoes. Well then. They're bound to have a history. Probably an even more intriguing history if we are talking about the oldest shoes owned by the rich and the famous.

"We're probably talking about an old pair of Wellington boots in the garage," I reason.

"I've thought about that. That's what they'll say. But will it be true? We'll get them to work on this. To really search. Maybe there'll be an old pair of pink silk ballet shoes in a trunk in the attic. From when they were children. If it's a girl we're talking about, obviously. Or, I don't know, hiking boots or football boots. Something that will tell a story. A story of the person they once were."

I know he's going to ask me. My oldest pair of shoes. That's easy. I don't own many pairs of shoes. I was reminded of that fact when we moved. I never have owned many pairs of shoes. So it's easy: my oldest still extant pair of shoes is a robustly sensible pair of black brogues that are my official sensibly robust good shoes and I wear them about four times a year on occasions when robust good sense is called for. They were bought for me by a girlfriend in 1989.

"You haven't really thought this one through at all, have you Jules?"

I thought for a second he was going to contest this. I thought he was going to protest bitterly. And actually, as I begin to sense his reply coming, and I begin to get an inkling of its meekness, I'm astounded at myself for the impatience I've just shown him.

"No," he admits. Just that: "No."

And it's true. On Pathfinder sheet 334, there's still no mention of Alt na Shellach by the River Lochay. No matter how carefully you examine the map, there's nothing even remotely resembling that name, though some of the

streams draining into the river start with the same (or almost the same) formulation. For instance, Allt na h-Iolaire, which flows into Allt Dhuin Croisg, which in turn flows into the River Lochay at pretty much the point marked as Alt na Shellach on Annabella's map in The 39 Steps.

It doesn't mean it doesn't exist, of course. Nor does it mean it has never existed. But whether it ever existed or not is probably the sort of thing you can only find out by actually getting up off your backside and going there. Also, I should really find out what Alt na Shellach means in Gaelic, I suppose. Because there is probably a joke here – there usually is where Hitchcock's concerned. Usually a totally uncharming smutty joke.

The strangest thing about this Through the Looking Glass feeling is the realisation that for ages, they've been trying to push Charlie through too. To where, I didn't exactly know.

A lot of the people who saw Charlie in a professional capacity over the first year or 18 months or so would at one stage or another introduce a mirror to the proceedings. I'm not talking so much about the people at senior end of the medical spectrum but those lower down – nurses, for instance, and the various people wheeled in to take an early stab at sensory and neurological assessments. And the tendency was even more marked among the various tribes of care workers to whom Charlie was introduced for various reasons.

I know that there is an element of the routine in all of this. If you are interested in interacting with and observing small children, you're likely to want to introduce all sorts of things that will catch their eyes. Toys, shiny objects, mirrors.

But for me, it seemed to go beyond that with Charlie. There was something mediaeval and superstitious and metaphysical about the way they invited Charlie to contemplate her own image. It was as if they wanted to confront Charlie with her own oddity and to see how she reacted. Or rather her soul. How her soul reacted. That's what they wanted to confront. It was a test for her soul. There was something primitive and fetishistic in this – some residual memory here of Red Indians starting at the image they see when they come face to face with a pioneer's looking glass for the first time. And yes, there seemed to be something of the witch finder or the changeling seeker in the women (sly, furtive, trembling with terrible anticipation) who were keenest to use mirrors on Charlie. They wanted to show Charlie's soul the body in which it was housed. They wanted the truth of a reaction to this knowledge. And maybe also they believed this was a first step in exorcising the demons that had made Charlie as she was.

At least that's how it felt – because the introduction of the mirror was always a moment charged with significance. Charged with expectation. Like when we went to see the woman whose details were given to us by a charity specialising in finding day carers and child minders for disabled infants. This woman lived in one of the dilapidated old brick-built London County Council tenement blocks bang opposite the Hackney Empire. It didn't look promising from the outside but inside, her flat was scrubbed, almost clinically clean.

She was a massive woman, blubbery, with dimpled flesh hanging from her arms and I couldn't help thinking of The Bearded Lady, though there was no evidence of a beard. In fact, her lank hair was thinning. She had thick-lensed glasses in heavy frames (caught at certain angles, her eyes loomed ominously) and she wrinkled her nose as she stared at you through them. The morning we visited her, she was looking after a little Down's Syndrome girl.

We wanted to find out what she thought of Charlie and whether she (the childminder) thought she could help kick start her (Charlie's) development. If so, we were hoping she would consider taking her on a few days a week. This woman had no medical qualifications but she was regarded as something of a minor miracle worker by the charity people and the social work people we'd been in contact with.

I don't know why, but all the time we were there (not longer than an hour, I suppose) I kept thinking of the Messiah of Brick Lane. And other unlikely manifestations. Maybe there was something truly awesome about this middle-aged woman, this worker of miracles who responded to you blankly, blandly, wrinkling her nose, talking sometimes to a space about two inches above the top of your head.

But anyway, we'd been there about five minutes when she suggested we put Charlie on the floor. So we did and she lay there inertly. And then from nowhere the woman produced this mirror about two foot square in size, unframed, propped it against the sofa and rolled Charlie over so that she was lying there staring at her own image.

Charlie was unmoved. She lay there complacently, regarding herself.

The woman explained (she explained it to a point a few inches above my head and then to a similar point a couple of inches above Beth's head) that mirrors were a great source of stimulus for Special Needs children. It sort of made sense. I mean, of course it made sense.

She'd had great results through the use of mirrors, she explained.

Not long after we'd left her flat, halfway down the building's three double flights of external brick stairs, we decided that maybe she wasn't going to be right for Charlie after all.

There's a picture of Charlie just a few days old, when Beth's father was still alive. His hair is white, very white in fact, against the dark green, almost black, of the evergreen vegetation behind. It was taken in the garden at Northfield Road. All newborn babies look pathetic and flimsy and scrunched up and dis-tressed. It's just that ours had a leg sticking out straight, as straight as if it had been splinted. And the outer end of a naso-gastric feeding tube taped to her face. You can't make too many definitive conclusions about the shape of the skull because the skulls of all new born babies look a little distorted. Don't they?

She's not exactly happy. In the photo.

I'm still not sure if the photographs help you understand. Help us understand, I mean, looking back, that we managed to lose quite a few friends around this time. They seemed just to melt away. That was, and is, basically, surprising. A cause of wonderment. We'd regarded some of them as very good friends indeed.

The thing is that right from the start, we genuinely thought Charlie was beautiful. No two ways about it. We said as much. So, yes, I think that this belief − this *certainty* − distressed one or two people.

Three days or so after she was born, around noon, a doctor we had never seen before arrived in our room. (We'd been given a room off the ward by then, so unusual and, I suppose, perplexing was our case.) Would we mind if some students looked on while he examined Charlie? No, on balance. Not being churlish would always, on balance, represent the line of least resistance. That was our view in those early days. And I suppose we both suspected that if we'd said no they'd have applied all sorts of subtle and not so subtle pressures to get what they wanted. We steeled ourselves to be cheerfully cooperative.

So in they trouped, about half a dozen of them, slightly awkward, slightly sheepish. They were not all students. One had a camera. Would we mind if a medical photographer took some pictures of Charlie?

No, on balance.

I would have to sign a form, he said. This, I told him, would not be not a problem.

So the doctor took off Charlie's towelling romper suit and began tugging her arms and legs this way and that, pulling and stretching, bending, stretching again. She didn't much care for this and she let everyone know and the cries she made were distressing. Many of the examinations Charlie suffered in those first few days basically consisted of seemingly arbitrary manhandling. It's like maybe we should have sold tickets. Big man in white coat wrestling tiny purblind shrew. At least they refrained from getting up there on the bed and pinning her down with their knees.

So the doctor wrestled. The photographer photographed. Limbs, torso, head, the sum of the parts. The students, arced around the foot of the bed, looked on impassively.

The doctor congratulated us on the fact that some of the contractures seemed already to be loosening. She was uncrumpling. Already. Two days was it? Three? Look, she could almost lie flat. Flat on her back. He used his hands to sculpt details in the air as he tried to convey to his students a vivid picture of Charlie's posture at birth.

And then they were done. Oh, except the consent form. If I could please sign. I took the form and looked it over.

"And what exactly am I agreeing to?"

"That the photographs can be used for research purposes and for the teaching of medical professionals."

I stared at the form. I looked up. I stared at the form again. Then I screwed my face up a little. I pondered. I knew I had them. An audience. "Well," I sighed. "I suppose so. Just as long as you don't sell them to Hello magazine."

I though that this would help things along. Lighten things up.

And they did laugh. The students mainly. They laughed.

But there was a dreadful pause before they laughed.

As they all trouped out again I watched them expectantly. Actually, tell the truth, I was more curious than expectant. About the students, I mean. The doctor gave curt professional thanks. The photographer melted away, as photographers do. But the students. I thought that, either collectively or singly, jointly or severally, they'd nod or make some sort of acknowledgement as they left. Only one of them did. The rest failed to meet my eye.

And I knew why. They were thinking of the pause before their laugher rather than their laughter itself. I knew what the silence before the laughter was all about. That tiny silence that stretched forever. I knew what it meant. It was as good as a sharp intake of breath. Or no – it was something far more raw and resonant than that. An intake of breath is no more and no less than a puny form of scolding. This silence, insignificant you might think and barely perceptible, lasting less than a second probably, was something huge, something instinctive, something hard wired into human nature.

Instinctive, that's the point. Instinctive and thus unchallengeable. Their instincts told them that there are things you can't laugh about. Shouldn't laugh about. Things you can't joke about, not even at one remove. No matter how obliquely.

The fact that my daughter is a medical exhibit.

Not funny.

Not even close to being funny.

Unless of course you see the joke. And laugh.

It wasn't polite laughter. Or nervous. I'm pretty sure we made comedy contact. It's just that the laughter was late.

Mid-afternoon, I took a bus to the station. It took for ever.

Strangely, there's a Guinness ad in the film. A replica of a Guinness ad was one of things I bought, along with the video of The 39 Steps, to give as a birthday present to my father. The one I gave him was one of the famous Toucan ones. One of the *Guinness is Good For You* series. Why a toucan, incidentally?

 What natural link is there between a dark ale and a tropical bird?

But the ad in the film obviously predates the Toucan campaign, which must have started in the 1940s or 50s. No, the one in the film, glimpsed at the station as Hannay makes his escape on a train from King's Cross, merely says, *Guinness Time*.

It's not there now. Not that I actually looked for it that afternoon as I dropped by the ticket office to get timetables and information about trains to (and within) Scotland.

More than anything, it intrigues me. This Colin-John Toby connection. Or rather, its *reinvention*. It's so unlikely. It's so very improbable. And that's not the only thing that's nagging at me where Colin's concerned. For the first time in as long as I can remember, I'm interested in Colin. More than that, I'm intrigued. Intrigued enough, it seems, to call him quite by accident.

"Colin."

"Hey," he says. "Hey."

He sounds slightly out of breath.

"I was thinking."

"Oh yeah?" he says.

"Nothing."

And actually, the really interesting thing about Colin is something I spotted the other day at his flat. Just as we were getting ready to go out again and find Itchycoo Park, he popped to the loo and I flopped into the big easy chair – the only comfortable piece of furniture in his whole flat. Except that it wasn't, on this occasion, comfortable. There were all sorts of newspapers and magazines on it. And underneath them, one of Colin's books. It was a Record Collectors' Complete UK Discography and it was open at an artist beginning with the letter N. Nilsson, as it happens. Which made me smile. So anyway, I looked down the column and came up with the information that Without You was released by Nilsson's record label, RCA, in the UK in January 1972.

Which clearly has to be wrong, doesn't it? The very earliest I bought it, I reckon, was late April when, I reckon again, it was number one in the charts. Those dates just don't add up, do they? Maybe Colin, for totally different reasons, doubts the accuracy of his book. Maybe not. Strange he said nothing though. Strange that he actually said he'd not had time to look it up.

"Go on. What were you about to say?" he insists.

"It's nothing," I tell him, adding: "I had a call from John."

"Yeah? John Toby?"

"The same. Strange little chap, isn't he?"

"Oh? Is he?"

"Completely fucking useless."

"Oh?"

"Don't you think so?"

A pause. I can almost hear him thinking. "Well. I dunno," he says at last.

"I told him thanks but no thanks."

"Oh, did you? Why?"

"Oh, and Colin."

"Yeah?"

I was going to say something. Then I changed my mind. "No, it's okay. Forget it."

The thing is, it was easy for uncle Tom to sell The 39 Steps to me. It was, we knew instinctively, an Edinburgh film. It features Waverley Station, or something purporting to be Waverley Station. But even more importantly, it has a spectacular bit of cliffhanging action set on the Forth Bridge. This, even for me watching the film in the mid 60s, was somehow intoxicating – that's our bridge, that is. Look. Our symbol. The token of our tribe.

And now, to top it all, the secret that uncle Tom was able to reveal to me. He told me it in all sincerity. There was no twinkle in his eye. I would have remembered.

It was secret.

Like the fact that there were secrets in the film.

Adventures were about secrets.

This was exciting. This was awesome.

The excitement was about knowing a secret and it filled you with pride because it was an Edinburgh secret. A secret encoded into the very stone of our city. Now I felt I was almost part of the action.

At some point I must have made yet another attempt to tell Beth about the article. But she just laughed. The thing that really got her going was my description of my working method. She knew she shouldn't really be laughing so she hugged herself and then to top it all, she got a fit of the giggles.

She shook her head. She'd already been shaking her head when I first noticed that she was laughing; but now she began shaking her head more vigorously. She turned away slightly and raised a hand in protest or warning. This was clearly a dangerously funny notion she was struggling with.

"What? What is it?"

I must have been smiling too but I suppose my eyes must have narrowed as well.

"What? Tell me."

She managed to draw breath between the shakings of her head. "No," she said at last. "It doesn't matter."

"Oh well then," I said, turning as if to leave the room.

"It's just…"

I hovered on the threshold, listening as if to a distant emptiness.

"It's just that. It's. The way you write articles. It's sometimes like the way you buy presents."

And yes, obviously, the film I saw this time around on video isn't the same film as the film I saw all those years ago on television with uncle Tom. We're more attuned to misogyny these days. For instance, almost without exception, male-female relationships portrayed in the film are failures and many of them are thoroughly nasty failures. Some of it is unthinking knockabout in the Music Hall tradition – for instance, the milkman who helps Hannay only when he starts to believe that Hannay is dodging the husband of his (Hannay's) mistress.

And there are stock in trade archetypes when it comes to more overt titillation. Like the scene in which Hannay is sharing his railway compartment with two lingerie salesmen, who embarrass the fourth occupant of the compartment – a priest – by examining and discussing various items of intimate apparel ("brassieres and pink elastic pantee belts") from their travelling samples.

And where sex is concerned there's another little timeslip.

Mrs Simpson.

As Hannay and Annabella enter the lobby of Hannay's Portland Place apartment block, he goes over to the board displaying the names of the flats in the

block. He wants to flip the slide across to show that he's now in. And what's the name at the top of the board?

Mrs Simpson.

Mrs Simpson was of course the most scandalous woman of the 1930s. She was the woman who bewitched a prince, soon to be King, and threatened to bring down the British monarchy. These days it's hard to fathom how and why. In the archive material she looks hatchet-faced. Hard-eyed, pointy-chinned. Witch-like. Unattractive and charmless. But Edward was besotted and he was prepared to stick by her even though it was clear that in doing so he risked all.

Gossip, mostly malicious gossip, had an easy explanation for this seemingly inexplicable situation. She was mind-blowingly good in bed, having learned almost unimaginable sexual techniques in the brothels of Shanghai. Some even said that (s)he was in fact a hermaphrodite perfectly designed to satisfy the needs of a basically homosexual Edward.

Mrs Simpson. The harlot at the heart of the British establishment. A little over a year after the release of The 39 Steps, Edward, who became King in January 1936, decided to marry the newly-divorced Mrs Simpson, thus making it inevitable that he would have to abdicate. He did, on 10 December 1936.

Yet the name would have been meaningless to the film's original 1935 audience – newspapers suppressed all mention of her right up until the scandal broke in 1936. It's an odd little detail though. Did Hitchcock *know*?

And what, while we're on this subject, are we to make of Annabella Smith? Your classic femme fatale? Women spies, according to tradition, are basically clever whores. International women of mystery, expert purveyors of the Wagon Lit blow job. Traders in pillow talk. As Annabella grabs hold of Hannay in the

Music Hall melee after the gun has gone off, her first words are, "May I come home with you."

> Smith: May I come home with you?
> Hannay: What's the idea?
> Smith: Well I like to.
> Hannay: Well it's your funeral. Come on, there's a bus.

Yeah, right. The bus. And if that wasn't flaccid enough, when they get back to his flat, the whole business really goes limp. There's all that spy thriller stuff about switching or not switching lights on. The telephoning ringing. And then? And then he cooks her a big fish. A big haddock. "Do you like haddock?" he asks. It's enormous. An alarmingly large fish. It has been filleted and opened out, its two halves still joined, spread flat like a butterfly the size of an omelette. He takes it out of the old cast iron fridge that actually looks like a safe (except for the Queen Anne furniture-like styling of its feet) where it's been lying uncovered on a plate and, a long-ashed cigarette still dangling from his lips, he

slaps it in a pan. It's Donat's most oafish moment in the whole film – and who knows, his whole career. It serves to underline the fact that there are absolutely no sexual overtones or undertones or any sorts of tones at all at this point in the film. It's an asexual situation. Despite the fish.

Well I like to. Like to what, dear?

I'll bet you, though, that uncle Tom thought this was the sexiest film he'd ever seen in his life. The sexiest and most sophisticated. We're a million miles away from pornography obviously. You can't imagine it physically arousing an audience, even a 1930s audience. Yet I'll bet it teased them, threatening to turn them on and teasing them with the idea of being turned on. I'll be they gasped inwardly at the audacity of it all – not at the explicitness of the behaviour it portrays but the blasé, free and easy flippancy that Hannay eventually aspires to.

And actually, come to think of it, there are a couple of occasions when much of the audience was probably very definitely aroused. At one point, not long after they've been handcuffed together, Hannay and Pamela are on the run – reluctantly on her part, obviously, because she still believes Hannay to be a murderer. So she's frosty and cold towards him. Which somehow makes it all the more interesting when they fall together and roll into a ditch. It's acted out in a contrived, stagey, highly mannered fashion (and they've monkeyed about with the film too, I think, speeding it up or something) and despite that or perhaps because of that you can see that this was, or was meant to be, a highly charged incident. And I mean it sort of still is. Rolling together in a ditch.

The other instance is more blatant – the scene in the hotel where Pamela takes off her stocking to dry them, again while she's handcuffed to Hannay. We see close-ups of Hannay's hand hovering sensually over her leg as she peels back the silk. So, come to think of it, maybe it was, in a more inhibited age, absolutely first rank wet dream material.

But there's no escaping it: the film Tom originally saw in the cinema when he was 35 years old was an entirely different film to the one we watched together on television in the late 60s.

Which brings us to the handcuffs. Absolutely. The handcuffs. They're the creepiest thing about the whole production. Hitchcock is The Fat Boy in Pickwick Papers, the one who says, *I wants to make your flesh creep.* The 39 Steps is the fantasy film of an emotional retard. I mean, come on, isn't it? The fantasy of a smutty schoolboy who grew up sweating more than he ought to. Robert Donat and Madeleine Carroll met for the first time at 8.30 am on the 11th of January 1935, the first day of shooting. No long-winded and elaborate rehearsals in those days. In fact, Madeleine Carroll had been signed up to play her part only two days previously. So at 8.30 they meet and within minutes, Hitchcock has slapped a pair of handcuffs on them – because (so he says) the first scenes he wants to run through are the intimate moments they share when joined at the wrist. After all, the handcuff scenes are central to the romantic plotline, which is arguably the heart of the film.

So they have a run-through and then Hitchcock tells them to take a break; but he disappears before unlocking the handcuffs. And then when he does return, many minutes later, he goes through this elaborate routine of apologising profusely for leaving them like that and he rushes out again to get the key so he can free them. Another long delay. This time he comes back and says he's mislaid the key, but bear with him, he'll get it all sorted out as soon as he can. That's the last they see of him that day.

They sit together on some steps backstage, feeling increasingly miserable, humiliated, distressed and isolated. It doesn't make things any easier that the crew seem pointedly to be ignoring them. But there's a reason for this – and it's not the obvious one. Little did they know that, far from being snooty and aloof, the crew were actually on the verge of mutiny – and they were on the verge of mutiny because they were sickened by the fact that Hitchcock had asked them to spy on his handcuffed stars. At first his intentions were (slightly) veiled – he'd merely ask people in passing if they'd witnessed anything noteworthy or unusual passing between Donat and Carroll. But by the afternoon, he was asking for more detailed information. Had anyone spoken much to the pair? Overheard any of their conversations? Had the two actors been flirting? Or had they been uncomfortable about this enforced intimacy? Had either or both wanted to go to the bathroom for instance? If so, how had they managed?

Eventually, in the late afternoon, they were freed.

This whole episode is usually presented as a prime early example of Hitchcock's genius at work. Not only was this a classic piece of twinkling mischief (they say) but it was also a brilliant way of confronting actors with the reality of a situation they'd have to play out before the cameras. An enforced bit of method acting research, if you like.

It wasn't the only known instance of a Hitchcock practical joke involving handcuffs. On another film he had a bet with one of his technicians about whether the technician would be brave enough to spend the night alone in the studio. He accepted the challenge and allowed himself to be handcuffed to an immovable piece of equipment. Before leaving that night, Hitchcock offered the man a glass of brandy to help steel him for the lonely ordeal ahead. Generous, you might think, except that Hitchcock had laced the brandy with a strong laxative. (A lot of Hitchcock's practical jokes involved strong laxatives.) When the crew arrived the next morning, they found the man still bound, weak and very distressed, his clothing badly soiled, slumped in a mess of his own excrement.

There was a sadistic side to Hitchcock. It has been well documented. It adds a certain frisson to the sexuality of some of his films. That too has been well documented. It's true that there's not much shit in his films. But his sexual imagination is the sexual imagination of a man who would play practical jokes involving handcuffs or strong laxatives. Or, of course, both.

It's sex for Boy Scouts. And after all, there are no women in the original Buchan novel, not a one.

***

The long and the short of it is I'm being immersed in the 1930s. It begins naturally, somehow. It's like a string of images or even just words. Rupert the Bear, Tiger Lily, autogyros. Shanghai obviously. I say obviously but I haven't a clue why Shanghai. Except maybe that sometimes thinking of Tiger Lily makes me think of Shanghai. A place of oriental intrigue.

I don't know. The decline of the Gold Standard. Flying machines – not just the autogyro but Zeppelins and speed record machines like the Supermarine, the aeroplane that was to evolve into the Spitfire. All sorts of fast machines. Trains and cars too. The Queen Mary.

Art deco and Poirot. Baggy suits, kipper ties and Raymond Chandler. The Wizard of Oz. All sorts of Hollywood camp in garish colour. Walt Disney cartoons.

Dan Dare, frozen peas, the planet Pluto.

Mechano.

And uncle Tom. Definitely uncle Tom.

Uncle Tom more than my father, though father was born in 1929 so the 1930s were his first decade. He had a fort and tin soldiers and a clockwork motorboat as streamlined as a Supermarine Spitfire. So father has always been wreathed in the faintest of wisps of the 30s.

But yes, uncle Tom more than my father.

And so we waited. We waited, the warnings of wasps sounding distantly in our ears, sometimes so faint you could hardly hear them at all, sometimes closer. Clouds of wasps, like shadows of sound. Sometimes things went in slow motion, sometimes they were a blur. Sometimes we were the ones going in slow motion. Sometimes it was everybody else.

For a while, it seemed that there was more coming than going; and then for another while, it was the other way around. And sometimes, in the in-between times, it seemed as if there were moments, I don't know how long, but moments certainly, of absolute silence and stillness. Absolute clarity. Where you could hear your own clothes rustling though you were not moving; where you could hear your hair grow.

And in that nervous stillness, the main question that we asked ourselves was: *Would we be able to love her?*

Actually, that's not true. There's no way I can say *we* in this instance. I couldn't say for sure what was in Beth's head. She was full of morphine at this point. Cold, harsh, serene morphine. But I bet she thought she knew she could love the daughter we were waiting for. The daughter we were destined to wait for. I bet she'd say she knew even then that she couldn't wait to get her and start loving her.

So we waited. We waited to see if we were to love her.

And here's a thing. Two lingerie salesmen sharing a railway compartment with Hannay and a priest. The salesmen are interested in horse racing. Well they would be, wouldn't they?

So when the train gets to Edinburgh, the salesmen are keen to get a newspaper because they want to know whether a horse called Bachelor's Button won a race that afternoon – which is rather handy from the point of the view of the plot because the newspaper turns out to be important in cranking up the tension (suspected-murderer Hannay's picture is on page 1 though the other occupants of the carriage don't appear to spot this).

The thing, though, is that the newspaper device is, in some respects, horribly laboured. It's narrative by numbers. You can just see Hitchcock hosting the meeting in his blue silk pyjamas. So, gentlemen, we have our fugitive in a train compartment. How do we proceed from here? Well, let's see. Mmm. How about this? At some point, someone in the compartment produces a newspaper and this newspaper has Hannay's picture splashed all over the front page. But no – how about this? Hannay buys the paper en route. He buys it off a platform newsboy when the train stops at Waverley. He's anxious. Has the news already travelled? Yes it has. It's a nice touch, don't you think, because the newspaper is not only a threat to Hannay but it also reminds us that the world is an ever-smaller place. The paper will make people think about the wonders of telegraphic technology and meditate on the long arm of the law.

But hang on.

Yes.

Listen.

How much more powerful it would be if it isn't Hannay who buys the paper. The threat is brought *to* him – much more unpredictable and uncontrollable. If it was his paper, he'd just throw it away. How about this – the other occupants of the carriage buy the newspaper? They unwittingly introduce this threat to Hannay into the carriage.

But how? Why? They're not anxious for news of the outside world are they? After all, they've just been wittering on about pantee belts.

We need something that's time sensitive and that has the power to affect them directly and substantially.

Like share prices?

No, they're only salesmen, remember.

Yes, that's true.

OK. Here's the thing.

Yes?

They're big horseracing aficionados. They want to know if Bachelor's Button romped home. They've got money on him.

Money. Oh yes, I see. That will work then, won't it?

Perhaps. Perhaps it works. The truth is, I've never quite known what to make of horse racing. To me, all horses look the same.

I've never known anyone who's been into horse racing. I know there's a mountain of evidence to the contrary (television coverage, newspapers, book-makers shops everywhere and just the sheer volumes of money spent on gambling each year), but I can't really believe that horseracing really interests anyone apart from feckless losers. Homeless alcoholics, mainly.

So its presence as a backdrop (or a plot device or even as a topic of conversation) in films and books has always sort of mystified me. At best it comes across as a stagey convention, a stale archetype of British life. And it's worse than stale, it's completely phoney – because though it's a cliché everyone recognises, it's one that has absolutely no bearing whatsoever on real life. I mean, people on trains don't discuss the odds and the runners and riders in that day's horse races. Not in real life they don't. Or have I been missing something here?

In any case. I have no interest in horse racing and know nothing about it.

Except for one thing. I may have mentioned it in passing earlier: I just happen to know that the Derby, which is always run on the first Wednesday in June (or was until it was moved relatively recently to the first *Saturday* in June) was, in 1936, run on the last Wednesday in May. The 27th, same day as The Queen Mary was scheduled to leave on her maiden voyage.

Among the favourites in the weeks running up to the event were two of Lord Astor's horses, Rhodes Scholar and Pay Up and three owned by the Aga

Khan: Bala Hissar, Taj Akbar and Mahmoud.

See what I mean? Names, meaningless names.

The week before the race, one clear favourite had emerged: Taj Akbar, at odds of 6-1, which was to be ridden by champion jockey, Gordon Richards. Richards, unaccountably, had never won the Derby before and it was reckoned that his name was on it this year. Whichever way you looked at it, you had to admit this was a great opportunity because Taj Akbar was a magnificent horse.

I can hear Beth calling me. She is in Charlie's room.

"Come and see this," she shouts.

Charlie isn't here. She's at the child-minder's. So obviously this isn't a Charlie thing. A first steps moment or something like that. Nor can I sense that something is wrong. There's no distress or urgency in her voice. There is, in fact, a hint of laughter.

She is looking out of the window. Out and down. Charlie's room is upstairs at the back and from her window we can see into some of the neighbouring gardens on either side. Beth is pointing. Pointing and smiling, on the verge of giggles. She is pointing at a boy, fifteen or sixteen years old maybe, standing up on a swing, swinging vigorously, riding high into the air on each beat. Even from up here we can hear the chains creaking. Nothing unusual about a boy on a swing, you might think. Except he's in the full Hasid gear. The long black coat, the Homburg hat. And he's tall. As full grown as a man.

It does look funny. Surreal, really.

So I tell her about the idea I'd had, by coincidence, just the day before. "I thought maybe they should have a Hasid games. Just like the Olympics, except that for every event, they have to wear full costume. Can you imagine it? The marathon. The pole vault. Even the swimming events or high diving."

This gives her pause. She doesn't know whether this should be funny or not. As I've said, we have problems about this. We never really know if it's right to laugh at the Hasids. Whether we should find them funny. Whether some of their beliefs and practices are just downright absurd or worse. We talk about it quite a lot. I think it's a shame that the Hasid children, especially the boys, aren't allowed more of a childhood and sometimes she says this is anti-Semitic of me. She sees a dividing line between being amused by something and outright mockery; she usually comes down on the side of respecting cultural differences.

Maybe she's right. I don't know. I really don't know.

***

Scores of people took Charlie's picture over the first few months – and I'm not even counting the countless x-ray sessions and scans she was put through. The strangest of all was at Great Ormond Street Hospital (or Gosh – the staff shorten it to a breathless acronym without any apparent hint of irony, and somehow the ghost of an exclamation mark always loiters. Gosh!) during the first major assessment when we stayed in the hospital (all three of us camped out in one cramped little room) for a whole week.

Somewhere off the beaten track in that sprawling town of little deaths and illnesses (if memory serves I think it's actually at the end of a long corridor on the top floor of one of the buildings) there is a photographic studio. Like everything at Great Ormond Street this studio is a big production. There's mountains of equipment, backdrops, drapes, props and it feels a little like a film set and still more like a rehearsal studio.

The resident medical photographer has this incredibly impatient (not so say brusque) attitude. This is hardly uncommon. You can expect that pretty much  everywhere in the National Health Service but at Great Ormond Street it's ten times worse because they're such precious bloody prima donnas. They expect, basically, to be worshipped. They've all been on Blue Peter or had their picture in the Women's Weeklies or joshed with Rolf Harris during one of his Christmas Morning Specials. The bloody parents and patients are merely the price they have to pay. You're damned lucky you've got them – and on balance really they'd rather you didn't ever forget it.

Anyway, they erected an overhead camera, put Charlie on a mat and threw her around a bit to get some interesting posture shots. And when that had been done to their satisfaction, they focused in on her head and face. And yes, obviously you feel great disquiet at the way they treat people. It sits heavily in the pit of your stomach. But you don't say very much because you've sort of been traumatised by the wait you've just had in the corridor outside. All the way down the corridor are examples of the photographer's work, blown up to massive, dominating proportions. Usually they're in the form of Diptychs. Before and after. Before plastic surgery; after plastic surgery. The faces of children with the most grotesque and disfiguring types of syndrome.

I suppose it's all meant to reassure you. To show you what's possible. But the truth is it merely reinforces the gothic nature of the whole experience. Its terrible, heart-rending nature. You realise this is real. You *really are* in a freak show now. And yet there are children a hundred times worse than Charlie. A thousand times worse. You're the lucky ones.

And for a fleeting second you realise that the Hello magazine joke, made weeks before, wasn't a joke at all. You regret even the merest notion of making jokes. Because, suddenly, one thing is now clear in your head, absolutely crystal clear – you are henceforth determined to be the model patient. Or rather, the model family of the patient. In an instant, a time interval equal to the fastest shutter speed on the medical photographer's camera, you have become chastened and pious. You have accepted into your heart the knowledge that there's got to be a damned good medical reason why they need all these photographs.

So that's the photography thing. It's not at all like the mirror thing, really, but, in the same way that tribesmen fear for the theft of their souls, you can't help feeling there's some spooky voodoo at play here too.

And actually, what I said earlier isn't true. When I was talking about that weird little bit in the film when Hannay and Annabella enter Hannay's living room.

The one with the decorators' dust sheets draped over everything. The curtainless room. I said that as the mirror is turning, as Hannay is turning it to the wall, it catches an image of Annabella.

That's not true. It's not true at all. The fact of the matter is that we start with her image captured within the glass and then Hannay turns the mirror so that the image is lost.

Do you reckon they thought long and hard about that shot?

Is that precisely the sort of thing that film directors, even film directors way back when film was indisputably superficial and disposable, thought long and hard about?

Meanwhile, a remarkable thing was about to happen. That evening, I saw a man called Jack Palmer on telly. He was getting on a bit. In his 80s probably, with yellowing teeth. But lively nonetheless. He could still twinkle. The perky, never-say-die spirit of an old trouper always ready to show willing, the jovial insecurity of someone who'd perhaps spent some time on the fringes of showbiz. For some reason, BBC2 was running a series of brief – 5 minutes at most – slots before the news each night. People from the film industry or minor celebrities from other fields, explaining how or why a particular film changed their life. The format was an interview cut with clips from the film in question. And there he was, Jack Palmer, founder of the Palmer Film Archive, talking about some old film.

I rang Jules.

"Jules. Where are you?"

"At home."

"Good. Are you watching telly?"

"No."

"Well put it on. Quick."

A small sniff of laughter.

"What?"

"I don't have a television, remember."

He was absolutely right. I'll give him that. He genuinely didn't have a television. He used to have an old black and white portable that he rested on the top of a pile of books. The sort of a telly with a loop of an aerial on the back that you can fiddle with all night and still not get a decent picture. And in fact the picture faded away over the course of a couple of months, way back, until it finally disappeared altogether. It just died. Now, whenever Jules spent any leisure time in front of a screen it involved computer games. He was especially addicted to one where you enacted the whole course of the Battle of Britain in absurd detail. He'd been playing it forever and he was only up to dawn on day four. He was doing well though – the future was safe in his hands.

Meanwhile I was staring at Jack Palmer, the aged keeper of a genuine film archive, sitting being interviewed in a dark labyrinth of celluloid. Or at least in seemed that way. You never can be sure about these things – maybe this was contrived, stagey, a set. Anyway, there he is, in a plastic bucket chair set on bare floorboards, in a big splash of spotlight; and in the fringes of half light beyond there is a shelf on which we can make out film canisters. Beyond that – darkness.

"Oh well. I called because there's a guy called Jack Palmer on BBC2. He has a film archive. Ever heard of it?"

It's true. It looks too stagey. The shelves, for instance. Am I mistaken, or are they wooden? Like bookshelves? Am I imagining that?

"Course I have. The Palmer Film Archive. It's the biggest privately held film archive in London. It's only down the road in Islington."

"What!"

"What?"

"You didn't think to tell me?"

"What?"

"I'm doing a piece on film heritage and I'm looking for a neat way into a lost world and you don't think to tell me there's a doorway ten minutes away? You don't think to tell me that?"

"Keep you hair on. What are you getting so upset about?"

"You. Don't you care about the Feature Factory?"

"Factory Features."

"Whatever. Well? Don't you?"

"Oh I see. I get it. You're trying to say that your idea, *your idea*, is in some way important in the whole scheme of things. Is that it? Whereas."

"Whereas what?"

"Whereas I'm really bored with this whole conversation."

I think I beat him to the draw. I think I got my phone down before he managed to hit the red button on his mobile.

But anyway, fate had intervened. As it does sometimes.

And first thing the very next day, it intervened again. I picked up the phone and a voice started gabbling.

"Hello Robbie, how are you," I said when I got a word in edgeways. Robbie was certainly speeding. Sometimes he inhales far too much helium.

"Just checking you're still okay for the end of the week."

"Sure," I said. "Absolutely."

"Good," he said.

"What?" I added. "The end of the week what?"

"The article of course."

"The article of course."

"We agreed Friday. And in view of what happened last time I thought I'd better check we were on schedule."

"Friday? Yes of course."

"You're sure?"

"Yes."

"Absolutely sure?"

"Look Robbie, this is not a problem. It's just not a problem."

Shit.

Oh shit.

Chapter six

It didn't take me long to find out about the Palmer Film Archive. They had a whole page ad in the Creative Services Directory.

I called their number and asked to speak to Jack Palmer.

Actually, I didn't get that far. I only managed, "Can I speak to Jack P…" before I was transferred by the girl on the switchboard. It rang a couple of times again and then someone picked up and said hello. You could tell immediately that this wasn't Jack Palmer. It was a bloke but the voice, even in saying that one word, *hello*, was too young.

"Could I speak to Jack Palmer please?"

"Who's calling?"

This is crap. This is fundamentally crap. *Who's calling?* Because you know that you're almost certainly going to be fobbed off. Unless you're someone that this guy thinks Jack Palmer will want to speak to, you're going to be told that Jack Palmer isn't available right now. He's in a meeting. Or not able to come to the phone right now. Or he's just too gaga ever to be allowed near a phone these days. Or whatever.

We both know that Jack Palmer is either sitting there doing his pools coupon or he's genuinely not there – he's taking it easy at home today because he's been semi-retired anyway for years now. Or something.

So I tell this call-screener my name and then I add one of my routine little legends. I tell him I'm from a well-known film magazine, one that I have indeed written for, but only on two occasions and they were both negligible articles and the last of them was over two years ago. This time, though, it doesn't help. It just injects a new note of suspicion (with rogue harmonics of nervousness) into the proceedings.

"Oh yes?" he says. "Maybe I can help," he adds, in the most unhelpful voice you've ever heard. And then, perhaps realising that actually, on balance, he doesn't really want to help, he again he changes tack. "Can I ask what this is regarding?"

"It's just…" And at this point you realise that perhaps your cover story needs working on. You're not at all confident of its durability, its combat readiness. The truth is… the truth is that you want something very general (to visit the Archive and drink in its atmosphere, if indeed it has an atmosphere) and yet something that seems incredibly specific (a lead that will uncover the incredible untold story of the fate of a small fragment of the true 39 Steps) but when you come to think of it, this second angle is also phenomenally vague. And so you find yourself coming out with something lame about having seen Jack Palmer on telly last night, adding: "I'd never heard of the Palmer Film Archive before. I suppose I'm interesting in finding out more."

"We could send you our brochure."

And before you know it, the guy on the other end of the line has taken your address and promised to pop a brochure in the post and he's successfully got rid of you, probably all inside a couple of minutes at most, and this was not what you hoped for or expected or wanted at all.

I mean, do stockings need drying? They'd dry naturally within minutes, seconds even, of coming into the warm. Wouldn't they? They'd dry on your legs. As opposed to a heavy tweed jacket or a skirt for instance. That would be sopping wet and would take some real drying.

That's what you'd take off to dry.

I mean, taking your stockings off to dry them. It's the ultimate prick tease isn't it?

Maybe stockings retained more moisture in the 1930s. Things were recognisable but different in the 1930s; all sorts of aspects of the familiar were basically in prototype back then.

Aunt Mary and uncle Tom were more or less as old as the century, so the 1930s were their thirties. The prime of their lives. And this, their golden decade,

was obviously put into perspective and given an even more golden glow by the decade that followed. Not that they had a bad war. Tom was too old (or medically unfit, perhaps, because of his eye condition) to fight and aunt Mary was involved, I think, in the most interesting work that she ever did in her life. Something to do with an agricultural science establishment. War work of a sort. Not that she was a scientist. Far from it. Aunt Mary was incredibly scatterbrained. It was probably a slightly more genteel version of being a land girl.

Their house at Murrayfield was a 1930s house – a bungalow with discreet art deco hints in the plasterwork of cornices and the design of the tiled fireplaces. Solid and honest stuff with just a hint of something more ambitious, more design-conscious – a passing nod in the direction of the Queen Mary or the streamlined zing of the last great era of pre-war railway design. In other words, modern in its day; and to our eyes, somehow quaint without being positively ancient.

When they moved from Murrayfield, they moved to another bungalow, this time just on the city limits out the Glasgow Road; and here too there were hints of the 30s in the tiling and in the designs of windows and doors.

And there was of course a powerful aura of the 1930s in the bric a brac that moved with them. An art deco teasmade (square clockface: very daring) that must have been a wedding present; a bakelite wireless that seemed as big as a drinks cabinet. Clocks, lampshades, cutlery. Books, even – all of Tom's books were musty and mildewed but, again, clearly not ancient. Cloth bound, their boards slightly warped, they spoke of manly pre-war exploits and pursuits, of fishing and cricket and of rugby and of the glory that was motoring. They spoke of a solid Conservative Scottishness. Tom was, after all, an elder of the Kirk.

And I think that the notion of Tom's resourcefulness also dates back to the 1930s – though of course there is no way for me to be sure of this. Tom's aura of resourcefulness was partly down to the fact that he was a fairly decent hunter. Despite his bad eye, he shot every rabbit that came within a hundred yards of his vegetable patch and he would always return with trout or salmon any time he got near a river.

So that was partly it – but I think it went well beyond that. They always ate well. Tom cooked epic roasts and Mary could always be relied upon to come up with legendary puddings. Very sweet, always – and she had bags of powdery (in fact, it looked like angelically pure weedkiller or something) glucose in the cupboard that she would allow you to sprinkle even on the sickliest, creamiest plateful of strawberries-cream-and-meringue. The thing was, you had the feeling that they had always eaten well, even in adversity. The contrast was with Nan and one of the other aunts, Meg. Even when they were well off, Nan and Meg seemed to scrimp and save – because, you felt, they had somehow got into the habit of scrimping and saving.

I don't want to give the impression that Tom was in some way like Pop Larkin in the H.E. Bates books, because he wasn't like that at all. He wasn't a happy-go-lucky ducker and diver, a benign rogue with a big heart; he was a far more severe character, a harder and less generous spirit. But there were lots of stories of him getting onto a motorbike and driving off down to Lauder in the borders and coming back with a whole ham shank. He was resourceful in that he knew the right people here and there. He had fundamental horse sense and an instant rapport with the earthier sorts of characters – the sorts of characters that made father, say, slightly uneasy.

I always found this slightly impressive. Even more so now, looking back.

Tom was a genius, come to think of it, when it came to boiling a ham shank. The meat would just fall off the bone and then he'd make a pile of sandwiches with white bread and tons of butter, mustard compulsory. He'd mix it himself using a tin of Colman's mustard powder. And mustard *really was* compulsory. He once caught me trying to make a ham sandwich without mustard and he was furious. I don't think he was joking, either.

Mustardy ham sandwich. Summer evening. A glass of cold beer. Tennent's lager probably. For years, he was the only person I'd ever come across who drank lager, though father said that ladies drank it in pubs. Me and my brother obviously didn't get lager, lager was for grown ups, but father joined him now and then. Father's standard drink was whisky and American ginger, which didn't strike me as a particularly 1930s drink. Not that there's any reason it should be.

Neither was the Tennent's lager, I suppose, a 1930s drink.

The ham shank idea was. In my mind it was and is. An old fashioned thing that isn't ancient.

Strange thing, really.

Between eight and nine, that's when you catch John. He'll be at home. There will be something cooking. He will not as yet have slipped out to his local.

"John?"

"The same."

"John. I've been thinking…"

I suppose I was half expecting to be punished. Paid back, to be precise, for being offhand with him that last time we talked. I'd forgotten it never really works that way with people like John Toby. Actually, he acted as if our previous conversation had only just been a couple of minutes ago and had been interrupted by something unforeseen, like someone coming to the door. I often wonder about people who (seem to) act as if the world is exactly the way they imagine it. Is that strength of character? Or just plain madness?

"Now," he said. "Now. I have something you want. Correct? And you have something I want."

"Yes?"

"Yeah," he confirmed.

"What?"

"I want you to tell me what this is really about."

"About?"

"You've got it."

My first thought was that he'd lost it. Lost it completely. "Sorry, John. Sorry to be so boring, but the truth is that I'm just researching a magazine article."

"Okay," he said. Meaning: if you insist.

"Tell you what, John. We should maybe meet up."

And the odd thing was, my first thought when I put the phone down was, *Should I call Colin?*

It must have been between Christmas and New Year, I suppose. I can't remember the exact year. All I can remember is that it was the last really ferocious winter we ever had. So, yes, it was cold. It was just me in the flat. No-one knew I was there. I'd come back early, before term started, to do a bit of reading maybe, to find a bit of quiet time – and I certainly didn't expect anyone would track me down. I sat bundled up in about four pullovers, sitting in an abraded old leather armchair in front of one of those old fashioned gas fires, one of those warhorse old things with ceramic honeycomb elements, a fire you'd take a naked flame too and eventually it would light with a *crump*.

So absolutely, I lit the fire.

And then the doorbell rang.

It was Colin.

"You eaten?"

I had. It was early afternoon, maybe just gone one, but I had. I pretended it was the most natural thing in the world that he should find me here and he, for his part, pretended to find my total lack of surprise equally unremarkable.

"Good," he said. "Grab a coat."

I did as I was told. He seemed to be in that sort of mood. The sort of enigmatic yet compellingly decisively mood where he's clearly not going to answer any of your questions nor is he going to take no for an answer. So you might as well play along.

He drove for over an hour and I haven't the faintest idea in which direction. Something makes me want to say that we drove into Fife but I have no real reason for believing that's the case. We chatted and laughed and joked about all sorts of other stuff while he drove but not once did I ask him what all this was

about and not once did he give even the slightest of hints that he wanted to tell me anything. You just got the feeling that he was being enigmatic for a reason and you'd probably appreciate it in the end. It was like a "surprise, surprise" thing but not quite – somehow not as glowing and smug. He wasn't hugging himself with his own cleverness, neither did he seem filled with gleeful anticipation. It was all very matter-of-fact.

And then he was pulling into a layby. The road wasn't exactly busy but by no means was it a cart track. An A road I should think.

We overlooked an arena-like topography – on one side of the road the ground fell away into a bowl of open, snow-covered ground defined by the curving edge of a wood a couple of hundred yards away. The intervening ground down in the bowl seemed painfully bare and bright. Bright from the ground up. There'd been a couple of hours of thin sunshine the day before and a mini thaw had taken place, revealing the black branches of trees here and there and the odd patch of dark ground – some green too, the glimpsed green of evergreen trees and clumps of grass. But the snow was still dominant, pervasive, unremitting, impossibly white and gently luminescent; and it was the strangest of lights, because though the ground was bright with whiteness, the sky above was grey and heavy with the prospect of more snow. The whole scene was unnaturally still.

From the layby the embankment sloped away steeply, a descent of thirty of forty feet and then we were in the arena. From down here, the treeline seemed more pervasive, encroaching, reaching round at its margins to embrace you, an enclosing darkness of trees. Some firs and pines but mainly summer trees – bare sycamores and limes, elder and ash.

I suddenly had a keen sense of deja vu. I had been on a winter walk here with my parents. Here or somewhere very like here. Somewhere, I realised with devastating clarity, with snow and bare winter trees.

And I had a second vision. That maybe Colin had brought me here to this white arena in order to fight a duel. Pistols probably. Old fashioned, antique firearms with flintlocks. We'd walk our allotted paces with pistols at our chests, then, slowly, deliberately we'd turn, each extend an arm, fire.

Crump.

And one of us would fall, having taken a bullet, and whichever one of us it was would lie chill on the snow, a rill of blood reddening its whiteness.

It didn't happen. We stood there for a moment, each in our own silent thoughts; and then we moved off.

"You warm enough?"

Colin was well wrapped up. Appropriately dressed for a walk in winter woodland. I was wearing a threadbare West German airforce greatcoat that looked really stupid outside of certain parts of certain cities – and not too clever there either.

"Yes," I said, though I was already feeling cold, the sort of cold that you know for sure is starting to eat into your bones.

"It's okay," he said. "It's not far."

We were going uphill now, fairly gently, but there were slipping points. I was starting to lose my faith. My faith in the possibilities of this whole enterprise, whatever it was. My faith in Colin to deliver. I was no longer the slightest bit intrigued.

And then suddenly we were there. We were on it before we – or me at least – realised it. What had at first seemed a thicker part of the forest, a darkening of the screen of trees, was in fact an ivy covered fragment of a wall. And there were even more substantial fragments beyond – dark, greenish, mossy, broken architectures, structures picked out in edgings and icings of snow.

Colin was playing it cool, as if this was nothing really. Which in fact it was. "I came upon it yesterday," he sort of explained.

I'm not sure he had his camera with him. I think he probably did. It was about then that he was getting into photography in a really big way. He'd begun roaming around looking for subjects, locations.

He clambered about a bit, climbing on mounds of rubble, hauling himself through the massively silled holes in walls where windows had once been. And I, to show willing, clambered about a little bit too. The light – ambient, source-less, muted – also seemed contrived, almost as if we were indoors.

"The thing is," he said, "it's not marked on the map."

"What is it?"

"Well that's just it," he said. "What do you reckon?"

By now I'd have lit a cigarette.

"It's a lovely pile of stones, Colin. It must make you very happy."

"But what do you reckon?"

"I don't know. It's not a church or a castle, is it."

"How old?"

I began to sense there was something wrong with this place. Something... not quite sinister exactly but unsettling. It was only when we were back in the car that I worked out what it was. Or what I thought it was. There was no litter. No evidence that anybody had been there recently. No blackened eye of an abandoned fire, no sooty black flamelicks up a wall. No cigarette ends, used condoms, cigarette packets, paper tissues. The moss was thick, undisturbed.

"Probably newer than you think," I said at last. The masonry still had a fair degree of definition. These were not the time-eaten stones and eroded outlines of an ancient monument. And I had a hunch. I don't know very much about architecture but I had a sense of the Victorian here. I said as much.

"And what is it?" he asked. He pitched it as a leading question. He'd slipped into slightly superior mode, filled with the supercilious smugness of a teacher following the Socratic method. Sherlock to my Watson. Maybe I still hoped that this was all going to lead somewhere — that the pay-off would be worth it. Not that I cared really. All I could think about was a warm bar somewhere and the medicinal whisky he was going to buy me when all of this was over.

I shrugged. "A house? A mansion?"

He nodded. A thoughtful sort of a nod — as if he was disappointed with the lack of inspiration in the answer. Disappointed but (sadly) unsurprised. In fact, I'd probably shown myself unworthy of any further encouragment. And the strange thing was that I shared his sadness. I started to get the feeling that something important was happening here and I was betraying it. I was letting him down badly. I don't know why.

But more than anything else I was cold. My ability to concentrate was evaporating, like the grey plumes our breaths made. I'm sure he could see I was in no mood for this. So he turned and walked off and I drifted after him. As we trudged (he probably didn't trudge but I certainly did) I sank almost immediately into a blackly pessimistic mood. I knew somehow that we'd get back to the layby and the car wouldn't be there. Or it wouldn't start. I could sense an adventure coming on, an adventure I wouldn't like.

In the end, my worst fears were unfounded — if we discount the fact that I failed to convince him we needed a drink on the way back. Every time I pointed out a likely pub looming on the road ahead he'd look sceptical.

He dropped me on the main road about two blocks from the flat. It was the middle of the afternoon and already twilight. It had begun to snow again. It would snow heavily for hours, days probably. Huge snowflakes; snowflakes bigger than eiderdown feathers, taking an age to fall in the still air. There was a cheerfulness in the lights of the shops in the parade round the corner, a warmth and a sense of community in the lights coming on in all the tenements of the neighbourhood. A sense of a world drawing in on itself. And yet there was a wildness and a rawness too. Something uncanny. I felt intoxicated.

He did tell me later, I think. I'm pretty sure I'm not making this up. Years later. In passing. I asked him one time if he remembered that day we walked to the ruin in the woods. "Oh yes," he said. "The folly."

The folly.

That was all.

Morse code is featured in lots of films, apparently. It signifies (or used to signify) urgency and operational importance. In The 39 Steps, the da dit dit dah of Morse transmission overlays a stilted little shot that follows Hannay's escape from the train onto the Forth Bridge. We see Hannay clinging to a steel column, then the camera lets us look down all those hundreds of feet to the

concrete pier and the waters of the firth below. When the camera eventually pans back, Hannay has gone. No explanation. Are we to believe he has fallen to his death? Should we fear for him? Do we?

Then comes a long, undeviating shot of the bridge, with a squat little tug or a ferryboat crossing in the background to show this isn't a still. A long undeviating shot with just Morse code on the soundtrack. A shot that says manhunt. Big manhunt. National manhunt.

And the Morse, decoded, says: *Height five foot ten, small moustache, last seen wearing a dark suit but he may have obtained a change of clothing.*

You don't need to know that, because at the close of the shot we also hear this read in an announcer's voice. Not so much a newsreader voice, more a "calling all stations" voice. Bizarre. Exposition or what? We will indeed shortly see Hannay obtain a change of clothing. Are we so stupid that we need preparing for this eventuality?

But yes, the truth was that Tom had something of a squint. Of course it would have been so much more comic — I mean there might have been so many more comic possibilities — if uncle Tom's bad eye meant he never managed to shoot a single hare or rabbit though he was continually loosing off buckshot at them day after day. Rabbits unscathed, hares completely blasé as they lifted carrots with impunity from his garden at Golf Hall.

On bad days you sometimes felt there was something in him of that cross-eyed US silent comedy actor. Will Something? Earp? Twerp? Glances. He could never really do glances.

On the other hand, in their Morse code messages, maybe the police really do speculate on the propensity of fugitives to slip into something more comfortable.

They sent a brochure. I sent back a letter in which I mentioned an article I was doing on e-cinema and said that I'd come to realise I knew next to nothing about celluloid and it would be incredibly helpful and interesting for me to visit the Archive and see what they did and get a feel for this whole celluloid thing.

And by return of post I got a reply. I was an incredibly starchy, uptight letter from someone who signed herself Caroline Palmer.

"I'm writing in response to your letter to my father," it began.

Fair enough, I thought. Family firm. Under her signature was the legend, Client Services Director.

"As I am sure you will understand, he is a busy man..."

Certainly. Busy man. And?

And, basically, he has no time to respond to the sort of footling request outlined in my letter, which, she implies, is in any case, vague and rather confused. If I wanted to learn about the basic mechanics of the film industry, there were surely nightclasses somewhere or other designed to furnish me with exactly the sort of knowledge I required.

I bristled at that. I don't mind admitting it. Instantly, I had a vision of me petrol bombing the Palmer Film Archive. Reducing it to ash. I'd stay to watch it burn down, an anonymous face in the crowd. Maybe Jules would be there too. In his hand he'd have a brick rescued from the devastation of Gainsborough Film Studios and he'd lob this brick at a fireman, even though this fireman was in the legitimate pursuit of his firefighting duties. We'd gasp along with the rest of the crowd as the roof of the Palmer Film Archive building collapsed into the body of the inferno, sending up a volcanic shower of sparks.

I didn't do this, in the end. I made no petrol bombs. Instead, I did the next best thing. I sat down to write a letter dripping with poisonous sarcasm. A scathing, coruscating broadside. A letter designed to ruin her day if not her week. This Caroline Palmer woman. A letter that would make her gasp, a letter that would make her hand tremble as she read it. An evil letter.

I didn't send it. I didn't even finish it. Somewhere towards the end, I thought better of it. I had a change of heart.

No, I thought. No. I could now see this Caroline Palmer woman. I imagined her in her 40s or 50s. A spinster. A neurotic loser. It would give me far greater pleasure to get what I wanted from her. So I wrote a letter that was slightly superior without being patronising. I regretted the fact that she had been unable to understand the nature of my request – the fault was surely all mine. Perhaps she would allow me to remedy this. I would endeavour to make things as clear for her as I could.

It was, I reflected, surely in the interest of all those who still worked with celluloid to promote an interest in (and to foster a knowledge of) this most precious medium. It could do no harm for me to visit the Archive and to learn a little of what it did by way of preserving film. And who knows, it might even be to the Archive's direct benefit. Although I couldn't envisage writing anything touching on the activities of the Archive in the very near future – who knew what the future might hold. Etc, etc.

It was a work of art; and I hugged myself with pleasure as I recognised this simple fact. It was an absolute pinned-on certainty that this would do the trick. She might not like it, especially if she detected any undercurrent of bumptious sarcasm, but she'd respond to this sort of gentle pressure. She'd pass this back up to her father and I'd be given an exaggeratedly cheerful invitation to pay a brief visit to the Archive within the next few days. And they wouldn't regret it. Genuinely. Because I'd be perfectly charming and they would warm to me and I'd warm to them and we would both wonder what the previous hints of spikiness had been all about.

And of course there was just a chance that Caroline Palmer wasn't a neurotic spinster in her 50s. Maybe in actual fact she genuinely was the flat-shoed keeper of the keys of the labyrinth. The blonde girl I was destined to meet at the end of this road. Maybe that much was true also, if only I'd let myself recognise it.

The change of clothes is important to the storyline in The 39 Steps. It's not exactly a change of clothes as it happens, though. It's just a change of coat. But it's a lucky change of coat because it saves Hannay's life.

***

A letter fired right back from the Palmer Film Archive. It wasn't from Jack Palmer. It wasn't even from Caroline Palmer. It was from a Jo Dawson. She (he?) thanked me for my recent letter to Caroline Palmer, which she had passed on for her (him?) to deal with. S/he explained that s/he (Jo Dawson) was the Archive's sales and marketing manager and that it was normally his (or her) job to deal with press inquiries. It was routine in these instances, s/he continued, to ask the journalist concerned to send in details of their credentials. A Curriculum Vitae, perhaps, and some examples of recent work. They also noted that I was purporting to be a freelance journalist. Could they therefore have a letter from my commissioning editor explaining the precise nature of the brief I was working on.

She was also, in case I was interested, including details of courses run by the Archive for film school students and other interested parties. These courses were in part about acquiring the skills necessary to be entrusted to handle Archive film (the Archive would not loan film to anyone who had not achieved qualifications in this area) but also included a more general basic background about the characteristics and care of celluloid. There were two options – the short course, of one morning's duration, at £50; and the two day course at £175. I would doubtless be more interested in the shorter course at £50. An application form was included.

Well.

Fuck my old boots.

Astonishing. Quite, quite astonishing.

Hannay has taken this coat from a crofter, played by John Laurie, who has given him shelter for the night. Or rather, he didn't exactly take it. It is given to him by the crofter's wife when it becomes apparent that her husband has betrayed him (Hannay) and the police are closing in. She forces it on him as he prepares to make a dash for it into the dangerous night.

The next day, Hannay is wearing the coat when he is shot by the spymaster, Professor Jordan. He survives because the bullet lodges in a bible in the inside breast pocket of the coat – clearly a Sunday best coat.

Which, for some, is an elegant irony. The crofter has betrayed Hannay for all the wrong reasons – he fears, probably quite correctly, that his wife is strongly attracted to Hannay; but more simply and importantly, he wants the reward offered for Hannay's capture. Greed he has led him to betray the rules of

Highland hospitality. It's mean and low. So, this crofter is a mean spirited Gael and we all know that Gaels get their mean spiritedness from their brand of religion, a severe form of Presbyterianism. Thus – the thick book in the breast pocket of the coat mends what the crofter has sought to break.

And this acquires even greater resonance when the crofter, who is the sort who makes it his God-fearing business to terrorise his wife, beats her when he realises that the coat has gone.

Domestic violence springing from religious fundamentalism equals just about the worst form of hypocrisy there is. So the bullet stopping bible is a nice touch. We like that.

John Laurie is obviously a link between The 39 Steps and Dad's Army, where he played Frazer, an apocalyptic harbinger of doom who, when not in Home Guard uniform, is an undertaker.

Maybe we, we as in the Scots, should disapprove of Laurie. Laurie played an important part in reinforcing the notion of the Scots as mean-minded pinched Presbyterians. Querulously pessimistic. Negative. Catchphrase: It willna work. And it's true, all Scots, for whatever reason, have a bit of that in them. It's something you recognise with surprise when you move away from Scotland. And it's odd because we think of ourselves as the ultimate engineers. Engineers are can-do people prepared to think the unthinkable. Aren't they?

Anyway, the thing is that Beth is spectacularly clumsy. The first evening I went out with her, she smashed a wineglass when, trying to put a beer glass down but not looking at what she was doing, she brought the beer glass smartly down on top of the wineglass. It amused me at the time that she sort of pretended it hadn't happened at all, even though there was all this broken glass now strewn across the table. It took her minutes to acknowledge it and then it was like "Where has all this broken glass come from? It's outrageous."

And she still breaks glasses at the rate of about one a week. She spills soup on the carpet and trips over everything. Every time there's an accident, even a tiny mishap, she screams. Sometimes it's a small little squeal but often a full blown scream. I tend to ignore screams now. She badly stubbed her toe once and fell and bashed her head and of course she screamed and I didn't come running and she was absolutely furious and I told her I barely even register it when she screams because she screams nearly every day.

Maybe it would drive Jules mad if I dropped him a line suggesting he researches a piece about coats in films. Because. No, hang on. Who's idea was it in the first place? The coats thing. The general coats thing?

It was mine wasn't it?

But anyway, I sat down right away and began writing a reply. Not to this Jo Whatsits but to Caroline Palmer. I was fired up, obviously, much more fired up than when I was contemplating that first evil letter a few days back – but, oddly, I couldn't quite bring myself to let them have it with both barrels. And the strangest thing was that a small part of me genuinely believed that I wanted to help them – I just couldn't get my head round the stupidity of their attitude. So my first attempt at a reply was incredibly pompous. In it, I revealed how many calls I tended to get from public relations companies desperate to inter-est me in their clients. People who were crying out for me to meet their movers and shakers, people who fantasised about attracting even the briefest of passing interest, people who'd crawl on their hands and knees over broken glass to pay me to listen.

The second version was more to the point. Scary, but, yes, very much to the point. It was addressed once more to Caroline Palmer.

Crikey, I chirped. What a very queer letter I received from your assistant. Was there perhaps some mistake? It has been a long time since I was last asked to audition. Who'd have though that the Palmer Film Archive, in all its glory, would have such rigorous standards? I would like to oblige, I really would, but on this occasion I was going to have to decline. I hoped that this didn't come as a shock to them. But there they had it. They'd have to take me at face value or not at all. And of course I still believed they would find the time and energy to see me. Yours, ever hopefully, etc etc.

And again I waited.

"Colin," I said. "Thought you should know. Colin?"

"Hang on," he said. "Hang on will you."

There was a muffled rustling, wrestling noise in the background. The line was open and clear, them smothered. Open, smothered. The rustling sounded almost nylony. Tough nylon weave like tarpaulin or canvas.

"Colin?"

"Hang on. Look, can I call you back?"

"Yeah. OK."

I put the phone down. What else could I do?

Ben Turpin. That's his name. The squinty eyed silent comedy actor. Ben Turpin.

I didn't have to wait all that long for John Toby – and any waiting I did do was down to me because I was early. We'd arranged to meet In the Camden Head at lunchtime. He was doing the Camden Passage market that day. The sun was shining so I sat out in the beer garden (the garden word is used here to denote a brick patio-barbeque type area) out front.

And suddenly, almost miraculously (because I thought I had been vigilant in looking out for him) they were upon me. It was as if they had coalesced out of

thin air. I say *they* because (and I hadn't even considered this as the remotest of possibilities) he had brought Kate.

I hadn't been prepared for that. It brought me out in a glassy smile.

Kate, squinting from the sun, unnecessarily so, for she had her sunglasses with her (she was letting them dangle by one leg from the fingers of her left hand). She was wearing a loose cotton print dress, white mainly but with flecks and strokes of strong colour. It dazzled. John was in a tubby polo shirt, his bomber jacket (a nasty shade of caramel brown) over his arm. He had his sun-glasses perched up on his forehead, which made me smile; but he wasn't squint-ing. Not a bit of it.

Me with my glassy smile.

"So here you are."

So here they were. John with his waxworks skin and his oiled-back jet black hair and Kate a Modigliani model with screwed up eyes and a blinding white dress. The sun beat down. The flower baskets round the pub's windows spilled colour and scent, a sunshade flapped languorously in a lick of breeze.

"What can I get you?" said John.

I lifted an almost empty glass for him to see. "Another orange," I said.

He grimaced theatrically.

"Yeah, okay," I conceded. "A beer."

"Katy?" he said, taking my glass anyway.

"Mineral water," she said. This almost sounded sulky. It was hard to tell though – by now she'd parked herself (it was one of those A-frame wooden picnic tables) but she wasn't sitting in properly so she basically still had her back to me.

John was giving her the double-take treatment too, glancing at me with that mischievous little twinkle in his eye, as if for moral support.

"Mineral water," she said again, plainly. Matter of fact.

And he just turned and headed off into the bar, the twinkle fading from his eye as if for all the world it had never been there. Matter of fact.

Now I knew that I feared being left alone with Kate. She'd turned slightly now but we were still at cross purposes – we still hadn't said a word to each other. And so maybe it was a game. A battle of wills. Or maybe not. Who knows? Maybe she hadn't even noticed there was someone else with her at the same table. She was squinting into the middle distance. I let her be for a while.

I was the first to crack though. Of that there's no doubt.

"Bright, isn't it?" I said at last. I was looking at her dress. "A lovely day, of course, but…"

"So this was your idea?"

"This?" And obviously, this whole situation was hugely ironic. Not so long ago perhaps my heart would have leapt, seeing Kate unsettled and somehow disgruntled. She shook her head; and then shook it a second time, more vigorously. And another silence fell between us.

I lit a cigarette and offered her the packet, amused at myself for not remembering if she smoked or not. She merely stared at the packet until I took it away. Then she put her sunglasses on. Deftly and definitively, she put them on. And she turned to face me at last. "I suppose that you and John are going to embark on yet another of your infamous sessions."

Again, it was plainly said. Gently, almost. Quietly. With great restraint. But unmistakably withering. I think my jaw must have dropped. My mouth opened but nothing came out. I was absolutely outraged by the sheer mind-numbing wrongness of this statement. I had never, ever, been a drinking pal of John's. I had never, ever, embarked on a session with him, famous or otherwise. Was she in her right mind? Did she even remember who I was?

So I suppose I just stared at her, mildly hurt, wondering if she was pulling my leg. All I could see were my metallic reflections in the dark of her glasses. And I suppose we were frozen like that until John loomed up with three glasses clustered in two hands, some menus wedged under his arm, packets of crisps in his mouth. Still, though, we couldn't settle. Not long after he'd squeezed in at the table, making the drinks slop, Kate stood up without a word – and we both watched, both, I imagine, admiring her tall elegance as she picked her way between the tables and made her way through the pub's tall doors into a cavernous coolness within.

John seemed thoughtful. He lit a long thin cigarillo and as he exhaled he narrowed his eyes, for all the world like a natterjack Clint Eastwood.

"What do you reckon?"

"What do you mean?"

He shrugged aggressively. "What do you reckon?"

He was, I supposed, still staring after her, tracing the space she had vacated.

"Is she doing the market too?" I asked. John took another drag on his cigarillo. "Here, I mean," I added, nodding in what I took to be the general direction of the covered market just up the lane.

He still didn't answer. Not directly at any rate. "You fancy going on after this?" he asked.

"On?"

"On. You know. Couple more beers. Catch up. We haven't had a chance to have a natter in years."

"Can't I'm afraid John. I'm nightmare busy just now."

He smiled at that. A smile that said, *I could easily persuade you.*

When Kate got back to the table, I offered to take our lunch order into to the counter. I didn't exactly hurry back.

We talked about a lot of inconsequential things over lunch – politics, love, death, religion. That sort of thing. And again it was Kate who surprised. She didn't direct the conversation (at least I don't think so) but she certainly had plenty to say. She babbled, she fizzed, and more than once there was a real feeling of anger about what she was saying. A really passionate intensity. A vehemence. All of which I'd never really seen in her before. And I'd certainly never seen her animated about things like politics or world affairs or whatever. It was almost as if there was a resentment breaking out at every pore – and the target was irrelevant. Time after time she'd break in with a contribution beginning, "I hate the way that…"

Was she spoiling for a fight? In all honestly, I couldn't really tell.

And so lunchtime passed. I only had a couple of drinks. I felt virtuous. And cool, I suppose. Bodily, physically cool, but also detached. I didn't say much to John, though I hinted a couple of times that we might actually get down to business at some stage. I wanted to be tactful, though. I didn't know if our business was the sort of thing he wanted discussed in front of Kate. I know this sounds flimsy, because we weren't exactly about to plan a bank robbery or anything – but John is one of those geezer types who's always got a handful of irons in the fire (any number of which might be interrelated in any number of arcane ways) and considers it, on a point of absolute principle, a bad policy move for his dearheart to know anything whatsoever about his doings. He'd probably feel that any breach of this need-to-know policy would strike right to the very heart of his masculinity.

So I failed to draw him out. And then, suddenly, we were saying our goodbyes. It must have been about half two. No later. I said I was heading back along to the tube station; they, obviously, were headed the other way. I watched them go. Derby and Joan, in their own sort of way, I thought. They'd almost been swallowed up by the crowds at the gloomy far end of the alley when I sensed Kate turning back. She came running. There was madness in her eyes. A real wildness. She grabbed my arm and stared intently into my eyes, as if searching there for something.

"We must talk," she said.

And then she had spun round and was off up the alley again. I couldn't see any sign of John. She must have sent him on ahead.

***

In fact it took me ages to get home that afternoon. It was after 5.30 by the time I returned. Beth was heating up Charlie's dinner and Charlie was strapped into her high chair. I came in and kissed her head. She nodded; and then she nodded some more. And then she was nodding non-stop, almost compulsively.

Sometimes she would do this. She'd find a movement she could do and then repeat it ad infinitum because, seemingly, doing it felt good. Because it was doing *something*.

Not long ago this would have irritated me. But now I understood. I kissed her head again, right on the top, the most goldenmost top. And she kept nodding. She was happy and I was happy because she was happy.

"Do you want to feed her?" Beth asked pointedly, leadingly.

"No," I said. "Maybe in a minute. I've got a couple of calls to make."

Which was true. Which was always technically true.

So I went upstairs to my office at the top of the house. And yet I didn't manage to pick up the phone. It was roasting up there in my Hell Hole – it faces due west and takes the afternoon sun full on. I sat there staring at the grain of the desktop, sweat trickling at my temples, and I thought about Kate.

I thought of two things, I suppose, two related things. How so many people used to court her. It was one of those elemental things; a fact of life. Everybody sort of flirted with her a bit; and even John was amused and flattered by it because it was always done in good part. But it was more than flirting too. There was somehow a serious component to it. Like Platonic or Courtly Love. A chivalrous thing. I don't know.

So that was one thought. The other was about how sweet she had always been. I know *sweet* is an all-round inadequate word but it sort of hits the mark too in a very uncomplicated way. By *sweet* I suppose I mean charming and gracious and generously amused by everyone and everything. But I also mean slightly more than that.

Those were the two things I was thinking.

And eventually I forced myself to pick up the phone and someone answered and I said, *Robbie? Robbie. Maybe we should talk. I think we should talk.*

Chapter seven

Our Long March to Hackney Town Hall. To call it Our Long March to Hackney Town Hall is not entirely ironic, though in the end the literal march, the bit we did with all the others, the one-foot-in-front-of-the-other march... that bit was just over half a mile. Half a mile, straggling down the middle of a road while they held the traffic up for us, our ritual chanting led by a man with a howling megaphone. Down Pembury Road to that nightmare junction with Dalston Lane, left wheel into that last little bit of Amhurst Road to Hackney Central Station and then the remaining hundred yards or so up Mare Street to the Town Hall.

It's hugely unsettling walking down the middle of roads you vaguely know. That completely new perspective on your world. Even more unsettling when you're with a whole group of people and you're making a noise and everybody is looking at you. When people come to the edge of the kerb to stare at you they'll quite often have their arms folded. They'll try to look blasé and nonchalant, sceptical even — sceptical about the whole hysterical waste of time you've obviously signed up to — but they also look sour. As if they want to dismiss you with a pettish swipe of their hand.

I suppose, in the past, that's also the way I've looked if I've stopped to watch a demonstration go by. Not that I can actually remember ever having stopped to watch a demonstration go by. I've certainly never been in one before — a proper march that is. I was once part of an ugly mob that surrounded the university administration building while some committee or other was meeting inside to deliberate which faculties should bear the brunt of budget cuts.

Somehow, though, that doesn't really count. The truth is I was a virgin. I felt somewhat sheepish about the whole business, though I think I tried to look as if I were enjoying myself in a decent, reserved sort of a way. I was determined not to cringe inwardly at this whole business – because in any case I was marching for my daughter. Some cars honked their horns in support; others – the majority – were so furious at the hold up that they had to look away. Or so help them. People waved from the tops of buses, though. We marched.

We'd arranged to meet at the south east corner of Hackney Downs. Assemble. Not meet. The plan was to *assemble* at 5 so we could move off at 5.30. And of course it was the usual story. We arrived at just after 5 and there was no one there. Not a soul. We stared off across the park scanning for others approaching. Anyone with a pushchair.

There was no-one with a pushchair in the whole park, never mind one heading our way.

It was one of those special, ordained, improbable times of the day and of the year. A still balminess in the air. The trees were heavy with leaf, the park had been recently mown and though the clumps of clippings were turning brown there was still that intoxicating sweetness of cut grass in the air. And an empty sort of silence. Not a complete silence – Hackney, after all, lay all around us – but a localised silence. A pocket of quiet with us, me, Beth, Charlie, at its eye. A heavy silence. It was all too perfect. Ominously perfect, in fact – because of course there were now flutings of panic in our heads and in our hearts. We'd got it wrong. We'd come to the wrong place. Or got the time wrong.

How shameful that prospect always seems. That you've let everyone else down. Let yourself down. Worse, proved to the world how basically stupid you are. You feel the weight of things – buildings mainly, pulling in at you. Things distort. Colours bend and drag. Things threaten to become rubbery. But glassy too. Fisheyedlens. The world warps.

And within five minutes, the panic turned to embarrassment. Because when the first part of our escort, four Bobbies in a Panda car, turned up we were still the only people there, ready and waiting, assembled. The Panda was one of the really old fashioned types. One of the dinky models. Four burly blokes in a tiny little motor. A toytown car bursting with Beefy Bobbies. They were staring at us, I'm sure they were staring at us.

We tried to make ourselves look like more of An Host by not looking at each other as we talked; we talked, in fact, to the park, to the world outside our intimacy, as if surveying a sea of friendly faces.

But of course people did start to arrive. We'd just got this whole demonstration etiquette thing horribly wrong, that's all. There was a sudden burst of activity at about twenty past. Not only did lots of fellow demonstrators appear as if from nowhere but the main part of our police escort turned up too – one of those white police vans with that grille thing that can be lowered like a visor over the windscreen.

This was the business.

It was only half full of coppers, the Bill, the *Filth*, but these were the boys, hardened front line troops who'd once been the backbone of the Special Patrol Group and who'd surely seen action in conflict zones as far apart as Brixton and Tottenham. Respect. And after all we – the Hackney Mums of Disabled Kids Against the Cuts – were not to be taken lightly.

Their leader, a man with scrambled egg on the peak of his cap... No, hang on, I'm making that up. He didn't have a cap on. He had nothing on his head and he was in shirt sleeves actually. But I think he was a sergeant. I think he had epaulettes on his shirt. He got out of the van, came over, nimble on his feet for such a top-heavy bear of a man, and seemed to be making some sort of announcement to the assembled group. There must have been about 50 of us there by now but we'd somehow found ourselves on the fringes. We couldn't hear a word.

"Sshhh."

"What's he saying? What's he saying?"

"Ssshh. Maybe I could hear if you'd just shut up."

Word travelled back through the crowd.

"He says there's no hurry," said someone turning to pass on the message, nodding now in the direction of the white van. The Filth were sitting in there, eating sandwiches from their greaseproof paper parcels, which lay open across their laps.

"Bastards."

It was at this point that the rumours started. They pulsed and thrilled through the crowd. I'd witnessed this sort of thing before – at Glastonbury, in football crowds, at parties, in clubs and even at railway station barriers – but I've never seen it happen so intensely. Spasms, ripples, convulsions of our common body.

A Member of Parliament was expected to join us; there were deputations from other Boroughs on their way, representations from national children's groups and other charities were expected. Most touching of all, a special contingent – a disabled children's crusade – had set off hours ago from the Ferncliff Centre and they had seriously miscalculated the time it would take to reach the assembly point because some of the children were insisting on trying to walk with their sticks and in their walking frames rather than being pushed in wheelchairs. It was our duty to wait for them.

A heady sort of excitement in the air, screeching silently. I was one of only three blokes there. It felt like I was in that scene in Monty Python's Life of Brian where the women put on beards so they can take part in a stoning.

But no-one came. No-one extra. It was just us. No deputations, representations, crusades. And somehow, when the time came, this plain fact was accepted by all and sundry without comment. When the escort motorcycle arrived to lead us forth from the park (it was ridden with an impressively deft precision, acting as a pilot fish at the head of the column until we approached a junction, when it would zoom ahead to stop the traffic for us), there were just the usual suspects. Thirty or so mums, at least as many disabled kids plus their brothers and sisters and a handful of hangers-on.

One of the other blokes was a hanger-on. Actually that's not at all true or fair. He was the one with the megaphone. He was from the Socialist Workers Party and had clearly done this sort of thing before. Without him we'd have been lucky to reach the end of the street. We'd still be milling about at the entrance to the park, just inside the gate, by the pool of tarmac where the paths converge, the frayed corner of the park where the grass is all patchy under the trees and the by-laws noticeboard is blank, has been for years, and the railings are all kicked in and buckled.

And the police, of course. The police too. The police would have got us on our way, they'd have seen to that. They were there to shepherd us. That was their job and they'd have done it, by hook or by crook. We'd almost certainly have straggled to the end of the street. But it would have happened in silence if it weren't for the SWP guy. The megaphone. The chants.

"What Do We Want?"

"No Cuts!"

And the banners and placards. He was responsible for the majority of those. He'd turned up with all the gear. Blank placards. Felt tip pens. You had to admire it. The organisation and the commitment. Between them, the SWP and the police, they pulled us through.

Charlie was in the luridly-coloured nylon-and-metal frame backpack. A sort of portable breeches-buoy. I think it was the last time we ever tried to use it – save for on holiday a few weeks later. She was starting to get to the point where her weight wouldn't be managed: she couldn't hang on to me, her arms being too constricted to reach round my neck and without that contact, it was really awkward to balance her. She had no strength in her back, no rigidity in her spine. So she was like a huge bag of apples – she just kept flopping from side to side or crumpling up into the most horrible twisted positions and it was eventually an agony for both of us.

But for now it was just about manageable. I could feel her breath on my neck, hear the hoarseness of her chesty breathing.

So we marched, Charlie on my back, and it felt weird but not as exposed and uncomfortable as I'd imagined. And yes, the weirdness came partly from the surreal novelty of being on show in a public thoroughfare. That was the rawest of the realities here. The rawest part of the experience. I suddenly felt as if I'd come out without my trousers on. But I mean, that was the whole point, wasn't it? To go on show. To make a show of yourself. To make a public protes-tation of your pain and anger. Your seriousness. Your intent. And maybe that's where the surge of adrenaline came from. The whole self consciousness of it. It's hard to be ironic or post modern when you're on a march. I suppose that's the point too.

So what did we want?

No cuts obviously.

We weren't normally political. Except of course for the fact that Beth had studied politics. And had been a Labour Party activist in the 1980s. Aside from that, nothing. Not a sausage. But we were prepared to be political about the Ferncliff; in fact it had become bigger than that, bigger than politics, it had become almost a matter of life and death.

The Ferncliff was (perhaps still is) a nursery school and day centre for at-risk, disabled and special needs kids and their families. It was run by Bernardo's but largely funded from the social services budget (not the education budget: that was more than half the problem) of the London Borough of Hackney. Now its future was being threatened by cuts.

The thing was, it was perfect for Charlie – at least for nursery and the transition to primary school, which she was of course approaching. And Charlie was on the verge of great things. Everyone could see that. She just needed the right help.

You don't need medical or social services qualifications to judge a place like the Ferncliff, though, as is often the case when you visit the places wherein dwell the mutant, the incomplete, the mentally handicapped, the heteromorphs of humanity, your first impression isn't great. Your heart tends to sink. Or at least mine does. It plummets. You can feel the swoop of it in your stomach. It happened there, the first time, at the Ferncliff.

As we entered the main hall, that glassy sunlit space, a plain floor area like a gymnasium, we could see, somewhere near the middle, surrounded by nothingness, a woman feeding a child. The child was in some sort of support, a special wheelchair maybe, I don't know, I wasn't looking at that. I was looking, I suppose, at his helplessness. A boy of five or six or seven. He was partially reclined and completely incapable. I mean absolutely incapable. There was no life in his limbs, his head lolled, his mouth lay slackly open. Even his eyes were dull, unresponsive. The woman was ladling spoonfuls of some form of pulp into his mouth and much of the pulp just oozed out again. Occasionally he would swallow and she would smile.

We were left waiting there while someone went to get the director. Charlie was with us. We were expected. The woman and the boy got on with things. A late breakfast, this must have been. It was ten o'clock.

So we waited. We shuffled.

Or perhaps we acted as if this were not part of our world and we talked to Charlie in that slightly patronising too-loud manner that parents adopt towards their children when they're using them as props That hard, blank tone they adopt when they're not really engaging – when they're talking *at* their children to reassure themselves. Charlie's capacity for conversation, at this stage, let's be frank, was limited in any case.

And this is the thing, this is how it happens: when the woman who ran the Ferncliff (director, I think, was her title, though I can't be sure and indeed I am even more ashamed to say that I have completely forgotten her name) came out to greet us, she pulled us into the unsettling scene, the one we had been ignoring, the surreal tableau, as distant to us moments earlier as a snowscene within a paperweight. She pulled us into it. And she introduced us. She introduced us to the child and she introduced us to the woman who was feeding the child. She did it as if it were the most natural thing in the world.

And I suppose that it was.

We said hello to the woman and we said hello to the boy. I think he moaned. This is the way it happens. When you go to one of these special schools or clinics or day centres something will happen to make your head swim. Something that is almost too much for you to process, something that assaults your senses; and sometimes you're almost overwhelmed, it's trippy, you're losing it, you're shaky, you want to cover your eyes and sit down.

And just when you've got a grip on the freakshow feeling, the portents of fear, phobia, revulsion; and just when you've started to tell yourself that this is probably as difficult as it gets and that the rest of your visit here will merely be harrowing, then along comes a woman and pulls you right into the epicentre of it all and turns it into a, pardon my French, tea party. And you will feel better for it, you know you will, it's not that hard. Nor, you tell yourself, should it be.

You begin to act as if this is the most natural thing in the world.

After we'd made our peace with the paraplegic boy we were invited by the director into her office. So we went in and we sat perched on your standard office-issue wood-frame armchairs, Charlie between our chairs in her buggy. And the sinking, swooping feeling returned. Because there was something slightly freakish about this woman. This director whose name I have forgotten. A hint of facial hair – a faint shadowing of a moustache, some wiry hairs on her chin. Actually, to tell the truth, she reminded me a bit of aunt Mary. Aunt Mary towards the end of her life, after Tom had died, just before she went into the home. That distracted, lop-sided smile, though aunt Mary's was never as pronounced as this.

She – the Ferncliff woman, though this much applies to aunt Mary too – was small. Elfin-like. An ageing sort of elfin. She wore darkframed spectacles. Untreated streaks of grey raced crazily through her dark and brittle hair. I don't know about her age. Somewhere over 50. And the thing was that she had a slight squint – so slight that it crept up on you unawares – and the corner of her mouth was turned down as if she'd just been punched there and was about to spit out some teeth. The whole effect, especially the downturned mouth, was exaggerated when she talked.

We thought… What we'd originally thought… The reason we were here…
Take this slowly.

What we thought was that we'd try to find a place where Charlie could get the sort of stimulation that you'd get at an ordinary nursery plus the specialist treatment she needed but in an environment that… that's to say… an environment that was not too grotesque. Sounds disgraceful when you try to explain it, try to put it down in black and white. But that's the truth of it. Not too grotesque. In some of these places, these gloomy, cluttered, introverted places, the best thing you can often hear is a strained sort of silence. It's a hopeless sort of silence. We'd already seen special schools absolutely pervaded by, saturated in, hopelessness. Even when they emulate the sounds you'd expect – the distant sound of a piano chording some cheerful rondo or occasional salvos of laughter – there is something eldritch about these places. And yes, usually it's the silence that gets you – a cold, flat silence, a minatory silence. And if the surface is scratched now and then it's by cries, wails, moans. The thing was, and I know in some ways this sounds terrible, we didn't want Charlie to grow up in a madhouse. We believed she would become hopeless too. Whereas, when in company of bright kids, kids we knew, the children of friends and neighbours, she brightened immeasurably.

We were prepared to be fight for her. And it's true that, sitting in that office, with the woman with the slightly awry smile, my instincts were turning against the Ferncliff. But Beth knew better. She always does. She'd listened to what people said about the place. She'd done her research. She knew that this woman wasn't grotesque. She was sunlight. She was as bright as this building, with its vast acres of skylight – it had a glass roof, not just over the assembly area, the gymnasium-like space where we'd seen the boy being fed, but in a large measure over the two classrooms too. It wasn't just light, it was love; and you began to feel that this love came from her, this flawed woman. You started to feel there was something of the nun or the saint about her.

In most of the other places we'd visited, the staff were more or less demoralised. They smiled but inside you sensed they were pinched and angry. This was somehow very different. And the thing was that they were all properly trained. Charlie could get the specialist treatment she needed – the continuing programme of physiotherapy that was to free up her joints; also the extra stuff like speech therapy and special play. Everyone was trained in the use of Makaton, the sign language developed for kids with delayed speech development. Here she would find the stimulating environment she now needed. Because there was a mix. Not all the children were special needs, some were underprivileged in other ways, at risk, or were the siblings of special needs cases here. What's more the staff-pupil ratio was workable. A huge worry was that Charlie, being both immobile and unable to talk, would just get sidelined in a big class. She was so placid that she wouldn't protest.

But this was right. Right in all particulars. Because Charlie loved it. Anyone could see that. Me, Beth, the principal, the teachers and helpers, most of whom fussed over Charlie. One of the teachers in particular seemed to strike up an instant rapport with her. She was comfortable. At ease. At home. This could work.

After our interview, the head took us back out into the bright assembly area.

We were very interested. Interested in Charlie coming here, we said.

She explained that there was a waiting list and that there were no places at that moment. But some might open up in the autumn.

We wanted to go onto the waiting list immediately.

But there was one absolutely vital consideration.

"Yes?" she said.

We'd been told that if Charlie got the right sort of what they called early intervention, then it would vastly improve her chances of walking.

She smiled at us, a patient sort of smile.

Had they had any… well had they had any cases like Charlie's, where the right sort of expertise in physiotherapy was so important?

"Oh yes," she said, as if dismissing these as questions of no consequence. "Yes of course."

So were any of the current kids in that category?

No, she said. Not at the moment. There was one little boy who couldn't walk when he first came. But the thing is he can now.

She smiled at us.

Her mouth was twisted all out of shape on one side. But it was a sweet smile. It really was. You have no idea how sweet.

We almost wept, the two of us, as we talked about it on the way home. And – I know this sounds awful and clichéd and banal, but there is really no other way of putting it – our hearts sang.

And this was the point… She looked as if she'd learned not just to cope with but to transcend disability. She herself had beaten it. That was the whole point. We wanted to send Charlie to a special school to make her normal. The

Ferncliff performed wonders. It performed miracles. I suppose we were marching for that miracle.

Of course we knew, as we marched, that we had already lost. When I say, *of course*, and when I say *we*, I'm not exactly being totally honest. I mean *I*, not necessarily *we*. I can only speak for me. The thing is, I can't believe that protests can change the minds of politicians. Or very rarely. Certainly not when the protest comes from kids and mums and the bloke from the SWP. They, the councillors of the London Borough of Hackney, had decided months ago – before any of this had become a public issue. It was done and dusted. They were withdrawing funds from the Ferncliff. No amount of rational argument about the merits of the place (and the more you looked into this, the more awesome its track record became) would save it. We were making a gesture. It had to be done, naturally. The gesture had to be made. But to burn large amounts of emotional capital on the march seemed folly to me.

I expect many on the march would have hated me if I'd said that. Perhaps. That's something you can never know.

So, anyway, we marched to the town hall and fell out in front of its steps. Big steps, Greek temple steps, fanning out from the front doors of the hall. Most of

us sat down on these steps. Lots of people were already there, many others were joining; because ours wasn't the only march – others, organised by similar protest groups, were scheduled to converge here. This was to be a festival of protest – because a crisis meeting of Hackney Council, where it would attempt to make emergency measures which would keep it technically solvent, was due to take place that evening. I say technically solvent, because actually it had been flirting with bankruptcy for months.

Beth knew lots of the people there. She had been one of the organisers of our march and had done a lot of lobbying work, cajoling people into writing letters to their counsellors, MPs and other interested parties. She'd also done a bit of media work too, for instance appearing on local TV. So I was introduced, as an incidental, to a whole stream of faces that smiled at me and passed on – and in the end I was barely making eye contact.

Someone said they were hungry. And then everyone in Beth's little coterie realised that they were hungry too. In fact they were starving.

I said I could go for chips. It would be a relief to be useful.

Almost as soon as I said it, I realised this might be a mistake. Not a mistake as such, more of a faux pas. Were chips in any way appropriate? Was there a political dimension to chips? Did marchers eat chips? Did Hackney's modern mums eat chips?

So, stupidly I said I'd go for chips.

There was a silence. A silence, I think, of astonishment.

Then one of them giggled. It was a girlish giggle.

"Chips?" she said. She breathed the word reverently, passionately, as if hushing it to sleep. I don't think I've ever heard the word said so warmly, so lovingly.

Then the others were giggling too. And tutting as if scandalised by their own naughtiness.

"Oooooh. Chips."

"Oh God. Yes. Ohgodyes… Chips."

They were, they reckoned, ever so hungry. And they had earned it. They had earned some sort of remission. They'd pre-paid. They were in credit.

So I was despatched.

"Plenty of vinegar," someone shouted after me.

"Vinegar? Ketchup!" shouted another.

Behind me as I walked I could hear the debate continuing boisterously.

"Both. Get two. Both," I heard a fading voice shout after me as I threaded my way down the crowds on the steps.

I headed back up Mare Street.

I don't know what made me go into the lobby of the Hackney Empire as I passed. Maybe it was just the fact that its doors were open. Maybe I was taking advantage of any excuse to prolong my errand. So I went in and stood there for a while in the empty stillness of the lobby, taking it all in. Shabby plush, here and there a shiny surface of metal, the smells of Brasso and stale carpet. I gave it the once over, as if I were some sort of architectural tourist. Not that I actually cared much for late Victorian theatrical architecture and interior décor, you understand. I was basically loitering.

The person in front of me in the chip shop queue asked for a Family Portion of chips. Which I thought sounded good. So I asked for the same.

"Actually, no. Can you make it two?"

"Two?"

"Yes two."

"Family portions?"

"You sure mate?"

"Of course I'm sure."

That probably sounded a little more aggressive than I'd intended.

"You have to wait," he added.

Which I did.

And 20 minutes later I realised what all the palaver about the Family Portions had been about. And I realised why I'd had to wait so long for more chips to be fried. My first inkling was when they asked me for £3. £3 was a lot for chips, especially on Mare Street, Hackney. But I paid him without any fuss because sometimes the line of least resistance is the right line, and he lifted three boxes onto the counter. One obviously was for the guy in front of me, who'd also been waiting all this time. And two for me. They were as big as shoe boxes and they were absolutely crammed with chips. It took ages to slosh enough vinegar into one and ketchup into the other, to make it look as if I'd actually bothered.

Because – and here's the really pathetic bit – you pull this trick with yourself where you say that she is only mildly disabled or will, in the long run, only be mildly disabled, she's not properly disabled, she's disabled only a bit, she'll be able to shake herself out of it, just as soon as she's got a foothold or a handhold on normality.

Needless to say, although everyone fell on the chips when I brought them back to the steps, we didn't manage to finish them. Not even close. We even tried that thing where you offer the boxes up to the multitudes and you end up feeling like Jesus Christ. A couple of times we watched the boxes bobbing and weaving down through the white water of the crowd – but they made their back each time.

Beth ranged far and wide; I sat there, not even trying to be sociable, staring out at the traffic passing along Mare Street, not really quite sure if I were a part of this. I was unmoved by the frisson that electrified the crowd every time a counsellor began threading his way up the steps to enter the Hall. Or the light-headedness when councillors came back out and made their way amongst us, making a show, I suppose, of being available to petition and open to persuasion. Which would have been impressive were it not for the fact that the ones who did come among us, the mob, were all committed supporters of our side, apparently.

And then I sensed that someone had sat down on the step next to me. It was Liz, Charlie's feeding and speech therapist who'd become a good friend of Beth's.

She handed me a flier. She did it awkwardly, furtively almost; and I started at it blankly.

"I went into the lobby of the Hackney Empire just up there," she said. And then she added, as if reflectively: "It's odd seeing it so empty, with daylight outside. I was just curious."

I said nothing.

"And anyway," she added after a while. "I found that."

It was a sheet of A5, advertising a night of film at the Empire.

EMPIRE FLICKS 1901-1999

Described below was a programme of old film clips courtesy of the Palmer Film Archive, much of it filmed in, or relevant to, Hackney. Like old newsreel footage. Troops returning from the Boer War. That sort of thing. Plus clips of feature films shot in and around the Hackney Empire itself. Including The 39 Steps.

"You're writing something about The 39 Steps, aren't you?"

I turned to her. It was the first time I'd faced her since she'd sat down. Her skin seemed luxuriantly pale, save for a smattering of delicately-coloured freckles that spread themselves on either side of her nose. I almost caught her eye but she evaded me, bending even further over her raised-up knees, looking down at her feet on the lower step. Sensible shoes, flat shoes.

"You are, aren't you?" she insisted.

"How did you know that?"

"Beth told me."

Yes, well, I suppose she did. It sometimes amused (and always mystified) me as to the sorts of intelligence she'd pass on as a matter of course.

I gave Liz back the flier.

"Yes. It's true. At least it was. It didn't work out. Thanks though."

So it was true. True that the music hall at the start of the film was indeed the Hackney Empire. And that the first stilted conversation between Hannay and Annabella takes place outside on Mare Street.

Obviously, in the film we're not meant to identify that the theatre is in Hackney as such – though we're clearly meant to understand we're in a rough old place. Strange though – what would Hannay be doing in Hackney? How would a visitor to London from Canada end up in Hackney? Hackney, after all, is one of London's twilight zones, neither fish not fowl. It's not north London, neither is it the East End. It's by no means easy to get to. It has no tube, is poorly served by buses and its railway stations are on lines that link only to the hubs of other twilight zones.

On the other hand, the fact that Robert Donat, Hitchcock and the crew were once right here in Hackney is not without interest. Come to think of it, Hitchcock makes his customary cameo appearance boarding a bus right opposite where I was sat at that point.

The steps were beginning to get cold. They were beginning to be sore and unforgiving, leaning back as I was on my elbows, my spine lightly resting on the cutting corner of the step behind. I sprawled there, watching for Hitchcock to come along and board his bus.

And I wondered whether I'd been rude to Liz. Sometimes it works out this way. It gets all tangled up. Things come along in the wrong sequence. For instance, if I'd not heard of the Palmer Film Archive before, I'd have hugged her and loved her for ever.

Beth came back and sat with me at some point. She was buzzing. A politico opposed to the Council's current doings had promised to get her into the gallery of the debating chamber to witness the historic events unfold. I was to go back home with Charlie and put her to bed.

That was the nub of it: I wasn't really listening.

"Are you listening?"

I thought for a moment about that one. I sat up.

"We could all go," I told her. "All three of us."

I suppose I mean Scotland. A trip. A sort of holiday.

"What!"

She was staring at me. She was horrified, basically.

It's strange to think, looking back, that I didn't count the number of steps at Hackney Town Hall. It didn't even occur to me. Equally strange is the fact that I've got no desire to go and do it now. No desire whatsoever.

The next bit is slightly surreal. So surreal, in fact, that I'm not entirely sure it happened at all. Tuesday this is. 9.30. I pick up the phone and it's someone saying they're the director of the archive section of the British Film Institute. She says she's only just found my letter (she's been on holiday) and she knew that her assistant had already replied to it – but could I ignore that reply?

Did I want to come in? Today? This morning?

I'd originally written asking if the Institute kept any memorabilia or arte-facts relating to pre-War British cinema, especially The 39 Steps. And back came the rather perfunctory reply that they didn't. But the archive director (now that she was back from holiday) had a hunch that this wasn't the case (confusion had occurred due to re-cataloguing and some items in the Institute's care had perhaps dropped off the system).

Yesterday, Monday, she had (from her own personal curiosity as much as any-thing else) checked out this hunch and had indeed found that there was a package of material relating to the film. Did I want to examine it?

I called a cab.

Within 15 minutes it had arrived.

And here's a thing. On the doormat, as I left, I found a letter waiting for me, freshly delivered. I read it in the cab. Ages ago, I had written to the Scottish Tourist Board asking for details of the area around Killin and asking also if they knew of anyone I could contact to find out more about the location shooting of The 39 Steps back in the 1930s. This was, I acknowledged, what they call a long shot and I hadn't expected much in reply. But here it was: a little booklet called Scotland On Film, which had lots of stills from feature films shot in Scotland set alongside modern photographs of the same scenes. There were several pictures of Hannay scampering about Glen Coe with police scampering after him.

Glen Coe isn't exactly near to Killin – or to the other real places actually identified in the film, Bridge of Orchy and Inverary. But then they're not exactly a million miles away either. When Hannay arrives at the croft kept by the scrimpet Scots character played by John Laurie, he is told that it's 40 miles to Alt na Shellach, which doesn't tell us very much. Killin, and therefore the fictional Alt na Shellach, is barely over 40 miles from the outskirts of Glasgow. Such a big country; and yet so small. But who knows whether there was even the vaguest topographical conception in the mind of Hitchcock or his writer Charles Bennett?

And it just so happens that the figure 40 came easily to Bennett or Hitchcock or both. The John Laurie character tells Hannay that a chauffeur who works at a local house has been there for 40 years – longer, as Hannay points out, than the motor car had been around. Later, when Hannay is captured (and just before he escapes, handcuffed to Pamela) we find out that they're being taken to Inverary, which is 39+1 miles away. (Estimated journey time by car, incidentally: two hours.)

So who cares? As we've discussed before, the setting isn't really Scotland at all. No. It is (or, when Pamela and Hannay go on the run handcuffed together, it will become) Arcadia. Or Illyria, Arcadia's wilder cousin. It has no miles.

But anyway, the main point is that the chase scenes out on the moor weren't shot near Killin. Killin, after all, is just a word on a page, one of Hitchcock's punning little jokes (where you go after a killin', geddit?). And perhaps, come to think of it, Alt na Shellach, or a name very like it, is to be found near Glen Coe. Stranger things have been found to be true.

Colin once drove up right to the top of a mountain. Me and my girlfriend at that time went with him. It, the mountain, probably wasn't a million miles away from Killin, come to think of it. It was two or three thousand feet tall, this mountain. Colin had a beat-up old Ford Cortina at that point and he said it was possible to drive it right up to the top, or almost the top, using the tracks used by the shepherds. And of course everyone laughed at him and of course he had to prove it could be done. Three of us – me, my girlfriend and one other

– accompanied him. I hated the whole business. In particular I hated the bleakness and desolation of the scene that awaited us at the mist-shrouded mountaintop with the light failing.

And the great thing – great but funny too – is the fact that the moorland chase sequence includes a shot of an autogyro, one of those string and sealing wax precursors to the helicopter. This autogyro is supposedly tracking Hannay from the skies. The glimpse we're given of this autogyro is funny – funny as in  quaintly, sentimentally amusing – because it's a model, a studio mock up, and a not very convincing one at that. But there's also something awesome about it too.

To tell the truth, I find the whole notion of the autogyro awesome. The autogyro is the 30s vision of a future that never happened.

You can (and in fact they often did for the newsreels) land an autogyro on the roof of a skyscraper. You can land one in a tennis court. The autogyro, as the ads and features and newsreels predicted, would herald an age of mass aviation.

Rupert Bear annuals, right up into the 1960s, when I was reading them, often featured storylines involving autogyros. By then, I suppose, the autogyro was there as piece of arcane and exotic machinery. The autogyro was something that a strange (yet, of course, benign) English eccentric would own. He would park it on the lawn outside his cottage on the edge of the village. By the 60s I suppose it represented an inspired combination of the old-fashioned and the technologically magical. Like Dr Who's Tardis. It's a magical oddity. A throwback to what was once the future.

Sometimes, when I believe that I am less stubborn now that I have ever been in my entire life, I remember Colin, the mountain and the Cortina. Nothing on earth would persuade me to drive up a mountain now. Nothing.

That evening, the evening of the day I had my crash meeting at the BFI, I could hear the phone in my little office up under the eaves. It must have been about 10.30. The door was pulled to (Charlie's bedroom wasn't far and sometimes the phone could wake her) so it sounded very faint. By the time I got to the phone, it had stopped ringing. Whoever it was had declined to leave a message. I called 1471. "Sorry," said the recorded message, "the last caller withheld their number."

I'd been wondering for days whether she was actually going to call. And if so, when. Kate, I mean.

So I sat up there until well after midnight, drinking wine.

My little office encyclopaedia – the one I bought for 50p almost 20 years ago, the one with the sum total of human knowledge shoehorned into one volume – has an entry about the autogyro and its inventor, a brilliant Spanish mathematician called Juan de la Cierva. His first autogyro made its maiden flight on 9 June 1923. "For nearly ten years during the 30s and 40s, autogyros made hundreds of mail delivery flights from the roofs of post offices in many US cities," the entry says. "However, the arrival of the helicopter closed this niche and the commercial autogyro perished."

But let's settle on the 1930s. Let's agree that the autogyro is one of the archetypal images of that decade.

At some point I must have admitted defeat. I picked up the phone and dialled his number.

"Colin," I said.

"Yes," he said.

"I thought you were going to call me back," I said.

"When?" he asked.

"The other day," I said. "You were wrestling with something, it sounded like. Perhaps a child's paddling pool. And you said…"

"Inflated or only partially inflated?"

"Does it matter?"

"No."

"Anyway, you said you'd call me straight back."

"And did I?"

"No. That's the point. Of course you didn't. That's why I'm calling you."

"Oh yes," he said. "I remember. Every time I tried to call you, you were engaged."

"I was *engaged*?"

"Well yes, you must have been. Why else wouldn't I have got through? You said yourself we hadn't talked."

" …"

"Anyway, what did you want?" he asked, brazenly.

"I, er…"

I'd had a thought.

"I, er…" I began again. "I, er…" I was hot, my palms were sweating up, my face was red. "Look Colin. Can I call you back?"

And of course, that's it. The encyclopaedias. Of course. It's obvious. It's been nagging at me for days. That's where all the stuff about the 1930s comes from. Not my current, tatty, second-hand encyclopaedia but the old family encyclopaedia. The Standard Encyclopaedia. Or rather the Standard Reference Books, of which the encyclopaedia was just one. It was the main one, of course, but there were another five or so. There was a dictionary. There was a volume on home medicine. Another (this seems a bit bizarre but I'm pretty sure I'm not making this up) on human psychology. And I think there might have been one on motoring and car maintenance but I'm not sure.

They were sort of softbacks – a binding I've only ever seen elsewhere on bibles. Thin card covered with a sort of flimsy plastic-type stuff impressed with wrinkles to make it look sort of like leather.

Something in the binding (maybe the plastic, maybe the glue used on the spine, I don't know) proved addictive to our first dog, a Labrador-ish mongrel named Honey after one of the Blue Peter guide dogs for the blind. Given half a chance, she'd fall on one of the volumes and begin worrying it, tearing out frenzies of saliva-pulped shreds. Over the years, her war of attrition on the Standard Reference Collection reduced it to tattered tooth- and claw-scarred fragments.

But here's the point: our edition of the Standard Reference Collection was published in the early 30s. It had been father's father's. He probably got given it as a newspaper subscription incentive. Probably by the Daily Express. That's how hundreds of thousands of homes acquired encyclopaedias in the late 20s and early 30s.

We used those books a lot. The encyclopaedia especially. For homework. It was a great shortcut. Sometimes, on a particularly slow Sunday for instance, you might even pick it off the shelf and lie on the floor leafing through its pages. Looking at the pictures.

Poor, shadowy reproductions of photographs.

Some of the pictures were weird.

Some were funny.

Some, actually, were scary. Genuinely scary. The world portrayed in that book was severe and unforgiving. So much so that it actually seemed like an artefact from a parallel universe.

I hadn't exactly forgotten the Palmer archive either. Unfinished business one way or another. So I called. I called and I asked to speak to Caroline Palmer. This time the girl on reception asked who I was and I told her.

"What company shall I say?"

"No company."

The line went dead for a very long while. And then it was ringing again. Twice. It rang twice. And a woman answered.

"Caroline Palmer's office."

"Can I speak to Caroline?"

"Oh…" Confusion at the other end. The mouthpiece was muffled, then some rustling noises and the receiver was put down briefly and then it was picked up again. "Oh… hang on. Hello? Yes. Can I take a message for her?"

"No. It's okay. No." And then, my resolve returning: "Yes. Actually, yes… It's just that I wrote to her recently. I just wonder if she received the letter."

"Who is this again?"

There was something wrong here. Something false. Something pathetically phoney. Some very bad acting. I could sense it. But I told her. I told her who I was again.

"Yes," she said immediately. "She got your letter."

"Oh. Are you sure?"

"Yes. Yes I'm sure." There was a silence now. A genuine pause, a strained connection; and then, in a voice that was flat and hard and surly, she admitted: "This is Caroline Palmer." In the silence that followed I could sense her growing discomfort. And then: "Yes I did get your letter," she said, and I could sense that she'd just slid past some sort of point of no return. "Yes I did get your letter," she repeated. "And I'll have to say, to be honest, I didn't like its tone, quite frankly."

"Really, Caroline? It's tone?"

"Yes."

"But apart from its tone. What do you reckon? On balance. Taking every-thing into consideration."

"What?"

"I'm asking you what you think about what I said."

"Look, I'm sorry," she lied. "I have another call waiting."

I think I waited another two days before submitting my application form. I chose the full two day course, filled in all the relevant details and even enclosed a cheque, though money wasn't actually requested at this stage.

Also, the thing is that uncle Tom was an archetypal Scot because he originally trained as an engineer. Just after the First World War, he joined Brown Brothers and worked on torpedo systems for the Navy.

Which is of course why he was such a success at Murrayfield. The engineering background. He did stuff that no-one would do today. You can't really make comparisons because what he did was relatively low tech but it's not just that. For instance, when the Scottish Rugby Union decided it might be a good idea to have proper terracing in its national stadium, Uncle Tom put a team of workmen together and they did it themselves one summer.

There was the existing stand down one touchline. The other three sides of the ground were earthen mounds. In other words, when Tom and his team accepted the challenge to lay tiers of concrete steps on these mounds, they were taking on something epic. No-one these days would be so stupid. No-one these days would be so brave.

Uncle Tom was also one of the first groundsmen to do something to stop the pitch getting waterlogged. He designed a build a system of culverts and drains. Again, not rocket science, but he was the first to care enough to do something.

And, perhaps most famously, he was one of the first groundsmen to lay undersoil heating. The summer after I was born they ploughed up the pitch and laid electric wires in the soil six inches or so beneath the surface. Never again would an international match at Murrayfield (the international rugby stadium furthest from the equator, on the same latitude as ice-bound Hudson's Bay, more northerly than Moscow) be under threat from frost.

Not that it often was. Seriously under threat from frost. An international match, I mean.

Because this is the main part of Tom's legend.

It is the legend of the salamanders.

I gave in. I called John and Kate's number. I called at 10 pm. Unfortunately, I got John.

"Well, well, well," he said. "Are we ready to do business then?"

I laughed, despite myself. I told him I wasn't sure any more.

I rubbed a finger against a thumb at her ear, making a quietly sibilant dry grass sound. She reacted. She smiled and she turned her head, trying to see what was going on. I was standing behind her, obviously, so she wouldn't be able to see my hands. She wouldn't be able to see when I had begun rubbing my thumb and finger together at her ear.

I tried her other ear. She reacted again, this time cringeing slightly, as if convinced I was going to tickle her neck. Her neck, especially just below their ears, was ultra sensitive to tickling. She tried to hunch her shoulders up. She giggled her anticipatory giggle.

This was the test I used on myself, when one of my ears was blocked with wax. Sibilance is the part of the range that you lose first.

So this was my test.

Beth had come back in tears from Great Ormond Street. At GOSH they had told her that Charlie was (possibly profoundly) deaf. They were wondering why she wasn't talking yet; and having failed to get any reaction when they rang little bells and squeezed squeaky toys behind her head, they hooked her up to this multimillion pound hearing tester.

And then told us she was basically deaf.

There was some slight measurable nervous activity, apparently, in response to the lower frequencies. But it was likely that all she could hear was a vague sort of echoey rumbling.

So Beth, obviously, was in tears.

"I don't think I can bear it," she said. Said is inadequate. The words were wrenched from her. A keening. "She can't move, she can't suck, her skull's deformed. And now she's deaf. I don't think I can take it."

This was in the kitchen at Northfield Road. The big kitchen with the dining area with black and white vinyl tiling on the floor. Not chequered. Mainly white with a few black.

The thing was, we both knew she wasn't deaf.

Beth had told them to give Charlie time to react. When they were ringing their bells and squeezing their squeaky toys. She said she was sometimes slow to react, especially when she was in alien surroundings, when she'd sort of freeze. And Charlie was, she reminded them, physically constrained by her condition.

They're brilliant at GOSH. When you point something out to them, especially the bleedin' obvious, they smile at you. It's the idiot smile. They have every right to give you the idiot smile because they are the elite. The crème de la crème. We appreciate that.

So, she was deaf.

Oh well.

It was amazing how quickly the white vinyl tiles became scuffed. In the kitchen at Northfield Road. It's strange. Every time I recall this scene I see the tiles on the floor really clearly. Close up – or as close up as you'd see them naturally, bending over from a chair to pick up something that had fallen on the floor.

And so, yes, I called him yet again. Colin. I said I was confused. Maybe. Something was nagging at me. I wanted to be clear in my own mind how I'd got to this situation.

"What situation?"

"That's it. I don't exactly know."

"And?"

"And, well, I met up with them the other day."

"Them?"

"John and Kate."

"What do you mean? Met up with them? Why?"

"You know why. It was your idea. Suddenly John Toby is an expert on The 39 Steps too."

"Too?"

"Well, you know. Just about everyone these days is an expert on The 39 Steps."

"Like who?"

"Like. Oh, I don't know." I suddenly felt very tired. "Colin. What's happening with John and Kate?"

He gave a little sniff of laughter. "Listen," he said.

I listened. Nothing.

And then he: "Look. Forget The 39 fucking Steps, will you?"

I didn't know how to answer that.

"Will you?" he repeated.

"Colin. What the fuck is wrong with you?"

He sighed. A big sigh. A sigh that could burn whole cities. Then meekly, the lamb followed the lion. "There's something I have to tell you."

Another long silence.

"Look. What's the time now?" he asked.

"Mid morning. Why?"

"I'm meeting some people early evening. Why don't I come in on an earlier train? Meet you somewhere around six maybe."

What he had to say to me could only be said face to face, he said. There were lots of better things I could be doing with my time than trekking into town and back to hear the full facts of the matter concerning John Toby. So I objected. I objected feebly but he insisted. And we compromised: I persuaded him to make it mid to late afternoon rather than early evening. I needed to be home by six, I told him.

One time, in getting her out of the car, Beth managed to get Charlie's naso-gastric feeding tube snagged around the car door handle; and as she lifted her out, the tube – a couple of feet of it reaching down through her nasal passage, down the back of her throat and into her tummy – was yanked out through her nose.

Now *that's* clumsy.

He was coming in via Charing Cross, so he'd suggested meeting in Victoria Embankment Gardens. We didn't agree anything more specific than that – and I'd sort of assumed that the place would be deserted when I got there – save perhaps for someone sitting on a park bench eating a packet of crisps, a someone who would turn out on closer inspection to be Colin.

But I was wrong. The place was packed. Busy. And yet not busy. Less frantically busy than a beach, for instance. It was instead busy in a mellow, melted sort of a way. People were strewn like debris, clustered here and there for sure, but basically strewn. It was clear they had, the majority of them, been lazing here since lunchtime at the very least – some of them were drunk and some of them were merely grogged on the day's heat. And it seemed as if they all knew each other; either that or they were part of some wider conspiracy. Also, it looked suspiciously for a moment as if these were the beautiful people, assembled somehow *en masse*, as happens all too rarely these days, apparently.

The grass was brown-parched in parts, green and speckled with daisies in others; there was a smell of wetted earth, richly fragrant, like patchouli oil; flowers, fronds; and from somewhere not visible there was the sound of jazz – a sort of Parisian style jazz, I think, with an accordion slinking sensuously. It sounded nearish and live – a real band, the splashes of cymbal were very here and now – but I couldn't even pin down its general direction. Strangest thing of all was the fact I kept imagining there was a Punch and Judy show nearby. I kept feeling its presence, behind me or just outside the periphery of my vision. All I'd have to do was turn my head and there it would be.

I lost count of the number of times I had to step back out of the delusion. It was almost a hallucination, so persistent was it. This Punch and Judy show. By now the band were playing the Mr Memory theme tune from the Music Hall scene.

I had a dreadful premonition, as if someone had died. As if Colin in particular had died. And as it turned out, this wasn't as silly as it sounds – though I wasn't to find that out quite yet.

I walked up and down for over half an hour. And then I went up to the concourse of Charing Cross station (cooler, echoey, glassy, but somehow not at all

like a swimming baths for all that), waited for the next Greenwich train to get in, and scanned the faces coming off the platform. Then I went back down to the park and walked back and forward a couple more times, picking my way around chatting circles of cross-legged people and between the stretched out bodies of sunbathers.

I don't know how much she needed intensive care. I mean, I don't know if she was actually ever in danger. I think it was a precaution thing. Or maybe what I'd overheard walking past Broadhurst and that other consultant in the hospital corridor was true. True, I mean, of Charlie. Maybe at that stage they really did suspect she was the hopeless case they had been discussing.

I was allowed into neo-natal intensive care at noon the day after she was born. Almost exactly 24 hours, in fact, after she was born. 25 hours, 10 minutes. Beth was still woozy on the ward upstairs. Woozy and distraught and disorientated. She was watching a frantic version of herself frozen within an opaque casing of morphine.

Charlie was in a perspex tank. It didn't have a lid – it wasn't a ventilator – but she was wired up to all sorts of machinery, just like equipment under test in an engineering lab.

Charlie was unconscious. "Asleep," they reassured me with one of those professional smiles.

I put my little finger into her tiny hand. A very wrinkled hand. I don't know if I'm making this up, I don't know if this is just a story I tell myself, but anyway, her fingers closer ever so slightly around mine.

I didn't even ask how she was doing.

For we were still waiting.

This was just one of those dreams, one of those strange scenes within the whole waiting thing.

I became aware of two other families gathered around perspex tanks across the room. Both boxes had lids, both were hooked up to respirators. Both families looked awful. Dishevelled, frazzled, some of them clearly hadn't slept in days. All the time I was in there, in intensive care, I was as aware of them as I was of Charlie. Two disbelieving families. In both cases there seemed to be something posed and stagey about the way they were each grouped around their perspex tank. It reminded me of something from a renaissance painting – a deposition of Christ perhaps – or a Rembrandt. Something melodramatic and yet restrained. A cosmic tragedy underplayed. Knowingly underplayed.

I don't know. There was an aura of imminent death in that room. An unmistakable aura of imminent death. I suppose that's obvious, isn't it?

Charlie's stiff little fingers closing ever so gently, almost imperceptibly about mine.

The nurses smiling.

The thing was that the nurses, they didn't just smile at you, they seemed to smile *through* you.

I wondered if the intensive care nurses practised their smiles. They were good. All of them. They gave good smile. A sweet smile with just enough of a hint of a frown in it. Solicitous. Profound. Just the merest hint of moistness twinkling there in their eyes. A smile that salves broken hearts. A smile that goes out to you, goes with you. A piquant smile, flattering in its appreciation of your bravery, your strength of character. Dammit, they all but envy you this opportunity to show what you're made of.

They're smiling though also, briefly, for a fleeting instant, they're staring. Staring at you.

I wasn't allowed to stay for very long.

All the time I was there, one record was playing on the radio. The radio was away over in the corner somewhere and it was turned down very low, almost below the threshold of perception. It was playing Walking On Broken Glass by Annie Lennox.

So I can't have been allowed to stay for very long.

As long as a pop song. Three minutes. Three minutes and something seconds.

It was as if I were just, for formality's sake, being allowed to check out the merchandise. To confirm that it existed. That it was still here.

And it was.

A nurse smiled at me and took me by the elbow and smiled at me and led me away.

Chapter eight

I'd been working pretty steadily on the lawn all summer. At first, the notion was merely to level up the really bad cracks and depressions and hollows and improve the quality of the soil so that across the whole lawn, the fork would go in easily at least three inches or so. But even that limited goal wasn't as achievable as I'd thought.

I'd come across patches where the fork would hardly penetrate the ground at all, even when well watered. So I started digging small exploratory holes to see what was there. What I found basically were little pockets of barely buried building rubble – probably, I reckoned from the amount of richly glazed tiling that I found, dating back to the building's original construction in the 1890s. This was extremely irritating but explained a lot. I didn't have to be a genius to work out that the patchiest, most blighted bits of the lawn seemed to coincide with the areas of buried rubble.

The fact that no-one down the years had made the slightest bit of effort to make the garden slightly less of a building site was suddenly very irritating. But at least I had got to the root of the problem. On the other hand, I should have given up, just as every owner of the house for over a century had obviously given up and settled for a puny, threadbare patch of grass out there.

But all summer I worked away. On good days I took off my shirt and laboured with the sun on my back. I liked feeling the warmth of the sun and my own warmth too, the warmth in my arms and my shoulders and my chest and even across my stomach. I felt the re-emergence of muscles I'd forgotten were there. Strenuous digging would straighten your head – and then empty it utterly.

Some days I'd get caught in showers. The sun would go in, clouds would slide across the sky and the garden would darken – and yet I'd dig on, the rain now falling on my bare back and shoulders, and I'd be completely oblivious. Some days I'd dig for hours, mindlessly. Some days I'd dig bits I'd already dug before. Sometimes I'd look up to the sky and realise that it was evening and I'd stretch, arching as I pressed fists into the small of my back and there'd be the tiniest of insects hovering in the air around me.

I learned to appreciate the easy working of my muscles, the feeling of substance that it gave you, and the honest sweat.

So the truth was that I had been evoking his spirit for weeks now. Not weeks, months.

Tom was a night person at the best of times, a man with little regard for sleep, who just didn't rate it, a man who'd pace away the small hours and still rise before dawn. In the week before a Murrayfield international, though, he would hardly sleep at all. He would sip it, graze its surface, but only for form's sake. He ran entirely on worry.

He was up and out at all hours checking his thermometers. And he had loads of thermometers. Air temperature thermometers, ground surface thermometers, soil temperature thermometers, deep subsoil temperature thermometers. He had thermometers in situ, he had sheds full of backup thermometers. He had them on and by the pitch itself and he'd have a duplicate set on the small patch of lawn by his bungalow at the edge of the stadium grounds – so that if he did go to bed he could nip out every so often through the night and check ground temperatures without having to walk over to the stadium itself.

That was risky, of course, and not really to be advised, because the conditions at pitch level within the stadium were not the same conditions as experienced by his small patch of lawn. The stadium conditions were exceptional. Unique even. For the stadium was a frost lens. It captured cold air, which sank heavily, like icy syrup over the terracing steps, and oozed over the pitch. Tom could almost hear it in the night, 200 yards away as he (pretended) to sleep.

So, actually, he usually went over to the stadium and checked.

Tom had an uncanny instinct for frost. He could hear it in birdsong, in the way the dawn chorus becomes brittle and super clear. He could hear it in the silent openness of the skies. He could hear it in the sparkling stars. He could hear it in the ring of footsteps on a distant pavement. He could smell it in evening air, through the plumes of people's breaths, yeasty with whisky and cigarettes after a party or a family gathering; he could smell it through the scent of women's perfume and the muskiness in the folds of their fur coats as they said goodbye on the doorstep. Frost's scent was a clean scent. An absence of scent.

Frost was a constant, a given. Tom could look across an undulating expanse of grass and tell you which areas would whiten first and which would be the first to thaw. On a golf course he'd stop, retrace his steps and tamp a stretch of ground (usually a barely visible gully, the faintest snaking fold in seemingly flat ground) with his heel, sounding it, reading its history of compacted winter deadness even in daisy strewn spring.

In the days counting down to a match I don't suppose he actually needed the Met Office reports passed on to him from the SRU offices in the main stand. Or the regular, almost hourly outlook reports relayed to him throughout the day from RAF Turnhouse.

It was like D-Day and yet it was not like D-Day because D-Day was a thing that could be postponed.

And if, in the days before the laying of the electric blanket, the thermometers began dipping below 40 degrees Fahrenheit, he would begin sending out for straw. Tons of it, trailerloads of it. And Tom and his team of men, supplemented by as many volunteers as he could whistle up, would grab pitchforks and begin hoiking it onto the pitch. It takes a lot of straw to cover a rugby pitch, perhaps an inch deep in straw. A lot of work. And it takes even more work to remove all that straw on the morning of a game, with kick off at 2pm and the turnstiles open at noon.

He would head for the Grassmarket. The Grassmarket was notorious in those days – that's where the working men's hostels were. Doss houses. The Grassmarket was where the alkies hung out. There, in front of the hostels, he made his pitch. A fair morning's work for a fair day's pay, heaving straw. To be paid when the job was done. Not a second before. No, no advances. No drinking on the job. But free entrance to the game, of course. Few took him up on that bit of the offer. They were in the bars of Roseburn well before the match kicked off.

But sometimes the thermometers would dip well below 30 degrees Fahrenheit and when the mercury drops that low then straw is just not enough – not even good, feisty, decomposing, humidly-alive straw.

And that's where the salamanders came in.

Salamanders were part of family lore. The word resonated with our pride for what Tom had once done and what he had once been. It was a word that resonated with his ingenuity – an ingenuity we liked to think we could also claim as our own.

It was a word that might lie at the heart of anecdotes.

"And if it was really bad," father would tell a crowd of the usual suspects at the golf club bar, "in would come the salamanders."

Even those familiar with father's repertoire might have forgotten what the salamanders were. And someone was bound to ask. They'd do it just to fill the expectant pause that father had manufactured and was hell bent on maintaining. They'd do it just to humour him. And they'd do it in the half suspicion that they might regret it. They could detect an undercurrent of mild one-upmanship here.

And so, yes, someone would ask what the salamanders were, again.

"What!" he'd say. "You don't know about the salamanders?" A pause. And this was it: we were in the domain of tradecraft here. The esoteric knowledge of the inner circle. Father would take in his audience, gauge the quality of their attentiveness. "How do you think he did it all those years? This was before the blanket was laid, mind. And never an international match called off. Never once. Even in Arctic conditions. Black ice everywhere, the city at a standstill and still the match goes ahead. How do you think he did it?"

Growing up, the word confused me, though. In fact, I found it profoundly unsettling. I knew a salamander was a lizard. Perhaps. Maybe it was some sort of a dinosaur – a primaeval creature, one of those scaly things that roamed the earth when it was young. Or no – salamanders were maybe mythical beasts.

But one way or another, the point was that they were creatures of the fire. Perhaps uncle Tom perhaps threw handfuls of these lizards into the furnace deep beneath the Murrayfield stands. Perhaps he shovelled them into the boiler like the footplate stoker of a steam train. Green when they went in, white hot when they came out; then cooling to a glowing red as the scuttled about the frost-bound Murrayfield pitch, giving it their warmth.

Or perhaps not. Instead, maybe salamanders were braziers. Big braziers. Massive things. I never saw them, obviously, because when I was less than a year old I helped lay the electric blanket, and the electric blanket removed for ever the need for salamanders, but I have heard them talked about so much that I can just about visualise them. We're not talking about crude, mediaeval, cast iron grates in which you'd heap wood or coals. No. We're talking of something more sophisticated. Rugged, industrial, but sophisticated. Smudge pots. Metal hookahs with pipes and tubes. Cylindrical affairs on big cauldron bases. Very tall pillar boxes. Mini incinerator chimneys topped with reflectors shaped like coolie hats – akin to the patio heater type things used by bars and restaurants on cold days to make their pavement tables usable. Gas fired or kerosene things that reeked like jet engines.

He hired them, I think from market gardens. Or orchards.

But as for the canvas half of the equation, I haven't a clue. Because apparently he set out the salamanders under big tents. I used to imagine, wishful thinking, that he hired the stuff from circuses. That he erected big tops on the pitch. But they were probably just marquees. The sorts of marquees one would hire if one were hosting a wedding reception on one's lawn. He'd erect these marquees over the worst spots, the pressure points, the frost's focal areas. And then, within each marquee, he'd set up an array of salamanders. And light them. And leave them lit. Burning for days before an international until the heat soaked deeply into the surface of the soil.

The salamanders were smoky and gave out an eerie light. They had to be watched through the night.

I would have done that. I'd have volunteered. Under great cathedrals of canvas, in perpetual twilight. I'd have watched them.

It took days for it to dawn on me. And the dawning hardened into full day when I watched the film's opening scenes once again. The Music Hall in The 39 Steps. It's not the Hackney Empire at all.

Not the exterior at any rate. The interior – yes, maybe. You'd have to do a bit more detective work to come to any sort of definitive conclusion about that. But the real Hackney Empire doesn't have a façade or an exit doorway even remotely similar to the one featured in the film. And then of course there's the small matter of them crossing the road and hopping onto a bus. A number 25 bus. Which doesn't actually go anywhere near Mare Street. Not as such.

Close, but no cigar. It is arguably your archetypal East End bus, the 25. It comes from Ilford and goes all the way down the Romford Road (skirting pretty close to Itchycoo Park, as it happens) to Stratford. Then Bow, Mile End, Stepney Green, Whitechapel and Aldgate before entering the City and taking in the Bank before heading off towards the West End. The closest it comes to the Hackney Empire is when it passes the end of Cambridge Heath Road between Stepney and Whitechapel. But from there, you're still looking at a mile or so northwards through Bethnal Green before you hit Mare Street. (And in any case there's an important taxonomy at stake here because as any resident of Hackney will tell you, and as I've mentioned previously, Hackney isn't in the East End. It has some E numbers in its postcodes but it's not in *The* East End.)

So it's obvious, isn't it? They filmed the interiors in the Hackney Empire and then they took all their equipment down to the Mile End road where they'd found a suitable Music Hall exterior to use. Either that or they mocked the whole thing up in a studio and borrowed a bus to drive through the set.

Coincidences begin piling up. It's true. Or rather, maybe you're surrounded by just as much coincidence as you ever were but it's just you become far more alive to it.

Like when Martyn turned up. He said he was at a loose end. This was lunchtime on Sunday. He had a horrible hangover but he'd woken up and couldn't get back to sleep so he'd gone to get the newspapers and had had some breakfast. And then, still feeling a bit ropey, he decided it might be best if he vegetated for a bit. Specially if there was a film or something worth watching on telly.

And there was. Or so he thought.

The Carlton Cinema channel. The 39 Steps. Brilliant.

My heart leaped slightly when he said that. In a flash I could foresee some sort of conversation that would end with me telling him something of the project I'd embarked upon. But then just as quickly, I realised it wasn't going to work out that way.

"It's like one of those films that you always remember as brilliant but when you start watching it you realise it's a bit…"

It's a bit… The three dots are a transition to the mime he now launches into. Or the pastiche. Or whatever. It's brilliant. It's spot on.

He acts out two people meeting, shaking hands. He acts both parts, wheeling back and forward between the two roles.

"How do you do?"

"Yes, how do you do?"

It's like one of those cod government information films that Harry Enfield used to do. The wonky eyelines, the jump-cut editing and more than anything, the wooden body postures, the lifeless, self-conscious delivery of the lines, the wonky inflexions. The improbability, the unnaturalness of the dialogue. The strange sort of stilted, emotionally constipated world being portrayed.

Martyn is absolutely spot on.

Despite myself, despite the feeling that I'm betraying a faithful old friend, I join in.

"Would you like me. To cook you some. Fish?"

"Yes I'd love. Some fish. Haddock. Do you have some. Haddock."

It's so spot on. And yet, equally, so unfair.

I've never actually been on a 25 bus. The 73 is more my style. In fact, I caught one, a 73, the next day. No, not the next day. Maybe it was the day after.

It was time for me to have it out with Robbie. We'd had a bit of a set-to the other day, as you'd expect. He tore a strip off me. And yet, in an odd sort of way, I won him round. It was not my fault, after all, that the project had acquired the kind of unstoppable momentum that it had. It was hardly my fault that it would take more time to do it justice. I think Robbie always understands that it's maybe worthwhile cutting me some extra slack now and again.

But sometimes it's awkward with Robbie, that can't be denied. Now and then I feel he's pestering me – he wants too much of me. Like with this new magazine he's been planning for months now. He keeps telling me little bits and pieces about it and asks what I think or whether I've got any ideas. Or maybe I know someone, he'll add, who might, say, want to write a column or something for it. A few weeks back I'm sure he was on the verge of asking me to edit it for him. Which would have been rich. And I'm sure he actually will at some point get round to offering me the job, which will be embarrassing because I won't know what to say.

So. That's always the difficulty where Robbie's concerned. Keeping his expectations down to more realistic levels. That's the awkward bit.

Whereas The 39 Bus. The 39 is your Clapham Junction to Camden Town bus.

I reckoned the odds on Kate doing the Camden Passage market two weeks in a row weren't great. But no. I was wrong. I'd left with plenty of time to spare before my meeting with Robbie and bussed it on a 73 down Essex Road – and there she was, sitting at her stall. It wasn't yet mid morning and the market (if you could actually call such a bedraggled enclave of stalls just off the pavement a market as such) was quiet; and she was so still that she might have been med-

itating. She didn't even notice me the first time I walked past her stall. And in fact the truth is that I nearly kept on walking. But I didn't. I doubled back and pretended to browse among the bric-a-brac of a couple of stalls right behind hers.

And it was strange because one minute the place was empty and the next minute when I looked up again and it was almost crowded. It was as if someone had called *ACTION* and lots of clock-work extras had been turned loose. In a way it made life sort of easier – I didn't feel so exposed as I approached her stall the second time. But I suppose I must have got the timing horribly wrong. Because. Well.

She looked up. I said: "Hello Kate."

She didn't say anything, I don't really think she had time to say anything, because, almost immediately, I added: "You said we should talk."

At which point I met her eye again and I realised (or noticed for the first time) that there was panic there. Real panic. She was speechless with panic. And then she began shaking her head. It was a vigorous yet nervous gesture. Not quite under control but clearly emphatic. Her eyes were saying: *Not now. For god's sake not now.*

I smiled. An ironic, rather world-weary smile. Then, as I turned away, I paused and I made it quite apparent that I had paused. A pause that told her there was so much I could say; so much I deserved to say, had a right to say. And yet I was willing to forego that right. I hoped she was aware of the nature of the gesture I was making.

And then I was gone.

I've never been a gambler if the truth be known. Obviously I know it's not true what some people say about horseracing – that it's basically a sport followed by homeless alcoholics. Losers basically. It's a big economy, I know that. And actu-ally, the truth is that I've been to the Derby, on a corporate jolly. I drank so much I was sick in the queue for the station afterwards. But I didn't manage to place a bet. At one point I tried to put £1 each way on a strongly fancied favourite.

"Fuck off," swore the trackside bookie. Just that. "Fuck off." He didn't even deign to look down at me – his eyes never left off scanning the crowd. His lips hardly moved, that was the thing. "Fuck off," he rasped, a hoarse aside, out of the corner of his mouth.

So yes, 1936. Rhodes Scholar, Pay Up, Bala Hissar, Taj Akbar and Mahmoud. And also Boswell, Noble King and Thankerton. Taj Akbar was the early favourite: the Aga Khan's horses were in fine form and Gordon Richards was just bound to win a Derby sooner rather than later.

Some observers were impressed with the performance of another Aga Khan horse, Mahmoud, during a run-out alongside Taj Akbar on the gallops on Thursday 21 May – but it wasn't a true trial and the form books tended to indicate that both Pay Up and Taj Akbar were likely to have the edge over the likes of Mahmoud. The omens were not good for Mahmoud because Mahmoud was a grey colt; and, as all the newspapers were pointing out, a grey colt had not won the Derby in 116 years.

In any case, those in the know were starting to have a sneaking suspicion that it might not be the Aga Khan's year after all. It might just be Lord Astor's year instead. By the Saturday, 23 May, the odds on Astor's horse Pay Up were starting to shorten:

Taj Akbar	6-1
Pay Up	13-2
Noble King	7-1
Boswell	13-1
Bala Hissar	100-7
Mahmoud	100-6

Still the reckoning was that it was actually the most open Derby in years, and the going could be absolutely crucial. The course was brutally hard. Like a car park.

Kate spooked me that morning in the market. I don't mind admitting that. So I don't know how I came to be in the bookshop across the other end of Islington Green that morning. Maybe I was just wandering around, half-dazed. But this is where another minor miracle was destined to take place.

It's as if I'm led straight to the right bay and the right shelf. It's a shelf in a spectacularly messy cul-de-sac, a bay of books that apparently hadn't been tidied or sorted (I think "faced" is the technical term) or dusted in months. Books had even spilled onto the floor and had been left there.

Down at the end, facing me by now, at the bottom of the cul-de-sac, between books on film on one side and art, fashion and design on the other, were the pop music books. Clearly they'd been here for years, some of them, so frayed and dog-eared were they, their covers creased, their corners bent back. But this is where I found it, nestling among the glittering biographies of a handful of blandly poptastic Elton John-like characters and the anthologies of post-modern cultural essays. Here it was. The Bumper Book of British Pop. It was one of those wonderfully hybrid books that defy any attempts at pigeon-holing. It sort of looked at first sight like a reference book. But you soon realised it wasn't at all organised or comprehensive. It basically stole bits and pieces from all the other books on the shelves round about. Star biographies, essays on musical styles and influences, summaries of the trends within partic-ular decades. It was a huge big floppy softback, like a computer software manual, but inside it felt more like a coffee table masterwork than a manual: it was beautifully produced, with sumptuous colour reproductions on richly glossy paper.

I should have bought it, I really should.

But I didn't.

Towards the back of this book there was a section called Chart Trivia, which listed every single British No 1 since 1955. With dates.

And there it was at last. Without You by Nilsson. There it was, sandwiched between Son of my Father by Chicory Tip and Amazing Grace by the Royal Scots Dragoon Guards. Possibly the only pipe band hit in the world. Ever.

But there it was. Without You. It climbed to the top of the charts on 11 March 1972 and stayed there for an impressive five weeks, being displaced by the pipes and drums on 15 April.

Yes, I should have bought it. Instead, I sat on the floor of that long forgot-ten bay of books and I recorded all the relevant information in my diary.

When I'd finished, I felt incredibly pleased with myself.

I even put the book back in its right place on the shelf.

Like a car park. Or a frost hard rugby pitch.

***

Robbie's outfit is based in Shoreditch and his offices are exactly as you'd guess – an open plan converted loft with anaemically pale pine floorboards. Robbie got in at exactly the right time, when Shoreditch was only just getting an inkling that it could steal some of the trendy credentials being worked up by its little brother, Hoxton. So he got his converted loft dirt cheap and when they first moved in there was just a handful of them huddled down in one corner of what seemed a ridiculously extravagant space. Now the place is like a hive obviously and they never did get round to ordering a pool table.

I only worked briefly with Robbie many years ago on a magazine with offices on Wardour Street. They were the coolest offices I ever worked in, not just because they were in the middle of Soho, but because there was a pool table. Right in the middle of the floor, with all the desks arranged round it. That, I thought when I first saw it, is style. I'd have put a hell of a lot of money on Robbie having a pool table in his Shoreditch loft.

Shoreditch offices are so open plan that the meeting room is usually out in a corridor. And Robbie certainly isn't radical enough to buck this trend. So, the corridor it is; a fat bit of the corridor round behind the stairwell, but a corridor nonetheless. It's a nook into which they've introduced an extravagantly oval table and there's a huge chunk of old photographic equipment (an enlarger, I think, with a downward-pointing lens and an abraded leather sleeve with concertina like pleats and folds) bang in the middle of this table. A centrepiece. How they conduct a proper meeting with lots of people round this table is anybody's guess. You can envisage all sorts of craning, peering and stretching going on.

Anyway, this time it's just me and Robbie. If you don't count the people who drift past now and then – the coffee machine's down this end of the building, obviously.

We talk for about half an hour about all sorts of stuff that Robbie might want me to do in the future. He doesn't even mention our little misunderstanding about deadlines. He says he's really excited about this new title he's going to launch and I say it sounds exciting, yes, I'm really excited about it too. I ask if an editor has been appointed yet. "Soon," he says. "Soon." An enigmatic little, reflective little smile. And then the oddest thing.

"What was the name of that that guy I met a few months back? A mate of yours."

I didn't know what he meant. So he reminded me. We'd gatecrashed the

Christmas party of a production company and we'd bumped into Robbie there. We being me and Jules.

"He did some stuff for Variety, didn't he?"

"One of their European spin-offs, yes. I don't think…"

"Have you got a number for him?"

"He's very busy these days."

"He wouldn't mind me calling him, would he?"

"I think he's setting up a company or something," I said. "No," I added. "No. Can't see why not."

And so I gave Robbie Jules's number.

And then that appears to be it. I'd been assuming that Robbie would want some sort of update on the piece I'm working on. I mean, we both know he'll love it. But he seems to be winding things up. He looks at his watch then glances at his personal organiser.

So it's time to tell him something he should know. Something he will understand.

"To tell the truth," I tell him, "I've sort of managed to get myself stuck in the 1930s."

He stares at me.

I reckon I can tell Robbie this because he can probably sort of understand. He has a pretty left-field sort of track record. For instance, there was that famous occasion when he was sent to interview Ted Turner, the cable TV king and inventor of CNN. He (Robbie) flew over to Atlanta to do the interview, which went pretty well by all accounts, and then… and then he just disappeared. As the days went by, people began to get worried. They checked with the airline and discovered that he hadn't used the return half of his ticket. As far as the passport and immigration people knew, he hadn't left the country. The police on both sides of the Atlantic began to get involved. His parents and his girlfriend began to make plans to fly to Atlanta.

And then, two weeks after he'd originally been due to fly back, he called and left a message. Not with his parents, not with his girlfriend, not with his editor. He called in the middle of the night, London time, and left a message with the security guy manning the front desk of the magazine's office block. He chatted with him for ages, so the story goes. He dictated a long message.

He was holed up in the Chelsea Hotel, Manhattan, if anyone cared to know. He'd started a novel. It was set partly in the Chelsea Hotel and involved not

0016

just its current residents but the ghosts of past ones too. It was set also on the road and in the dark heart of America. It was going well. He didn't know when he'd be back.

Actually he arrived back within 24 hours.

Strangely, no-one ever asked him about the novel.

So now he's staring at me, stroking his chin and nodding sagely. "Stuck in the 1930s?" He doesn't actually say the "huh" at the end but I can hear it all the same.

"Yes," I tell him. "Yeah." Actually, I'm warming to this now. "It's like, something happens to you when you have a child." I usually steer well clear of this subject where Robbie's concerned. It's not that he doesn't want to talk about Charlie and our particular circumstances, which he knows a little of, it's just that (as I maybe said earlier) children, all children, occupy a place to which he'd rather not go.

But I plough on into this, regardless. "It's like, you start to realise you have a past beyond your past. Beyond your own individual past, that is. It all starts to connect up. You remember bits of your own life that you've forgotten. And you remember stuff about your dad and you realise suddenly that particular memories happened when he was almost exactly the same age that you are now. And it connects even further because you are able sort of to colonise his memories too and make more sense of stuff that he's told you in the past or tells you now. And stuff that other relatives have told you too. It all, well it's like I said, it all starts to connect up."

He's looking at me sceptically. He's trying to work out if I'm taking the piss or not. I don't know if I said before, but I have this sort of reputation for pulling people's legs. I mimic people, I take them off, I send them up. He's wondering now if maybe there's a joke here. He's wondering if the joke's on him.

And I'm glad of that because I'd begun to hear myself towards the end of that little spiel and it sounded horribly homespun.

"So it's like a bridge?" he says, as if he's in on the joke, whatever it is.

"Absolutely," I agree, enthusiastically. This is going roaringly well.

"Back to the Thirties?"

"Yup."

"Which is where you're now stuck?"

"Can't seem to get away."

"You know what?" he says. He's chuckling now. "It sounds a bit like

Brigadoon."

I hadn't thought of that before. It does. Or one of those timeslip comedies or sitcoms. It does. It really does. I'd started to think of this as significant – a journey into nostalgia perhaps, but a meaningful one, revelatory, apocalyptic. But no. This is pure light entertainment.

He stares at me. Blankly. Unsympathetically. "You know what," he says at last, as if determined to lead me back to somewhere more familiar, somewhere in the here and now. "You know on that piece you've been doing. I was thinking. You should talk to some people at the BFI."

Quite. My BFI visit had been a huge disappointment. I suppose I should have told you that already. They sat me down in the main reading room of the library there at Stephen Street and told me that it might take a few minutes for the materials to be made available. If I wouldn't mind waiting. They'd call me to the desk when everything was ready.

It was like a dinky version of a university library. A section of shelves, a section of microfiche readers in front of the main librarian's counter and a zone of tables and chairs (spartan, pine largely) in rows and ranks. White walls, white security lattices over the windows, white polystyrene ceiling tiles, white plastic ducting running here, there and everywhere.

Apart from me, there were two others haunting the pine furniture zone. I couldn't work either of them out. The girl was in her mid twenties and looked, I thought, a little bit like a South American Indian. She had coffee coloured skin and dark hair, slightly crinkled but longish. She was wearing a US college sweatshirt, tight beige cords and trainers – but the best touch was the plain red gypsy (or pirate) headscarf she'd stretched tight over her forehead and tied at the nape of her neck. She dragged her feet dreadfully, so badly in fact that I thought maybe she was disabled in some way. But no, she was just incredibly lethargic. And she couldn't settle either. Two or three times she got up from the book she was supposedly taking notes from and wandered off into the shelves. Then she'd some back minutes (seconds, probably) later, sit in behind her book again but almost immediately turn her head to gaze out of the window.

Was she a postgraduate student or something? Somehow I couldn't see it. Or merely waiting for an adventure to happen to her?

The bloke was really weird. He was a pocket-sized version of Henry Kissinger – stately, dark haired, dark jowls, dark frames to his glasses – wearing the most disgusting jacket I have ever seen. A check (plaid?) pattern in two shades of brown – diarrhoea and solid stool. You could tell that it was mean to be both discreet (tasteful in a tweedy, subfusc sort of a way) and yet at the same time, somehow flamboyant. It was truly nauseating. I came to the conclusion that he must be the editor of a Luxembourg-based film magazine that received funding from some European Union cultural fund. But I might have been wrong about that.

As I waited – 20 minutes or more – I speculated on what sort of story it would take to bring us three together. In real life I mean. The debilitated student, the Euro-culture editor, me. How our paths might cross. Until I realised, with a sinking heart that we had to all intents and purposes already been brought together in this room. Dialogue could easily have been added. I mean, really easily.

So I turned my attention to the staff – but neither of the middle aged women behind the desk looked like they had the potential to land parts in the film of the book of my article. One of them, though, was heading towards me, I now realised. She had in her hand a large sized (the next up from A4, whatever that is) padded envelope. The first part, obviously, of the collection of 39 Steps material.

She laid it on my table. I thanked her. She turned to go.

"Excuse me," I said. "How much more is there?" I was conscious of the need to plan my time.

"More?" she said. "This is it."

And she was gone.

And there it was. All this palaver (I instantly regretted the taxi fare) for a padded bag. Inside: a script of The 39 Steps and a folder of microfiche film of newspaper reviews from around the times both of its press premier (6 June 1935) and its official cinematic release (25 November 1935).

I suppose I should have been more excited about the script than I was. It was an early version of the shooting script and it diverged from the finished film in a number of mildly interesting ways. For instance, in the script, Mr Memory is asked who won the 1935 Derby. Which obviously has to be changed – the 1935 Derby was run on 5 June 1935, the day before the film's press premier.

And in this version, the dialogue outside the Hackney Empire is actually more convincing too.

WOMAN: Quick, come on – there's a bus.
HANNAY: Sure, but where?
WOMAN: Where do you live?
HANNAY: Portland Place.
WOMAN: That will do.

Or perhaps not.

And best of all, Kinreach. In the stage (or camera) directions for Annabella's map-in-hand operatic dying gesture, the village we focus in on is called Kinreach, not Killin. But there's an asterisk beside this Kinreach name. It's a badly drawn eight-pointed asterisk like a squashed spider. Down at the bottom of the page there's a similarly badly drawn asterisk, beside which is written the legend, KILLIN.

And obviously, Kinreach, like Alt na Shellach, doesn't exist in the real world.

But the asterisk and the capital letters? The hand of Hitchcock? And could he not do asterisks?

It was while I was poring over this particular page that I noticed a hair. A short (may half inch long) dark hair, tucked right in at the binding. I managed to tease it out with the cap of my biro. Who did it belong to? Hitchcock, Bennett, the producer Michael Balcon, Robert Donat?

It was a spooky sort of moment until I realised I'd had my hair cut the day before. I was probably still moulting the debris. I pushed the hair back into its hiding place

The most amusing thing to discover, though, when you get your hands on the original script, is the fact that it's typed in green.

Green?

Why?

What's that about?

It made me think of Hitchcock's taste in strong laxatives.

Of course it was unfair. And maybe I should have pursued this point with Martyn at the time. If only I had thought of it. What he was saying was that the film is highly stylised. And yes it's true that it is full of all sorts of Music Hall nonsense and stock characters. Easily embarrassed priests, travellers in women's underwear, nudge-nudge milkmen; not to mention the whole paraphernalia of shady spies, treacherous toffs, plodding policemen and femmes fatales. On the other hand, I suppose the point is that, when it comes down to it, underwear catalogues really were trouser stiffeners in the 1930s and people in train compartments really did talk about race horses. Didn't they?

I don't think you could ever say that there was anything truly heroic about Tom. In fact, there was always something slightly risible about him. Something ungainly. Even when we were very small we felt instinctively that he wasn't the sort of person in which you could place all your trust. Something about him made us wary.

And it wasn't necessarily the fact that he could be physically dangerous. When he tickled it would hurt. He would grab hold, trapping you completely, and it wasn't so much that the tickling was too rough, which it usually was, but the fact that he was so strong – and struggling to free yourself would inevitably be bruising. And he was immensely strong. He gave horrendous Chinese burns and if you made a fuss he'd complain to mother or Nan that you were surely soft because he'd hardly touched you. If he'd used even a tenth of his strength, he would imply, *then* there would have been something to complain about. Even as an old man, and for me and my brother he was always an old or oldish man, because when we were born he was already in his late 50s… even as an old man, he played rough; and there is something slightly scary about an old man who can grab you with animal-like suddenness and hold you with super-human strength. A man with a hook nose, a white toothbrush moustache and one dulled eye that squints deadly at you. There was something dreadfully con-tradictory in that squint. Something comical in the outlandish way that Ben Turpin was comical. Yet something grotesque too. Something mildly freakish and eerie.

And yet we loved him in a perverse way, because we could sense that he loved us, loved us to bits, would die for us. Tom and Mary were childless and of their two nieces, mother was by far the favourite. We knew we were favoured.

And it didn't help, I suppose, that father was such a ruthless observer of Tom's foibles. Children don't need much encouragement to mock or hold mockery in their hearts, especially when we could already see Tom's weaknesses our-selves. Of course we could.

That last time me and Charlie and Beth were up at my parents (probably that time at father's birthday) and my brother and my niece and nephew, Emma and Gregor, were there, we all played cards after dinner. A simple sweepstakes game called Newmarket. And when father overlooked a card he should have played and gee'd a round, my brother turned to him and in that querulous tone he has, the one where his voice leaps an octave, he complained: "You're as bad as uncle Tom."

It was bizarre to hear that accusation again. A decade (in all probability much more than a decade) after we had last heard it. Spooky in a way. Once upon a time, in the 70s probably, it had been common family currency. Any ponderous duffer was accused of being worse than uncle Tom. Any ditherer. Anyone whose grasp of detail was less than secure.

Worse than uncle Tom.

These things are never exactly fair.

But it wasn't that so much. It wasn't his tendency, due to the defects in his eyesight, to struggle with anything fiddly. Tom's weaknesses, the things in the end that made it all but impossible to look up to him, were those that father was thinking of when he called him (never to his face, of course) an "old woman".

And he was of course. Strangely, unaccountably, he was an old woman. Nothing to do with the fact that he lacked emotional intelligence. Nothing to do with the fact that he was dangerously fond and foolish on the one hand and yet terribly brittle and unaccommodating on the other. Yes, it was true that Tom was an Elder of the Kirk. Yet he wasn't half as severe as you'd expect from an Elder of the Kirk. The Elders of Tom's generation could be unpleasant in the extreme, uncompromising theopaths, full of sinew-and-spittle pomposity and a white knuckled wrathfulness that could make them tremble with explosive anger. Tom wasn't at all like that – he always came across as the modest and reluctant holder of office, a man who served because he'd been asked and it was somehow his duty – although it was true he did have a capacity for riding a high horse now and then.

But he was basically sentimental when you got right down to it. He could be hurt, easily hurt, by the smallest things. His wasn't a very fluid personality. He wasn't very imaginative in the sense of being able to gauge emotions or be alive to the subtleties of certain situations. He wasn't a diplomat, he wasn't a leader in social situations.

But so what?

No, the thing that made him an old woman was his indecisiveness and his openness to bullying by his wife and her sisters. Bullying is perhaps the wrong word. But they had an ability to make him do things against his better judgement, such as it was. He was an old woman because he was pushed around by old women.

When Tom's weakness inconvenienced father, it infuriated him. Most commonly this involved transport mix ups connected with family gatherings. Tom and father were the only ones in the family with cars, so shuttling all the aunts around sometimes took a bit of organising. Tom and father would divide up the task. But more often than not he'd arrive at one of the aunt's houses, say aunt Meg's, to find that she'd already left, Tom had picked her up. He'd done it because Nan and Mary had been talking and had decided it would be best if they tweaked the arrangements slightly and then ganged up on Tom to implement their revised plan. Tom would give in but he'd conveniently forget to phone father to confess this fact. So in the end Tom would tell father that he, father, had got it wrong and that he, Tom, was just doing what had been agreed all along.

Even as a child, you see through that sort of thing.

Especially as, very infrequently, Tom would try to dig his heels in and lose. It would happen most publicly when it involved Nan. He'd have a wheedly, inconsequential opening skirmish then choose the wrong ground on which to fight and select the worst tactics. You just had to cringe slightly and feel for him.

But what also infuriated father was that they still deferred to him on mundane practical matters. Things needing fixing or looking at. They'd leave it until Tom arrived. Father wasn't good enough. He was the second best in this department, the oily rag not the engineer. And of course Tom was completely useless. He couldn't change a fuse, what with his eyesight. But they'd happily sit for days with half the house in darkness, not allowing father to so much as open the fuse box until Tom could have a look at it and when he did have a look at it days later he'd tell them that the fuse probably needed changing. And then father would come along a few days after that that, the next weekend probably, and change the fuse.

I don't know. Maybe it was merely their way of managing Tom. A little flattery buys a lot of command.

Or maybe it was just habit.

And yet, for all his strangeness, for all his unheroic traits, there was still something robustly admirable about him and a hint of something almost exotic.

Something comfortingly old-fashioned, something that had all but died out or had been diminished. It was something pre-war, something of the 30s and before. The last resonance of a High Victorian Scottishness. An outdoorsiness. The Hannay type of character. Or at least Hannay as Buchan conceived of him: a man at home in the outdoors, a shooting and fishing man, a man of physical hardness, a self-sufficient man.

That notion died in the Second World War. Strangely, perhaps, it had just about survived the First World War, the war in which Baden Powell culture, Boy's Own, Boy Scout culture, the culture of naively romantic jingoism, was most cruelly exposed. Hannay, Buchan's Hannay, was already dying in the 30s, killed by the sort of flippancy that gives The 39 Steps its whole tone. Killed, in fact, by Hitchcock's Hannay. But his avatar was still there, somehow, in the austere ruggedness of uncle Tom's domestic interiors (aunt Mary's influence on the décor of their houses was minimal, restricted to most discreet of frills) and on his modest bookshelves.

For instance, Tom as gardener. And he was a very keen gardener. But it wasn't gardening in the modern sense of gardening as exterior décor. No. There was something uncompromising about Tom's gardening. For instance, he had a big roller, the type they used to use on cricket wickets and he'd haul it back and forward across his lawn, like a circus strong man hauling a truck. And in the beds at the back he grew vegetables. Potatoes and carrots. The sorts of vegetables you can eat with something you have just shot.

The thing is that Hitchcock is a litter lout. Take a look at Hitchcock's appearance in The 39 Steps. His cameo. As the 25 bus pulls up outside the Music Hall he's in a group of passers-by. He's the fat one throwing something away. It looks a bit like a cigarette packet.

He throws it down with a certain contemptuous arrogance.

I don't think he is acting.

That other day, the Sunday when Martyn came round, he ended up helping me with some chores round the house. Or at least he pretended to for a while and then sort of faded away. Sunday morning. A vacuous, vacant, blowy sort of a bright day. One of those renegades from early spring that sometimes managed to pop up in summer. Beth had given me a whole list of things to do – all those small, irritating jobs that you somehow never get round to – and I was basically pottering my way down the list. One of the jobs was to put up a couple of pictures in the hall so I dug out some picture hooks and my hammer from the toolbox.

And then it occurred to me that I didn't know where Beth wanted the pictures hung. Not exactly. And it would seem a shame to make holes in the plaster in the wrong place when I could get her to show me just what she wanted. I suppose that's when I realised that the house had become supernaturally quiet.

So I crept upstairs. Sometimes, if Charlie falls asleep Beth will manage to carry her upstairs without waking her and put her onto her (Charlie's) bed. She (Beth) will then go and lie down on our bed and with any luck will be able to get off to sleep herself.

But Charlie was not on her bed. Neither was Beth on ours. So I crept downstairs again. They were in the living room, on the sofa under the travelling rug, fast asleep, Charlie on the inside. Beth on the outside. In fact it looked a little precarious, especially as the seat sloped considerably and the back was considerably lower than the front. It looked not only as if Charlie was already wedged in against the back cushions, but that Beth might just roll down on top of her at any moment.

That's when I thought of it again. What I'd said to her in the hospital that day, the first day, Charlie's first day on this world, a matter of hours into what was turning into a nightmare. About not letting this ruin her life. Was that it? Did I actually say the word, *ruin*? Anyway… about what I'd said. What I'd meant.

And I looked down. And there, hung loosely from my hand, was the hammer. It was held head down, in a minimum of grip, just enough for me to be able to heft it and swing it jauntily as I walked. So I looked down at this hammer, my hammer, and I thought.

I don't know how long I stood there.

But eventually I left them.

Or I think I did.

They didn't wake up for hours. Charlie woke first and then woke Beth.

In the schools we visit there is usually a hydrotherapy pool. Hydrotherapy pools exercise a strange fascination – and I'm always expecting the worst. Because one of the spookiest of the pictures in the medical section of the Standard

Encyclopaedia (and in general this section was a chamber of horrors, though there were no illustrations of blood and guts, just an insane theatre-of-cruelty atmosphere suffusing each and every image) was of a woman being lowered into a hydrotherapy pool, strapped into a rigid and unforgiving chair.

It gave me the willies, it really did. It's almost like a swimming pool, except that it's not as big as a swimming pool. It's only about ten feet wide. It's deep though. It's as deep (or even deeper) than the deep end of a swimming pool, you can sense that. The woman being lowered in is an emaciated woman with

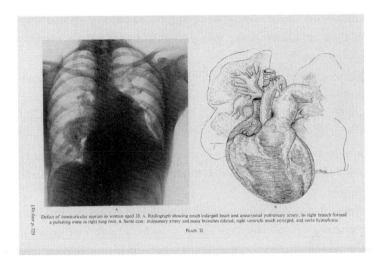

Defect of interauricular septum in woman aged 35. A. Radiograph showing much enlarged heart and aneurysmal pulmonary artery; its right branch formed a pulsating mass in right lung root. B. Same case: pulmonary artery and main branches dilated, right ventricle much enlarged, and aorta hypoplastic

PLATE 11

withered limbs. Mid-40s? Mid-50s? Hard to tell. She is wearing a dark all-in-one bathing costume, one of the old fashioned designs that cover the legs down to the just above the knees.

She strapped in, as I say. She's trying her best not to look terrified but you can tell that she is. In fact, she could be disturbed, clinically disturbed. The attendants are slightly out of focus and partially in shadow. In fact, there seems to be a shadow over the whole plate, an inky miasma that makes the scene all the more sinister.

The strapped-in emaciated woman is descending into the inky water.
I can remember the caption. Just one word. Hydrotherapy.

But actually, the hydrotherapy pool of a special needs school is often the cheeriest place on site.

***

She says: "You OK?"

"Yes. Why? I think so."

Beth is staring at me, her head slightly aslant. She's frowning a little but there's also a playful, amused sort of a look in her eyes. Sceptical and amused.

"You look tired, that's all."

Charlie is strapped into her high chair. I kiss her on the forehead. Beth's back at the hob, heating Telly Tubby spaghetti in tomato sauce for Charlie's tea. I can hear the spoon stirring against the sides of the pan, a cheerful little enamelled pan, scarlet on the outside, white within. Charlie is mouthing something, a fragment of a word maybe, and tapping the surface of her table with her spoon.

"Maybe I am."

"What?"

"Tired."

"Yes. You look tired."

"Yes. I had an odd sort of a day."

"Oh? Oh well. Do you want to feed Charlie?"

"Maybe in a minute. I want to nip up and see if I've any messages."

Beth pouts slightly. "Oh okay. What was odd about it?"

"What?"

"Your day."

"Oh... nothing. I'll tell you later."

There's a message from Robbie telling me not to worry about things. He says I looked jaded. But didn't I tell him that? Didn't I tell him that I was exactly that?

Does he think I'm sick or something?

She must have sneaked up on me. I was still sitting up there under the eaves, my head in my hands. It must have looked as if I was thinking dark thoughts. But she didn't say anything. Not about dark thoughts.

"Who's John Toby?" she asked.

"John Toby? Why?"

"It's just that he called me earlier."

"He called *you*?"

"Yeah, that's what I said."

"I..." What I was trying to say was: *I don't understand.*

"Why did you give him my number?"

We both work from home, so we each have a work number. I hadn't given hers to John Toby though. I thought about this. I frowned with thought. "I haven't," I said. "Hang on. This is bizarre. He called *you*?"

"Yes."

I shook my head. "Who is he?" she insisted.

"Oh, it doesn't matter. He's just a contact."

"A contact?"

"Yes."

"Who you gave my number to?"

"No. I've told you. What did he say anyway?"

She handed me a post-it note. There was a date. The name of a pub. A time. "Oh yes," she said. "And he said to bring £50 too."

Chapter nine

I'm close now, I can sense that. I'd been sure for a while now that John Toby
would turn up something special. Now I can feel it in my water.

What I couldn't have predicted was the fracas that night in the pub. And the
bizarre fact that it might have been my fault. That, I didn't foresee. But I'd been
distracted. Incredible as this may seem, there was about to be another break-
through on a completely unrelated front.

And all sorts of other stuff was happening too. Because, all of a sudden, the
summer holidays were upon us. Our fortnight in Devon. And just before we
go, there's the small matter of the biggest day to date in Charlie's life. Okay –
the second or third biggest day in Charlie's life to date. One of the biggest. Her
milestone assessment at the Neurological Institute. The day on which her (and
our) future will be unlocked. Laid bare.

At some point around now, I get a strange handshake from my father. It's like
a dream, this – but of course it actually happened. We're leaving somewhere and
we're saying goodbye to them. Usually when we leave I shake father's hand
then get a kiss and a hug from mother. This time there's something awkward
and self-conscious about the way father shapes up for the handshake. So I sort
of know something is coming. And he doesn't offer his hand. Instead he says:
"Here. Give us your hand."

And it's only when I've done as he says that he makes his move. It's a two-
handed move, my hand becoming sandwiched in his. And at the very kernel of

this layered handshake, there is a little package. A hard little box. It's as if he were passing drugs or a secret note or something. Smuggled diamonds.

I don't know if he's joking with me, having me on. But anyway I play along and conceal the little package. I'm not sure who I conceal it from. Probably not Beth because as soon as we're on the road I open my hand. I'm looking at a flat little box. Roughly 56 mm by 107 mm and barely 14 mm deep. A classic container arrangement: cardboard tray with an overlapping lid. The inner tray is matt black, the lid a glossy orangey yellow colour with red and black lettering and graphics. It is stained and worn, and there are tape scars on the outer surfaces of all four of its shallow vertical sides – streaks where the orangey yellow has been stripped off by the tape, letting the dull off-white of the cardboard beneath show through.

The lettering says: Kodachrome. COLOUR FILM TRANSPARENCIES.

And adds: 'Kodachrome' is a trade mark.

Also, written in rather smudged fountain pen on the orangey yellow of the lid: B. Summer 1960.

Inside there are 20 slides, mounted.

One by one, I hold them up to the front windscreen and squint at them. The road rushes up at me through them. Or some of them at least. Many are too dark to see anything in or through. But I'm pretty sure what they are.

They are of me. Standing for the first time. Taking my first steps.

They were taken at Alnwickhill Road and Castle Avenue.

Celluloid. A box of it. A film. Sort of a film. A film frame by frame.

Me taking my first steps.

I don't know what to make of this at all.

Except that it spooks me.

And I can't work out what it means.

Are they trying to tell me something?

 I am desperate at this point. If I hadn't've been trapped inside a car hurtling down a motorway I would have made a break for it. I'd have caught that train. A fugitive. King's Cross, heading north. I'd have got off the train at Waverley Station and climbed the 39 steps out of the station towards Princes Street.

The amazing thing about that list of No1s from 1972 (I copied out the entire list) is how many of them I actually handled in one way or another, how many of them I actually placed on a turntable at the time. One friend, Neil Anderson, owned both Telegram Sam and Metal Guru by T Rex plus Take Me Bak 'ome and Mama Weer All Crazee Now by Slade as well as, incredibly, Son of my Father by Chicory Tip. (He must have been buying almost a single a week, now I come to think of it.) Dickie Barr (or maybe his big brother, David) owned School's Out by Alice Cooper. My brother owned both I'd Like to Teach the World to Sing by the New Seekers and the Amazing Graze pipe band embarrassment. I owned Mouldy Old Dough by Lieutenant Pigeon, which was equally embarrassing in its own way.

So why did Nilsson cause such ructions?

It's even more of a mystery now I come to think of it.

Why I'd not been allowed to buy it for myself in the first place, I mean.

I don't know how many times Charlie has been x-rayed. Scores of times. Her arms in general, her wrists, her hands; her head of course; her hips, her knees, her feet. Most times I'm in there with her to hold her in the right position and when I am, I'm wearing a lead overcoat.

They always say, the radiographers: "If dad could just slip this on."

Once, there was a slight delay for some reason. And I shouted over: "This lead overcoat. Could it stop a bullet?"

"Uh?"

This row of eyes surveyed me through the glass from the safety of the control room. At least three pairs of eyes: Beth and the two x-ray technicians. There was a muttering, as if they were conferring. Or maybe they were just trying to correct the fault that had caused the delay.

"What did you say?" shouted one of the radiographers.

"This lead coat. Could it stop a bullet?"

Again a pause; again the sound of radiographers conferring behind a screen.

"But bullets are made of lead too, aren't they?" came the reply.

I'm not sure that's the point really.

For those first days of her life, in intensive care, they kept her in a tank like a tadpole. It was bright in there, in the intensive care ward I mean, not just within the perspex tank. The ward was uniformly bright, it seemed to me, like in a hydroponic growing chamber. A bleached-out brightness where everything is flat, depthless, dimensionless, lacking definition.

And in this bliss-out of light, just the one black dot, maybe a full stop. And in that black dot, all that is malformed and fearful and terrifyingly tearful. All that is grotesque, all that reaches in and finds your soul squirming.

Your soul, frantic, writhing, squirming.

Often while we were waiting, I closed my eyes and looked into that black dot, as through the wrong end of a telescope. You ask yourself if. If she is thoroughly malformed. If she is mentally defective. If she dribbles and rolls her eyes. If she screams incessantly, moronically. If she is unlovely. If she tries to steal your life. If she promises to destroy you. If she becomes a terrible burden. Not so much physically but mentally. Psychically. But yes of course both, you cannot have one without the other – physically and mentally. Destroys you. If. So if.

If. Then. Love.

Love?

If.

Then.

Love.

If then could I?

We waited. We did. We waited in that ward, stone-like, while the world swarmed around us, nurses and doctors and patients and visitors. They time-lapsed, blurred. We waited on the ward while, like an image coalescing on a photographic plate, a child was formed from out of the void. A jelly becoming opaque in clear waters. Waiting. Time slowed, life's fluid becoming viscous.

I've always had paralysis dreams. Dreams where suddenly you're wading through treacle that's threatening to set. Or, even more terrifying, where the slow motion is happening in fresh air. Where all movement is thick and slow and deliberate. But full of terrible intent too. That's the thing. Where violence is achieved at the very threshold of paralysis. That's the terror.

And all the time a child was perhaps forming out of the void. A ripple, a wrinkle in the water, taking on a stringy sort of a substance.

So we waited.

And then there was Jules. Somehow I wasn't entirely convinced I should call him to warn him that Robbie might be calling him. No, not at all convinced.

The good news is that one morning a letter arrived from Sotheby's. I'd contacted all the major auction houses ages ago, obviously; but they'd not exactly been helpful. They'd not exactly gone out of their way to think laterally. But I mean, why should they? That's why this letter from Sotheby's, belated as it was, was so welcome. It was from the head of the Collector's Department who regretted that, although they occasionally had early British film memorabilia, and in fact a few years previously the Donat family had put a number of items up for sale, they'd had nothing recently. In any case most of the memorabilia they dealt in was in the form of posters, press packs and publicity stills. Not film or production materials.

But he could venture to suggest a couple of other avenues I could explore. Firstly, he said, I might try a number of small cinema and photography museums. He listed three, none of which I'd heard of and only one of which was in London. Secondly, there were, he said, a number of eclectic film magazines that carried classified ads – and occasionally, some of these could be very intriguing indeed.

So I went out and bought some film magazines and I scanned their classified sections. The ad that seemed most promising was a notice for a convention of film collectors at Central Hall, Westminster. It sounded like a major event. Well over a hundred stalls. It looked ideal – just the sort of place to pick up the sort of lead I was looking for. Only one problem. The convention had taken place on the Saturday just passed.

Which was bloody typical. But there was a phone number at the bottom of the ad. I called it. A woman answered.

"Oh hello," I said. "I've just seen an ad for Saturday's film convention in a magazine. I know I've missed it but I'm interested in finding out more."

"Oh," she said. "Oh." She seemed totally thrown.

"Have I called the right number?"

"Oh," she said. "Oh yes. Yes you have." She seemed slightly dotty. Vacant. A slightly quavery voice. Like someone's elderly mother who's been left holding the fort with a set of instructions she isn't at all sure she understands. "He's not here you see." I can smell her house from here – it's stale with pets, little rat-like terriers probably. Obviously the guy – the guy I'm after – is a middle-aged guy still living with his mother. He's an obsessive. A hobbyist. A sad collector.

"Are you an…" She searches for the word. And at last it comes tumbling. "Are you an exhibitor?"

No. No I'm not.

Her son, the exhibition coordinator, is away on business. While he's away, inquiries are being directed to Movie Music. It's a shop. In London somewhere, she thinks. She'd give me the number but she can't make out the figures on the note. Can't make them out at all.

When Tom was due to retire, it came almost as a shock to them both – Mary and Tom – that they would have to move from the tied bungalow at Murrayfield. Not a shock in the sense that it had come totally out of the blue but a shock in the sense that they hadn't felt its reality, hadn't breathed it, hadn't admitted it into their souls, until it was almost upon them. There'd been a refusal to accept. I think I understood this at the time, even though I was pretty young. Nine or thereabouts.

Because spasms of exasperation pulsed back and forward across the whole family. There wasn't a row as such, not that I witnessed directly or was aware of, even obliquely. But the air was charged. There was no big summit meeting. Things didn't get done that way. Too explicit, too demonstrative, too con-frontational.

But there were conspiratorial exchanges each time someone left a room. Mother whispering something hoarsely to father when Tom popped out. Or Tom urging mother to say something to Nan when she came back with the tea things.

But the thing was, they were looking. Initially they were looking. To all intents and purposes it seemed as if they were looking for a new house they could buy. And for some reason, I always seemed to be dragged along. This was probably because they'd asked father to help them. To give prospective properties the once over. And so we all went. Father, mother, me, Graeme. Well, you do, don't you? I've found that out. You become a package. You travel as a team.

Almost without exception, the properties I saw with them were gloomy and sinister. At least one was completely derelict – tiles missing off the roof, broken glass in the windows, holes in the floor. They tended to smell of diseased pets or of damp (the dampness of mildewed clothes or carpets or curtains). Mangy, dogbreath houses. One in particular seemed particularly evil. But maybe it felt particularly evil solely because of the timing – we went to see it towards dusk on a supernaturally still spring day. One of those days that's beautifully poised between the seasons, neither one thing nor the other but strangely both.

This was a Saturday evening. They'd picked up the keys from the estate agent's office that afternoon. The house was a quiet area near the zoo. On the hill there, just off the Corstorphine Road. A decent area. But the house was weird. A bungalow, not that you know it was a bungalow from the street.

Actually, to be more accurate, it wasn't a street, it was a cul-de-sac. A steeply sloping cul-de-sac. And the house was right at the top, in the middle of the dead end, commanding the slope, facing back down the hill. Except that it wasn't. It should have been but it wasn't. It commanded nothing because it was hidden. It was almost completely overgrown. There were tall trees in the garden, pines or firs, I think; and bushes bursting forth from under their low-ermost branches. You sort of had to force your way in, as in a fairy story. And the almost comic aspect to this was the fact that the gardens of all the other houses on the cul-de-sac were so prim, so etched, so naked in comparison.

We forced our way up the front path, through the briars. When you got through, it was like being in another world. Behind the curtain. Secret. Dark, basically.

Tom fumbled with the keys, a whole bunch of them. They didn't seem to be working. Either they didn't fit or they wouldn't turn. He stood under the awning of the front porch with that baffled, slightly amused look on his face, methodically going through them in sequence for a second time. And while he cursed and struggled, the rest of us made a complete circuit of the outside walls, peering where possible in the windows. Father had brought Nan's torch, the torch she kept in the kitchen drawer. As its beams probed the bungalow's empty rooms from outside it felt like we were breaking and entering, which was fun in a perverse sort of a way.

Then father lost patience and went back round the front to the porch where he gently relieved Tom of the keys. Not that Tom was being completely useless – it also took father a while to find the right keys and get the locks to tumble.

We didn't stay long. It was almost totally dark by now, especially within that little fir copse, and the house was freezing.

Mary especially wanted to leave. She said it sent a shiver down her spine.

And it was true. It did.

That dark, tree-oppressed house seemed evil for all sorts of reasons. It stood for something. A blight perhaps. A broken dream. A bad outcome. Your worst fears. Something like that. You just knew you didn't want a part of it. You didn't want to touch it lest something rubbed off on you.

I think it was the last house they looked at for a while.

The last one they looked at with a view to buying.

Because the truth was. The god's honest truth was they hadn't made an adequate provision. And Tom was now 67 years old. He was 67 years old and had been living in a tied house for decades and he'd made no real provision for the day when he'd have to retire and look for somewhere else to live. Provision. That was Nan's word. Others used it too when talking (urgently, conspiratorially) about the Mary and Tom situation but it was mainly Nan's word. She gave it the grandeur it deserved, a grandeur that no-one else seemed able to honour.

There was a period when all sorts of solutions were proposed. The family clubbing together to help raise more finance. Aunt Meg moving in with Nan and Mary and Tom taking Meg's house. Mary and Tom moving in with Meg. Or Nan.

This was the point at which the conspiratorial whispers reached their greatest intensity.

And in the end, I suppose, they were lucky. They ended up at Golf Hall.

Directory Inquiries. Yes, Movie Music does indeed exist. I call the number several times but no answer. I call directory inquiries again and get an address. I consult my A-Z. Bloomsbury. Bloomsbury-ish. Actually it is a couple of blocks away from Great Ormond Street. I hurry out, my jacket trailing after me like a streamer and catch a bus just down from the library on Stamford Hill.

They pulled strings to get Mary and Tom the house at Golf Hall. *They* being, I suppose, various office holders of the Scottish Rugby Union. This was never stated openly of course – this was another of those things you had to decode from eavesdropping on all sorts of cryptic exchanges between adults.

Because Golf Hall was basically a council house. Which was in itself more than a little shaming. Whatever our material circumstances (and across the extended family there was a broad spectrum) we were nothing if not proud. We didn't require handouts or charity. We didn't sponge off the state.

And here were Mary and Tom not only sponging off the state but also abusing the system. Or having the system abused for them. They'd not only jumped all sorts of queues but had landed one of the council's most desirable properties. Even though there were none so deserving as Mary and Tom – given the service they had rendered to the city in their years as keepers of the national stadium – there was something not quite right about this. Something we should perhaps be ashamed off, something that could make grown-ups lower their voices to a whisper. And after all, he wasn't exactly a public servant.

Golf Hall was hardly a palace if you looked at it coldly and critically – but that was hardly the point, was it? On the other hand, everyone felt immense relief. Golf Hall was a bungalow, it had its own garden and it was almost in the country. In fact it was almost out of town altogether – out the Glasgow Road past the Maybury roundabout, which, within living memory, had been the old city boundary.

But it was hardly the cheeriest of locations. For a couple of miles at least along the south side of the Glasgow Road there was a high wall overhung by a dense layer of trees This side of the road always seemed dark, gloomy and damp – and we were always aware that somewhere behind the wall was Gogarburn Mental Hospital, where the loonies lived.

The north side of the road was more sparsely wooded – and behind its verge of tree and hedge the land fell away in gently undulating arable fields to the perimeter of Turnhouse Airport. Golf Hall was on this north side of the Glasgow Road about a mile beyond the Maybury roundabout, set just back from the road, hidden slightly behind a patchy screen of bushes and trees.

It felt marginal and precarious, yet hemmed in by the busy main road, which was on its way to becoming a dual carriageway feed for the M8. (To turn into the driveway, you had to cut across a stream of really fast moving traffic, a manoeuvre that, in the end was to cost uncle Tom his driving licence.) In all the years we visited there, I can remember only once going on what you could call a country walk. There were no rights of way through the arable land and each individual field was jealously fenced off. You had to walk a half mile or so down the Glasgow Road to find the sort of rural lane that you'd want to take a walk down.

For all the advantages it offered (a decent-sized garden probably topped this list from Tom's point of view) there was something eerie about the place. Something spooky and forlorn, almost in exactly the same way that the over-grown house at the head of the cul-de-sac had been forlorn. You had the feeling that life's marginalised, eldritch and demonic souls would be drawn to its isolation. Nature's wild spirits.

And indeed they did have odd people calling at their door. People, often bloody or hysterical or both, who'd been involved in accidents further up the Glasgow Road and had staggered or crawled in search of a telephone. And of course there was a steady stream of itinerants, vagrants, tramps, beggars. Travelling salesmen looking for directions, dishevelled strangers looking for petrol in the middle of the night. Tinkers and carnival folk.

Aunt Mary especially would be nervous when patients escaped, as they reg-ularly did, from Gogarburn – and in that respect there was an Arsenic and Old Lace atmosphere about the place. Or something of the Wild West. They had the house at the end of the universe. Darkness at the edge of town. Weird scenes.

Mary always said jokingly, in that disconcerting way she had of seeming both heart-flutteringly vulnerable and almost cynically ready to embrace the inevitable, that they'd be murdered in their beds.

The place was even more forlorn for the fact that there was a plot of derelict land right next door. There had once been a building there – you could see the ruined traces of its walls and the building had clearly had a cellar because there it was, exposed for all to see. A brick lined pit, the bricks still covered here and there with glazed plaster; a pit filling with moss and slime and mouldering leaves, with the odd weed establishing a foothold through the foundation cement.

The pit was fascinating (in that it represented the dark innards, the secret heart of a building, a secret that somehow you felt you shouldn't ever see because this exposure was an awesomely blatant form of nakedness) and scary too because you could imagine yourself falling in there and not being able to climb out again. No-one would hear you calling, even when your shouts became screams. Not even from Golf Hall – where you learned to expect the macabre and your antennae were finely tuned to its immanence.

Elder trees grew in the derelict plot, a good three or four of them, each fully mature and richly productive. By late summer each year they would be bowed down with fruit, swarms of berries that had transformed miraculously from green to bronze to purple to shiny black. Uncle Tom harvested them each autumn and turned them into wine, which we would drink on his birthday the next spring. A girlfriend who drank it one year whispered to me that it tasted of graveyards.

The house too was cold and clammy. The spare bedroom, where visitors coats were always laid out on the bed, smelled of damp and the perfume of old ladies. Or no, not perfume – more a soap or pot pourri smell. It was always cold and forbidding in that tiny front bedroom, even in summer. In winter it made your teeth chatter and made plumes of your breath as you prepared to go home, coated, bored now and willing mother and father to hurry their farewells. It was an immensely bleak room, with its single weak lightbulb hanging from the ceiling within a dusty, floral-pattern, tasselled lightshade. If anyone had ever slept in that room, they would have been dead when they woke the next morning.

Golf Hall was flimsy, jerry build. You could always sense that. Even as a child you knew you could almost punch a hole in the walls (in contrast, Murrayfield was hugely robust, build like an electricity substation). But Golf Hall's atmosphere of austerity was somehow appropriate. Although they had always eaten well, Mary and Tom had always flirted with asceticism when it came to the other good things of life. They represented a rough hewn, honest simplicity, if that doesn't sound almost sentimental. Nothing exotic here. For instance, there was little evidence of travel – or any other form of broadened horizons, come to that. The only trace of luxury was in the bathroom where there was always a cake, a large cake at that, of Cusson's Imperial Leather soap. I loved the lingering smell of it on my hands after I had washed them.

Movie Music doesn't convince me at all. It is clearly a front. Or no – more outrageous than that. It has clearly been got up in the last hour or so, for some dubious purpose, that purpose being, more likely than not, to take me for a fool. It makes charity shops seem slick. It's flimsy in the way that those £1

World shops are flimsy. Those injection-moulded Aladdin's Caves that squat vacant leases. Flimsy and marginal.

And yet in another way it isn't flimsy at all. Not in the slightest. As if it had always been here; had *always* been marginal. It is neat and disciplined. Puritanical. It has rejected everything that is superficial. Thus the brown office-style carpet tiles on the floor, some of which are curling at their corners; thus the plain walls decorated here and there by posters held up by thumbs of blu-tack.

Actually, the thing it resembles most is a hole-in-the-wall record store. Because everything is displayed on jerry-built browser shelves. Not just the records themselves – and vinyl long players are its speciality – but also books, cigarette cards, magazines. On the main floor and in the basement too. Down a flight of cracked, maroon-painted cement steps there is a whitewashed cube of a basement that smells of cellar mould, disinfectant and faint traces of cigarette smoke. Harshly-lit. And actually it isn't disinfectant – it's more like that weapons-grade bleach they use to unclog sewers.

Movie Music. I hadn't realised that just about every film ever made has put out an album of its soundtrack. It's like an obscure tax dodge. They press a couple of dozen albums as a matter of routine. No-one buys them and they all end up here at Movie Music.

So I browse. And when the shop is suitably quiet I go up to the counter and offer up my cover story. The one about my father. How he used to be a projectionist. In a cinema. How I want to score him some celluloid. For his birthday, like. The 39 Steps. An original.

"Oh yeah?" is the reply.

The guy behind the counter is distinctly unimpressed with me. I am distinctly unimpressed with him. We are unimpressed with each other. He is playing the part of bohemian shop assistant. Lightly camp, slightly theatrical. Combat rock – fatigues and a plain shirt – with a parodic touch of flamboyance in the pale blue and mauve Paisley cravat. Bags of attitude. Jarvis Cocker style black framed spectacles. And do I detent traces of a Welsh accent?

So, could he help me?

He looks at me blankly, as if he hasn't heard. And then he seems to begin busying himself with stuff under the counter. I am not at all sure how patient I am prepared to be.

"You couldn't point me in the right direction?"

"Mmmm?" Again he looks up briefly, as if slightly surprised I am still there. "The 39 Steps," I remind him.

"Yes." This is his show. He tunes in and out, as if not really of this world. And then he smiles at his own cleverness. "Yes. Actually. Yes I can, as it happens."

I am aware now of his smell. The tobacco smoke on his breath; the staleness of scummy soap suds escaping from within the folds of his clothes.

"There's a guy. I'm trying to think of his name. Based in the Midlands I think? Nottingham? Coventry? Dudley? Somewhere like that."

There is something else too. Not a smell. A feeling – a certainty, as it happens – that almost all of his energy is being wasted on mastering a huge anger. Enormous anger. Anger as big as a bus. As big as a building. Or a whole city. Anger that will only ever surface now and then in hints of sarcasm and the mildest of sardonic self-deprecation. It is terrible, this insight. I suddenly just want to turn and walk away.

"No. Hang on. That's his name. Dudley. Dudley Griffiths."

"Dudley. Dudley Griffiths," I parrot. "Do you know how I can contact him?"

"No." He's shaking his head again and he's gone back to the figures in his copy book, drawing a biro lightly down its columns, feigning instant additions, leading it lightly, delicately, as if pulling a needle and thread. "No," he repeats. "We just see him in here from time to time. He's your man though."

I always wondered why Tom never planted some form of hedge around the perimeter of the back garden at Golf Hall. On one side there was the waste land, which was overgrown, obviously, not least with the elder trees. And the back of the house defined the south side of the garden. But the other two sides were completely open. There was a wire fence, maybe three or foot feet high. And then the field. In winter it was flat and barren, dull brown earth curving away into the distance. In summer there was wheat, turning from green to gold as it grew.

But it always seemed incredibly exposed.

And then I worked it out.

At Murrayfield, the bungalow had been hemmed in by hedges. Huge hedges. Twelve feet high. They formed a little compound of the house and its outhouses, including the First Aid Station, and the garden. The tallest and thickest privet hedge you've ever seen. All to keep the bungalow from prying eyes on match days.

Of course. It was obvious. At Golf Hall, he wanted to see as far as he could see. The bay windows of the living room at the back looked out across the garden at the wheatfield, which fell away towards the airport and RAF Turnhouse. A pair of binoculars stood on the window sill. The big front lens was missing from one side, which of course Tom wouldn't miss, given he only really had decent sight in one eye.

There were maybe two flights a day from Turnhouse in those days. You couldn't actually see the runway or the aerodrome buildings – they were just within the fold of the land – but that actually made a take-off more majestic and spectacular. You always knew it was coming because the props would wind up into an ear-piercing high pitched whine that seemed oppressive from even a mile away. And then it (a Viscount or a Vanguard) would begin to rise sluggishly above swaying tides of corn, the plane's heat-hazed image rippling in the one good lens of the binoculars. It would whine low and lazy out to the south west, as if reluctant to let go of the land.

Sometimes Tom had his short wave radio on and if you were lucky with the tuning, you could hear what the pilots were saying to each other and to air traffic control. Or so he said. He also said it was illegal to do it, which was why we never heard this demonstrated.

Dudley Griffiths. Yes. He was my man. Within days I'd confirmed this inescapable truth. I'd cross-referenced his name, running it by a couple of sources I'd tracked down via the classified sections of another couple of magazines, the sorts of magazines that carry ads for companies trading in all sorts of stuff for 8mm film enthusiasts – projection equipment, film stock and developing services, for instance. But, interestingly, these companies also sold 8mm versions of classic films. That in itself seemed a fruitful line of inquiry.

So I made some calls. All these firms were outside London and most were actually in the Midlands, which for some reason seemed promising. None of them knew anything about original prints of The 39 Steps. But had they heard of this Griffiths guy? Yes, actually, now that I mentioned it.

"How can I get hold of him?" I asked one of these 8mm dealers. He gave one of those annoying little dry laughs designed to make you feel stupid. "You won't," he replied in a broad Brummie accent. "He'll contact you."

Tosser.

The other 8mm guy was much more helpful. Griffiths, he reckoned, used to be in the business big time – 8, 16, 39mm, stock, facilities, lighting, camera hire, professional production back-up, the lot. Worked a lot with Zenith Films in the old days. Inspector Morse, that sort of thing. He'd heard that maybe Griffiths traded memorabilia on a mail order basis these days but there were hundreds of people doing that and it was all done pretty much anonymously. He reckoned, though, that at one time this Griffiths character had a company called Trent Films. It was based in Nottingham, or just outside, if his memory served.

It did. I called directories and got an address and a phone number.

Which of course I dialled.

The short wave radio was a retirement present.

I don't know how many times I dialled that number over the next few days. It just rang and rang. I'd let it ring so long that the line would eventually go dead. I'd let it ring so long that the line melted. I'd dial the number and not even bother holding the receiver to my ear, leaving it on the desk on the off chance that if someone did pick up, I'd hear.

I imagined hundreds of scenarios. Phones ringing in empty rooms; phones ringing in deserted buildings. I even remembered that spooky story (it might even have been part of the *Hitchcock Presents* series on television) of the only man to survive a global nuclear war. This last man alive is so lonely that he decides to commit suicide. He climbs to the top of a tall building and throws himself off – and as he's plummeting past the 39th floor, he hears a telephone ringing.

In the end I gave up. Or almost gave up. I wrote to the address I'd been given by directory inquiries. I enclosed a brief note outlining (rather succinctly, I thought) my cover story. I'd had plenty of practice at it now. So much so, in fact, that I pretty much believed it was true. I was looking for a birthday present for my father.

On the Sunday, 24 May, 1936, it rained. It wasn't exactly a torrential downpour but it did rain for several hours. A course official was moved to say that if there were 12 more hours of rain before the race then the going would be perfect. Not everyone shared his optimism: Rhodes Scholar (a horse that found hard going really punishing) was scratched on veterinary advice. Lord Astor now only had one horse in the race – Pay Up.

On the Monday, the first confident forecasts were made as to the probable conditions on race day. It was likely to be bright but chilly and no more rain was expected. The going would remain firm.

Also on the Monday, the first large contingents of gypsies began arriving on the Downs – and as was customary, gypsies being supposed to have great horse sense as well as uncanny clairvoyant powers, newspaper reporters were sent out to canvas their views as to the outcome of the race. The gypsies seemed to be of one mind. Pay Up. By Monday night Pay Up had edged into the position of favourite, just ahead of Taj Akbar and Noble King. The forecasters were right. Wednesday, 27 May, 1936, Derby Day, dawned bright and chilly. The going was firm. So firm was it, in fact, that rumours began circulating that Taj Akbar had fallen lame at a run-out the previous morning. Still, its price held

fairly well – though there was an interesting late contender for the smart money. Punters arriving at the racecourse were putting large amounts of money behind Boswell for some reason.

Yes. Golf Hall. But Tom was still at Murrayfield when we watched The 39 Steps together. The more I think about it, the more confident I am of that. Which would make it some time before the spring of 1968. Tom on an armchair drawn close to the rented television in Nan's front room, an armchair an antimacassar and its casters in bakelite caster cups to protect the carpet from wear. Uncle Tom wearing a tweedy sports jacket, grey flannels, Argyll socks and brogues, his legs stretched out before him and crossed at his ankles. Me in his shadow, wobbling on the pouffe that was like an Islamic big bass drum, riding it, fingers latched under the cord round its midriff, holding tight like a pillion passenger. Brother completing the Great Chain of Being, sprawled, elbows on the floor, hands supporting his chin, then wriggling, rolling around, unable to concentrate for more than 30 seconds at a stretch.

Uncle Tom leaning over to explain what the 39 steps really were.

Me listening, awestruck, but with my eyes still glued to the screen.

And then one evening, returning late – later than expected, the sort of late that throws domestic arrangements up in the air and leaves in their place only a fiery frostiness – I saw there were almost a dozen messages on my answering machine. My heart always sinks when I see that. It usually means something somewhere has gone horribly wrong.

Not in this instance. One of the messages was from someone called Jerry Verneau. (Vernaud? Vernot? I'm only guessing here: the line was very bad. Or maybe it was my machine that was failing.) He worked with Dudley Griffiths, he said. He'd found my letter very interesting. Perhaps we could talk further. He left a number and something made me dial it there and then. Somehow I knew he'd be there and he'd pick up, even though it was late. And sometimes even I have hunches which turn out to be right – because he was and he did.

I expected yet another highly-strung hobbyist. One of those obsessive types who come across all brusque and brittle on the phone, even when they're trying to be friendly. But no, not a bit of it. Jerry turns out to major in superficially cheery matiness delivered in a sort of hospital radio drawl. He's affecting this horribly 1970s transatlantic showbiz patter and desperately trying to hide the textures of a more indigenous accent – Manchester, it sounded like.

Anyway, there's lots of cringe-making small talk and repartee – lame, jokey, slightly ingratiating, slightly creepy – as he eases himself into the conversation. Not that there is much of a conversation, actually. He talks a little about The 39 Steps. What he likes about it. There are many things he likes about it. General things. Its style. Its tone. Its sheer panache.

And how it was a great shame, wasn't it? A shame that classics like The 39 Steps were almost becoming forgotten. They were just not part of people's frames of reference any more. And of course at its heart was this crazy notion that anything in black and white can't be any good. Or that people just won't watch black and white films on TV. Or even worse – the belief that anything made more than five years ago was just completely worth forgetting about.

It made him mad.

Anyway, he says, we should meet up.

Yes, I agree. Great. Why not, I add. But could he actually help me? You know, about the film.

He laughs. One of those knowing laughs. One of those *leave it to me, don't be naïve* sorts of laughs. One of those stale little laughs.

"There's a film collectors' convention at a place called Westminster Hall…"

"Oh," I sigh. It's a big sigh. A deflation. "Oh I know. We've missed it."

"What?"

"It was last week."

"Oh good, so you know it then?"

"No."

"I thought…" Consternation in his voice now. An urgency. And you sense this is the real him – because when this frustration breaks through into his voice, the fake drawl really wears thin. "I thought you said…"

"Well, yes, I've heard about it. I saw an ad for it in a film magazine. But we've missed it. It was a while back."

That smooth little laugh returns, rich yet mordant, like malt whisky.

"There's one a month."

"Every month?"

"Yes indeedy. Our stall is usually on the stage. Ask for me there."

The prelude to violence is preternaturally still. I had known that since I was small. I had always known it. It was, is, an instinct.

At Golf Hall, the 1930s existed most powerfully at the level of the fine detail. For instance, they had a soda siphon and a table top cigarette lighter, silver, a minia-ture urn crossed with an Aladdin's lamp, ornate with vaguely classical designs: tassels, braidings, wreathings of

tiny leaves in bas-relief. Which gave it a fastidious delicacy. Yet it was chunky as a hand grenade too.

When the young wife (played by a suitably young Peggy Ashcroft) of the crofter (the mean one played by John Laurie) offers Hannay her husband's coat, he hesitates.

"He'll not ill-treat you?"

And she reassures him: "He'll pray at me but no more."

But it's not true. Later, when the crofter can't find his bible... and then realises that he can't find his bible because it was in his coat pocket and the coat (it dawns slowly) has also gone, he scares an admission from his wife, whose voice we hear off screen.

Eyes staring, he exits the frame in the general direction of the voice. And then we hear the sound of a hit, a very palpable hit. It's meatier than a slap.

It's not the sort of thing Hitchcock could show on screen. The physical contact, I mean. It's too raw. You can make light comedy from a scuffle in a Music Hall, you can form a fantasy from a spy thriller plot in which several people die, you can create a melodramatic frisson from a young woman being stabbed in the back in a dark flat in the dead of night. You can even have Hannay joking about a fictitious uncle who murdered his many wives. But in a 1930s film there was no way you could show a young woman being slapped about a bit by her misery of a husband.

But at least this much is true: the arithmetic here is straightforward.

39

3 + 9= 12

1 + 2= 3

3 x 13= 39

39 = 40 - 1

1939 is the year in which the old world ended. Buchan had no way of knowing he would die in 1939. Which of course he did.

I was not quite 39 when Charlie was born. I gave the Nilsson single to my father for his 43rd birthday. But. Which. What I mean to say is. It is a difference of four years.

***

We bickered all the way to our appointment at the Neurological Institute. It didn't help that the first time we set out we got halfway and had to turn around. We'd been asked to bring some appropriate seating for Charlie – something that would support her and enable her to do the intelligence and perception tests they were going to give her – and we'd reached the Angel before we remembered. Remembered that we'd forgotten. So we drove all the way back again, both of us absolutely fuming.

And then set out a second time.

Not that we were late. Or yes, technically we were a few minutes late but two of the assessment team were delayed and didn't actually turn up themselves until 40 minutes after the assessment was scheduled to begin. And they didn't see us right away even after they'd arrived.

But we weren't to know that. We weren't to know that as we bowled around Coram's Fields and rolled into Mecklenburg Square, taking the corner just a little too sharply. It was an absolutely gorgeous day – a more-or-less cloudless sky, just the hint of a stirring breeze and the towering plane trees around square at their fullest and most glorious. The sort of day that you just know is going to glow.

We had been given permission to park in the visitors' bay right by the clinic's entrance steps. So we did. Somehow it seemed a struggle to get everything out of the car, Charlie into her buggy and gather together everything we needed. A handful of children – seven or eight year-olds – watched us through the railings from under the trees in the park. They were dirty and ragged and bedraggled, like Third World children, and they held onto the bars and pressed their faces to them and stretched their arms through.

And then I realised they were calling to us. One of them had a can of Fanta. He stretched it towards us through the railings. At first I didn't realise what he was trying to do. Then the penny dropped. He was trying to sell it to us. Instantly, that brought me down again. I'd felt these kids were, I don't know, almost picturesque, a summer city scene you meet feel nostalgic about if you came across the pictures in a Hulton Getty picture library catalogue. But now I felt disgust and indignation. They spooked me, those kids, on this day of days for Charlie. They were like birds of ill omen.

"Mister. Mister."

Hands through the railings. Runny noses.

"Mister."

50p. They wanted 50p.

"It's chilled," they kept insisting. "It's cold. Feel. You can feel it if you like."

In the end, Jules called me. I was just about to go out again, as it happens. I was just about to meet John Toby. I pick up the phone and there's this silence. It's a live silence though; an embodied silence. It's a silence with space at the other end. And in that space, I can sense Jules. I don't know how.

"Hello?"

You wait a couple of seconds. Maybe it's one of those too-clever-by-half phones and they've pushed speed dial and they haven't had time to put the receiver to their ear.

"Helloa?"

But I can sense someone on the other end, someone struggling to say something.

And then when the words came they're almost a croak: "Do you mean the dirty decade? The yellow decade? The miserable decade, the dark decade?"

"Jules." I am cheerful. I greet him with an exclamation mark: "Jules!"

"The decade of unemployment, hunger, desperation, depression. Of appeasement. Of Fascists and National Socialists. Of Hitler and Mussolini and Mosley."

He's angry. A tense sort of anger, a quivering resentment. An anger that's not quite been wholly unlocked. Or focused. An anger unsure of its legitimacy or scope.

"Jules. What on earth are you on about?"

There's another pause. And when he speaks again there's more disappointment than anger in his voice. A sullenness, a flatness. And somehow that's worse than the anger.

"What you were saying the other day. About the 30s. About Hercule Poirot and Rupert fucking Bear and Just William and the Graf Zeppelin and how fucking fascinating the whole thing was."

There's nothing I can say. I'm pretty sure he doesn't want me to say anything at this stage. There is nothing that can be said.

"It's all crap, isn't it?" I'm pretty sure this is a real question, not a rhetorical one, but I'm still not sure where to take this. So I give one of those little laughs, one of those huffs, one of those plosive little sighs.

And he goes on, though you can sense he's starting to lose momentum: "It's all crap. That's all I called to say really. It's like... I was thinking about it and I thought... this is pure. It's like... it's crap isn't it? It's just crap. Pure crap. That's all I wanted to say really. How are you, anyway?"

I am fine, just fine.

But we don't have much to say to each other after that, really.

That night, I met John Toby in the pub of his choice. And what was to follow was my fault probably. I've never been very good a noticing when people are drunk. They usually have to do something really obvious – reel about a bit, upset people's drinks, fall over, crash into tables, be sick, that sort of thing – before I'll generally catch on.

Like there'll be a group of us standing at a party and someone will come up and start talking to us and when they've gone, someone will say, "Christ she was smashed, wasn't she?"

And I'll go: "Oh was she?"

And they'll go: "Uh? Hello." And laugh in an aggressively cliquey way.

Some people use this as evidence that I'm just very unobservant in general. I'm not sure that's true. I'm not sure that's true at all. It's just that we all tend to notice different things. And anyway, maybe it's because I tend to think the best of people. Or at least I'm not always looking to find fault.

So to cut a long story short, I don't really have a clue how drunk John was that evening. He'd left a message for me to meet him in the Flying Fox, E2, and to bring £50 with me. My heart sank when I traced the pub's address and then located it on the A–Z – because it was in one of those warrens of streets leading into Brick lane. I automatically assumed (as you would) that it would be one of John's pikey East End boozers with framed photos of boxers, their signatures illegible, on the walls and an air of genial menace from behind the bar. The sort of pub where everything's been worn down to a buffed ragamuffin sort of a finish. A patina of the rough and ready. The John you'd get in that sort of establishment would be very different to the John you'd get in somewhere (to put it in his terms) more poncey.

But I was wrong, or sort of wrong. The Flying Fox was a bit bistro. A big room with tables lining its inner shell and a few out on the main floor – but they looked sort of lost because it was such a big area of floor. Varnished pine boards; and the whole place felt airy and bright, what with early evening sunlight streaming in through expansive plate glass windows, filtering through the cigarette smoke and making the dust motes dance. It was the sort of place that boasted food – baguettes, club sandwiches, chips that they even dared to call fries – and a wine list in a little plastic folder on the bar.

And yet there was something oppressive about the place too. You can sometimes tell when a pub's had a heavy afternoon. It's not just the amount of smoke in the air or the amount of froth ringed glasses still on the tables and it's not just the expression on the faces of those who've survived. It's an aura, an atmosphere.

I felt pissed the moment I entered.

It was moderately busy even though it had just gone six. And there was John at the bar, holding court to a ring of the usual suspects. A couple were rough old geezers John's age or older but the rest were younger – between 25 and 35 and mostly down at heel and underfed. Not John's regular sorts of mates at all, I'd have said. It had the feeling of an after-market wind-down session – but like I say, I don't really know if he was already drunk or not. I only know it was about to turn into one of those evenings that you'll always remember – in the general if not in the particular.

Because everything seemed larger than life. Right from the moment I walked in. I was greeted by the whole crowd (there must have been a good ten of them including John) as a long lost brother. Lots of backslapping and what can we get you to drink. They were lining them up on the bar top for me. Lagers and nips of whisky too.

"What's the celebration?" I asked and they laughed at that as if it was just the funniest thing.

Almost everything I said was funny, in fact, so I must have been on pretty good form. Because I did relax into the whole thing pretty quickly even though John was perhaps acting a little oddly. A couple of times I caught him staring right at me, a curious, dispassionate look on his face. A cold sort of a look.

And then at one point we hit one of those freak moments when all of the conversations – and there just have been at least three on the go at any one time in our little group at the bar – hit a lull at the same time. And again I became aware that John was staring at me. But this time he said something too.

"The 39 Steps," he said.

I must have nodded, slightly alarmed that he was seemingly going to conduct business so publicly; yet relaxed enough to be past caring.

"One of the earliest films by Alfred…" He paused theatrically. He still had his eyes on me but it was as if he expected someone else to furnish the end to his sentence. Someone else, I somehow knew, other than me. But no-one helped him out and he had to nail it himself. He did it in a voice that made clear how much we had all disappointed him. A careworn, almost sarcastic aside: " …Hitchcock."

In the brief pause that followed I thought I could feel a general sense of embarrassment. I felt that, after a decent little interval, someone would say something and we'd all jump at that something, whatever it was, as a way of pretending John's little performance hadn't actually happened at all. But maybe it was just me that was embarrassed, because no-one said anything. We were an island of silence within the bar's ambience of background chatter.

"Released in 1935," he continued in that unforgiving voice. There must have been a sheepish look on my face by now. But the strange thing was that, though John was saying this stuff at me, no-one turned to see what my reaction was. They were spellbound by him, by his performance. "Starring Madeleine Carroll and Robert Donat, screenplay by Charles Bennett from a novel by John Buchan."

Another pause. How much longer was this going on?

He soon answered that. Because now he lifted his beerglass from the bar and (there was no hint of a toast or even a nod) and drained the rest of its contents; and as if by magic, as if at this signal, everyone slipped straight right back into conversation again. And I slipped off to the loo because I'd suddenly been over-taken by a maverick sort of nervous excitement and my bladder felt painfully full.

I suppose there was something false about the whole atmosphere – but maybe no more false than you'd expect when you meet up with a whole crowd of people you've never met before. I sort of assumed that everyone would piss off at some stage and me and John would be able to sit down and have a quiet chat and conclude our business, whatever it was. Strangely, though, John didn't seem to have anything with him in the way of merchandise.

I was perfectly happy though. I'd relaxed into the whole thing pretty quickly – I seemed to be on pretty decent form and this, by and large, was a good crowd, even if I could see that some of them were maybe coiled just that little bit too tight. A good crowd – all except John, of course.

At one stage he walked me out of the circle and made me bend my head to his. "You got that £50?" he whispered hoarsely.

So I got out my wallet and opened it and as I did so, his hand was in it. It was the deftest thing. He filleted all the notes before I realised what was happening. There was a good deal more that £50 in there. Closer to £100 in fact. He counted it out. Then he pocketed the lot. Then, smart as you like, he put my wallet back in my breast pocket. He slapped me on the cheek as he stepped back to take his place at the bar. That little aftershave double smack that's half praise, half reminder of what's what.

I was angry at that. The whole cheek smacking bit. And as the resentment festered I clammed up. Which in turn made me feel like I was even more of a target. I was well gone by then but a couple of times I got the "cat got your tongue" mocking treatment when I failed to keep up with the conversation.

Then someone asked John if I always had this much trouble holding my liquor and I could sense laughter and the fact that I'd merely coloured and was grinning sheepishly in the hope they'd turn their attention elsewhere. Maybe I was slurring my speech more that I realised. But somehow I got renewed Dutch courage from the laughter and started pitching in once more. That's when I noticed that John was mimicking me now and then. The first time I cottoned on I frowned and stared at him and there was a brief frisson of embarrassment round the group but thereafter he did it more or less brazenly (that was half the joke, what with me being unsure of how to react) and soon there was no embarrassment, just knowing grins.

So I decided to go. Just as soon as I'd finished my beer. I'd leave. It seemed to be getting darker outside and the place was filling up so our crowd was being absorbed and was just part of the larger crowd and it was harder to hear what people were saying. Not that I was contributing much.

And then it happened. I don't know what exactly because the detail remains blurred. All I can say is that John suddenly had me by the collar of my polo shirt. A fearsomely tight hold. My collar in his fist. And then, not letting go at any point of my collar, he jabbed this fist up into my chin a couple of times. When this sort of thing happens to me all I can feel is nausea. So that's probably what I felt now. Sheer incomprehension. The sickness of fear. But I think I must have tried to swat his arm away. The next thing I know is I'm on the floor, winded and disorientated.

And it's the oddest thing. When I managed to haul myself up, half the bar seemed to be fighting. Really vicious, frantic stuff. It seemed much brighter now as if the lights had been dimmed before but now someone had turned them up full. And I just stood there. It was a war zone, there were people being bottled and glassed and there was a splintering of wood and crashing and screaming, a complete frenzy, and I just stood there. Stunned, I suppose.

At one stage there might have been a girl screaming, *A knife, a knife, he's got a knife*, but I don't know at what stage that might have been and I'm not at all sure I heard it at all, actually. Maybe that's one of the sorts of things you make up, almost without knowing it, much later.

But anyway, suddenly everything decided to burst out onto the street. Everyone spilled out, they streamed out, like there'd been cabin depressurisation and the maelstrom was being sucked out through the main door. It seemed natural, shaking though I now was, that I should follow, if even just to bear witness. But as I moved in that general direction I felt a hand grab my elbow and hold tight. I wheeled round. It was one of John's mates, one of the older ones, in his mid 40s maybe. I hadn't really said much to him all evening and now more than ever I thought I recognised something sinister in him. He had a lean, ferrety face. A hungry face. He was not a big man. Scrawny. But totally unscrupulous, you could see that. He scared me. Especially now.

He said nothing at first, merely wagging his finger at me in silent admonition. And then, as he led me back across the bar, he said something. He said, with a slight burr of an Irish accent: "John thinks someone's screwing his bird."

And then he stopped, we stopped, and he looked straight at me. "The cunt," he said, shaking his head emphatically.

There couldn't have been more than half a dozen people left in the bar (and it was amazing how surreally peaceful it looked, despite the overturned tables and broken furniture and splinters of wood and broken glass and smears of blood) and they all seemed paralysed, fearfully looking over to the door yet too scared to leave. John's mate steered me right round the bar towards the toilets and here (I'd not even noticed before) was a side door. He pushed me through into the night and followed. He had me by the elbow again.

He steered me on a labyrinthine route and as we walked I tried to work it all out. Put all the bits in their rightful position. Which is exactly the sort of thing you should be doing when you're dead drunk and in a mild state of shock. I kept imagining I could hear the muffled sounds of a streetfight several

 blocks away. A scuffling intensity. A ringing hint of bright steel. The scattering of boxes and bin bags and fruit crates. But the truth is I heard nothing, not even a police siren. And my companion said nothing. Or nothing new at any rate, though at one point he did say, "the cunt" again with what seemed like great bitterness – and as he did so he shook his head sorrowfully once more. By now the evening was clammy, not cold really but not exactly warm; and there were hints that a summer mist was about to descend. One of those opalescent evening mists that soak up the streetlights. He accompanied me all the way to Aldgate East tube and when we got under its canopy he pointed inside and nodded and raised his eyebrows as if I were stupid.

It was as if I were dreaming it all.

As he turned to go, he did a little salute, forefinger to eyebrow, with a hint of a finger-pointing flourish at the finish; and at that stage he seemed like the Lone Ranger or something.

"The cunt," he said with what seemed a great bitterness.

Chapter ten

We still believed it was possible to go on holiday. By go on holiday, I mean what most people mean by go on holiday. An adventure and an escape and a cure. A consumer good. Of course we believed. We believed in all sorts of things.

We chose (for good enough reasons) as our holiday destination a picturesque spot at the frayed edge of the world. Actually, that doesn't really convey it at all. Though there was much that was frayed and ragged and unkempt all around – brown, blasted moorland falling abruptly off a crumbling range of cliffs into the sea – we were down in the cosy bit. A little Shangri-La, a Lost World, fragrant with honeysuckle and rambling roses. A combe-notched gap in the cliff line, a tiny bay with a village at its back. From up on the clifftops above the village you could look back inland and wonder at this deep gash in the land: this snake of a combe, heavily wooded, dense as jungle, cutting its way down out of the high interior, deepening and darkening as it sought the sea and our village, a seemingly sunken village, an overgrown huddle of buildings; church, smuggler's snug, school refurbished as craft centre.

At low tide the waters drew back to reveal a rocky arena: to one side a weed strewn shelf pocked with anemone pools; on the other, a rougher range of fallen domino slabs, wave beaten boulders, exposed and broken strata, like a vast yard of monumental builder's rubble. In between, a twisting thread of wrinkled lugworm sand that led you to the low water's edge. Further out, at the corners of the bay, there were crumbling stacks of quartz and mica (a light grey that hinted at silver and flirted with white), rocks fractured at the margins into teeth and precarious columns, arches and shallow scoops of caves.

The only road in came down the length of the combe and you just knew without being told that it was the sort of village that got cut off in winter snows. To the east, a couple of miles walk over the clifftop path, in the next combe along, there was a larger town; the next combe to the west, again by the clifftop path, held the lost domain. Uninhabited, treeless, it was a smaller but steeper ravine filled with dense tangles of gorse through which there was a labyrinth of pathways. Its colouring, dark green specked with an infinity of intense yellow firebursts, was almost hypnotic; and as you stared down into it from the hillside way above, you became aware of small figures, waylaid cliff path hikers no doubt, in one and twos, appearing and disappearing as they made their way through this dark green maze.

It was all too good to be true. We'd rented a black-beamed doll's house with lead-latticed oriole windows, a warren of a house that creaked and groaned like a sailing ship, a house with low ceilings and leaning rooms, with twists and turns, hidden steps and half-landings, split levels, a house whose front door gave out onto a shingled courtyard right beside the village tearooms and whose back door led, through a porch large enough to be called a sun room, to a garden whose three ascending terraces cut broad strips of uneven lawn into the first gentle slopes of the valley's side. At the far end of the garden there was an impossibly well-composed bit of biscuit tin scenery. Not too far off, a lone pine – a tall, rugged beanstalk of a tree, its bare trunk rising plain and true for what seemed like hundreds of feet before cutting into the strata of its own needles – and beyond, a cliff line sinking jaggedly at an angle into the sea. A stunning simplicity of sea, tree, cliff.

So yes, too good. Too right. Too obvious.

We'd argued horribly on the way down; and yet the clouds lifted on the morning of our first day and by the time the sun had cleared the tree line, far up at the rim of the combe, we were filled with a cheerful levity, a naïve under-standing that we would, each day, march forth into each rosy dawn. Because of course we were absolutely determined to go walking. To do walks. To wander, explore, marvel at scenery, take the air on breezy clifftops, follow woodland trails, strike out on expeditions – there, lunch and back – to country pubs hidden in tree choked hollows in the hinterland of the moor tops.

Actually, that first morning, it took us an eternity to get going. We had decided on a short exploratory walk up onto the cliff path to the west. So when we'd got ourselves organised and laden with picnic provisions, we set off with Charlie in the carrier – the aluminium and nylon fabric frame we'd used on the Hackney Town Hall march. For at least a quarter of a mile, all went gloriously well. And then, before we'd reached the edge of the village, it all started to unravel. As it had been on the march, and as it had been on last year's holiday too, the frame was proving a problem for Charlie. She basically sagged into it until she became intolerably cramped and twisted out of shape and started to scream blue murder. She just didn't have the strength to sit tall in this saddle. Not yet, at any rate; not yet, we reckoned. Not quite yet.

But we were determined. We made it to the clifftop in a dozen short stages, stopping to extract her from the frame every hundred yards or so. It was agony, absolute agony, for me as well as Charlie. The sinews and muscles of my shoulder and neck were twisted and pulled ragged. We had our picnic on the first patch of clifftop green we came upon, a stone's throw from the path, almost within sight of our house. It felt like a victory though, a victory of sorts; and we told ourselves, privately, inwardly, that if we took things gradually, by the end of the week, Charlie would have more stamina.

On day two we set off with Charlie in the backpack frame again; and again she was screaming blue murder before we'd got through the village. This time we decided to go back and set forth a second time with Charlie in her lightweight buggy. The logic (unspoken, but clearly understood) was that by breaking her in gently, one day in the back pack, one day off, we were more likely to get there in the end. The stamina would come. So we pushed her in her buggy up the west road and onto the path. And when the going got too steep or rough and wheels just wouldn't do, we took her out of the buggy and I carried her babe-in-arms style and Beth folded the buggy and carried it until the path became smooth enough for us to set it down once more. And thus we made it fairly easily to our picnic spot of the day before.

Then we pushed on. The clifftop path seemed promising. True, it was rocky and stony but it was wide and though not exactly even, the gradients, as far as we could see, didn't seem too steep. So we set off. We must have pushed on for about a half mile even though the first few yards should have told us all we should have needed to know. It was a huge struggle to get the buggy moving at all, so rutted and jagged and loose underfoot was the path – and when we did get it moving, it rattled and shook so violently that it seemed that it was on the verge of disintegrating. As for Charlie, all shook up, she was beyond screaming blue murder and was merely white faced and wide eyed with terror. She was probably a bit stunned too because, despite all our best efforts, her head kept lolling against one of the buggy's metal side spars, so her skull was getting a good old rattling too.

Once we had conceded and turned about, it took us hours to return to our clifftop picnic base, our square one. We had to stop and take a seat every time we came across a bench, which was every hundred yards or so. Other walkers (and this section was thick with hikers in shorts, rubber-soled walking boots, clear plastic map-pouches, compass mounts dangling from cords round their necks) always smiled when they saw us on the move. On the boneshaking move. We must have looked surreal. Out of place. Or sort of quaint. And rather thick. So yes, they smiled but always in a strained sort of narrow-eyed way, as if to say, *What the fuck are those fuckwits doing up here with a buggy like that?*

On the third day, we decided we'd go with the buggy again but this time stick to tarmac. The track out of the village to the west was almost as good as a road (in fact now I think of it, it *was* a road, giving access to a handful of houses scattered up the steeper reaches of the combe's side, overlooking the bay). According to the map, as the road cleared the combe and levelled out, it cut inland – and if we were lucky it might be a smooth surface the whole way.

It was; but as the day unfolded we weren't to look on that as good fortune. Because it meant we made good progress and were miles away from home when we hit trouble. Down by the bay the weather was bright and breezy and it seemed to be developing into one of those open, blowy days with scatterings of cloud – whole fleets of it cruising serenely across the sky, borne steadily before the breeze.

And we assumed, naturally, that it would be blowier up on the tops, clear of the sheltering wall of the valley. We were wrong. The weather had other plans altogether. The wind dropped, the clouds evaporated; and as we pushed on into mid morning, the temperature began to soar. Perversely, it was probably hotter up on higher ground because here there was no shade – there was the occasional puny tree by the roadside but for the most part the road was hemmed in by high hedgerows that cast no shadow from an overhead sun. Suddenly the whole world was blanketed in an unnatural silence – a silence that seemed all the more oppressive for the fact that when we turned and looked back we could still see glimpses of the sea, deep blue now and glinting where waves caught fragments of sunlight. You sort of wished to hear the sound of the waves

– as if, in this uncanny silence, that alone could cool you down.

It dawned very slowly on us that, although Charlie was wearing a floppy sun hat and had on her achingly-cute baby sunglasses, the ones with the fluorescent yellow plastic frames, she was going to be in real trouble if we continued as we'd been doing. She as already showing signs of distress. She was thirsty and obviously in this heat there was no way we could get enough liquid into her quickly enough because she still drank very very slowly. Also, in her sleeveless yellow summer dress, her arms were bare; and despite the smothering of sun tan lotion she'd been given, she was probably getting sunburned too. We had to find shade – and soon.

"We have to go back."

"Yes," I agreed bloodlessly. How had this crisis suddenly ambushed us? How on earth had we let this happen? I felt sort of paralysed.

"What?" she asked, when I remained motionless. As in: What is it?

"The irony," I said. "The irony is that we're probably only a hundred yards or so from shade."

"What?"

"The other side of this hedgerow there's probably a field and across the other side of that field will be the treeline. You know – the top edge of the woods above our house."

And actually, now I came to think of it, though we'd come a long way round, I was probably nearer the truth than I'd initially calculated. We were probably right above our sailing ship cottage. Meanwhile, Beth was surveying the hedge. It was at least ten foot tall and dense with prickly stuff like hawthorn. She looked it up and down in barely concealed contempt, gave me an angry glare, and then (pointedly) began ministering to Charlie.

"Actually," I said, grasping at straws. "Didn't we pass a gap in the hedge a while back?"

She looked up and gave me another angry glare. It was turning out to be *all my fault.* "Come on," I said, striding back off down the road, a picture of inspirational leadership.

And, bizarrely, I was right. Not a quarter of a mile down the road in the direction we'd come, there was a gap in the hedge. And yes, though there was a stile in the gap, we managed to manhandle the buggy over. It took a lot of effort, it pained us mightily, Charlie must have been scared to death; and if anyone had seen the whole business it must have seemed pathetically comic. A grim struggle owing more than a little to the memory of Laurel and Hardy. At one point we got stuck, me and Beth on either side of the stile each holding one end of the buggy above our heads, Charlie lying in it staring straight up into the sky, whimpering in terror. But we did it. We manhandled her into the field.

Our mistake was probably to feel victorious at this stage. Smug almost. Because, yes, the treeline was a hundred yards away. Salvation. And the thing was, we'd struck on the most magical little corner of the world. The view was breathtaking. As your gaze swept round towards the sea the land began to fall away steeply and, due to the way that terrain was folded, tucking the trees and the heart of the village out of sight, it looked as if you could run down to the edge of the field and drop straight into the sea. It was spectacular, the way the view opened out like this – and further round you could even see part of the other side of the valley, with fragments of its outlying rooftops and ivied chimney stacks peeking through a broken blanket of green shade. And the thing that made it just all too perfect was the field itself. It had clearly been left undisturbed for months – it was lush, the grass almost knee high, and there were poppies growing in it, vivid spots and splashes of red in the rich green. Smallers spots of yellow flowers too. It was a stunning view, doubly arresting because we had come upon it so unexpectedly.

All of which contributed to the nature of the defeat. All of which, in fact, actually underlined the true nature of the defeat. Pointed it up. Made it inescapable. Because, in this most magical of places, this loveliest of locations, I should at least have been allowed the dignity of pushing my daughter, in her buggy, a few score yards to the shade we were seeking. We were not (I decreed to myself and to the spirit of all that was just and right and proper) going to be made to feel alien here, we were not going to be excluded even from this. This simple pleasure. This simple act of being. I swore that it was just not going to happen.

And yet it did. Because of course the buggy wouldn't go through the long grass. It was like trying to cycle across the powder dry sand of a beach. It was like attacking a jungle with one of those old manual lawn mowers. It stuck fast. You had to pull one yard back to push two yards forward. And I did. I lost it. Completely lost it. Almost immediately I flew into a frenzy. I charged at it, charged at it, charged at it. I'm amazed, actually, that Charlie didn't make more noise than she did; and she made a lot of noise, I'm pretty sure about that. Beth as well. Me too, I suppose. There was a lot of yelling and shouting and scream-ing in that too-perfect summer field, that field tilted crazily over a blue and sparkling sea. All three of us, we tore at midday's supernatural silence.

The sun beat down, it scorched us all, Charlie most of all. I knew that. I knew she was burning up, within sight of the shade.

But still I charged at it, charged at it, charged at it.

I don't know if I collapsed or if I merely pretended to collapse or if there's really any difference. But the next thing I can remember, I'm lying splayed out on my back, arms and legs spread, staring into the sun.

I lay there what seemed a long time, until Beth started to get scared. Charlie was still crying. She was crying miserably.

In the end, the real end, we carried her across the field, the buggy back-tilted again, level with the ground like a stretcher so she lay staring up into the sky. I don't know what she saw there, if anything.

The odd thing about that day is that it began raining almost out of nowhere. We lay stunned for a while when we reached the first shady fringes of the wood. Then, as we recovered, as we drank in the cooler air, we moved slightly further in to a spot beneath a huge spreading tree, a beech I think, where we could all sit comfortably (line abreast, staring out into the arena of our recent defeat). We were all still stunned, quiet, everything internalised, each privately contemplating what the day so far had delivered.

And then, when we had finished our lunch, we took one last look into the sun-filled field (it was still oppressively hot out there, and getting hotter, you could tell that from the way tall grasses round the fringes of the field blazed goldenly) before moving off down the valley slope into the deeper wood.

It took us the best part of an hour to reach the valley floor with its gurgling stream and its woodland path that zig-zagged from one bank to the other, crossing and recrossing the stream on a series of slatted bridges. The best part of an hour – because again, obviously, we had to carry Charlie and the buggy most of the way, this time slip-sliding on muddy, mossy slopes fretted with exposed tree roots. We felt increasingly foolish and furtive, anxious that someone might see us in all our ridiculousness, trying to manoeuvre a buggy heavy with child over an assault course. And maybe also that furtiveness had something to do with the hushed quality of the sound and the dank green

quality of the light as we descended deeper. It was as if we were spiriting something away. A changeling, perhaps. We hushed our voices and held our collec-
tive breath and everything seemed muffled, a smokiness somehow hanging in
the air. The spirit of the woods smelled mouldy but fresh too. Toadstools. Mud
and nettles. And yes, if someone then had come to us and held forth about the
spirit of the woods we would have listened deeply because we were part way
to being spooked.

So here we were at last, down on the valley floor, about half a mile upstream
from the village, we reckoned, the worst of it over. We rested up, Charlie glad
to be sitting quietly in her buggy now it wasn't being borne headlong on a
white water ride, me and Beth sitting with our backs against the broad trunk
of a tree.

And it was here that we were properly spooked.

A rush of fear as we became aware of something. A noise. A noise gaining
on us. An energy, a raw force; and we were terribly unprepared. We'd already
been blown away. We had nothing left. And yet here came this thing. There was
an uncanny mischievousness in its animation, in its very vitality. Suddenly it was
around us on all sides. Or no – above us.

A high rustling.

I laughed. Beth's eyes widened, perhaps at the hubris in this laugh. We had
been living so long at the edge of the apocalypse.

"What? What is it?"

"It's only gone and started raining."

And sometimes it was like that. Apparently. Someone told us that the deeper
combes have their own weather; and perhaps it's true.

We didn't come out at all the next day.

For the rest of the holiday, the furthest we ever made it under our own steam
was to our hidden platform. Yes, there were day trips, exploratory forays by car.
One to a National Trust garden nestled like a green oasis in a sheltered moorland rift. A garden with its arbours and trellis arches and ponds alive with flitting dragonflies. We spent ages by the side of one of those ponds, mesmerised
almost by these insects, electric blue against the green-black clarity of the pond
and its underwater forests of weed. We were never sure if Charlie could see
them too. She was very tired that day, her eyes blank.

But anyway, the point is we got out and about a bit. Certainly we did.

Mainly, though, before Beth stopped going out at all, we'd head for the cliff top. Our hidden platform. Actually, it wasn't all that hidden either. In truth it was hardly a stone's throw from the picnic spot we'd made it to on the first day. Our observation platform, our green, was just a little bit further round, a bit further off the pathway – in fact, almost doubled back under it. There was a little copse that came almost to the cliff's edge just at the point where the land seemed to fall away towards the cornerstones of the bay; and from the main path it didn't look all that promising, a dead end; but if you were sufficiently curious you'd hit upon our spot. No-one ever did, though – in all the hours we spent there, not another soul appeared.

It was an oval area, hardly larger than your average garden lawn, seemingly cut into the cliff. A ledge, sort of, though it was far bigger than a mere ledge. And it was a perfect vantage point – inland, to your right, the leaf-camouflaged village; straight ahead, the bay; to your left, the cliff margins shelving to the open sea; directly below, stacks and arches and fissures cut from crumbly micas. Up there, on our platform, it felt as if this had been created just for us.

We said little to each other when we were up there and Charlie was nearly always silent – though on some days this was actually a worry, so dreadfully limp and still was she. Nor (and this is a source of wonder, looking back) did we ever read up there, though between us we had a crate of holiday books to get through and this was surely the perfect place. We each just gazed, either inwardly or outwardly. And we'd go there even when the weather was dodgy: if just to take in the view for half an hour in the cold before heading back, probably to the pub far below for lunch. Sometimes you could track weather out in the channel, like some elemental air traffic controller, watching a squall curving landward till its first spots began to patter against the clear plastic bubble of the rain cover we clipped to Charlie's buggy.

On warmer days I'd lie with the side of my head pillowed on the turf, taking in the world. Some days the sea was almost Aegean in the intensity of its colours. Clear glassy greens and greys in the surging masses of inshore water between rock channels at the cliff base. Darker browny greens further from the shore where reefs of weed swayed closer to the surface. Then deeper blues, almost purples. Further out towards the horizon, aquamarines and turquoises.

Some days, you'd stare so intently at the sky that it would begin to lose colour and become lighter than the air itself. There'd be flossy hints of cloud here and there; and at places on the horizon it seemed as if blue had become totally bleached into white.

Often, I'd stare into the dense weave of long grass, the last tangled fringe between our green ledge and the precipitous slopes beyond. I suppose I started to find it a source of great awe and wonder that there could be so many different plants in just one short section of this fringe. The grasses alone – there were hundreds of different varieties, from broadblades to tall, barley-like ears; long sheaves and fallen hanks of unkempt hair; wisps of gossamer and spiky porcupine quills, like chives. The flowers too, previously unseen but now becoming etched into your consciousness. Hyper real in their intense detail. Baby ferns, buttercups, tiny blue flowers almost as small as pinheads, purple flowers on twisty haulms, yellow starbursts, mauve miniatures like Parma violets. And the whole dense mass alive with insects. Lacy winged things. Ladybirds. Pale winged butterflies alighting delicately and flitting on.

"It was a golf course at one time, did you know that?"

I told her this one afternoon. Sometimes there's a long delay and you can never be exactly sure why. Beth is slightly deaf in one ear, so sometimes it can be that. It genuinely can. Or if she's depressed it can seem to take an age for her to find the energy to bring herself to the edge of a reply. But sometimes it's what my mother would call sheer bloodymindedness. On the other hand, often it's just down to the fact that what I've just said is so mind numbingly banal that it doesn't deserve anything better than silence.

"What was a golf course?" she replied, unable or unwilling to hide the flat boredom in her voice.

"That," I said standing and turning to face inland – the rough, gorsy scrub on the bank behind us and further over, the copse. Actually the copse, I'd only just twigged, was basically an oblong enclosure of privet that had been allowed to grow out over years, probably decades. "All of that. The downland on the tops here. As far inland as the track and almost as far over as the lost domain."

I was waving my hand over to the west along the coast in the vague general direction of the next valley – the steep ravine, the gorse bush combe along the coast. And because she remained silent, I continued: "It was designed by James Braid. There's a couple of lines about it in that little pamphlet we got in the church hall."

Still no response, though I could hardly blame her. The pamphlet was a history of the valley, compiled by a local archivist from interviews with the village's oldest living inhabitant. Since finding this document, I'd come close to irritating her once or twice by quoting facts from it. It wasn't that she wasn't interested in local history – more the feeling, I expect, that this was yet another territory I'd moved quickly to colonise unconditionally as my own. And I could see that talking about golf wasn't necessarily a good idea either.

But no, I wasn't going to stop now – because it had all sort of clicked. It had come together. "That copse back there. The thing is, it isn't really a copse. That's to say, I mean it is. It is now. But originally it was a privet hedge. In fact, I'm almost certain it was. I'll bet it went round the club house. Round the back. The back and the sides. The front would have been open so it had a view. I'll bet you."

She didn't know who James Braid was, obviously. I mean, who does? The only reason I know is because I spent part of my childhood in the twin villages of Elie and Earlsferry in Fife, where we, me and my brother, learned to play golf.

And one of the bits of golfing lore that became entangled with our lives was the legendary story of James Braid, one of the triumvirate of great Open winners in the first couple of decades of the 20th Century. James Braid was born in Earlsferry. He learned his stuff on Elie links. But that wasn't all. In Edinburgh, we lived on the edge of the Braid Hills, which was our run-of-the-mill, sea-less Elie. Our inexhaustible tract of land to explore. We had the run of it, even though it contained two public golf courses, and you had to know the danger areas, acquiring an instinct for when it wasn't safe to break cover. These golf courses were designed, of course, by James Braid. Gorse-choked, hillside golf courses, teetering, clinging precipice-like over the city. So, although I gave up playing golf when I reached the age of 16 or 17, and though it has never really been my friend, all sorts of notions coalesced when I learned that Braid was woven into this part of the country too.

I began spending a lot of time up there. There on our observation platform. The thing that really baffled me about this clifftop golf course (in existence from 1906 as a nine hole course, redesigned by Braid as a fully fledged 18 hole course in 1921, finally decommissioned, if that is the right word, in 1956) was that not a single trace of it remained as far as I could see.

It was mindboggling. It defeated me completely.

1956. They took away the flags and the tee markers, I imagined, and let the sheep back in. And at some stage, they must have demolished the clubhouse. Or perhaps it didn't need demolishing. It had been, I was told, a wooden building with a verandah, which boasted wonderful views along the coast – and it wouldn't have taken many winter gales and salty squalls to turn it into matchwood. I couldn't even find evidence of foundations within the vestiges of the privet enclosure; but, on the other hand, the whole area within the privet enclosure was pretty densely overgrown.

At one point I went down to the smugglers' snug and asked about the golf course. The woman behind the bar disappeared through the back to find, I supposed, someone who'd be able to help.

It was quiet and dark in that low-beamed old pub and the brightness of its sunlit garden was framed in its open doorway. I could sense flowers, mote-like insects drifting in the sleepy air, a warm silence.

I waited.

You could tell that the lay of the land was right for a golf course. It would have been a pretty flat, open, treeless course, in the classic Scottish seaside links style – with rough the only real hazard off the fairways. You could imagine there were maybe half a dozen holes up by the cliff edge, maybe only three actually bordering on it, with greens almost projecting out into fresh air. The rest of the course would have headed inland, with the terrain falling away gently towards the turn. But I couldn't with any confidence locate a single green. There were lots of mounds and hollows that might be the vestiges of bunkers – but the evidence was profoundly unsatisfying. The mounds were low, the hollows shallow.

And even when the pattern of these mounds and hollows was set in a telltale configuration, nowhere could I detect roughly circular areas of perfectly flat ground, circular areas which might yield evidence of a green.

It was hugely frustrating.

And yet, on the other hand, this complete lack of any trace whatsoever, this complete absence of evidence, made the ghostliness of the whole business more intense. I spent hours stomping back and forth with my head bent, scanning the ground as it scrolled beneath my feet. Sometimes I even got down on my hands and knees and crawled across long forgotten fairways. I presumed. Maybe I was crawling along them. Up them. Or down them.

In a way it was awesome, supernatural. That a physical feature, a landscape feature, a big project like a golf course can so completely and utterly disappear.

So, yes, I suppose I was the golf course detective.

You have a whole different perspective when you lie on your stomach staring into the ground, trying to spot a golf course. A golf course is the last thing you'll see. You see the infinite variety of the structures, shapes, forms that grass becomes; or rather, the structures, shapes and forms that become grass. You become aware of the immensely deep strata that grass can weave. Far below the topmost cropped fringes of this fescue jungle, you can dimly perceive an undergrowth of mosses and clovers and plantains. And within this whole ecosystem, a menagerie of beetles and centipedes and ticks. The whole ground, the whole surface, is itching.

Tons of droppings, like strewn pebbles, some of them clinging together in spawnlike colonies. Sheep? Or Rabbits? Or both? Each dropping a dark liquorice brown but with a lustre, like the carapace of a beetle, a lustre that hints at the subdued surface sheen of more exotic colours. Metallic mauves, oilfilm greens and blues, sombre spectra.

It must be a Calvinist thing. I've never really thought about it before but it must be. That whole judgemental thing. We always believed we were the generation finally to break the Calvinist thing – that we had started out with (at most) Calvinist Lite and then had proceeded to laugh even that off. But perhaps, looking back, we overestimated its residual powers, the persistence of its strain. Its judgemental nature. Basically. Judgemental and uncompromising. The seemingly ineradicable belief that, when you come down to it, there are no such things as accidents. And I don't just mean the glass spilling accidents that Beth is spectacularly prone to. I mean the belief that things in a larger sense are pre-ordained. And that the pre-ordination is inexorably linked to character. Destiny and character is as one.

Not to mention the untiring self-examination in search of falsehood. And again, this goes far beyond the mere telling of tales. Far beyond fibbing. This, too, is about character.

What doe he say in the film? The man Hannay is seeking for near Killin. The man with the top of a finger missing. What does he tell Hannay? "I'm not what I seem." Is that it? Or, "I must continue to be seen as I seem?"

And I suppose when it comes down to it we should have read more into the sunsets. We should have had our suspicions; they should have been cause for thought. The sunsets could have been disturbing, if looked at in a certain way. Actually, when I say we, I almost certainly mean I. Beth wasn't interested in the sunsets, no matter how often I tried to drag her out into the garden in order to bear witness.

Day after day in the second week it happened. No matter what the rest of the day had been like, come late afternoon, black clouds would bulk up and on would come the rain, usually pretty heavily. And you'd be certain it was on for the duration. Night after night, you'd be wrong. Night after night after night, the cloud broke up and eventually dissolved, just in time for a sunset to unfurl out to sea, making a dramatic silhouette of the lonesome pine tree. And because the rain was still fresh in the air, the colours were somehow even more lurid – chrome yellows and eggy oranges and crimson lakes – watery colours that splashed and smeared and ran. It was true – they were screaming drama queens, those sunsets. Outrageous, really.

I'd sit out there after dinner with the rest of the bottle of wine (and some-times it would even be a second bottle of wine) sitting on a moulded white plastic garden chair at a moulded white plastic table, smoking the occasional cigarette while the darkness gathered about me.

I don't know why I didn't see then that these sunsets were actually more than outrageous. They were angry wounds, dyspeptic, ulcerous even.

***

And it was true I was getting ferocious heartburns. So ferocious sometimes I felt like I should lie down or something. It was eating me up. And the whole osteopath thing got a toehold again somehow. Using Charlie's carry harness had tortured my shoulder and the base of my neck; and the whole business was made much worse by the fact that the rooms were hardly six feet floor to ceiling and the door lintels gave five foot clearance if you were luckily. So I was basically stooping the whole time indoors. My neck ached and I'd get a stabbing pain if I tried to turn it too quickly, which of course happens the whole time when you have a sore neck; and it's even worse, obviously, if you overcompensate and try to walk about all stiffly.

"You should see the osteopath. I'm telling you."

I attempt to ignore this.

"He fixes my back just like that."

"For the last time. Will you listen? Will you? It's not my back. I don't have a problem with my back. It's my neck that's sore. It's from stooping the whole time and sleeping in that awful hammock of a bed next to that draughty window. Do you understand? It's not my back."

And then of course, the day after trying to push the buggy across the long grass in the field, I woke up with a twinge in my buttock. Not my back, my buttock. Dead center on the nate. But I spend most of the day straightening and stretching and arching my back to combat the twinge.

"You should see the osteopath. I'm telling you."

I didn't hear this. I'd have been incandescent with rage if I'd heard this.

And actually, it was a lie, what I said earlier. About how the clouds had lifted on the morning of our first day here; and how we'd stepped forth in an innocently cheerfully mood. The truth was we'd just had a ferocious argument about Charlie.

Because. Because, well, this is the truth. Here.

Beth had decided we had to redouble all our efforts as far as physio was concerned. Usually we gave Charlie a full session of stretches (on legs and arms) after she'd had her breakfast. Then if she was up to it, she'd go in her standing frame (we'd brought it with us, naturally, but even when disassembled it was a bugger finding room in the car for all those awkwardly shaped bits, especially the base, which was like the base of a flightcase, a big solid board on casters) for 20 minutes or maybe more.

Now, Beth had decided, peremptorily, without any discussion, to intensify the regime. There would be one session after breakfast and another some time in the afternoon, schedule allowing. Or no, in fact, second thoughts, henceforth the schedule was to be constructed around this afternoon session.

To me, this seemed a desperate move.

We all needed a break from the grind. All of us, Charlie included. And didn't she realise that we'd end up doing nothing and going nowhere if we had to commit ourselves to a session absolutely religiously, every afternoon? And the thing was, when it came down to it, we were actually talking about early afternoon, weren't we? Because any later and the whole business would start eating into Charlie's tea time schedule.

We had this discussion on the morning of the first day. She said her piece and I said mine. She gave me a black look. She looked terrible. Grey and drawn and haggard. She said some stuff and I listened and then, trembling, I went for a short walk until I had gathered myself. And then we had breakfast as if nothing had happened.

Except, of course, for the fact that it was taken in complete silence.

The day before we left, I was up on the cliff top, not on our observation platform but on the other side, the east side. The terrain over this side was far more severe and uncompromising. On the west there was a good deal of slippage and crumbling, the land crashed to the sea in steps, all of them big drops admittedly, but steps nonetheless. On the east side there were just cliffs pure and simple. Vertical; or even more severe than vertical, with the top edge clearly overhanging the cliff base. If you could face going anywhere near the edge, you'd feel yourself (your weight, your sheer destiny) suspended above milky cliff wash far below.

I'm usually terrible with heights. I can't bring myself to come closer than three decent strides from an edge. Just don't have the head for it. But that day, that Friday morning, something made me flirt with it. I walked the plank. I walked out onto a bowsprit of rock, a narrow overhang like some gantry suspended over the bay. I looked down. And there below me was the bay's most audacious monument – a quartzy pillar of rock, white one minute, silver the next as the light took it. On top of the pillar, a perfect round of grass. From up here I could see it was like the tip of a snooker cue, chalked green instead of blue, domed slightly but perfect in its symmetries.

Bang in the middle of the green, lord of all it surveyed, was a white heron. I suppose that's what made
me edge out there despite everything. That heron.
The tide was racing in across the rocks (from up here
the rock shelf looked foul, a gnarled and pocked and
fissured wasteland, stained luridly with sea lichens and
spongy sea mosses) and soon it would be foaming at
the pillar's base. That alone would be worth watching,
that closure. But it was the bird that drew me to the
edge. Its whiteness and its stillness. The white of its
plumage was an intense white – softer yet more light-
saturated than the whiteness of the daisies that grew
in the grass of the stack around it, softer yet more
luminous than the white of the whitecaps racing in
on the tide.

I edged out onto the promontory, inch by inch;
and as I did so, the breeze seemed to stiffen, tearing at
the tide, chasing ragged tatters of cloud across the sky,
becoming blustery even. And I, I was edging out into
it. Gulls were planing, soaring cutting extravagant arcs
in the air; the wind was turning the sweat on my forehead to a dusting of stinging salt. The sea became big,
bigger, vast – some sort of improbable, unfathomable
meniscus. I couldn't catalogue its colours or take a
census of its whitecaps, though, because I wasn't looking at the sea. Not
directly. I was looking at the heron.

I'd made it to the edge. I told myself I'd move when the heron moved. Then
and not before. I'd take my cue from the white bird.

Because. Because the thing is, we'd come down here on a Saturday. Two days
before, the Thursday, the Thursday afternoon in fact, Charlie and Beth had been
at the Conductive Education Centre. The people who specialise in making
cerebral palsy sufferers walk. But this wasn't about them, as it happens.

Beth had taken Charlie there for what I think was the last of three assessment sessions and the physio, the regular physio, our physio went too this time,
so she could show the Conductive Education people the sorts of equipment

Charlie used (her standing frame and especially important, her seating) and how it should be best set up.

Charlie doesn't have cerebral palsy; but the Ferncliff Centre having been denied us, we hoped she might instead be able to attend the Centre on a part time basis, starting perhaps in the autumn. It had got to the stage where all sorts of practicalities needed thrashing out.

And at one stage Beth was explaining to the Conductive Education people the operations that Charlie was probably going to need on her feet and perhaps her hips and whatever. How would that whole medical schedule fit around what they did here, potentially? And how might it affect their prognosis? How long did they think it would be before Charlie was walking?

They were non-committal. Pouts, shrugs. They couldn't say for sure. And then the meeting was over and Beth and the physio found themselves alone in the room (Charlie was there too, naturally), packing up all the equipment. And Beth chose that point to tell the physio she was worried about how stiff Charlie's legs had been recently, it was particularly noticeable when we tried to do the standard bend and stretch exercises with her. What should we be doing? She was worried at this stage that if we didn't do enough or didn't do the right thing (or didn't do enough of the right thing or things) then Charlie might lose the chance of ever being able to walk.

She'd said it jokingly. Or not exactly jokingly, but as if this was an unimaginable scenario really.

And the physio, our physio, laid her hand on Beth's arm. "Beth," she said. It was somewhere between a reassurance and a plea. "Beth," she said. "I really wouldn't get my hopes up about that."

That was the point. That was the real point. And still the bird did not move. Seagulls soared, arced, planed. The wind stung my face. I was out there where I had no right to be. And I realised I was half crouching, had been beginning to crouch, almost imperceptibly, for some time now, except now my knees were trembling. Soon, I knew, I would be shaking uncontrollably.

Somehow or another, I made it down onto my knees. And then I was down on all fours. Maybe people saw me there like that and maybe they laughed at me. Each time previously I had been up here, I had seen other people out here on this little spit of rock, even maybe a foot or so further towards its tapering point, standing quite blithely, scanning the far horizon. And here was I down on all fours, shaking uncontrollably, trying to edge back off it like a feeble old man.

And still the heron had not moved.

But I knew now. I knew what I would find.

So when at last I had reversed far enough from the edge and I was able to stand, I turned and ran.

The truth is that on that first day, Beth hadn't wanted to set forth at all. She had wanted to stay in and do physio on Charlie's legs all day. She wanted to fit in 20 sessions a day every day of the holiday and even then that wouldn't have been enough. And that's why every time I did physio it was wrong, clearly wrong. She wanted to stay in all day and do physio or shout at me doing physio wrongly, so wrongly in fact that I was crippling my own daughter.

And then, after the first week, there was no longer the same sort of insistence on us doing physio 20 times a day. And maybe we had begun slipping into the black.

So I ran. I ran and I ran; and when I reached the house, I burst in.

Charlie was awake but slightly dazed. Maybe I woke her. She was laid flat across an armchair on a nest of cushions. Beth was lying on the sofa facing inwards, her face smothered. I stood there above them both. It's like that time I was standing above the two of them sleeping on the sofa in our living room at home, standing above them with a hammer dangling loosely from my hand, held just firmly enough to feel its heft. Except now, perhaps appropriately, I have no hammer in my hand.

And all I can think about is the sofa. The material is horrible. The fabric has a raised pattern, vaguely floral in design. The suite – a sofa and two chairs – looks as if it has been upholstered by the members of a beginners' class in embroidery.

And then I hear a sound. It's a sound that confuses me, much in the same way as the sound of rain in the trees confused and surprised us that day as we struggled home through the forest with the buggy.

It is the sound of snoring.

Beth is snoring.

That's when I realised that it was me who'd done myself a mischief. What with my precipitous descent from the cliff tops. I was sweaty, out of breath, trembly again, but this time from the run. I had a vague notion that I might actually be sick. And in fact I did manage to gag up a little bit off the top; but it hardly got past my throat and I was able to swallow it back down. That's when the heartburn came raging. I had to step outside. I went out the back onto the middle terrace and sat in one of those moulded white plastic garden chairs. The wind was still whippy but the day had an over-exposed feel to it now; with the sun burning full-on in the hard blue gaps between scudding clouds. A dry fever was clutching at me. I felt stung and scratchy. But I sat out there, the sweat drying on my tee-shirt, until the trembling stopped and I felt solid enough to have a cigarette.

Chapter eleven

The Neurological Institute report was there when we got back. We saw it straight away in the mountain of mail behind the door, it sort of leapt out at us, but neither of us had the courage to open it. Instead, I did the usual thing I do when I come back from holiday. I wandered round the house, marvelling at its strange, warm, dusty smell, noting quizzically how its dimensions seem to have altered subtly while we've been away.

There were other distractions too. Among the packages our next door neighbour had taken in for us was a square one in a tough cardboard flat pack about the size of a carpet tile. I knew what this was too – it was a copy of the Nilsson single Without You I'd tracked down via a mail order list.

"Just nipping upstairs to check my messages," I said.

She didn't really hear.

I was actually just nipping upstairs to see if I couldn't get my old Garrard record deck to work. But as it happened I did listen to my messages. Or rather to my message. Message singular. Two weeks away and only one measly message.

It was from Robbie and it was long and rambling and, it seemed to me, terribly confused. Either he had been trying to get in contact with Jules or he had not; either he had actually talked to Jules or he had not; either he had actually met up with Jules already or he had not: but anyway, one way or another, the message seemed to be that for some reason it was now up to me to fix up a time when me and Jules could meet up with Robbie for a spot of lunch maybe. I felt a terrible swooping sensation in my stomach.

It was late afternoon by then I suppose. Saturday. A vague hint of autumn was in the air. There was a spider building its web in the upper corner of the window casement, just on the other side of the glass. It worked steadily and accurately, with a spindly deftness. So of course I watched it. I don't know for how long – long enough to work out that it was probably for the best if I called Jules. Not that I really expected him to be contactable on a meek and mild Saturday afternoon towards the end of summer. But he was.

"Jules," I said.

"Er, um, ah," he said. "Er, um, ah, hello. So you *are* still there."

"Yeah?"

"I called over a week ago."

If he did, I thought, he declined to leave me a message.

"Yes. And? I've been on holiday, you tosser."

"Oh? You never told me that."

"Yes I did."

"Oh."

Of course I hadn't told him that. I mean, he wasn't my mum, was he?

"Anyway," said he.

"Anyway," said I.

"Anyway."

"Anyway."

"So, is that the news? You've been on holiday and now you're back."

"Yes, Jules, I had a lovely time, thank you for asking."

"Oh. Did you?"

"No."

"Oh."

"Yeah, well."

"So what do you want?"

"No. You first."

"What d'you mean, me first?"

"You said you'd called a week or so ago."

"Oh. That. No, yours is obviously more recent."

"Oh. Okay." Might as well, I thought – we were probably talking about the same thing. "Just to say, I hear Robbie's made contact at last."

"Robbie? Robbie who?"

"Robbie. You know. Remember me telling you about him?"

"No."

"No? Oh well."

"Is that it?"

"That's not why you called me then? The other week?"

"No."

"What then?"

"Oh, it's nothing really. When I called you, I'd just got back from a features meeting at The Observer."

"The Observer," I echoed, curious yet curiously sceptical.

"Yes," he said. "You won't believe this. You know that idea we talked about for an article? You know, the Blackpool one."

Was it Blackpool? Probably. Probably it was. The idea was I'd go to a holiday resort and maybe stay there for a week towards the end of the season. In fact, it was a bit like the motels idea. It would be an offbeat look at Blackpool through the eyes of the students who worked in bars, the chamber maids, the people who served in chip shops or emptied machines in the arcades – seasonal workers who'd be just about ready to pack up and go home. They'd maybe have a slightly jaded perspective. They'd have lots of stories to tell, lots of revealing little anecdotes that would maybe convey the real spirit of the place. Its dated seediness, its tackiness. It would be, well, poignant. Bittersweet.

"Yeah," I said, half statement, half question.

"Well, they bought it."

"They?"

"The Observer."

I still didn't quite believe it. I thought this was some sort of a practical joke. "Who? Who at the Observer?"

"You know that new features editor?" I did. He wasn't exactly new by then – actually he'd joined back in the spring. All I knew was he never returned anyone's calls. "Well, him. He bought it."

"You went in to see him?"

"Yeah. I talked to him on the phone, told him the idea and he asked me to come in. They see it as a photo piece. I've got a week up there with a photographer, all expenses paid and…"

"Hold on," I said. "Hold on." There was a pause. We both held on. "You sold them this idea?"

"Yeah."

"You. *You* sold them this idea?"

"Yeah."

"You cheeky sod."

"What?" He squeaked.

"It was my idea," I reminded him.

"No it wasn't."

"Yes it was."

"It wasn't."

"Was."

"Wasn't."

"Look, I'm telling you. It bloody well was. And for another thing, it wasn't even Blackpool."

"What! You're saying it was your idea but yours was a different one. Or what?"

"It was my idea. Except it was in…" Where exactly was it? Skegness? Torquay. Or no, Margate, it must have been somewhere like Margate.

"Except nothing," said Jules, storming back. "And actually, this proves it, doesn't it? Because I only told you about the idea after I showed you that article in one of the psychogeographical journals. You know, the piece about how Blackpool was actually the fabled coast of Bohemia."

"I can't believe it Jules. I can't believe you'd do this to me."

I can't remember who managed to get their phone down first. I think it was probably me. My reactions are far superior.

We didn't want anything more to do with the Neurological Institute. We didn't want to read their report. We didn't even want it lying unopened in our hallway. So we sort of pretended it wasn't there. We wanted to wipe all memories of our assessment day. This, this supposed landmark event, this defining event in Charlie's story, had been dismal. Thoroughly dismal. They, the people at the Institute, were worse than dismal. They were a complete and utter waste of time.

You learn to live with delays when you haunt the corridors of hospitals and clinics. You learn to live with the fact that you're never seen at the appointed time. The hour comes and passes and you begin chatting to one of the other families waiting out there on the benches in the corridor and you find out with a sinking heart that *they* should have been seen two hours ago. There are probably half a dozen people ahead of you in the queue. Or you'll arrive in good time to find that they have no record of the appointment whatsoever and it doesn't matter in the slightest that you can show them the letter they sent to you. They can take no responsibility for administrative errors. Go away now please thank you.

The letter summoning you always reminds you in bold capitals of how inconsiderate and antisocial and in fact downright irresponsible you're being if you're as much as one minute late. Because obviously if you keep a consultant waiting that amounts to a shameful waste of health service resources. So if anyone is going to have to do any hanging around, it's you, not the consultant. Which is sort of fair, isn't it? Isn't it?

In effect, they break you. You become feeble. You're like a supplicant in the court of a Dark Ages King – you'll take any scraps that fall to you and be bloody grateful for them.

But get this. For the team we were about to see at the Institute, we were the only business of the day. They were seeing no-one before us and no-one after us. Guess what? We were there at nine as requested. They didn't see us until a whisker before ten. So, yes, they were contemptible from start to finish. The waiting room was a disgrace too. You become inured to the depressed and depressing nature of waiting rooms, but this one was particularly unappetising – and it threw a shadow across the day, even though it was beautiful outside, with dappled sunlight streaming in the windows through plane trees and through the scissoring leaves, big as the fingers on giants' hands, of towering horsechestnuts.

There were lots of toys, of course. Oxfam-style toys crudely identified (in manic marker pen) as Institute property. The usual mean and shabby stuff. All

 except the dolls' house. We were drawn to this dolls' house – of course we were, as hundreds of people like us, fragile, hungry for hope, had probably been drawn to it down the years. It got us. Absolutely it got us.

Because it was the most beautiful doll's house I'd ever seen close up. It must have been about four foot tall

and just as much wide and it was a Georgian townhouse rendered in incredible detail – pillars, porticos, friezes, mouldings, window surrounds, chimney pots. It looked wonderfully well maintained and immaculately painted. The whole frontage opened on hinges that creaked substantially, like a cupboard door.

But, oh, the horror inside. It was a squat. A dosshouse, a thieves kitchen, a shooting gallery. There'd clearly been interior detail at some stage but hardly anything remained. Not a mantelpiece nor a mirror nor a light fitting. All torn out. It was grimy throughout; and the floor in one of the rooms was charred, the walls patterned with ugly black flame licks. It was the furniture that was most unsettling, though – an ugly collection of crude woodblocks and lumps of hardboard nailed together. That rough cube with battens like ice lolly sticks nailed to it was meant to be a chair, that slab of hardboard was a bed. And the scale was horribly *out* too – this furniture was huge as well as crude and clunky. You will say there are worse things in this naughty world, and of course you will be absolutely right, but there was something grotesque about opening up that beautiful façade and seeing what we saw. At that time, in that place. There was something hideous and doom-laden about it.

Its only inhabitant was a huge knitted woolly lamb and this woolly lamb was crammed, absolutely stuffed, into one of the smaller rooms. It wasn't easy extracting it. It had been wedged in there good and proper. Not by a child either. Or a freakishly strong child if it was a child.

When at last they decided it was time to see us, they ushered us into a cupboard. Actually, that's a lie – it was slightly larger than a cupboard because, after all, there were six of us to be accommodated. Three of them versus three of us. This, they said, was a preliminary chat to find out more about us – mum and dad and Charlie obviously. There was no apology or explanation for starting so late. (Though there was clearly no relevant excuse – they couldn't pretend, as most consultants regularly do, that they were behind schedule because they'd been called away to conduct an emergency operation. This was a research unit. This was what they did. This was *all* they did.)

Three of them. Two graceless birdlike women with rather brittle social skills and the third, the most junior one, who seemed more robust and real and warm but who was clearly so worried about her status that she was determined to be arrogant. The whole thing basically came across as an interrogation and we were so taken aback by the tone they'd set right from that start that we dropped pretty much into defensive mode. We were helping them with their inquiries – but only just. Actually, for a while it was all very very very bizarre. I felt as if I was on the verge of discovering what an anxiety attack is all about. It was like entering those first inkling stages of an acid trip.

Clumsy. That's the word. The whole thing was incredibly clumsy. Time and again it was clear that they hadn't read the case notes properly. Or more alarmingly, that their case notes were incomplete. Here we were in the presence of the elite of the elite, the crack specialists; and they clearly needed help tying their shoelaces. And yet there was a punctiliousness about them, as if their worst nightmare was the outside possibility that they might not be accorded the respect they clearly thought was due to them. The truth dawned slowly on us... no matter how academically gifted they were, they were way out of their depth when it came to dealing with real people.

Then they started asking a lot of questions about how we were coping, mum and dad, as parents; and that's when we started taking the game to them. At one point, Beth said that actually she felt let down by the medical profession. They were somewhat taken aback by this and they lined up to ask us the sort of leading "surely you're being rather harsh" questions designed to lead us gently from the error of our ways. And when we gave them the chapter and the verse, our litany of the inept and the insensitive and the arrogant and, yes, the downright clumsy, compiled more in sadness than in anger from day one, they squirmed in their chairs and retreated somewhat – but were still peevish and querulous for a while after that.

We had broken the most important rule that you have to obey if you're going to get that all important Good Parent gold star. To get the star and a patronising pat on the head you must be uncomplaining; you must bear up cheerfully. And here we were blaspheming.

They called time out; then, after a long break (during which Lisa, one of Charlie's care-workers, had arrived), we reconvened in a much larger room, a more clinicky sort of a room, wide, oblong, with all sorts of disabled kids' equipment and toys at each end. Lots of techie looking stuff too – gadgety type toys, computer display technologies and various forms of keyboards. In the middle, a nakedly empty space. A centre stage, a performance space. There were windows, and even the smallest amount of natural light was welcome after the interrogation cupboard; but it wasn't much of an improvement – these were meagre, shallow, fanlight slits of things running the length of the long wall,

right up by the ceiling. Through them you could just about see the tops of far-off trees; and even further off, wisps of cloud drifting in blue.

Under these windows, in the middle of the room, Charlie's high chair was set up and she was asked to perform. They put her through her paces much as you'd put a performing seal through its paces. They'd put three pictures out on the table in front of her. Which one was the sheep? She picked it out. Did she see the biscuit? She did. Could she pick it up? She could. Just about. They tested her ability to follow the trajectories of objects and to coordinate various hand movements. They did little bits of business, little acts of legerdemain and gauged if Charlie had followed what they had done. Could she see where the tiny white dot now was on the sheet of green baize? Yes, probably, if they gave her time.

She was really trying hard, really loving the challenge, I could see that. I was immensely proud of her. She was up for it. She could do all sorts of stuff I wasn't aware she could do. They worked her hard and she showed real willing. She performed. For an hour and a half. A gruelling hour and a half, especially as she was struggling to prove she could do stuff just at or beyond her range of abilities.

So yes, they worked her; and then they said there would be a short break. They trooped out leaving us in the room. Luckily, we'd brought half a packet of biscuits and a banana and some grapes – the little survival kit for Charlie that we tended to carry. She'd done brilliantly and it was lunchtime. Obviously they were going to let us go soon and we'd get her home for a proper late lunch but a biscuit and some grapes would tide her over. I mean, we were starving too. It was exhausting willing her to complete the tasks.

But suddenly they were back and without even so much as a preamble they had surrounded Charlie (who was still in her high chair) and were preparing to work her again. We were astounded. We (and we felt the odds were more in our favour now that Lisa, who after all had relevant expertise, was now sitting

in with us) pointed out that they weren't going to get the best out of Charlie – and thus an accurate picture – if they didn't give her a rest or at least time for lunch. But they were having none of it. With barely controlled patience, they reminded us that they were the experts and added, somewhat tartly, that they had a job to do and it just so happened that this job was fundamentally important for Charlie's future. They would be the judge of what a child was and was not capable of.

So they pushed on and Charlie fought valiantly. But she was going down under the onslaught. She was grinding to a halt. That's probably when we were at our most tearful, our eyes brimming. It was a torment knowing you should intervene but also knowing you should not.

And then the relief when they said it was almost over. But there was one last agony to endure. They put some matting on the floor then they asked us to undress Charlie. And then put her on the mat. Then they too were kneeling on the mat, surrounding her, crowding us out. Then they began to knead and maul her, seemingly at random. We'd seen Charlie being wrestled by doctors before; but seeing our pale, unorthodox child, her naked flesh blue-marbled, being pulled around by three witches, worrying at her as cats will toy with a mouse before dispatching it, was chilling.

And then they were done.

They stood, they stretched, they told us we could dress Charlie again.

Then they trooped out. We couldn't go quite just yet, they said. They were going to confer and then they'd be back to deliver a preliminary assessment.

So we waited.

It was 2.20.

We waited.

Charlie finished the rest of her food, such as it was. We hadn't brought very much for her because one way or another you expect a specialist children's unit to have the welfare of the child as a fairly high priority.

So we waited.

And waited.

It's shaming to think that we waited until 2.45 before even beginning to speculate about what had happened to them. It was Lisa who found out when she went to the loo.

When she got back her face was ashen.

"What's wrong?" asked Beth.

"You'll never guess," she said. "They're sitting in a staff room down the corridor gossiping and eating sandwiches."

I hooked the record deck up to the amplifier, plugged it in and pressed play. The turntable span. I put my new single on. I eased the stylus onto the vinyl's edge. The stylus seemed to take an age working its way in from the guide groove.

And then a groan. A low drone.

It took a while to realise what I'd done. I'd left the setting on 33.

But no. Hang on. There it was, the lever, set to 45. I flicked it back and forward but still the low droning groan continued. So I took the stylus off the  record and the record off the turntable. Then I let the turntable rotate again, flicking the lever between 45 and 33 in an increasingly manic fashion. An increasingly manic and desperate and futile fashion. Violence, I finally realised, probably wasn't going to work on this occasion. So then of course I had to start taking the deck apart.

At one stage, Charlie kept losing concentration. They couldn't get her to settle to the tasks they were setting her. She kept looking up at the high windows and trying to turn her head more fully in that direction.

"What is she looking at? She seems to be looking up at the windows," said one.

"Yes, I've noticed that," said another.

The room became uncannily vigilant as all three doctors observed Charlie, looking at her intently, then trying to follow her eyeline. It was as if they were holding their breath, expectant on the verge of some definitive revelation. In the distance, you could hear the screams and cries of children playing. Actually, perhaps the sounds weren't so distant. They were probably from the park just behind the Institute, the park bordered by the railings through which ragged urchins had earlier tried to sell us a can, chilled, of Fanta.

It was Beth who broke the spell. "It's the children playing," she said.

"She can hear them?"

"It would seem so, wouldn't it?" I said.

They observed her anew.

"Yes, yes it's true," one of them said. "Yes. Look. That's what she's doing. She can hear the children."

Charlie began nodding vigorously, as she does (mainly with relief) when people eventually catch on.

The three women, though, were exchanging glances among themselves. "But it says in the notes that she has problems with her hearing," one of them said. It was a remark directed at Beth. Actually, it wasn't so much of a remark as an accusation.

I was still tinkering when Beth came up, popped her head round the door, and said she was going to bed.

Okay, I said.

The head disappeared.

Then it reappeared again. "What are you doing anyway?"

"What does it look like I'm doing?"

"I don't know, do I."

I sighed pointedly. "I'm trying to fix this deck."

"What's wrong with it?"

"It won't play at 45."

"Why do you want it to play at 45?"

"So I can play singles."

She scrunched her face up. "But why do you want to play singles? I thought you taped all your singles ages ago."

This, as it happens, was true.

"It's a long story," I said.

"It never is."

"Huh?"

When people say it's a long story, it never is. It's usually a very short story. What they mean is, it's an embarrassing story."

"Well this isn't."

"No?"

She sat on the chair by my desk. I was squatting on the floor by the dismembered deck.

"No. As a matter of fact I want to fix the record deck so I can play my new single." I held it up to her for inspection.

"See," she said.

"What?"

"Talk about embarrassing."

"What!"

"Don't you remember that sketch they did on that TV comedy show? The one where the two women are listening to this single on the radio and they begin to sing along and they start competing with each other and in the end they're both howling like dogs."

As she was saying this, I was pulling the single away from her, closer to me. Closer to my face. It was as if I was seeing it for the first time. And it was true. I now had to face this fact – Without You was a dreadfully melodramatic, overblown production. Is that how my father had regarded it all those years ago? Had it *embarrassed* him? Was he just ashamed for me? As opposed to being enraged by my selfishness as I'd always thought.

And so I found myself telling the whole story, half in justification, I suppose. I told Beth that I was so besotted with the song (hearing it all the time on the radio, I suppose) when I was 13 that I felt I just absolutely must have it, the only problem being that my father's birthday was coming up and my pocket money wouldn't stretch to both a present and the single. And how I hit upon a solution whose neatness seemed just absolutely awesome. I would buy the single and give it to father for his birthday. Genius.

And I told her how I had given the single to father on the morning of his birthday and in the afternoon had hurried home to listen to it on the stereo on the sideboard in the dining room. And how I had not been able to find it on the old EPNS toast rack that held the family's 45s. And how at this point I had made discreet inquiries and had extracted from my mother the information that, before going to work, my father had thrown the single in the dustbin. And how (on the advice of my mother) I said nothing to my father about what may or may not have transpired vis a vis his birthday present and he said nothing to me; until, more than a week later, I gave my father a second birthday present. It was clay piggy bank I been working on all term at school and was now more or less finished, though the glazing hadn't fired as well as might be expected. I tried to give it to him one evening after tea.

"I've got you another birthday present," I said.

He merely stared at it in disbelief. So I put it on the coffee table.

"Happy birthday," I said.

"It's a bit late now," he replied, leaving the room.

I told Beth that nothing had been said since about this episode, all down the years, though there was surely much to be said.

"So in fact," said Beth, "this record actually represents a childhood trauma?" She wasn't being facetious. Just matter of fact.

I gave a little laugh. I shook my head, incredulously. "No," I said. "No."

But, yes, I called Jules again and left him a take-it-or-leave it message to meet up the next day, Monday, for lunch at Pizza Express on the Green.

On Monday morning I wrote to Jules too, as it happens. Actually, wrote is a bit misleading. I put a clipping in an envelope, no covering letter, no note, nothing, and addressed the envelope to him. It was inspired actually. Wholly appropriate and hugely funny. It was one of those little two column coupon response ads for a self-help course. I cut it out of the Guardian.

I.Q. of 145 Yet You Can't Remember People's Names?

ran the headline. You send off a fiver or something and they send you a little booklet with techniques for improving your memory.

I cut it out and put it in an envelope, which I addressed with the pen in my left hand. I was very pleased with the results. I chortled all the way to the post box. Then I wrote a letter to the editor of The Observer, complaining about the obvious dumbing down of his newspaper and informing him that I would no longer be purchasing it of a Sunday. The letter was short and to the point, crisp without being rude. I lamented in particular the decline in standards at the colour supplement, which week after week seemed to run endless "the way we live now" takes on unusual, obscure or forgotten aspects of contemporary Britain. These pieces were clearly meant to be quirky, wry and left field but they were in point of fact bland and banal.

I remained his humble servant.

I chortled all the way to the post box with that one too.

The 39 Steps: a coat, a pair of shoes, a fish.

And then the next time I looked, there was a hole in the spider's web outside my window and he (I don't know why but I started to think of him as a he) was repairing it. It was probably one of those holes that comes about because a fly has got caught in the web and the spider has wound it up in a silk cocoon and cut the cocoon put of the web and dragged it off to the larder, wherever that is. So he has to repair the hole where he cut the cocoon out.

I sat there.

He repaired the hole.

I waited for the phone to ring.

So yes, by the time the horses cantered round to the start, it had resolved itself into a two horse race. Pay Up versus Taj Akbar. Lord Astor versus His Highness the Aga Khan. Following the withdrawal of Rhodes Scholar, Pay Up was Astor's only horse in the race; and though the Aga had three runners, his number two jockey, Charlie Smirke, had decided he didn't want to ride the owner's second best prospect, Bala Hussar, and was switching to the owner's third best, Mahmoud. And those with money on Mahmoud must have been depressed by what they saw in the parade ring. Mahmoud was sweaty, nervous, jumpy even. He was filled with all the wrong sorts of energy and burning off the best of it before the race had even started.

So, yes, it was Pay Up versus Taj Akbar and though Pay Up was the popular favourite, many in the know were sure that this was going to be Gordon Richards' year at long last. After all, Taj Akbar was known to be pretty decent on hard going and the Epsom course was baked like a brick. The whole matter was simplified even further by what happened as they were called forward to come under orders. When Mahmoud, clearly still jumpy, was jostled by other horses, he bucked and kicked out, catching Thankerton on the knee and Thankerton's rider, Tommy Burns, on the mouth. If it had been anything more than a glancing blow, that would have been the end of Burns's day. His week come to that. And his teeth.

But he was only dazed. You could easily discount his chances though. And

Mahmoud's come to that. Or so you'd think. Actually, Thankerton nearly won the race. He had a real flier of a start, shooting straight into an eight lengths' lead, even though Burns had another bit of potentially disastrous bad luck when, as he came through to the front, a chalk stone flew up and caught him in the eye, temporarily (and almost permanently, it later turned out) blinding him in one eye.

Thankerton, ironically, was just about the only horse the crowd could see because the chasing pack was kicking up such a cloud of dust from the flinty ground. By Tattenham Corner, although the pack had made up ground, Thankerton was still well clear; but two horses in particular were closing the gap – Taj Akbar as expected and, bizarrely, Mahmoud. Richards had it all under control, though. He knew that Thankerton would tire up the hill to the finish and Taj Akbar, with its elegant stride compared to the low-slung, scampering, "daisy cutting" action of Mahmoud, could always do Mahmoud for raw pace.

But the thing was, he never had the chance. Richards miscalculated, basically. He was computing on the basis of softer ground, which was understandable in a way because the course was in the sort of stony condition that only comes along only once in every generation. Smirke, in contrast, got it absolutely spot on, realising that under these super fast conditions, you couldn't afford to play the classic waiting game. As they came up into the straight, Smirke gave Mahmoud a couple of tickles of the whip and he flew forward, overhauling Thankerton almost instantly and taking a lead that was to prove unassailable. As Smirke passed the finishing post he looked over his shoulder to see Taj Akbar, now in overdrive, gaining on him at truly awesome pace. If he'd been on Taj Akbar, Smirke remarked later, he'd have won the race by the time the rest of the field had reached Tattenham Corner.

Mahmoud. Yes, Mahmoud. This comes as no surprise to you now. You sort of knew it all along. Mahmoud won the 1936 Derby in the then record time of 2 minutes, 33 and ⅘ seconds. He was only the third grey to win the race since its first running in 1780, the other two being Gustavus in 1821 and Tagalie in 1912. A triumph not only for Mahmoud but also for Charlie Smirke, victorious in the chocolate and green colours of His Highness the Aga Khan. Smirke had almost given up the sport (and hope: he was reduced to sleeping rough) after being handed a Jockey Club ban in 1928 for allegedly "pulling" a favourite. The ban was rescinded only in 1933 and throughout the dark days, Smirke had vehemently protested his innocence. With much justification it

seems – the horse he had allegedly pulled was subsequently found to be "disturbed" and prone to spectacularly erratic behaviour.

Result and Starting prices
Mahmoud	100-8
Taj Akbar	6-1
Thankerton	33-1
Pay Up	5-1

The winner won by 3 lengths; ¾ of a length between second and third. It was the first time in 60 years that one owner had supplied the first two horses in the Derby. Both were also trained by Frank Butters.

The last time I'd been at Central Hall, Westminster, was to see Julian Cope. Cope and his band. In hindsight, this was always likely to be a mistake, because I was actually only a fan of Teardrop Explodes, which isn't exactly the same thing as being a fan of Julian Cope. And anyway I wasn't even an unreserved fan of Teardrop Explodes, just a huge fan of their second album, Wilder. I hated their first, Kilimanjaro, and they only made two albums. Plus I'd hardly heard anything that Julian Cope had done outside of those two albums. So I probably shouldn't have gone to a Cope gig with any great expectations. Except that he's one of those characters who, if they have any talent at all, it's in conjuring almost Messianic expectations out of nowhere and nothing.

But it turned out awful. Truly awful. Central Hall is not a performance venue. True, its conception is not a million miles away from that of a theatre – a raised stage sort of area projecting from the back wall, seating ranged back from it into the main body of the hall, balconies above. But it's too much of an echoing basilica, too much of a monumental stone cube, a cold box. You feel crushed by its epic aspirations, its gravity, its naked solidity, its sheer chunkiness. On the other hand, those qualities might make it an ideal venue for a sprawling indoor market. It would be like a temple for moneychangers.

So here I was again. It was a bitterly cold afternoon. One of those summer days that wouldn't surprise you at all if it had snow up its sleeve. Incessant drizzle since before dawn. Drizzle broken now and then by spells of mizzle. A fine gauze of droplets taking a long time to fall.

Not that this put off the tourists. They were massed thickly around the entrance to the abbey, with reinforcements moving up in more or less neatly organised battalions from the tube station. Japanese mainly, led from the front by umbrella-brandishing marshals.

I skipped up the steps of Central Hall unbuttoning my smugly sensible  cagoule, followed the signs past a deserted cash desk and, confused now and disorientated, I was in the midst of the film collectors' convention before I really knew it.

And hugely disappointed. Completely and utterly wrong-footed.

Because I'd got it wrong, hadn't I?

I imagined this convention spread over the vastness of the main hall like some neglected east European Bourse or a fleamarket in Istanbul. Something epic about it. Epic and mediaeval. I thought that I'd be confronted virtually by an infinity, an unfathomable richness. I wanted to feel a certainty that what I wanted was here if only I had the stamina to look and keep looking. Whereas in fact I found myself in the dinky version. The convention was housed in a side hall. It wasn't exactly a tiny hall but it was village church in comparison to the vast temple in my head. A village church by, say, the likes of a Hawksmoor. An elegantly classical space. A white room. More Masonic than Methodist – an austere simplicity and proportion about the space. White painted pillars, white walls, high clerestory windows down one side, with only the subtlest little plasterwork flourishes and curlicues to remind you that this place, however vaguely, had some sort of a higher purpose.

Long tables – boards on trestles – were set width-ways across the room, about ten banks of them, like hedges in a steeplechase. Trestles lining the inner walls too and the side aisle. One end of the room featured a stage area and this too had a stretch of tables across it. There was something faintly comical about this, because seated behind this barrier (halfway upstage naturally, so you could run their gauntlet) there was a perfectly spaced row of seated figures. They stared blankly into the body of the hall as if aloof, sitting in judgement, like a drama-free version of Leonardo's Last Supper. Or no – the Praesidium of the Supreme Soviet.

The floor of the hall was busy; there was a no-nonsense buzz about the place. Actually, it was even more intense than that. It swarmed, the room swarmed. The trestles were honeycombs, clinging with bees. And that in itself was surprising – I expected something a bit more refined, like an antiques fair, I suppose. This felt closer to a car boot sale. Some of the people here clearly had day jobs – proper shops with letter headings and VAT registration numbers – but they were easily outnumbered by those who traded mail order from back rooms. Or were the sorts of enthusiast who were here to here to swap doubles, suss out the market for bargains themselves and have a bit of a gossip.

I quickly realised, though, that they were dealing in the wrong sort of gear from the wrong era. There was some 60s stuff and lots of contemporary material, from the late 80s onwards. But the real focus, it seemed to me, was the 70s. That's what the real heat was all about. Star Wars, for instance. Tons of Star Wars freaks. But nothing from earlier days. Or hardly anything. Only the really cheesy stuff. Fred Astaire, Judy Garland stuff.

And you wouldn't believe the tat. A lot of merchandising spin-offs for instance. Darth Vader masks – and in fact whole fancy dress outfits. Toy car versions of James Bond's Aston Martin. Mickey Mouse watches. And then there was just a mountain of trashy card and wastepaper. Posters, bubble gum cards, old film magazines. Some people were even selling bootleg versions of films they'd taped off the television. And books. There were an awful lot of people trading books about film.

I picked my way towards the front (there was jostling, elbows were called for at some points) and as I looked up at the row of seated figures behind the long stretch of trestles on stage, I finally nailed them – they were actually like the official party of masters and guests at a school prize giving. So, one of these bored, stone-faced men (and they *were* all men) was my contact.

The stage was over three feet high, reached by a neat flight of wooden steps at each wing. I climbed up from the left, slightly nervous – as if by the very act of setting foot up here I had called attention to myself. Eyes, heads in the hall below would turn. I felt exposed. And the thing was that maybe other people felt this too because in all the time I'd been in the hall I'd not seen one other person browsing up here.

It was the same arrangement as down below in the rest of the hall – each section of trestle table was territory commanded by a different stallholder, but none were identified by name. So I just walked up to the one nearest me. "Jerry Verneau?" I asked.

The guy merely shrugged. He looked absolutely mortified. Mortified, I suppose, that anyone had even tried to talk to him. His part of this Last Supper

Prize Giving Praesidium tabletop – his zone – contained four very thumbed issues of an old film magazine. That was all. Believe me. That's all. Four old magazines protected by plastic folders. They were set out in a square formation. His fingers trembled nervously on the two nearest him.

He was desperate for me to go away.

So I asked all the way along the length of the table. It turned out that there were actually only five pitches up here – and at the last of them I got something of a result. Or almost.

"Jerry Verneau?"

"The pleasure's all mine Jerry," said the guy behind the table, rising and offering his hand. He'd been sitting slightly back from the table and he seemed terribly near the floor, slouched in one of those folding camping seats – the sort with stripy, garishly-coloured course-nylon-weave fabric and an aluminium frame that creaks horribly every time you shift your weight. When I see one, I always think *caravan*, which is probably my problem.

I took his hand and shook it, limply probably.

"No," I said. "I'm looking for Jerry."

"Oh," he said, dropping my hand. "Sorry."

Mahmoud. You died without being able to memorise that, Mr Memory.

No. Uncle Tom wouldn't deliberately have misled me. He was too sentimental. There was a stiffness about uncle Tom – a very 1930s quality that you recognise instantly when you watch a film like The 39 Steps. That's the point; that's the point I keep coming back to. If he ever indulged in mischief, he would telegraph it really obviously. He just didn't do deadpan. He probably thought that deadpan was dishonourable. Morally reprehensible. It's something to do with high moral seriousness.

As I left returned to the entrance hallway, the heavens opened. Straight ahead, across the immense gloom of the hallway (mausoleum-like, a cold stone immensity of its space), the main doors of the temple had been flung open for some reason. They revealed an intense patch of light, the light of the world beyond, and this light was alive with the downpour. It was spooky, this almost overpowering light though it was raining. Spooky to witness it across the dense ecclesiastical gloom of that vast, stone-enclosed space. My footsteps echoed as

I crossed towards that light and the seasurge sound of the rain lashing down.

I stood in the doorway, just over the threshold, not quite on the pavement, still within the shelter of the entrance portico. I'd not seen rain like it in years. Each time I thought it was letting up, it seemed to strain again and down it would come, more stinging and vicious than ever, sweeping and squalling in dense bands. It lashed so hard against the street that a light mist formed close to the ground, almost like theatrical drifts of dry ice, wisps of cold steam that wreathed and curled and were whipped away.

I watched this for perhaps twenty or so. No-one came and no-one went. The street was deserted. The world had taken cover. I watched until it became banal, this violent rainfall, incessant and unrelenting. I decided I'd walk, at least to the corner and back. Victoria Street was deserted. Only occasionally did a car pass, its tyres hissing on the streaming road. There were growing pools of floodwater along the lengths of the gutters.

I eventually turned back, I suppose. I returned once more to stand in the temple's entrance doors – still, uncannily to my mind, wedged wide open – and I smoked a cigarette. My fingers were so damp that I wet one side of the cig-arette as I fumbled it, coldly and clumsily, to my mouth.

I suppose I thought about a lot of things that day, while the world was empty.

On the Sunday nearest his 80th birthday, there was a birthday lunch for him at Golf Hall and most of the usual suspects tipped up. I was there with my girl-friend, a girl who, by then, I was living with. Nobody much approved of the fact that we were unmarried or *Living in Sin*, as they put it. Tom especially was *disappointed*. Which I suppose was predictable, him being an Elder of the Kirk and everything.

All of which meant that there were sometimes stresses and strains at family gatherings during this period – and indeed, before the end of the afternoon, my girlfriend had locked herself in the bathroom in floods of tears.

That was at least partially down to the amount of alcohol we ripped into that afternoon. All of us, or almost all of us. It turned into an epic session. Which is sort of an excuse and also not an excuse at all.

The truth is that I've never really known how to deal with this memory – because it's one of those instances where you feel immense guilt despite the fact that you are not guilty. It is one of those memories that can still keep me

awake at night. I feel its pain keenly. It can even ambush me now and then —
walking down a busy street, say, or on a tube train — and when it does, it can
make me cry out involuntarily. A sharp little half-suppressed cry. A cry that I
have learned not to apologise for or feel embarrassed about. There are only a
handful of memories that can do this. Certainly fewer that half a dozen.

The elderberry wine. The wine that a girlfriend (the very same one, probably, now I come to think of it) said reminded her of graveyards. The lunch had
started sedately, with proper, bought-in-the-supermarket wine being offered
sparingly, in keeping with the spirit of a Scottish Sabbath. It was almost certainly Riesling. Uncle Tom had a thing about German white wines, some of
which could be spectacularly sweet, cloyingly sweet, but on special occasions
he would stretch to an almost-decent Riesling. He probably had a couple of
bottles on hand.

Of course there were lots of toasts. And then I think the main course was delayed for some reason. So the supposedly good wine ran out and the elderberry was called into action pretty early on. A dangerous sign on its own. But then someone, probably father, would have made some sort of vaguely provocative comment. Something to the effect that a lot of rubbish was talked about wine, because it all tasted more or less the same. Which would have led to some sort of a tasting challenge. Tom had several vintages of his elderberry laid down. And in fact, now he came to think of it, the very latest vintage would now be available, if anyone was interested in tasting it. Elderberry nouveau.

We did. On balance we did. Me, my brother, father, the girls. Tom too, obviously. And the others, the old aunties and mother, became caught up in this too. Within 20 minutes or so, it had gone from a sober (ish) Sunday lunch to a raucous party. It was a riot – a civilised sort of a riot but a riot nonetheless. Just about anything anyone said turned out to be possibly the funniest thing that anyone had said, ever. The room rocked with loud laughter and suddenly we found we were all clinging to the table like shipwrecked sailors to a raft. The drunken hilarity reached its height when the apple pie pudding arrived and aunt Mary realised there was no fresh cream so we had to make do with aerosol cream.

And that absolutely brought the house down.

People were hurting. You could see it in their eyes. They were crying. Genuinely. They were troubled. In trouble. But they couldn't stop it. They were howling with laughter. Baying. Squealing. Squeaking. Braying. It was out of control. They couldn't stop.

I stopped them.

Tom was sitting at the head of the table. I was at the top end, at his left hand. I was doubling with a laughter that looked like tears.

I grabbed the sleeve of his jacket, probably because if I hadn't I'd have slipped away.

"We'll remember you party now," I said.

There was a twinkle in his eyes as he turned to me. They were already moist from all the laughter in the room but there was a mischievousness there too. A sentimental mischievousness. "Who says I'm going anywhere?" he said.

The next one I sent was clipped from the front page of the Times. Again it was

been to re...
at the sharp e...
Minister's spokesman said.

Ben Kingsley, who won an
Oscar for his depiction of
Gandhi, is made a knight for
services to drama.

...co.
...ces to the fil...
Further reports, p...
Leading
Review, p...

made a knight
a CBE

...neral in New York
...special recogni-
...ir "exceptional
...he 11 September
...which dozens of
...ned. They include
...ris, the Consul
...receives a knight-
...acan Taylor, the
...f Mission, who is

...wn

...t individuals, not
...d on computers.
...clear that she
...th plans drawn
...arling, the Sec-
...for Work and
...v benefit fraud
...,s to suspects'
...ounts. She has
...proposals for
...s.

...last acts in
...aw up guide-
...'s that they
...tients before
...entists, drugs
...hers and uni-
...to people's

...Mrs France
...g more high-
...ctor job before
...ssibly in her
...e such as polic-
...a Service.

...ncy

...n of the in-
...tomic policy."
...elp to create
...tity" among
...ded, giving a
...to European

...hes, page 3

EATHER

one of those ads you find across two columns down at the bottom corner of the page. Eight inches high by just over three inches across. The copy heading read:

WHY NOT BE A WRITER?

"As a freelance writer," the opening paragraph stated, "you can earn good money in your spare time, writing the stories, articles, books, scripts etc. that editors and publishers want." All you needed to do was sign up for the home study course. There was a FREE CALL telephone number, an email address or, if you preferred, a coupon to cut out. The testimonials from satisfied customers were superb. "My first three novels are all best sellers!" stated one with admirable restraint. "I was paid a £25,000 advance for my novel 'Red'," boasted another. (Red. Geddit?)

Again I addressed the enveloped left-handedly. To my dismay, it looked almost like presentable handwriting. I posted it just the same.

So, yes.

We'll remember your party now.

"Who says I'm going anywhere?" he replied, half-defiantly.

Sometimes, when it ambushes me, I can still hear him saying it. He had a very deep, rumbling voice for the most part, though it whistled slightly over sibilants. A silence grew. It wasn't sudden or instantaneous or anything. It just sort of arrived with a forlorn inevitability. I don't think anyone really knew why they'd stopped squealing and howling other than maybe having a vague sense that something had happened. A vague understanding that maybe something was up.

My eyes were widening.

Then the horror. The realisation. I could feel the smile draining from my face. I could feel the blood draining from my head.

I was sinking now.

I was ashamed. Not the shame of embarrassment but a cold shame that tasted of ashes. The shame that comes with the knowledge that something is lost.

The moment passed. Actually, I think it passed pretty rapidly, with an absolutely minimum of drama. The silence didn't last for long. People moved swiftly on. It was as if they'd caught the tiniest fragment of sense from something they knew they were never likely to understand and were unlikely to pursue. Ghosts and angels, signs in the sky of distant bad weather. The volume returned, the laughter eased in again, but maybe now it was less secure in itself. The hints of hysteria had gone; and somehow it was as if a forest fire had been blown out by an explosion.

Everyone was talking. Talking nonsense, talking over each other, talking to no-one and to anyone who would listen. All but myself and Tom, two people sat in silence, two people who'd failed to understand each other in a far more profound way.

It must have been half two, quarter to three when I returned to the convention. It was still busy, the place still buzzed, but the atmosphere was somehow just a fraction less intense. In the heart of the melee it looked as if there was less elbowing going on. I don't know why, but my mission suddenly seemed daunting again. It seemed as if everybody here knew everyone else and I was the only one not on the inside. And also, I decided, this was all a front – their real business wasn't film, it was something else entirely, something numinous, inexplicable yet horribly pernicious.

I found myself climbing the steps once more, up onto the stage. For some reason I walked right along its front, one side to the other, looking down into the hall, as if sizing up an audience. And then I walked back again until I was dead centre. A recklessness had taken hold of me. I just stood there, as if commanding people to look at me, yet somehow safe in the knowledge that were not going to. And of course they didn't. I lorded it over them for what seemed like ages.

I was in fact Hannay at the public meeting. The one where he's mistaken for the big shot politician they've invited to make a speech on behalf of the local Liberal candidate. Usually I cringe at this sort of thing in films, because they do it a lot don't they, acting out variations on your worst nightmares. And being thrust, unprepared, into the spotlight, is indeed one of my worst nightmares. I can imagine my blind panic and my staring eyes, my failure to speak, my inability to make even the tiniest noise, my trembling hands. I can hear a cringe-making silence, a heavy expectation, an awkward shuffling of feet, coughing, nervous tweaks in people's necks. The moment is cold, then it sweats – the temperature in the room leaps ten degrees. And then, with sweat trickling, the room freezes.

A clock ticks. They shoot you down.

Usually, as I said, I cringe at this sort of thing in films. But for some reason, the public meeting scene in The 39 Steps is okay. Don't ask me why.

I walked the line of tables again, asking for Jerry Verneau. Again, the same blank looks in response. I almost took it out on the guy on the end stall. The one sunk almost beneath the level of the table-top in his folding caravan chair. The one that looked like Randy Newman lookalike refugee from the 70s, with his bubble perm, beard and heavy black frame glasses.

"What is with you people?" I challenged.

He was wearing a red plaid shirt, which somehow made the beard and perm all the more unforgivable.

I picked up a book from his stall. I had a vague notion that the gesture would somehow look threatening. But he didn't really rise to the bait.

I wondered if it was still raining outside.

I told Beth I'd only be here for an hour or so. Somehow, though, the whole afternoon had gone. Soon the hall would be emptying, stalls packing up, a dog end feeling to the day. I could sense that already.

I put the book down. I turned to leave.

And then I came back again.

I picked up the book. And also a CD, almost at random. Beardy watched me do all of this, without comment.

"Twenty pound," he said.

I gave him a ten and two fives.

Then I turned to go.

I'd reached the top of the steps at the side when he called me back.

"Here," he said.

And yes, obviously I hadn't got the hang of this thing at all; because he was holding out a fiver. "Call it fifteen," he said.

And yet it remains true. True that it was Tom who implanted the most resonant piece of nonsense of the lot. My belief all these years that there are 39 steps between street level on Princes Street and the sunken concourse of Waverley

Station. Tom. Tom did it. Tom, who'd give you advance warning in triplicate if he was going to do anything as daring as pull your leg.

Him. He did it. He was the one.

"Who says I am going anywhere?" I don't know why I didn't take him to task right away. I don't mean I should have confronted him. Gently, though, I should have put him right. Just between us two, later. Or even at the table, quietly, unfraid of being overheard, yet simply and clearly. Or I could even have made a joke about it. Done it upfront and publicly.

Who says I am going anywhere?

But I was abject. I just felt profound dismay. It stopped me from functioning. Completely and utterly. I felt destroyed and I felt also that I had spoiled something too.

So, yes, I should have said something to him, absolutely I should – yet, on the other hand, I sometimes think it was a form of wisdom that stopped me from trying to untangle the misunderstanding. Something to do with not wanting to dig a deeper hole.

But it was cowardice. It boils down to cowardice.

"Jerry Verneau," says the voice. It's a vaguely familiar voice.

And I'm so confused that all I can say is: "What?" A really irritable, snappy *what?*

"I'm sorry about the other day at the film convention. I really am."

"What?"

"Beard and glasses. Westminster Hall on Saturday. The stall on stage."

I laugh. An insipid, sniffly, vaguely sarcastic laugh. I'd known all along and yet, somehow, hadn't known.

"It was you all the time then?"

"Yeah. Sort of, yeah."

"And the accent?"

"What do you mean?"

"That first time we talked on the phone you had a fake American accent, like, I don't know, a disc jockey."

And of course, I'd answered my own question yet again. But he answered it anyway, in his own way. Sincerely and matter-of-factly.

"That's just something I do now and then," he said.

I'd have deserved it hugely if he'd added, *for a joke*. Something I do now and then, *for a joke*. And I'd have deserved it even more if he'd gone on to explain to me what a joke was. I'd always somehow assumed that this guy, this Jerry Verneau, was a sad character living in a fantasy world. Maybe, though, I'd got that wrong. Maybe that was me.

Because he seems genuinely concerned. Like a big brother. And I can't help myself. "So?" I find myself asking. "What? You're really Dudley Griffiths?"

He laughs, but it's more of a sigh. "Sort of," he says, "sort of."

I don't say anything for a while. And I think he senses that this has to take its own time. But eventually, he says: "You still there?"

"Yes."

"I can give you the name of someone who almost certainly has what you're looking for. Or can probably help you. If this guy doesn't know, no-one will. But he's a bit eccentric and... he's a bit odd. I'll give you an address and you can write to him."

He got through a lot of shotgun cartridges but they were always kept in the same ancient box. It wasn't a big box either – its dimensions were roughly those of a bag of flour. Maybe slightly bigger. The cardboard it was made of was unusually thick. It was old, almost ancient, frayed, felt-like and soft at its edges and corners, its surfaces almost greasy, slightly shiny from centuries of handling. It was held together by massive staples, epic staples, and though they didn't seem to show signs of rust, a pink seepage tinged the cardboard around them.

Every time he bought new cartridges, he must have emptied them into this old box. So he must have liked it for some reason. He'd obviously been doing it for decades.

The box was in the cupboard by the kitchen door, near to where the gun lived, propped in its alcove. Sometimes though, the box was left out on the working surface. We were forbidden, absolutely forbidden, to touch this box of cartridges.

When we could – on summer afternoons, usually, when the grown-ups were taking tea outside on a ramshackle collection of ancient deckchairs and grey, brittle, desiccated wooden garden furniture – we sneaked back into the kitchen and took the lid off the box. It came smoothly, but with a hint of resistance, the elastic reticence of vacuum. And then they were revealed. We picked them out daintily, almost with reverence, fingering them nervously. The casings were orangey red, waxy; the caps were shiny bronze, almost golden.

We were forbidden, absolutely forbidden, to touch the gun too.

We weren't really interested in the gun.

Steven Danilo. That was the name he gave me. Steven Danilo. Was this, at last, the man at the core of this piece? Would this be the enigmatic character that I'd eventually interview? Was this the retired projectionist?

The thing is, Tom's words carried weight. I mean, despite everything. Despite his manifest flaws. His conceitedness. The sentimentality that belied his physical strength. And the foolish denial of his weaknesses. His words carried weight because he commanded the storm.

We grew up feeling that the stadium, Murrayfield Stadium, was in his back garden. That it belonged to him, that it was his fiefdom. And it was true. International matches took place in the grounds of his house. On his premises. Or so we thought. That's how it *felt* to us when we were small.

Sometimes, when we were old enough, we were allowed to attend. The whole family, of course, would turn up at his house at Murrayfield on match days. Family, friends, general hangers-on. Most were there for the crack and the pre-, during- and after-match drinking. They tended to cluster round the black and white television in Tom and Mary's living room during the game – with the windows open for added atmosphere if the weather would allow. Some of the men might wander over and squeeze their way onto the terracing if they felt like it. And there were always a half dozen or so tickets for the main stand too. These tickets were generally for seats right down at the touchline by the tunnel – in fact, they were for the second or third front row, right behind the team doctor and the replacements. To get to these seats we'd often come through the back of the stand, past the dressing rooms and out through the tunnel.

Even for an eight or a nine year old this was an awesome, almost terrifying experience. It was sort of thing that could leave you blasted and speechless for days. The dressing room area was scary enough. The corridor that separated the two teams was an area of intense activity. People with unchallengeable purpose coming and going, doors banging, people talking too fast and too loud, people spilling their nerves like blood. Just the sheer intensity of that zone was something that you couldn't possibly mistake even though you were just passing through. A mixture of fear and excitement and of… almost of panic. The smell of damp concrete, linament, turf, whisky, pipe smoke and something more, a metallic smell in the air that was almost a taste. A tanginess. It was as if something awful was about to happen As if someone was about to be executed or assassinated and no-one could or would do anything about it.

And then as you passed through this barely restrained hysteria you became aware that you had entered an area that was both sacred and awesome, an area that everyone seemed to be avoiding. They didn't even want to look in this direction. But you were walking into its loneliness and you were becoming aware that the differently-textured light at the end of the tunnel was… well, it was finality. The pitch, the stadium, the crowd, history, destiny. The end of the tunnel was an aperture, a rectangle of light that dilated slowly at first and then opened up alarmingly as you put one foot almost reluctantly in front of the other. The first sense you had of the crowd was of an intense density of movement, a mighty swarming. And indeed, all you could hear at this stage was a buzzing. A big murmur with a stinging edge to it.

Then it hit you. As you broke from the tunnel's mouth it hit you. A wall of noise. It fell like a wave, it burst in upon you, it filled your head. It was the rush you get when you have your ears syringed. And it had a heat too. It warmed your ears and your cheeks. And yet drained them too. It made you feel you were losing your balance or your sanity or both. You wanted to fall to the ground, to embrace it, to enfold yourself in it, curled in the foetal position. It was all too much. And yet (you sort of knew this), this was nothing near boiling point – the teams would not be out for a few minutes yet. This was as nothing; this wasn't the roar, this was just the anticipation of the roar. And yet you felt that all eyes were on you, that the crowd would at any second rouse itself and devour you, tearing you limb from limb.

For a child, this is as awesome as it gets. There was something raw and elemental here, something basic. Something pure and distilled. A ferocity, a violence. It was frightening, yes, but it was more than that. There was something fundamentally addictive at play here too. Something final, beyond argument, beyond good and evil. A reckoning.

This was Tom's. It was his doing. And so it was true. He was Master of the Apocalypse.

***

Steven Danilo. I got nothing from the name. Sometimes a name will give you an image. An aura. A sense of the person who might inhabit such a combination of letters.

But Steven Danilo?

I couldn't even get a feel for how old he was. And was that a Mediterranean name? Or east Europe? Or even African? My instinct said Balkans. But what did that mean even if it were true? That his family came here in 1914? Or 1939? Or during the Hungarian uprising of 1956? But so what?

The 39 Steps: a pair of handcuffs, a pair of stockings, a fish.

The aerosol can of whipped cream. At Tom's 80th birthday lunch. That's what really did for us. I only found out about this recently. Apparently, the propellant they used to use was nitrous oxide. Lots of it. Nitrous oxide just happens to be better known as laughing gas. By the time we'd all squirted cream on our apple pie, the room was absolutely drenched in laughing gas.

We didn't stand a chance.

And the awesomeness of the Murrayfield event was underlined by the fact that there were many casualties. You had more of a sense of this if you stayed back at the bungalow on a match day. Because one of the outbuildings was the First Aid Station. I think this was where the chickens were normally kept. (I've only just realised why we had chicken so often at Tom and Mary's when they were at Murrayfield. And why it tasted so good. We ate his chickens. He'd go out in the morning and wring a chicken's neck and at dinner we'd be eating it.) A low brick-built building like a barn separated from the main house by only a couple of yards.

In here on international days there were half a dozen cots (khaki canvas stretched on wooden frames, like army camp beds) on which the fallen were laid. When I was smaller especially, I would always sneak out and try to catch a glimpse of what was going on in here, though the St Andrew's ambulance men would always shoo you away. When I asked, I was always told that the men laid out in here had "passed out".

They always did the briskest business in the First Aid Station during the Welsh game. Eventually I was made to understand that this was something to do with the fact that some Welshmen could not "hold their drink". But this was always said with a great sense of amusement and fun. Everyone loved the Welsh game more than the others and the fact that the Welsh could not hold their drink was, I reckoned, something to do with this.

To be fair, the adults said, they gave it their all, the Welsh. After a week of it, who could blame them if they passed out? And it was true. The Welsh were in town all week and it was well known that they drank the pubs in Rose Street dry. On match day they staggered, an unsteady army, the two miles from the west end to the ground, stopping often for refreshment along the way.

We liked the Welsh.

The French were volatile and mercurial and they were cruel to animals, bringing cockerels all that way under their jackets to throw them on the pitch.

The English were insipid and bloodless and so desperate to prove themselves superior in every way that they made fools of themselves and came across as weak and humourless.

The Irish were a fractious rabble.

But the Welsh were passionate. They gave their all. They had real blood in their veins and they sang rousing songs as if their lives depended it. They came from down coal mines and had sneaked off to the game fourteen to a transit van and the foreman down the mine would pretend not to notice. Underground was a magical place. It was well known you only had to whistle down the pit and up would pop yet another prop forward with a flattened nose and cauliflower ears.

But they also became the worst for wear and passed out.

Though the area around Tom's bungalow was all fenced off, there was obviously a lot of coming and going through the back gate during a game, not least by the ambulance men. So anyone within the ground could come into his back garden – but why would they want to with the big game going on?

One day someone did though. It was a Welshman. The second half had just started. I could hear that. But I'd sneaked out to see what I could see through the back door of the First Aid Station. And there he was at the end of the garden path, just beyond the Station. He was slouching and unsteady on his feet. When he saw me he smiled and made some sort of a vague gesture. Of greeting perhaps. Then he said something. I couldn't understand what it was because he was Welsh but I could sense that he wanted something. He repeated himself, this time with more urgency.

And I. Well, I just turned and walked away. I went back inside. I went and watched the match on the television. I didn't tell anyone there was a Welshman outside in uncle Tom's back garden, a Welshman who wanted something. I couldn't really find a way of doing it. I was only seven or eight. If father had been there I would have whispered it in his ear. But father was at the match.

I thought he might still be there, the Welshman, later, after the game had finished. And that he might be angry with me because he probably believed I'd understood him and had gone to get what he wanted. But he wasn't there. He'd gone.

You could hear the last of the crowd tramping past, beyond the tall hedge. They were like an army on the march. They really were.

Sometimes, leaving the ground, they sang. And when they sang they moved the earth.

Once, only once as far as I remember, I was brave enough actually to go into the First Aid Station. If you hung around for long enough an opportunity would always present itself but usually I was too scared to take it. I'd always hesitate on the threshold. This time, though, was different. I took a step or two inside. It was spooky. Only one of the fallen men was asleep. The others were lying very quietly. Unnaturally quietly. As if deeply chastened. They stared upwards. There was nothing to see up there. Just rafters. And a row of three hanging lightbulbs surmounted by shades made of tin and shaped like cooliehats. The brickwork was white painted to a height of about four feet. And then above that it was painted a maroon colour that was almost the same shade as the original bricks. I always thought that was an odd thing to do. Painting something the same colour as it already was.

It was truly spooky in there. As if death was there, hesitating just behind me. I felt a mild sense of trauma, of shock. I felt faint. There, in that absolute stillness, the far-off noise of the crowd rising and falling and stirring, but no more really than a whisper, like the sound a distant sea might make.

It was like a field dressing station behind the front line.

So, yes, for a few days a year Tom was many things. Not just Master of the Apocalypse, the Frost Magus, a Prospero. But also a General. A Field Marshall. We, the children and the women left behind in the house while the match was on, were in his baggage train. The chickens too.

Who says I'm going anywhere? he said.

***

We opened it eventually. I mean we had to eventually, didn't we? When I say we, I mean she, obviously. Beth. Beth opened it.

I don't know how many days later this was. I was down in the kitchen waiting for the pasta to boil. She slapped the report onto the table in front of me and laughed a bitter laugh.

An ironic laugh that was not really a laugh at all.

"It's pathetic," she said. "Absolutely pathetic."

The Institute report. It was over 20 pages long and each page was black with laserjet ink. It looked a closely argued, thorough report. But it wasn't. It told us nothing we didn't know. In fact it got lots of things wrong; and it completely ignored lots of the points they said they were going to have a go at answering.

It was. It was pathetic. Absolutely pathetic. It was a joke.

It's not Jerry Verneau. Or Vernaut. Or any of the other variations I'd considered. Two weeks later, I'm looking at the credits on the back of the video case of The 39 Steps. And there it is. Of course. Verno. *Jerry Verno – traveller.* It's the name of the actor who played one of the men in the train compartment as Hannay heads north. One of the travellers in women's underwear. One of the horse racing enthusiasts. Which one was he? I wondered. Which of the two? The slightly vacant, complacent one; or the sparky one, the cheeky chappie with glasses?

But back a bit. Back a bit, in fact, to the end. It's sometimes only in hindsight that you recognise the endings to things. Because the ending often comes sooner than you think and way before you expect it to. It happens in the strangest and unlikeliest places. And in hindsight it turns out that the rest is merely a playing out of the consequences.

In this case the strangest and unlikeliest of places turns out to be Pizza Express. Pizza Express in Islington. Tuesday. Lunchtime. I was sure I was going to end up eating alone. Or waiting for an hour and then leaving, hungry. It was all so tenuous because at no stage had anyone actually talked to anyone else. Robbie had left a message on my machine telling me to organise it; I'd left a message for Jules telling him to be here; then I'd left another message for Robbie telling him what I'd done. But Robbie, I knew for sure, got really nervous and had nosebleeds on those rare occasions when he was forced to leave central London – and Islington, if not exactly the giddy limit, must have been a daunting prospect. And Jules. Jules had far too much on his plate, what with him planning to travel to Blackpool (Blackpool on the coast of Bohemia) the next morning. He was hardly going to have time to put in a routine credentials lunch for the likes of Robbie, now was he? Not now he had bigger things like the Observer in his sights.

Wrong. Wrong again. In the end it turned out rather crowded. For a start, the three of us managed to converge on the Pizza Express doorstep at exactly the same time. Robbie, larger than life and (as the cliché would have it) twice as loud, was wearing a summery ensemble that gave more than a passing nod in the direction of Hawaii; Jules, far more buttoned-down, smart-but-casual and rather chipper, in a laconic but cheekily iconoclastic mode. The ultra dry Jules. Me the grist to their mill.

We were given a table upstairs – the biggish one against the middle window, a vertigo special, right up against the plate glass. We sat down, we ordered drinks, we looked at menus, the small talk bumped along – mainly Robbie finding endless ways to show how he could be larger than life and Jules showing he could not only be dry but also supportive of larger than life characters. I was already surplus to requirements.

Which is why, I suppose, I let my eyes wander the room. And which is why, I also suppose, I saw him. Colin. He was right in the corner, sitting alone at an intimate little table for two. My immediate reaction was to blank him completely. I hadn't wholly rationalised this – but I instinctively understood that something complex and unforeseen had happened to our friendship (however fitful that friendship had become) and that this was neither the time nor the place for either of us to have to confront that fact.

So, yes, I blanked him. As best I could, I tuned in once more to Jules and Robbie. But all I did was nod and smile at the increasing deftness of their by-play. They'd cut me out of this transaction. Basically, I kept drifting.

I stood.

"Sorry," I said. "I've just seen an old friend."

Colin still wasn't aware of my presence. But at some point as I crossed the room he must have spotted me. And it was the oddest thing. I hadn't seen this coming at all. The look in his eyes. It wasn't loathing exactly, but close. Actually, he looked sick. Thoroughly sick. His face turned grey and he looked thoroughly beaten. Hastily, he began gathering up his things, such as they were. That tatty old combat jacket he'd had for at least a decade. A book, some newspapers. He smiled wanly at me as he passed. "I'm sorry," he said. "Bit of an emergency."

I don't know what I thought. I suppose I must have stood there staring at his vacated table for ages. I didn't really know where (or how) to go from here. It crossed my mind that the best strategy would be to follow him. It would save my face and get me out of what was shaping up to be an excruciatingly boring lunch. But I didn't. I turned about and returned to our table, massaging my forehead.

"What was that all about?" asked Robbie.

It was my turn to smile wanly.

And sit there uncomfortably for a while as Jules and Robbie picked up the thread of their conversation once more.

Things, though, were not about to get any better.

About ten minutes later, Kate appeared.

She'd obviously just that minute come up the stairs and had somehow stalled at the top and was rummaging about for something in her bag. At first I assumed she'd seen me from the street below, what with our table being right up against the window. I was wrong, obviously. The things is, I didn't realise she wore glasses these days – and that was what she was rummaging around for in her bag. So there I was, just sitting there, smiling at her; smiling in anticipation of the moment when our eyes would meet, wondering what sort of look there'd be on her face when they did. She found them eventually, her glasses; she put them on daintily, with charming awkwardness. Then she surveyed the room, frowning. Her eyes must have passed over me two or three times, me sitting there smiling at her in anticipation.

And then of course our eyes met, as they were bound to eventually. As was destined. But she coloured. She went the deepest red, right to the lobes of her ears. It was almost funny, really.

I don't know how long we stared at each other. Then she about–turned and disappeared off down the stairs. I followed. I caught up with her near the bottom of the stairs. Close enough to say her name without shouting it. A whisper really, a desperate stage whisper. "*Kate.*"

Kate.

She turned. And she whispered back at me. Except she did it with a violent intensity that was like some awesome natural force.

"Leave me alone."

Leave me alone.

Like something cornered. Something frantic. Something sick and ill and lonely.

And all I could think about, standing on that stair long after she had gone, was that she obviously needed me more than ever.

Chapter twelve

I don't know when I made my decision, in fact I'm not sure I ever did, not really, even though it had a certain inevitability about it. I can't say for sure there was any definitive point along the way when I admitted to myself that the game was up.

You'd think that the letter from the Palmer Film Archive might have been conclusive. But it wasn't. Because, yes, the Institute report wasn't the only feeble piece of correspondence waiting behind the door when we got back from holiday. In among the circulars and the junk mail and the bills and the chain letters there was a letter from Caroline Palmer. It read: "Thanks for applying for one of our courses – and apologies for the late reply. Currently, we have no fixed dates for our courses. But you are on our mailing list. Thank you for your interest. Caroline Palmer."

In other words: Read my lips.

No. The truth is I was still pushing on numbly into this territory, barely aware that my efforts were increasingly dissipated and futile. On the other hand, at one stage (quite in contrast to the alienation I'd felt at the convention at Westminster Hall) I almost began to feel I was becoming part of a community of sorts. Or at least I was beginning to appreciate that this *was* a community of sorts. I'd started to gauge its extent. Its depth, its width, the richness or otherwise of its connections. I suppose it came down to the fact that I was beginning to feel more at home with its vocabulary. Also, the same names were recurring. The same ideas, the same possibilities. And you'd start to feel cool, slightly swaggery, because someone would offer a suggestion and you could say, "No, I've tried her. She can't help."

The guy you're talking to will warm to you and he'll say: "Oh, how is she? I haven't talked to her in years."

And maybe he'll tell you about the last time they met. How they'd got really drunk together one evening at the Berlin Film Festival in the late 80s – this was just before the Wall came down of course.

And you'll chuckle along as if you were there. Because the point is – suddenly you are. Genuinely. You're there. And you tell him about a time you were drunk in Berlin – and he knows exactly the cellar bar you're talking about, the one with the battered old cigarette-burn piano standing up against a dirty bare brick wall near the corner. And the whole thing begins to cross-pollinate. There will be a touch of regret in his voice and you can sense that he was secretly in love with this woman – this woman that you had a brief chat with only last week – but nothing came of it for some reason.

So yes, I've lost count of how many people I've talked to now on this story. All sorts of people on the fringes of the film industry. The lower slopes, obviously. The distributors, the rights owners, the media owners, the cinema chains – cogs, small wheels, but people who nonetheless sometimes, despite all odds, know a little of the history of the industry they work in. Then there are the institutions. Your BFIs and your MOMIs. And there are also lots of other little museums and collections, either privately-owned or attached to universities and colleges. The Bill Douglas Centre For the History of Cinema and Popular Culture, for instance. It contains 18,000 books on cinema-related topics; 5000 periodicals, ranging from fan magazines to scholarly journals; 4000 postcards, including images of stars, studios and cinema buildings; 4000 still photographs of stars; 3000 items of sheet music related to films; 2500 programmes from film festivals and premieres, etc; 2200 cigarette cards; 500 records; 1400 items of press and publicity material; plus stereocards, stereotransparencies, toys, jigsaws, games, handbills, posters, greetings cards, letters, magic lanterns, magic lantern slides, zoetropes and praxinoscopes.

And in exactly the same way as I had been pestering people with a request that is just a little bit left field, a little bit outside their ken, on the periphery of their vision, so I too started to attract unsolicited mail. Your name gets out. Out and about. Someone, for instance, wrote to me about their collection (currently seeking lottery funding for a permanent housing) of cinema-related ashtrays.

Could I pass on their details to any relevant parties?

At one point I was invited to participate in activities in the ongoing campaign to draw attention to the plight of the ABC Cinema on Whiteladies Road, Bristol. This art deco cinema, which was built in 1921 and which still boasts (boasted?) its original ballroom, was given a Grade 2 listing in 1999 but the listing didn't stipulate what it can and cannot be used for. The campaign, backed by Keep Cinema Local, was to prevent the building being turned into a gym.

I don't know if they succeeded.

And then of course there are the traders, obviously – people with shops, people in the mail order business. Mavens, marketmakers, facilitators, salesmen. People in the optics business (selling, say, telescopes but also projectors and cameras and therefore all sorts of celluloid related products and peripherals), people in the consumer electronics business, people in the memorabilia and antiques and collectibles business. And whole hordes of archivists, both professional and amateur. Maybe I'd become – in my own modest way – a collector of these people.

The point is that you suddenly hit critical mass and these people are cross-referencing each other. You want to be blasé and sophisticated about this realisation but the truth is that it makes you warm inside. Suddenly you're connected. Or at least, you feel you're connected. You're not just in the city, you're downtown.

But we were waiting again. That's the inevitable truth of it. Still waiting. It was something less than waiting, as it goes – lethargy took us now and dragged us down. For days after we read the Institute report we did nothing with Charlie. We fed her and changed her and at an appropriate time took her and put her to bed, but for the most part we propped her up within a nest of cushions on the living room sofa and left her there watching videos. A lethargic miasma

seemed to have enveloped her too for she stared blankly at the screen, allowing the images merely to play across her greeny-brown eyes.

The eyes that were so blue when she was born. A deep blue, an intense blue, a more than natural blue, a blue of glass beads and lagoons and South Sea island rock pools. Even the whites of her eyes, so opalescently clean and uncorrupted, seemed even more pure for the fact that they were tinged with the palest of pale blues.

And then, when we managed to shake off a least some of the lethargy (it lasted less than a week in truth), we launched into a time of endless walks, taking it in turns to push Charlie in her buggy. These were silent walks, desperate walks, pursued without planning or discussion. We'd just seem to know – all three of us – that it was time to set off yet again. To head east towards the River Lea across Springfield Park, where our favourite tree, a voluminous yet delicately feathered green cloud of a walnut tree, was to be found; or south into Clissold and the chestnut avenue of Queen Elizabeth Walk; or round in a labyrinthine, rambling journey through baking and subdued streets, starting out westward and almost improbably – for it often felt as if we must have wandered by accident into new and other lives on those unfamiliar streets – winding our way back.

Silent, the three of us, a spooky little group.

Uncanny.

Stood at a crossing, say.

Waiting. Obviously waiting.

Mahmoud. Mahmoud's mother was Mah Mahal and Mah Mahal's mother was Mumtaz Mahal. Mumtaz Mahal (named after the Mughal empress in whose memory the Taj Mahal was built) was described by The Bloodstock Breeders Review as "wonderful, as near to perfection as imagination can conceive". Those who saw her race said that she was quite plainly "electrifying". Of these things are legends made.

There was, according to contemporary reports, a suitably "electric atmosphere" the evening she came up for auction in 1922. The consensus was that this spotted grey daughter of The

Tetrarch was the most perfect filly ever seen and it was no surprise when the bidding surged towards record levels. In the end, the Aga Khan paid 9100 guineas for her. He would not regret it for one minute. In her first year of racing (as a two-year-old) she won race after race after race in "facile fashion". Racegoers nicknamed her The Flying Filly because she was untouchable over sprint distances.

MAHMOUD ① (FR) gr. H, 1933 DP = 0-4-28-8-4 (44) DI = 0.69 CD = -0.27 - 11 Starts, 4 Wins, 2 Places, 2 Shows Career Earnings: $85,413

BLENHEIM (GB) br. 1927 [CS]	BLANDFORD (IRE) br. 1919 [C]	SWYNFORD (GB) dkb/br. 1907 [C]	JOHN O'GAUNT (GB) b. 1901	ISINGLASS (GB)	br. 1890
				LA FLECHE (GB)	dkb/br. 1889 *
			CANTERBURY PILGRIM (GB)* ch. 1893 Profile	TRISTAN (GB)	ch. 1878
				PILGRIMAGE (GB)	ch. 1875 *
		BLANCHE (GB)* b. 1912	WHITE EAGLE (GB) ch. 1905	GALLINULE (GB)	ch. 1884
				MERRY GAL (GB)	b. 1897
			BLACK CHERRY (GB)† br. 1892	BENDIGO (GB)	dkb/br. 1880
				BLACK DUCHESS (GB)	br. 1886 *
	MALVA (GB) b. 1919	CHARLES OMALLEY (GB) dkb/br. 1907	DESMOND (GB) blk/br. 1896	ST SIMON (GB)	br. 1881
				LABBESSE DE JOUARRE (GB)	blk. 1886
			GOODY TWO-SHOES (GB) b. 1899	ISINGLASS (GB)	br. 1890
				SANDAL (GB)	b. 1885
		WILD ARUM (GB) b. 1911	ROBERT LE DIABLE (FR) b. 1899	AYRSHIRE (GB)	br. 1885
				ROSE BAY (GB)	b. 1891
			MARLIACEA (GB) b. 1902	MARTAGON (GB)	b. 1887
				FLITTERS (GB)	b. 1893
MAH MAHAL (GB)* gr. 1928	GAINSBOROUGH (GB) b. 1915 [C]	BAYARDO (GB) b. 1906 [P]	BAY RONALD (GB) b. 1893	HAMPTON (GB)	b. 1872
				BLACK DUCHESS (GB)	br. 1886 *
			GALICIA (GB) dkb/br. 1898 Profile	GALOPIN (GB)	b. 1872
				ISOLETTA (GB)	b. 1891
		ROSEDROP (GB) ch. 1907	ST FRUSQUIN (GB) dkb/br. 1893	ST SIMON (GB)	br. 1881
				ISABEL (GB)	ch. 1879
			ROSALINE (GB) b. 1901	TRENTON (NZ)	br. 1881
				ROSALYS (GB)	b. 1894
	MUMTAZ MAHAL (GB)* gr. 1921 Profile	THE TETRARCH (IRE) gr. 1911 [I]	ROI HERODE (FR) gr. 1904	LE SAMARITAIN (FR)	gr. 1895
				ROXELANE (FR)	ch. 1894
			VAHREN (GB) ch. 1897	BONA VISTA (GB)	ch. 1889
				CASTANIA (GB)	ch. 1889
		LADY JOSEPHINE (GB)* ch. 1912	SUNDRIDGE (GB) ch. 1898	AMPHION (GB)	ch. 1886
				SIERRA (GB)	ch. 1889
			AMERICUS GIRL (GB) ch. 1905	AMERICUS (USA)	ch. 1892
				PALOTTA (GB)	ch. 1893

She wasn't a stayer, though. She couldn't make the transition to longer distances as a three year old. She went to stud instead.

Once you start noticing them you really start noticing them. They're everywhere. Almost every day in the paper there's a new angle, a new take, a slightly different slant.

Just send in the coupon. I must be sending one about every two days. It has almost become a habit. A routine.

Just round the corner, a couple of blocks away, was the hedge. We often passed it. The guy (it was tempting to call him "The Hedge" too) was always out there, clipping it, caressing it. A privet hedge. It must have been over ten feet tall and the guy had a little pair of aluminium step ladders so he could get up there and do some clipping on the top. Because the thing was, he was a topiarist. He cut shapes into the top layer of the hedge. Geometric shapes, mainly. At each end there was an attempt at a ball – like a cannonball on a parapet. And, just in a bit from the balls, we find a couple of cones. But right in the middle was an attempt at a.

At a.

The thing was we were never quite sure.

A duck, we thought at certain times of the day or year.

A cockerel maybe? Was he Spurs?

He was West Indian, in his 60s probably and he was sort of withered. There was fight in him, I mean of course there was, to be out there day after day (he almost lived out there on the pavement and even when friends were round they'd hang out there with him, sometimes fetching chairs from the kitchen to sit on); but he was also sort of colourless. His skin was going grey: dull and rough and dry like the skin of a ginger root. When you passed by, unashamedly looking at his hedge, giving it the once and maybe the twice over, he didn't ever acknowledge you, he always managed to evade your eye and he looked sort of sheepish.

And the thing was, the hedge was miserable. The front gardens here were on the north side of the terrace and the hedge was completely overshadowed. It must have got a couple of hours of sun around noon in the summer on a good day if it was lucky. So it was all puny and shrivelled and threadbare, its leaves dark, malformed, ill-nourished. In a couple of places there were holes. Big holes. Not just so as you could see right through. I mean you could put your arm through without a scratch.

It was mangy. His shapes were ragged.

I wondered how long he had been struggling with this hedge. How many decades.

"It's pathetic. I mean it's beyond belief, isn't it?" I said. "Why would anyone want to put so much effort into something like that, with absolutely obviously no prospect of getting anywhere? Does he not actually see his hedge? I mean, what is the point?"

"Yes," said Beth, looking at me strangely. "Why would anyone want to do something as stupid as that?"

I looked often into Charlie's eyes. I was looking for many things. Me, I suppose. I was looking for me. Intelligence, I also suppose. Evidence of a basic spark, a seed. But mostly in wonder. And of course it is true that I have never felt anything as intense as the feeling I have for Charlie. It is something beyond love. Way beyond love. It is scary sometimes in its intensity. And yes, part of it is the surety that here is someone for whom you'd lay down your life. In the past, when I've heard people saying this sort of thing, I've always thought it sounded hollow and sentimental. A sort of melodramatic hyperbole. But now I know.

She tolerates my stare. Usually. She knows it is a look of worship and she can appreciate that. Only rarely does she seem uncomfortable, writhing slightly in a way that makes you feel as if you've been playing mind games with her – and the strange thing is that she's often right. When you're merely trying to provoke a reaction, she can sense it. Not that this happens very often. Usually it's just plain worship.

The thing was, I still had relatively high hopes for what was still my best lead. I had written almost immediately to this Steven Danilo character, outlining my legend. My cover story. Somehow this story had become more and more elaborate over the weeks – I suppose, in a way, because I was struggling towards authenticity. My father (in reality born in 1929, remember) was, I had decided, too young for a central role in this. It must have been, I reckoned, *his* father who was the projectionist in the 1930s. But according to this latest version of the legend, my father spent a good deal of his formative years in the projectionist booth while his father worked. (How do you describe what a projectionist does? Project?) I hadn't yet decided why this was the case – why he wasn't at home with his mother where ideally he should have been.

Perhaps, though, my father (my fictional father that is, my cover story father) had exaggerated the amount of time he spent in the projectionist's booth during the 30s. You know how this can happen – over the years, a few wondrous hours or days can expand to fill whole childhoods.

Another oddity of this evolving legend was the fact that the family's Scottish heritage had completely disappeared. When I imagined the small cinema in which my father's father worked (I somehow couldn't bring myself to think of him as my grandfather – my real paternal grandfather owned a garage in Edinburgh, though not the one on Causewayside designed by Charles Rennie MacIntosh. Apologies to anyone who I've perhaps misled in the past), I saw a tiny cinema in the West Country. Possibly Newton Abbot, I thought, but it would need research to confirm this.

And then, towards the end of the 30s my fictional father's father had accepted the position of head projectionist at a newly built white stucco art deco cinema somewhere in the southeast. Not the de la Ware Pavillion – I was pretty sure of that. And not necessarily on the south coast. Perhaps suburban London, I reckoned. He'd arrived at this pinnacle of his career via the White Ladies Picture House, Whiteladies Road, Bristol. Perhaps (I was merely able to speculate – I hadn't got this bit clear yet) some incident during a screening had made The 39 Steps an important film for him. Whatever the reason, though, its importance couldn't be denied. Needless to say, it would mean so much to him to be able to get a copy of the film itself. Or any artefact that could evoke it powerfully. (I reckoned it might be too bizarre to mention anything directly. Like, for instance, the handcuffs.)

At one point, she might ask something seemingly innocuous like: "You okay?"

And I'd day something like: "Yes. Yeah… I mean."

Is it what I mean?

There's a silence in which we both consider this unstated question.

"We should talk," she says when this silence begins to warp and bow.

"Maybe."

"I mean we should, though, shouldn't we? Talk about it?"

"Talk? Yes. Talk. Let's talk. Let's talk about it. Why don't we?"

***

But it's true – in the days since we'd read the Institute report, running battles were erupting far more regularly and more intensely. But what do you say to someone who goes to bed three times a night?

She'll say she's tired and moan about the fact that there's nothing on telly anyway. "Night-night," she'll say.

"Night-night," you'll say.

And the door will hardly have closed behind her when she'll pop her head back in and the next thing she'll say will always begin, "Don't forget…"

Instructions follow. Something I must remember to do tonight. Wash something up. Find something. Put the rubbish out.

So, okay, yes. You've told me ten times already.

And then she goes to bed. Or so you think.

About ten minutes later you hear her step descending the stair. She comes into the living room and she faffs around. You daren't ask her what she's doing or what she's looking for because there's an edge to this performance, brief though it is. She'll get in the way of the telly a couple of times, not that you're actively watching it. And then she'll ask you a spectacularly inane question – and because it is so spectacularly inane you bite your tongue to buy time and patience so you might just be able to refrain from giving it the reply it deserves. So there's perhaps a little flare up about you not answering and then she'll be off upstairs again.

And then about five minutes later she'll be down once more. She's looking for a glass. The glass she was drinking bottled water out of earlier. And she'll take it away and, having filled it again from the bottle in the kitchen this time, she'll come back and open the door a fraction and stand there looking at the telly for a couple of minutes.

Hanging there on the threshold, wraithlike.

And then she'll go.

Direct descendants of Mahmoud were not as prolific as the descendants of his grandmother, Mumtaz Mahal. I don't know if this is self-evident given that one is a subset of the other – in that, by definition, direct descendants of Mahmoud are also direct descendants of Mumtaz Mahal. The only racehorse I could name until recently, Shergar, was a Mumtaz descendant. The Mumtaz genes live on throughout the bloodstock world, and if a horse has sprint pace to burn, it often comes through her line.

But the descendants of Mahmoud form one of the strongest subsets of the awesome Mumtaz inheritance. For instance:

Mahmoud begat Almahoud.

Almahoud begat Natalma.

Natalma begat Northern Dancer.

Northern Dancer begat Nijinsky.

Nijinsky was a Triple Crown winner – St Leger, 2000 Guineas, Derby.

When I was at school, our year boasted a very promising junior sprinter. He had national medals at 100 yards. He had a deep voice and a moustache even though he was only 13 or 14. The masters tagged him Nijinsky, a nickname they used with great warmth and affection. I always wondered what that was about. I actually thought it was something to do with the moustache.

And yet, there are more considered moments. Moments in which she might ask: "So, what, he committed suicide?"

"What? Who?"

"Your uncle Tom."

"What! What makes you say that?"

"What you were telling me the other day. About his shotgun. It felt sort of sinister. I thought. I thought it seemed to be leading up to. I thought what you were leading up to. Was. Well."

The Hasids were awesome when they swarmed in the streets around our house. There's always going to be a visceral excitement about seeing normally-quiet streets suddenly flooded with people. Something elemental, evocative of early civilisation, a time when cities were young. And maybe also it's an apocalyptic feeling – this is how the streets will run thickly with people when the end is nigh, this is how it will be when all of the houses empty up all of their people. But it's not just that, it's something more banal too – it's to do with the fact that when you see crowds and you can't explain why they're there, you begin to fret that you're missing out on something.

One way or another they, the Hasids *en masse*, exert their own peculiar gravitational pull. They generate their own electricity too. When they move in numbers they move *you*, they clear your head, sharpen the senses; they smell of tingle-tongue battery terminals, zinc and racecourses.

Like when you open your front door and notice that the pavement at the end of your path is dense with black coats and clusters of black hats. And now, having opened your door, you're *really* aware of the megaphone. In fact, it's obvious it's being used nearby. You've been hearing this megaphone peripherally for a good five minutes or so but the truth is that it really hasn't registered. Until now, it has seemed incidental – an impressionist soundscape produced by a march or a demo happening far away, perhaps converging on Hackney Town Hall. Or so far off in fact that it could be ten or even 20 years ago, for instance that funding cuts rally at university in the early 80s.

But no, it's here – not very far down the road from the end of your path. That's more than apparent now. It's not exactly threatening to invade your space – your postage stamp patch of front space is well hedged in. But it's clearly, in some ways, *close enough* – and your spontaneous gut reaction is to resent (however vaguely) the figures you see immediately in front of your house out there on the pavement. How dare they mass on your borders, on the threshold you share with the outside world?

But you are excited and almost flattered too that this unexpected commotion has landed on your patch. It doesn't stop you from being Bolshie as you push out onto the pavement though. And immediately you see that this is hardly the epicenter. Nowhere near. The crowd has coagulated most thickly down at the far end, way to your right. And it just so happens, you are going that way.

What's happening, it seems, is this. Down there, there's a Volvo estate double parked. Actually, that's not true at all. It isn't double parked so much as just plain stopped in the middle of the road – and given the fact that there are cars parked down both sides, it has effectively blocked the whole road off. The Volvo's offside front door is open and there's a tall Hasid there, standing on the sill of the open door, towering above the car's roof, and he has this little matchbox of a microphone cradled in the palm of his hand. He's in his thirties, maybe. Pale, serious, glasses. And a Homburg, obviously. The cord of the microphone stretches into the car's interior; and there's a cluster of small horn speakers taped to the front roofrack bar of the car. He speaks into his palm and the words come out big and metallic. They echo, bouncing back and forward between the houses – this terraced street, this gulch, this genteel ravine of sash windows and painted frontages and rowan trees.

First thought is that this is a political meeting. Not a demo as such. Not even a rally. More an ad hoc thing. A spontaneous public airing of a fundamental grievance. The crowd feels sort of galvanised or coiled, especially round the Volvo where it's at its densest. There's an energy epicenter here. Mobs, you can't help thinking, have hotspots like these. And it is an entirely male gathering, of course.

And yet you realise almost instantaneously that you're wrong in this assessment. This mob notion. Or at least you're only partly right. Because there's a melancholy in the speaker's voice as he addresses the crowd and you begin to plug into that melancholy – especially as you start moving move through the crowd.

Someone has died (you're almost willing to bet) in one of the houses down at the far end and this is the "home" bit of the funeral oration, the bit done in situ. It's as if everyone has just streamed out of the service and headed here to leave some sort of a mark on a particular bit of space.

Is this how it works?

But the thing is, I'm actually too arrogant to ask anyone what is going on. I merely leverage my way through, saying "excuse me" with the sort of hard edge to my voice that makes it a parody of politeness.

Eventually I catch up with a black woman doing the same – and we form a tacitly acknowledged double act as we cut a chord (geometrically speaking) across the fringe of the crowd's true core and begin to make faster progress as we break out the other side – there's less of a tail to the crowd down past the man with the microphone, and we are soon on the true fringes, where the hangers-on and passers-by stand and gawp. And we stop too, this black woman and me, and we look back. She smiles, shakes her head and rolls her eyes.

"I know," I say. "It's bizarre, isn't it?"

She rolls her eyes again. They are very yellow eyes. Her skin is bluish, dark and shiny, too shiny, like glass. She's a lot older than I'd first taken her for – a foolish early judgment because I could only see her from behind. But still. Her hair, wiry, sits low to the curve of her skull as if cropped; it's becoming patchy. Thinning. Seeing her from the front, that much is now evident. Her smile is big, full on, but there's an uncertainty, a wariness lurking somewhere in there too – as if she expects at any moment to be ordered to stop smiling.

We stand there as the swell of amplified words rises and falls, falls and rises. An annunciation. It might be something like that. A truth revealed to the world from a guy clinging to the side of a Volvo. One Day in Stamford Hill that

Changed the World.

"Yes," I say again. "Bizarre."

We move off. I go to the shops. When I return, less than five minutes later, the street is empty. Absolutely, unambiguously empty. Unsettlingly so – because there isn't the detritus that you see for instance in the streets around a stadium once a big sporting event has finished, the litter that confirms your suspicions that something has indeed happened. Here there is nothing. Except of course for the stuff that you expect to be here. The Volvo has gone but the usual parked cars are where they usually are. The houses and their gardens are as they ever were. But it is as if they have been etched clean. When filled with dark-dressed figures, the street seemed giant, epic: now it seems tiny and infinitely parochial.

Talk, yes, perhaps we should talk.

The reply was in coloured pencil. I kid you not. From Steven Danilo. The handwriting was coherent, if not exactly joined up. But still. Coloured pencil. A pale mauve colour. The message read:

> The rights to this film in the UK was owned by The Rank Organisation (now Carlton TV). I understand Rank junked all the old prints, and they have only retained a couple of good prints for the archives. They will never ever let a print come onto the market.

A longish message considering it was in mauve coloured pencil. Because the writing was huge. It took up most of two sides of a sheet (good quality, textured, with a watermark) of A4. On the one hand it seemed sort of sane and considered – and you'd certainly not want to hold a trivial little grammatical slip against anyone. Yet it screamed insanity and not just because it was written in coloured pencil.

First thing I did was to call the Carlton press office. Bit of a bizarre inquiry, I know, blah de blah, but does Carlton ever junk print copies of the films it owns the UK rights to? Did Rank? Yes it is a strange query blah de blah, what are you working on? None of your business, blah de blah.

The next day she gets back to me.

Not a simple matter, etc etc. The highest standards are always applied etc etc. Great care is always taken that nothing relating to the British cinematic heritage now under the stewardship of Carlton Communications plc is ever lost or destroyed etc etc. The archive continues to be well managed in partnership with the British Film Institute etcetera etcetera.

Or on the other hand, she might wade in with: "Don't do it like that."
  "Do what like what?"
  "That like that."
  "What on earth are you on about now?"
  "Is that the way you do her nappy?"
  "What on earth is your problem now?"
  "The other day I found limps of talc on her bottom."
  "Look. How long have I been doing her nappy now?"
  "In all the nooks and crannies."
  "If you're not happy with it you know what you can…"
  "Dry her properly first."
  "Beth!"
  "And don't put so much talc on. You put so much on that it goes lumpy."

I wrote back to Danilo. I thought you might be interested, I said, to hear how Carlton respond when you ask them even the most innocuous of questions about the old films in their archive. And then I related an edited version of the conversation I'd had with the press office. A lighthearted version designed to win his confidence and further collusion.

Danilo responded by sending me a photocopy of a couple of pages from a catalogue issued by, interestingly enough, Trent Films. It was a list of titles available in "Super 8 Sound" format. The 39 Steps wasn't on the list. Attached was a note bashed out on a very old and worn manual typewriter, its letters dancing and jumping nervously. Raggle taggle lines of leapfrog characters.

Look. The 39 Steps is available on super 8 sound and is very common but I do not have a copy neither have I seen one in a very long time.

Later that day, he phoned too. His voice seemed very English, very upper class. Of a certain era. That slightly debilitated drawl. It was reminiscent of one-time Tory MP and Telegraph editor, Bill Deedes: a slurring here and there that made you think of illness or a stroke. He spoke in snatched phrases that were punctuated by a laugh that was a cough or a cough that was really a laugh. A sound that crunched like footsteps on driveway gravel. "Look here," he began. And then he went off on a ramble. He seemed to be implying that I was slightly mad and had in some way been harassing him. He was now telling me, in the nicest way possible, as you would a harmless yet comic eccentric, to go away. He was prepared to be firm, it seemed to me, but he was also prepared to have a laugh about it too. Whatever *it* was.

"It's available you know. This film. You can buy it. It's not anything to do with me."

"I'm not really interested in buying it on eight millimetre or on video."

"Well that's entirely up to you."

"I've been told that you have a 35 millimetre copy. Or know where I can get one."

"Look, I sent you the catalogue."

"But that's just eight millimetre films, isn't it?"

"What do you mean anyway, you were told? Who by, for goodness sake?"

"I'm not sure they'd want me to say."

"Well," he laughed. "I dare say."

"Please believe me…"

"You're one of those practical jokers, aren't you?"

"No. Listen. This is important."

"I'm sure it is."

"No please, it's very important to me. It's not the Super 8 version I'm inter-

ested in. I need to find a 35 millimetre copy. An original copy."

"Well," he said," a sudden coldness entering his voice. "Good luck to you."

And then he put the phone down.

And luckily I was on the ball because I dialled 1471 immediately and got his number. It took me ages to find out that it was the number of a public phone box somewhere in Shropshire.

I'm not entirely sure, even now, why I called him again. John Toby. Our last meeting seemed a very distant, dreamlike memory. The soured, electric quality of the night, its seemingly ragged crescendo and my spectral exit from the scene. It all seemed very unreal and improbable. I didn't even know what had happened to him that night. If anything.

I didn't feel any anger where John was concerned. Or Kate, if it comes to that. That's the truth. I was past believing, probably. If anything, I merely wanted to patronise him. To have the last laugh. So, he had ripped me off. So, they had made a fool of me. So, yeah, how pathetic was that? And if there was any thought of the money, it was only the visceral excitement that grabbed me every time I visualised him offering to pay it back to me, the money, because I couldn't wait to just take it and throw it right back in his face. £50 – or actually more like £100 because hadn't he cleaned my wallet out that evening?

So I called him that evening.

I got the answering machine.

I suppose, one way or another, I was prepared.

"John? John. I think the time is right, my friend, for us to have another chat. You and me."

Not that I was going to delay for one second. He would or he wouldn't, it was as simple as that. There was no point hanging around. He'd call that next morning or he wasn't ever going to call at all.

The morning passed.

That afternoon, I began checking out. I unearthed my overnight bag from somewhere near the bottom of the wardrobe. I put it under my desk; and over the course of the rest of the day, in a subtle and unobtrusive manner, packed a few things in it. Toilet bag, some changes of underwear and socks. Four t-shirts. That lightweight cagoule that had saved my skin several times now. A hand-towel. Toothbrush, toothpaste. Puny really.

I told myself that if I woke up early enough, I'd do it. Because it would have to be done properly. In the darkest of dark before dawn. Which meant of course that the odds were against it because I'm terrible at getting up in the morning. Even if I woke up early enough, the likelihood was I'd just roll over and go back to sleep again.

But something made me. I slipped out of bed and dressed in the dark. I was just bucking the belt of my jeans when Beth rolled over.

"Where are you going?" she asked.

I froze, searching for an answer. But she was just talking in her sleep and soon she had drifted back down, even further below its surface.

And I crept up the little flight of five stairs from the top landing to my little office under the eaves where my overnight bag was hiding under my desk. There was a red light winking in the darkness of my office. My answering machine.

Steven Danilo obviously. This was destined to evolve into the sort of game where he thinks I'm pestering him when actually the truth is that he has become a nuisance to me and my sanity. I almost left the message unplayed. It was sort of academic now one way or the other. In the end though, I just couldn't resist. I closed my office door so that not even a murmur would be allowed to escape into the rest of the house. Then I pushed the play button.

It wasn't Steven Danilo. It was Kate.

She sounded very mechanical.

"I'll be in the Camden Head tomorrow just after opening time. I can't get away for long. Please, please don't mess me around."

Which was ironic really. I'd be a long way from the Camden Head by eleven. I was destined for the six o'clock train. I'd envisaged hitching a lift to the station on a milk float. There is one, honest. Sometimes if you've had a restless night, you'll hear it, the jolt and the clink of bottles when it moves off and then its electric purr then whirr then whine, getting increasingly high-pitched as it builds momentum. But I've never seen it though; I've never been up that early. We tried to find out where it came from so we could get milk delivered but no-one seemed to know.

Anyway, I couldn't wait for it now.

I set off down the street, tempted almost to whistle now I was underway. I slung my bag over my shoulder and held it there in what I took to be a jaunty fashion.

There were no shady characters smoking under the any of the streetlights down our street.

No-one shot at me and I shot at no-one.

There's something etched and super-real about stations first thing in the morning. It's like being given a sneak glimpse behind the scenes. Another world somehow more genuine than the façade world of show and spectacle. A world in the raw. Here are early morning workers crossing with the night shift, the twilight keepers of the infrastructure. Here you watch stuff being shunted around that you wouldn't normally notice being shunted around because too many people would be in the way.

I bought a ticket for the first train to where I was going, which was a neat trick because I didn't entirely know where I was going.

Then I went looking for a sight-line on the place where the Guinness ad had been in 1935.

As if it'd still be there.

I missed my train in the end. Ticket in hand, I stood at the barrier, incognito, under cover, and watched it go. It struck me now that perhaps I had success-fully shaken them off, whoever they were. If indeed anyone was following me. They'd be on board the train, stalking its corridors, sliding back compartment doors and none-too-subtly scanning the startled faces of occupants within. That train would be crossing the Forth Bridge before they'd realised their mistake – and doubtless it would be too late by then.

I made a couple of passes of the pub just after eleven, first one way, then the other. Nothing doing. So on the third pass, as if spontaneously, I went in.

I ordered a beer, thought better of that, and had a coke with ice and lemon instead. They were still opening up, basically. The cleaner was still there, vacu-uming in the far corner under the biggest mirror in the world.

I took my drink over to one of the window booths. I thought Kate might approve – it was a table we'd all sat at many times in the past.

And I freely admit that the more you think about it, the more it seems to be a tall tale. Perhaps the tallest tale I know. The most epic. But it happens to be true – uncle Tom basically built much of the old stadium himself. The stadium as was. When he took charge, there was a big brick-built stand along one touch-line. Around the other three sides there were basically earthworks. Earth and cinder banks stepped into shallow terraces by the use of railway sleepers held more or less in place by iron stakes. That was it: one grandstand plus a huge staple-shaped, sprawling slag heap round the rest of the pitch. So yes, Tom built over that – he made it a proper stadium. Him and a handful of men. They fixed the overall structure, anchored it, then poured cement and stones. They con-creted the terracing, step by step, tier by tier, and they put in proper crush bar-riers. They dug drains (the pitch was traditionally a quagmire before Tom sorted it out) and they put up a scoreboard on the top of the main terracing facing the stand. A matchwood signalbox it was, on stilts. They cut broad access gangways in sunken diagonals up the terracing – a design intended to help the police and stewards because you couldn't see much of the pitch from down in these channels – so (in theory at any rate) people would be less tempted to stand in there, blocking them. Down in these gangways, each expansive shelf of a step was scored with hatchings and it was done crudely, as if they (Tom and gang) had done it themselves with a broken old bit of a stick. Which in fact they probably did. In some ways the effect was pathetic, in others, as you thought about it, as it struck home to you, it was truly heroic.)

Tom and just a handful of men one summer. A summer in which no war was declared and no revolutions took place and no monarchs died and during which there were no major earthquakes – but an epic summer none the less.

Of course the terracing isn't there any more. There's a cantilevered steel bowl there now – but fragmentary traces of the grass banks at the back of the old terracing still exist there, like carelessly preserved vestigial traces of a Roman ruin. An ancient boundary wall, say. Hadrian's or the Antonine. Accidental archeology. It all seems improbable now. Unthinkable. Tom and a handful of men building a national sports stadium. Maybe you could say there was a different spirit abroad in those days. A sort of fearlessness. It helped that he was trained as an engineer of course. But they didn't think twice about doing it themselves. There is something awesome in that alone.

He laid the electric blanket too. This was much later, because on this occasion, as you know, I was there. I was sat on Tom's lap on the tractor, aged just over six months or so, when he cut the first furrow.

Wires underground.

He'd never have to worry about frost again.

The real scandal was that, a couple of years after Tom retired, a big match had to be postponed because the pitch was frozen. Tom was furious for weeks. Barely able to speak of anything else. Absolutely livid.

So were we.

The whole family.

Absolutely beside ourselves with rage.

Somehow we'd been treated with contempt.

It was the sort of thing that might make you weep.

They'd forgotten to switch the electric blanket on.

There was one barman and the cleaner, when I arrived. The cleaner left. A second barman arrived. He hovered about behind the bar for a while, making desultory conversation. He seemed slightly distracted and vague. It was hard to work out whether he outranked the first barman – the one who was actually doing stuff. They were both in their late 20s and seemed to have an edgy, slightly spiky friendship. Was the second barman feckless and useless and thus despised by the first barman? He'd arrived just slightly late and had done nothing yet but although the first barman seemed slightly taciturn, he hadn't rebuked the second barman so perhaps the second barman was the manager or something.

Anyway, he eventually disappeared off upstairs.

It shouldn't have been a surprise when it came, but it was. People had been talking about the end for months; and to see him, as I did just the one time in their new flat, was to feel the full force of the inevitable. He'd made it (he was already in place when we arrived) to the armchair in honour of our visit and it was pitiful because he just seemed to be this crumpled arrangement of clothes in the chair. Clothes with this shrunken head perched on top. Within the clothes was, you suspected, a loosely thrown together collection of bones. His skin, what you could see of it (hands, neck, jowls), was sagging. It hung loosely. His face was alarmingly blotchy. The hands too. Liverspots perhaps but bigger like bruises and darker like melanomas. The oxygen tank had been wheeled in beside the armchair and the clear plastic breathing mask was never far from his face.

The oxygen cylinder was the hardest thing to cope with. This inanimate object. It was somehow more eloquent than Tom's deteriorating form. It didn't belong. It didn't belong in a living room in a house; in fact, it didn't belong at all in the story of uncle Tom.

There was something surreal as well as threatening and weird and just plain chilling about this tank. It was three or four feet tall – much bigger than the tanks that scuba divers take down into the depths, strapped to their backs. It was held in a cradle, a metal framework of a scabbard, and the whole arrangement had two little trolley wheels at the bottom. The tank itself was scuffed and scraped and dented and blotchily discoloured and there were glue-bound scraps of paper left behind on its surface where previous labels had been (more or less successfully) removed. It was chipped; it clanked. It was uncouth. It was industrial. It had a red crinkled wheel at the top to open and close the valve. It was the sort of thing you'd expect to see in a welding shop, not a house.

It had, I suppose a commandingly sinister presence.

I can't remember how long they'd been in that flat. Years, certainly. Sometime in his mid to late 80s he became too infirm to drive and then they really had to move from Golf Hall because it was too far from civilisation, or the shops at least, and Mary couldn't drive. And then, it seems hardly any time after that, his legs gave in and he couldn't walk; soon after that it was his chest.

One Christmas, maybe just after they'd moved from Golf Hall, it was distressing having to help him up the path to our house, me on one side, father on the other, bearing his weight between us, his arms stretched across our shoulders. Father had fetched him in the car and though he (Tom) had a wheelchair – which he'd brought, obviously – he didn't want to be wheeled from the car to the house. He wanted to walk. Something to do with pride and dignity as he saw it, I suppose, though, it wasn't exactly dignified being hauled up the path like a badly wounded soldier, his shoes catching on the flagstones, dragging and bobbling and scuffling behind him, head hanging limply, chin on his chest.

It wasn't much of Christmas actually. Mary fell (down the stairs as it happens: she flew) and gashed her leg too and we had to take her to Casualty.

When the second barman came back down again he was all energy and boundless optimism and chat. He checked the float in the till. Then he noticed that one of the upside-down spirits bottles in the optic row was empty. So he took down the empty bottle and found a new one and inserted the optic and put it back up, all the time making a great fuss about the fact that he was changing it and that it was he, not anyone else, who had noticed that it was empty.

They'd moved back into the city, obviously. They found themselves in a brown and flyblown district of 1930s era corporation housing in that curdled, indeterminate zone between the inner city and the outskirts. Parks and trees to the northwest, a clotted artery of a major road with all its fumes and squalour and its magnetic ability to attract rubbish, pubs and blood, to the south. It was not far, as it happens, from Murrayfield, but no-one made much of the connection between uncle Tom and Murrayfield any more.

The process by which they'd ended up here was absolutely typical. For instance, it took them absolutely ages to be convinced that they were going to have to move from Golf Hall in the first place. Which again, as it had been when they had to find somewhere after Murrayfield, was frustrating for everybody trying to help them. But strings were pulled once more. They were offered a pretty decent flat fairly close to Mary's sisters (my Nan and my other great aunts) who all lived in Corstorphine. But they turned this down almost out of hand because the flat was too pokey and anyway, they didn't like the precise location all that much. They persisted obstinately in this view even when they were told that they'd actually been remarkably lucky to be offered a property as good as this (it was ranked as one of the best the council owned) and opportunities like this one didn't often come up.

But no, no thanks, they turned it down. And the next one and the one after that. And after that. By now, a pattern was emerging. Each flat was slightly worse than the one before – though they all met the basic requirements of being on the ground floor with wheelchair access to the flat itself and all the rooms inside. So in the end, they had no choice at all. Our man at the council informed us with great regret that they had to take the next flat they were offered or they would be removed from the list. Then they'd be evicted from Golf Hall – and because they were now homeless they'd both be put into an old people's home. Or homes.

So that was how they came to be in a dreary 1930s tenement block in a dreary, dun-rendered estate in west Edinburgh. It was hardly a slum – and actually the estate (or their bit of it) was cleaner, tidier, prouder and more resilient than scores of other seemingly identical estates I (or you) could think of. It was one of those housing schemes with Metroland era town planning stamped all over it. The overall design was a nesting of concentric circles cut by four radials meeting at a central crossroads, which had since been reconfigured clumsily as a mini roundabout. This was where the shopping parades were – lining the immediate approaches and wrapped around the four quarter-facades of the circus.

I bet the plans looked lovely at the time. The original architects' drawings. I'll bet they were all sunny, with loads of warm pastel colours set off by brilliant use of awesomely pure white space. Lots of tree foliage, like puffs of pale green cloud. Watercolour blue skies. Architecture as confectionary. And we all know, or we should all by now know, that it never quite works out that way. In reality it was brown. That dun rendering. A light brown that's like a grey that's become discoloured. Stained. A pale, insipid dirtiness. And though in some respects it wasn't at all bleak (it was far from being a heroin-raddled sink estate), it was ill-favoured in others. The whole place was cracked, as if someone had dropped it, in transit, somewhere along the way. The dun-coloured rendering was webbed with fissure lines or in some places it had just plain fallen off, revealing great continents of decaying brickwork on gable ends. And it was always windy there, especially around the central crossroads. It was that special outer-urban wind that's specific to only certain parts of town; an eddying wind that was created by H-bomb tests in the 1950s rather than fresh-minted by weather systems out in the Atlantic. It's the sort of wind that takes whatever litter there is and makes it swirl and scrape but never actually sends it anywhere. Swirling, scraping, mindlessly, for ever.

Dogs roamed, solitary or in two and threes. They quivered as they shat on the cracked paving stones outside the shops on the shopping parades. Many of the shops were boarded up, the rest were protected by wire mesh screens or aluminium pull-down shutters that were cack-handedly tagged with spray paint.

On bright Sundays in summer (through which the wind still swirled fitfully) you could hear flies buzzing. Insidiously, every step you took across the estate. Flies buzzing. So it didn't look (or feel) at all like a town planner's blueprint. The pale dirty brown of the buildings seemed always to stain the sky.

And I suppose, as far as Mary and Tom were concerned, no-one really knew what to say. I mean, what could you say? That it was a shame? A shame that they were living in less than gracious circumstances. This great servant to a sport, a city and a nation. I mean, could you ever say all that? And to whom?

It must have been after twenty past before anyone else came in. Not Kate. Just someone.

I stopped watching what was going on behind the bar. They were no longer putting on a show for me and me alone. The place was connected to the real world again and I was no longer an embarrassment. No longer the solitary customer who must be entertained.

I was waiting.

I was anonymous once more. And waiting.

And maybe it was another of those instances where time plays tricks on you.

One of those instances where nothing, not even the curl in a thread of smoke rising from an ashtray across the room, nor the flush of a distant toilet, nor the creak of a hanging basket swaying in the breeze outside will escape you. A waiting that swarmed with ifs and buts and forked paths.

A ladybird advanced doggedly across the hammered brass of the tabletop.

My scalp crawled.

They had gone there to die. This would be their last house. We knew that. We all knew that. (Did they know that?) Their last living space. It closed around them. Tom was increasingly ill; Mary was increasingly senile. The kitchen smelled awful. There was stuff rotting in cupboards and (albeit at a slightly slower rate) in the fridge too. That which didn't rot was burned or scorched or boiled dry by Mary at the cooker. She became incredibly forgetful and empty headed, much to Tom's distress. There were many minor accidents, a couple of small fires.

But they weren't uncomfortable. The flat wasn't damp. Not in the summer at any rate. It all sort of worked. It had hinge windows in metal frames and some of them weren't painted shut, so you could let some fresh air in. They had electricity and an indoor toilet and hot and cold running water. They had friendly neighbours, especially a young (mid 60s) guy upstairs who'd do all sorts of handyman little jobs for them.

Actually, I think I'll have a tomato juice this time. No, just a tomato juice. One of those mixer bottles if you have them. And actually, do you think I could have it in a wine glass? No. Just as it is. Yes. In an ordinary wine glass.

The highlight of an international weekend was of course the party in the SRU bar, which was a pretty substantial function room within the main stand. The main bar area had (I think: I hope I haven't dreamed this up) an area dotted with dainty little round tables, each surrounded by four chairs, a bit like a night club; and (again, I'm almost positive) a small dancefloor area beyond, towards the back. Just behind the main bar area there was a private suite used by "dignitaries" attending the match as guests of the SRU. If you were lucky, the head barman would allow you to see (no touching) the Queen's signature in the visitor's book. And even to glimpse the private toilet, dignitaries for the use of. It was all extremely pokey back there, even the suite's main sitting room.

After a match, dignitaries would meet the officials and players of both sides in the SRU bar and then the dignitaries would leave and the players and officials would have another couple of swift halves before heading off to the official dinner at one of the swanky hotels in the centre of town.

All this time, Tom would be out securing the ground, making sure that the whole crowd had left the premises. Having reassured himself on that point, the sign would be given for the big gates to be closed, then everyone on the ground staff would come back into the stadium to begin retrieving seat cushions from the pitch. These were foam rubber affairs (about the size of a box file but maybe slightly slimmer) covered in red or blue imitation leather and with carrying handles so they looked like utility issue handbags. Or actually, come to think of it, colourful sheet music cases. You hired them for a few shillings to stop yourself getting piles from the hard old bench seats in the stand – and the tradition was, after the end of the match, to hurl them spinning down towards the pitch. If you were sitting down the front you could get a thick ear if you didn't watch out. Meanwhile, we'd be tucking into a roast chicken dinner at the bungalow and the air throughout the whole house would already be laced with whisky fumes and thick with creamy cigarette smoke.

When the official SRU party had left, early evening this must have been now, Tom would come and get us and lead our party, a straggling crocodile tripping and chattering and laughing in the dark, across to the looming shadow that the stadium had become, now a formless yet massive double density in the black of night. We'd always be right up there at the front with Tom because we absolutely loved this bit. This was a secret perk even for the adults, so for us to be allowed to tag along was doubly exciting.

This was our reward. Our reward for being… well, just special people who knew or were related to Tom. We were *the* people. There was a great sense of privilege. The privilege of those who see behind the scenes, the people who're invited to the party after the party. Who get a glimpse of how the machine works. More than anything, I loved entering the stadium again. It was awesome to see how the nature of the beast could change in just a couple of hours. Compared to the earlier hysteria that seemed to sing in its very stones, you could sense that the stadium's energy had dissipated, that it had worn itself out, that it was (in grown-up terms – I obviously couldn't even conceive of such a concept back then) almost post coital, warmly relaxed, satisfied, yet sadly hollow.

And there was a ghostliness to our ascent into the bowels of the stand. We went up the side stairs, past the back-up generators and the boiler room, somehow off the beaten track, semi-secret, stealthy; and as we entered this inverted city, this overturned battleship, we were aware that it was still in the process of being closed down. It was switching off section by section – so we moved through a labyrinthine world of light and dark: stark contrasts, pools of harsh lighting, stretches of purblind blackness. We'd cast shadows before us along corridors; we'd pass seemingly cavernous rooms, fathomless darkness after fathomless darkness; or occasionally a distant door would form an aperture of light, casting a widening strip of light across a floor. Sometimes we'd have to cross just such a space, feeling our way towards the next splash of light, our legs numb, our feet probing, landing hesitantly as we followed the nonchalantly surefooted silhouette we knew was uncle Tom.

Once he stopped in one of the partially-lit kitchens just along the corridor from the function suite and tipped us the wink. Then he stepped forward and heaved open the massive hinged doors that (as our eyes adjusted) we could now make out looming above us, like steel bank vault doors. They were the doors to huge ovens. A draft of warm air escaped, bearing a fatty, slightly scorched smell. Inside, we could see from the light of his torch, there was tray upon tray of mutton pies and sausage rolls. Surplus to requirements. Uneaten. Though the ovens had been turned off, everything left inside had baked dry and there was a lot of blackened pastry in there. We gasped at the prodigality of this neglected feast. To show willing, however, and as an early gesture against waste, we each, me and my brother, ate some sausage rolls and filled our pockets with pies.

And then suddenly, out of this harshness, this crudely lit (or lit hardly at all) factory-like labyrinth (cement floors, bare brick walls, rough cast-iron pipework, paint-smothered girderwork), you pushed through a swing door and you were, astonishingly, front of house. Linoleum giving onto the almost shocking luxury of a carpet, lights blazing as if they were never ever switched off, which they probably weren't. And suddenly you were in the impossible glamour of the SRU bar – part social club, part cocktail bar on an ocean liner, The Queen Mary, say, in its heyday. Brasswork shone, wood had a rich sheen, glass glinted. There were potted parlour palms, panelling, framed pictures on the walls.

The drinks were free. I had a tomato juice in a wine glass. The juice came from those dinky little bottles (the ones you had to shake to disperse the sediment) that seemed hugely exotic and sophisticated and almost decadent. I was allowed a sip of mother's gin and bitter lemon. I was even allowed to help the barman, John, behind the bar. I loved the fact there were two sinks under the bar. You'd never have guessed, so well were they hidden beneath the bartop. In fact there were hundreds of things back there you'd never have guessed about. Equipment with obscure and intricate yet vaguely glamorous functions. I wanted it all. I wanted in particular to take home all the bottle caps that collected in the plastic attachment slung beneath the mounted bottle opener.

So I'd help for ten minutes or so and then John would send me away.

And at some point the music would come on.

It was Jimmy Shand and His Dance Band. Or something similar. An accordion band playing ceilidh classics. Heuchter Cheuchter music it was called. I always thought at the time that the music must have come from a radio someone had turned on; but now I come to think of it, that seems unlikely. It was too loud, too engineered, too *right* to have come courtesy of an outside agency. So maybe there was a public address system and maybe someone played some records through it. Or maybe I was right all along: maybe in the late 60s on Radio Scotland every Saturday evening there was wall to wall accordion music. It's the sort of thing I would research if I could be bothered.

Anyway, there it was. Some danced, some didn't; but everyone heuched.

Cambleton Loch, I wish you were whisky.

They were the best parties. Even though we had to leave early.

I would drink you dry.

And in fact everyone remembered Tom's parties.

She didn't say anything. She just perched herself on a stool across the table from me. Jeans, boots, a burgundy suede jacket I'd seen her in before, a darker t-shirt underneath. Her hair was up, held in a simple clasp, from which it cascaded in a tousled mess. Plain, utility Kate. Cowgirl Kate. And yet something glamorous and compelling about her too, scarily so, like a sexier, more voluptuous Katherine Hepburn.

So, no, she didn't say anything. She had a carrier bag – one of those flimsy, rustling things that you get from corner shops. And from within this bag, she produced an envelope. Brown, A4. It was fattish, more a package than an envelope. She placed the enveloped in the middle of the table with exaggerated emphasis. Then she crumpled up the carrier bag and let in fall to the floor where it began uncrumpling itself.

And now I became aware that she was staring at me. I smiled – thinly, I suspect. "Can't I get you a…"

She was shaking her head. And then she had stopped shaking her head and she was staring me out. Her face was set. Grim. Set hard. But also magnificently proud. Something crystalline about her, like a cut glass swan. Or maybe something more gelid. An ice sculpture.

I tried to smile once more. But definitely no response. She'd succeeded in spooking me and now she was also observing me. Marking, noting.

"Kate."

"I hope you're pleased with yourself."

I don't know if I frowned, or if I did, whether the frown was genuine or not. I don't know if my heart sank or the blood drained from my face. What could I say?

"Well?" she insisted. "Are you?"

It was somehow easier to return her stare now. I was beginning to realise that I'd never liked her. Not really. When it came down to it, there was something fundamentally ridiculous about her. Something you always tried to forgive or excuse but which in the end you just had to face up to. I'm not sure it pained me any more to admit it.

"I thought I left a message for John anyway."

"Then it was just as well I got there first, then wasn't it?"

I tutted, shook my head, pretended to give a dismissive little laugh.

Which she was onto like a flash. "Don't ever, ever think you can judge me. Or John for that matter." It was said with feeling. Hard hatred, but with a warmth that you knew might just spill if she said much more. "I want this to be an end to it. Do you understand?"

I don't know why I nodded. But I did.

And then suddenly, with a litheness bordering on violence, she was on her feet. I thought for a split second that she was going to slap me across the face – so strangely, so intensely was she acting. But before I really knew it, she had reached the door and had gone.

For what seemed like forever, I stared at the package she'd left on the table. Then I snatched it up and came running after her. I stopped just outside the pub door. She was a good twenty paces gone, striding purposefully away.

"Is this it?" I shouted, brandishing the envelope.

I meant, *Is this all there is?* But I didn't really mean that at all. Not really. I was asking her something different. I meant what I said.

I went and sat down by the canal if you must know. The bit you can access down off Duncan Street. The bench on the towpath there is almost hidden by the fringe of this big old tree, probably a willow. The fringe is like a bead curtain or something and it's cool under there. I just sat there watching the world go by, what there was of it; and it was a perfect late summer day – maybe, in fact it was technically autumn. It was quiet; but now and again a couple would come strolling along the towpath, studenty types mainly, hand in hand, blissed out in their own little hermetically sealed summers of love. They made me vaguely nostalgic – but not for anything in particular, nothing I could actually pin down.

So I sat there for what seemed like hours. I'd never been aware before that canal water moves. Ever so slowly. Like the minute hand of a clock.

***

At some point I must have opened the envelope. It contained three photographs and three documents. All three photographs featured Madeleine Carroll. So did the documents. Actually, the *document* word is a bit misleading. One of the items was actually Carroll's obituary article, torn from a newspaper, possibly the Telegraph. And then were some photocopied pages from a book – a memoir or autobiography, probably. Some old buffer reminiscing lamely about his life as a gamekeeper of one of England's big estates, cranking out laboured anecdotes about the various members of the great and the good he'd had a chance to observe at close quarters over the years. The extract I had here was about how Carroll's first husband courted her during her visits to the great house. How he wooed her in the great outdoors. Lots of walks together. The sharing of shy intimacies in the crackling silence of the great wood. Her girlish giggles. The flush of her cheeks as a game bird, breaking cover, surprises them. It all sounds rather tweedy and bloodless.

The last item is a letter (the original this time) to the editor of the Times written just after Carroll's death. It's possibly taking issue with something contained in the paper's obituary because it points out that Carroll had, contrary to popular belief, lived for many years in Spain. The signature is illegible, but beside it someone has written, ever so faintly, in pencil: *a cousin?*

I thought vaguely about whether they, John and Kate, were still laughing at me – whether this was worth £100. Or even £50. And whether I should actually just throw it all – the photos, the clipping, the photocopies, the letter – into the canal. I'd throw everything up in the air and let it all flutter down in a shower. A suitably dramatic gesture. But instead I put it all back in the envelope. Still, I weighed the package in an open palm, perhaps continuing to contemplate the splash it would make.

And then I put the envelope in the overnight bag and zipped the zip. In the end I did throw something in the canal but it wasn't the Madeleine Carroll file. It was my train ticket. It had been bent double in my wallet; now it was unfolding in my hand – an ultra slim U becoming a round-bottomed V. By the time I threw it, it had almost opened out into an L.

It landed on one of its flat faces. And then the most beautiful thing happened. It kept unbending – but faster now that it was soaking up water – until its whole extent lay perfectly flat on the surface of the water.

And then it sank.

Chapter thirteen

And that's it, if I'm being honest. There's not really much more to tell. Not really. My project, seemingly, had been saved. The game was afoot. I mean, yeah. Obviously.

I digested the contents of Kate's envelope secretly, as if they were intelligence reports. At my desk, a pool of light from an anglepoise, a soft rain outside in the silence of the night, pervasive and insistent and saturating.

Three photographs. Firstly, a picture of Madeleine Carroll walking along a Southampton quayside, having just arrived in England with her husband, Henri Lavorel. It is taken in darkness, presumably (because the quayside is seemingly deserted) early morning darkness, the two of them walking towards the camera, both carrying luggage, and Madeleine has turned her head slightly to look smilingly, perhaps adoringly, up at her husband as they walk. Henri, who is smiling self-consciously too, as if they have just shared a joke, looks slightly down and to his left. The caption information, pasted to the back of the print, is dated January 9th 1947. It says:

MADELEINE CARROLL IN ENGLAND.
British-born film star Madeleine Carroll and her French husband, Mr Henri Lavorel, were among the arrivals at Southampton today, Thursday, in the 'Queen Elizabeth'. After a night in London, Mr. And Mrs. Lavorel are going to their house outside Paris, taking with them Madeleine's mother, who lives in Kent.

It has been stamped several times on the back. One is the stamp of the main Reuter's office in Fleet Street. Another says: "DUPLICATE SENT 10 JAN TO PROVINCES." Someone, at a later date obviously, has written in blue china-graph pencil: "NOT PRESENT HUSBAND." And still later, an ominously stark word has been stamped in magenta: "DEAD." To which someone has added a date, 10/87.

The second photo, this time dated 17th November, 1947, shows Henri

Lavorel leaning forward to shake the hand of Bob Hope. Framed between the two men is Madeleine, who is looking at Bob and smiling the same smile that she wore in the Southampton dock picture, but now there seems to be something slightly strained about it. This time the caption, again pasted to the back of the photo, reads:

Madeleine Carroll, who recently returned to the United States from France, where she spent part of the war and post-war years, introducing her husband, French war-hero Henri Lavorel (right) to Bob Hope, in New York. Madeleine will return to Hollywood to resume her screen career.

This time the copyright stamp is that of Planet News Ltd, 3 Johnson's Court, London EC4. Again there's the "NOT PRESENT HUSBAND" in blue chinagraph and the red DEAD stamp.

The third photograph is a head and shoulders of Madeleine. It probably isn't a studio handout – she's wearing a hat and coat and the lighting is stark. The smile is here at its thinnest. But there's nothing in the background to suggest where she is. In transit somewhere, possibly. Again it's from Reuters and the caption is part of the facing side of the print. It says:

CARROLL; MARBELLA, SPAIN – Madeleine Carroll, the well-known actress of the thirties and forties, died 10/2 at her home outside Marbella, Spain. She died of natural causes a local hospital spokesman said. She was 81 years old. She is shown here in a 1940 file photo.

On the back, that same red DEAD stamp and the legend: "RETURN HARMSWORTH PHOTO LIBRARY FILED 6 OCT 1987."

I spent hours with these pictures and documents. I don't suppose I saw much of Beth or Charlie at this point. Beth would come and say goodnight to me there in my office, hesitating within the doorframe before leaving, and I'd sit on in a darkness lit only by a pool of light from a desk lamp. Sometimes, first thing in the morning, while the light was still no more than a grey hint in the thin cotton curtains, she'd find me there too. She'd stand there in the doorway, her face pale.

"What are you doing?" she'd say.

She looked sort of shamed.

It was obvious she was spying on me. I needed to be more careful.

I wasn't at all sure what to make of the photocopy. It was of a page of a book as I've said and the author was a gamekeeper on the estate (a rambling, moated manor house in Herefordshire, extensive woodlands) owned by the family of Carroll's first husband. By all accounts they visited often, from their courting days before their marriage in 1930 right up until they divorced either just before or just after the outbreak of the Second World War.

Other times when I was out shooting with the Colonel and the other guns, when we come to a wire fence I had the privilege of taking my jacket off and putting it over the barbed wire and then picking her up and lifting her over so she wouldn't scratch her legs. She was nothing to life — between eight and nine stone, ten perhaps. I was strong when I was a young man. I was fourteen stone two; I could chuck a bull by its tail over a fence! [...] A very pretty young lady she was with light yellow hair, but whether it was dyed or not I don't know. I was five foot eleven and three quarters so she'd be about five foot eight to be precise. She always wore skirts but I was far too shy to notice! That was in the good old days!

One time, when she managed to creep up on me and take me unawares, during the middle of the day this was, I had to lean forward over the papers and photographs, encircling them with an arm too. I thought I'd done it ever so subtly but I think I might have actually drawn attention to myself because her eyes kept flicking back and forwards between mine (I was still staring intently at her) and the desk — as if, if she were quick, she might take the papers I was hiding by surprise.

When it became obvious I was determined to face her down she turned, almost reluctantly, and disappeared from the doorway. And then she turned again and came back and this time came further into the room.

Her mouth set itself as if to say something — then she thought better of it and left me to it.

No attempt had been made to tidy up the ragged edges of the obituary column after it had been torn (roughly or carelessly or hastily: I couldn't say) from its page in the newspaper all those years ago. The newsprint had turned a yellowy brown. It was a fairly handsome article – over a third of a broadsheet page. No picture though.

The more I read it, and I read it a million times with a dogged stupidity, the more I wondered about the fact that I hadn't previously been interested in Madeleine Carroll. Not at all interested. Not even in the slightest. She seemed such an insipid and stilted creature, charmless and petty, self-centred, crazy for reassurance. All-round hard work, in other words. Cold on the outside with a shrill centre. And I don't mean the character she played in The 39 Steps. Or rather I suppose I had always sort of assumed that she *was* the character she played in The 39 Steps. I didn't reckon she was much of an actress – I didn't reckon there was this whole different person behind the mask. I didn't reckon she was a worker of magic, a chameleon. What you saw was pretty much what you saw.

And yet her story is… well, it has elements of the unexpected.

She was married four times. Hardly remarkable for an actress, you might argue. But she was married to four incredibly different men. Their very diversity makes you see her in an entirely different light.

First, Captain Phillip Astley, who we've already heard about. She was married to him from about 1931 to 1939 (the wording of the obituary is rather vague). By then she was in Hollywood and after what is usually called a whirlwind romance, she dumped Astley and married the actor Sterling Hayden. They met on the set of the now forgotten film, Bahama Passage. It was his first big part. She was his first leading lady.

Hayden was an incredible character. You'd recognise the face but be hard-pushed to name any of the films he appeared in, probably because almost all of them were dismal and also because he was mostly in supporting roles. Perhaps the two best known were Dr Strangelove (where he played General Jack Ripper) and The Godfather (where he was Police Captain McCluskey). But Hayden had more going for him than your average Hollywood actor – he'd been a Grand Banks fisherman and a merchant marine captain before, rather improbably, getting a screen test. But he was never totally enamoured of the whole Hollywood thing. When he tired of the business in the 1950s, and following an acrimonious divorce (not from Carroll, obviously, he was married to someone else by this time), he bought a schooner and set sail for the South Seas. He took his four kids with him, defying a court order in the process and getting front page coverage in the newspapers as a result. He wrote a book about it all, called *Wanderer*. And in fact he also wrote a critically acclaimed novel too. But all that was to come later.

Soon after marrying Carroll, and just prior to Pearl Harbour, he assumed the pseudonym John Hamilton, joined the Marines and was seconded to special operations. He ran guns up the Adriatic to Yugoslav partisans and was then parachuted into Croatia to take part in guerrilla raids. He was personally awarded the Silver Star by Tito. In the process he'd become a communist, which, again in the 1950s, was to land him before the House Un-America Activities Committee.

While Hayden was fighting in German-occupied Croatia, Carroll was doing her bit too. Although she was in California, obviously, the war touched her early on when her sister was killed in the Blitz in 1940 – and thereafter she became desperate to be released from her Paramount contract so she could return to Britain. She couldn't get out of studio commitments until 1942 but meanwhile she had been campaigning for American involvement in the war and had helped raise money for the merchant marine charity, the United Seamen's Service. When she was released by Paramount she adopted the Hamilton pseudonym, joined the Red Cross and returned to England in 1943, crossing to France after D-Day. She worked with severely wounded men and stayed on in Paris as a Red Cross liaison officer well after the end of the war. The marriage, though, didn't survive and presumably the years of separation didn't help – she divorced Hayden in 1945.

So that's marriages one and two: on the one hand, an English army officer, lord of the manor, and, we must presume, gentleman; on the other, a thoroughly Hemingway-esque firebrand of an actor. The third was different again. Henri Lavorel was a suave and sophisticated Frenchman – an unlikely war hero despite the 1947 photo caption describing him as such. Does this mean he was an active member of the French Resistance during the occupation? Or did he fight with the Free French? Whatever. The obituary refers to him only as a film director. And indeed there are three titles against his name in the reference books. 1. The Plotters. 2. It Happened in Paris. 3. Voyage to America. All from the early 1950s. I haven't seen them and haven't a clue what they're about but it doesn't take much to read these as titles as autobiographical: the first inspired by his wartime experiences; the second by his meeting and falling in love with Carroll in Paris in 1945; the third referring to their failed attempts to transplant their marriage to the States. And their shuttling back and forward across the

Atlantic perhaps tells its own unhappy story. Again, the obituary is vague on this point, but they had certainly divorced by 1950. Because that's when she married her last husband, Andrew Heiskell.

Heiskell was, in his own way, as big a character as her three previous husbands, if not exactly as glamorous. He was a magazine publisher, spending the last 20 years of his professional life as the chairman of Time Inc. He was (perhaps still is) one of New York's great and good, devoting large amounts of his time to good causes, charities, foundations and other "non-profit leadership roles".

She stayed married to Heiskell the longest – from 1950 to 1965 – and it was by him that she had her only child, Anne-Madeleine. This is easily the most frustrating part of the obituary, for it is again extremely vague. "She had been a virtual recluse since the death of her only daughter three years ago," it says.

The tactics changed. She began bringing me cups of tea. She never brings me cups of tea. Not all that way upstairs. Now, though, I was listening for her, feeling for her presence, weighing the house's internal gravity. You can sense the intentions of someone merely from the subtle shifts in ambience – walls warping, breathing more deeply, densities clotting. But my vigilance was never really tested. As she climbed the stairs she would make sure she made a racket somehow – so I could safely stow the Carroll material. By the time she reached my office, clattering, chattering, exaggeratedly cheerful, I'd be staring at my computer screen. A word document. An article for Robbie on e-cinema, half finished, late now, very late, miles late, stupidly late – and destined to get no further forward than half finished.

I'd stare at the random collection of words on-screen while Beth put the mug of tea on my desk to the right of the keyboard. And then she'd make some small talk and I'd contribute a little in response but appear distracted, totally absorbed (supposedly stuck, searching for the deftest way to phrase some idea I had only vaguely grasped, mildly irritated that it kept escaping me) in the article I was supposedly writing.

"Maybe," she said one time.

And I pretended I hadn't heard this – this one word hook I was supposed to swallow. But in the end it drove me to distraction, this *maybe* just hanging there in that small, airless room under the eaves.

"Mmm?" I said.

"Oh nothing," she said. "Are you very busy?" But this time she didn't wait for me to decide whether I was going to reply or not. "It's just. I was thinking. What I was thinking was that maybe with everything we've become a little isolated. We've *let* ourselves become a little isolated. Perhaps if you just made a little bit more effort."

"Me? This is my fault?" I wasn't entirely sure what "this" was exactly; but in my anger I'd let that pass.

"It's no-one's fault," she said.

But no. Hang on. I'm not sure that's true. The angry bit. I don't think I was actually angry at this point. I was more depressed than angry – depressed at the familiar pattern this seemed to be following. I certainly wasn't angry enough to point out to her that actually it was she who had vetoed the whole idea of having a housewarming party when we'd first moved here all those months ago; nor did I advance the argument that this decision more than anything else had set the tone for anything that may or may not have happened since.

"What about your friend from university? Colin isn't it? What about him, for instance? What's happened to him?"

I can't believe I didn't smile at this. I slumped back in my chair and pretended to consider. "Colin? Yes, Colin. I haven't seen him in ages. I wonder what did happen to him. I suppose we must have drifted apart."

"You used to talk about your friends from back then as if they were... as if they were..." She searched, unsuccessfully, for something apt.

"Yes I did, didn't I?"

And I suppose at this point she must have tuned in to the sarcasm in my voice because she turned immediately to a new target, one she probably considered a better bet.

"But what about Jules? You used to see him all the time."

Jules. Yes... Jules.

Jules, I had to admit, was a bit of a worry. He hadn't been returning my calls – and almost despite myself I'd begun assume that he was dead. I imagined that he'd had a fit or something and he was even now lying sprawled across the teetering labyrinth of books that takes up at least a third of his bedsit room. (And I mean it really is a like a labyrinth – like the maze at Hampton Court except it's only knee high. I think he likes to be able to walk among his books – and it's a challenge finding a pathway through this clutter in the summertime if you want to open a window, which is usually your first thought when you enter

Jules' room in summer.) He was dead, help not having arrived in time, but he was remarkably well-preserved; and he'd remain in that condition until we burst in, having broken the door down, when he'd start decomposing before our eyes at an alarming rate.

Or alternately, I imagined that he'd disappeared in sort of spooky circumstances. Walked straight off the edge of the map. Not a sign, not a note, nothing. Mail would be building up in his pigeon hole down in the communal hallway of that Addams Family building he lives in. Lived in.

I suppose this scenario built itself in my head over a couple of weeks or so. And then, quite matter of fact, I heard through a friend of a friend that Jules  was not exactly dead but that he very definitely *had* been drinking. He'd actually managed to get himself barred from the Horse. Jules is one of those people who claims he's a moderate drinker and who actually *is* a moderate drinker. He's the sort of person who absolutely *has* to be a moderate drinker. Because he can lose it so easily. So easily and quickly and catastrophically. He can lose it even if he has a moderate amount but has it too quickly. He becomes both volatile and sleepy. It's an odd combination and you always start to sense that there's something very petulant and fractious just below the surface.

Jules has friends in Clerkenwell, people he went to school with I think, who drink at the Horse – The White Horse – almost every night. Jules is usually gently sardonic about the unimaginative routine of their lives. But sometimes also he shows them off – like he's proud that he knows these geezers (actually most of them work in the City and they're a strange combination of the oafish and the trendy) who colonise a pub from six till nine most evenings and often till all hours. But the point is, if it's true, for Jules to get barred, properly barred, from the Horse, he must have been going in there a lot and he must have been making a complete arsehole of himself on a pretty regular and consistent basis.

Which is not a good sign where Jules is concerned.

You get the feeling that Jules works within narrower tolerances than most of us; and that outside of those tramlines he is the sort who could just start to unravel. Needlessly. Really stupidly. He looks slightly frazzled, what with that dense weave of light brown hair that always seems to tighten and warp into intensely furrowed waves. That sceptical arch of his eyebrows, the sardonic way one corner of his mouth turns down, just a flicker, as if he's mocking you internally. He's highly strung. He has a nervous, sensitive disposition. Sometimes he looks startled for days on end. He has that sort of insubstantiality that invariably attracts bullies.

"Jules, I'm afraid, has been a little depressed."

"What!"

"He's had a couple of paranoid episodes, to tell the truth."

"What? What do you mean?"

"It's sort of unfortunate really. He landed a really good gig from one of the nationals. Then the day he comes to submit the piece they tell him it's no longer required. They've decided to revamp the magazine. A change in editorial policy or something. And then, to cap it all, he's been getting what he believes is hate mail."

"Through the post?"

"That's the orthodox method of receiving hate mail, yes."

"Jesus!"

"All it is is clippings from newspapers. You know those little response ads. *Ever wanted to write for a living.* That sort of thing. Correspondence courses. Anyway. At one point he thought it was something to do with a couple of really heavy geezers he met and sort of interviewed for the article while he was up in Blackpool."

"Blackpool?"

"It's a long story. These geezers were in the fruit machine business. Arcade stuff. And Jules got it into his head that, realising that they'd probably been indiscreet, they'd put a contract out on him."

"And have they?"

"I don't know, do I?" Jeezy peeps. Talk about stupid questions. "Do I look like a geezer in the arcade business? It's probably just some practical joke."

"What!"

"Yeah, you know, a joke. Remember jokes? Someone just pulling his leg."

"Don't be stupid." She was brimming with indignation now. "What sort of a person would even think of doing a thing like that?"

So, yes, the obituary piece says: *She had been a virtual recluse since the death of her only daughter three years ago.* And that's it. How did the daughter die, for heaven's sake? How old was she? Anything between 19 and 34, presumably. But let's assume late 20s, early 30s. (She married Heiskell when she was 45 or 46, so let's assume she conceived straight away – in 1950. Making her daughter 33 or 34 when she died.) So what happened? An accident? Illness? Does anyone know? The only sure thing is that Carroll took it very badly. What does "virtual recluse" mean? Did she become this overnight? Is that when she decided to go to Spain? Or was she living there already?

Why didn't she stay in the States? After all, she was granted US citizenship in 1943. And surely Anne-Madeleine grew up in the States. Wouldn't she want to live near her father? Wouldn't Heiskell want that? Wouldn't they all want that?

And why Spain anyway? Carroll (real name, O'Carroll) had an Irish father and a French mother. She read French at Birmingham University. She taught French at a girl's school in Hove before becoming an actress. She worked in Paris during and just after the war. She'd had a French husband.

Maybe the weather was better in Spain.

Marbella.

My parents used to go there on their holidays.

Actually, she lived in a little place just outside Marbella, called San Pedro. She was suffering from pancreatic cancer.

2 October 1987. It was a Friday.

My memories of the actual row itself are pretty hazy to be honest. I think the truth is that it, the row, took ages to achieve anything like critical mass – it ebbed and flowed all morning and at any moment in the early stages, the first hour and a half, say, it could easily have petered out and been quickly forgotten. A non-event. But I suppose neither of us had had much sleep the previous two or three nights – me because I'd been attempting to follow the Carroll documents to their inevitable conclusion; and Beth because Charlie had been having some really badly disturbed nights.

And it was one of those rolling rows where there's a brief little skirmish of really bitter sniping, ending with one of the snipers storming out of the room, delivering in the process a lethal, absolutely definitive parting shot (or, failing that, slamming the door). And then, five minutes later, the one who has just left will come stomping back with "and another thing," and it will all kick off again and now it will be the turn of the-one-who'd-been-left-behind-the-last-time to storm out, again probably slamming the door behind them.

And so, for hours, it rolled on from room to room, simmering always on the verge of violence. I can't even remember what had started it – except that maybe she had reverted to stealthy ways and had perhaps crept up on me unawares, me and my Carroll files, and I was probably dozing, less than half asleep, my arms spread across the papers on the desk before me, my head on my arms. And she probably really startled me – and I probably stumbled into wakefulness, ashamed now but not at all sure why I should be ashamed, and so, therefore, when it comes down to it, in the final reckoning, actually ashamed of the fact that I was ashamed.

And so it came to this.

Everything, the routine humiliations and frustrations and disappointments and agonies, focused into a few distilled drops of poison. It reached a stage just the other side of name-calling where some home truths are exchanged. Bringing me to the point, I suppose, where I make a great show of barely controlling myself, barely restraining myself from the use of violence. And on to that point where you hear yourself saying (out loud at last: you have said it a million times in the secrecy of your head), saying:

"Right. That's it. I'm leaving."

Inevitably, I suppose, there was a silence at this point. We were both white-faced with anger. And perhaps, now, at last, shock. Trembling shock. And yet, hadn't this been where were headed? Had been headed for an eternity now.

We were in the kitchen at this point. As I took a step back, for some reason I reached out behind me and felt for something I knew would be there on the table. When my hand encountered it it felt bulky and, in a lightweight sort of a way, substantial. It was a camera. It had packed-up a couple of days into our holiday – almost, in fact, on the first occasion we'd tried to use it – and I'd only just had it repaired. So anyway, I picked it up, this camera; and the truth is, at that point, I felt like cracking her over the head with it. I didn't though. Instead I found myself brandishing it in her face, as if it symbolised everything that lay between us. Or as if it summed up everything I was trying to say at that point. Which wasn't much of substance, as it happens.

I was basically swearing at her. Mindlessly. I was calling her names. She was just staring at me with that expression of tearful sweet hurt that some women have had perfected since time immemorial. And then she, yes, this is it, she said:

"Are you going to see her?"

"What?"

"Now. Is that where you're going? To meet her?"

This wasn't exactly new, as it happens. Right from the very start, since before we began living together, I'd say something innocuous like, *I'm just nipping into town for a while, I'll only be a couple of hours.* And she'd say, joking but not really joking: "Are you meeting her?"

"Who?"

"Her."

"What do you mean?"

"Your girlfriend."

At first I'd reassure her – that there was and could not be anyone else. That she was not to be so silly. But then, as time passed, each time the accusation resurfaced (as it was to do now and then, inconstantly), it began to seem genuinely silly. Very silly indeed. And so I'd learn say something breezy like, *Yes, that's right, I'm meeting her.* And sometimes that would be enough to underline the ridiculousness of the whole thing; but on other occasions she'd say, *You're only saying that so that when it turns out to be true, you can say you never actually lied.*

But this time when she said it, this almost routine accusation, I said nothing in reply. Not right away, at any rate. I walked the length of the hall and opened the front door. Then I turned and came a few paces back toward her. And again I brandished the camera as if it somehow bestowed authority.

"You," I said definitively, in a voice that was hard-edged rather than loud. "You are pathetic."

And when I left, I left the front door wide open. That was somehow more satisfying than slamming it. As I walked down the street, I wondered how long it would be before she would bring herself to close it.

So. Yes. Anyway. Here's a thing. The fact was. Is. The fact is, Tom wasn't even Scottish. That was the strangest thing I discovered after he died. Not on his father's side at any rate – I don't know anything about his mother. His father was a professional cricketer from Yorkshire, in an era when teams were generally made up of Gentlemen and Players. The gentlemen played to amuse themselves but they needed footsoldiers to do some of the dirty work, which would include ensuring they won the odd match. So they employed people who weren't half bad at the game. Professional players.

Some time after the 1914-18 war he was attracted north of the border to play for one of the Edinburgh teams. There was more cricket than you'd think played in Scotland back then. And indeed it's still true – there's a surprising amount of cricket still played in Scotland. So anyway, he came and he stayed.

For many professionals, it was a natural evolution to go from player to groundsman and he first took on that role at Inverleith, the ground used for rugby internationals at that time. And then I presume he transferred to Murrayfield when that became the national stadium. Maybe it was more complicated than that. Whatever. It became a family thing. Tom followed in his father's footsteps. He too became groundsman of the national stadium.

But it was weird discovering he was a Yorkshireman. Or at any rate had Yorkshire blood in his veins. Tom who was so passionate and proud about all things Scottish, not just the nation's prowess on the rugby field. Tom who got me interested in watching The 39 Steps because it was a "Scottish" film.

It was funny in a way. Confusing. But funny.

Almost immediately, as I walked, I became reacquainted with the terrible burden of the limitless. It almost bowed me down. I had to force myself to take deep breaths, great draughts that tended to end in sighs. And yet, as I continued down the street, I was buoyed by that hollow sense of freedom you feel when you've no particular place to go. I didn't hear the front door being closed. It certainly wasn't slammed and anyway by the time she might have reached the threshold, even if she'd half-followed me down the hall, I'd have been too far away to hear anything definitive. Not that I was listening really.

I suppose I must have got home just before midnight on the day he died. I wasn't exactly drunk but I wasn't exactly stone cold sober either as it happens. Not in the best of moods. Not in the calmest of moods. There was a message on my machine from mother saying he had died earlier that day. I was already in a hyper sort of phase – I mean generally, during that whole period of my life – but when I heard the message I was immediately overtaken by a demonic urgency; one of those squalls of insistent bloody-mindedness, one of those moods where you are absolutely adamant that things shall happen this day. Or this hour.

So I phoned my parents' house right away – waking mother of course. She'd only just managed to get to sleep after an extremely distressing day. As Tom's niece she had to take responsibility because Mary was long past being able to cope (and I know this sounds patronising and monstrous in some ways, but I don't think she really understood the reality of Tom's death). So I phoned mother and we talked for ten minutes or so and she was very patient with me. I know I will never have that sort of patience. We agreed to talk again the next day when she would have a clearer idea about when the funeral would be.

And at that point I should have gone to bed. But I did not.

I phoned the *Scotsman* newspaper. I phoned the *Scotsman* and I asked for the night editor. He came to the phone almost immediately and I asked him, arrogantly, militantly, if he was planning to do anything special in the way of an obituary for Tom Sellars, who had died earlier that day.

"Possibly," he said hesitantly. "Quite possibly."

If I'd been in a more stable frame of mind, I'd have been aware of the cautious reservation in his voice. I'd have admitted the possibility that he hadn't heard of Tom Sellars nor was he aware of any plans to run even the simplest and most modest of obituary articles, never mind some more fitting tribute to him. Whoever he was.

"Possibly. Quite possibly."

And momentarily I was gratified.

Then he began asking questions. Who was I, for instance, if I didn't mind him asking?

I told him who I was and then there was a bit of confusion when I tried to explain to him that I was calling from London, which he found difficult to comprehend for some reason. Calling from London at one in the morning about some old boy who'd died in Edinburgh? Preposterous.

But then he began asking about uncle Tom. And maybe it's true that actually I *did* realise he didn't really know what the hell I was talking about. Because I really started giving Tom the hard sell. His importance to Scottish rugby in general and Murrayfield Stadium in particular. And this guy, the night editor of the *Scotsman*, probably bored, on a quiet news night, sleepy, listened intelligently and asked intelligent questions. He kept me on the line for half and hour, maybe 45 minutes.

Or did I keep him? In any case, I was selling. Or pushing. I know this because I found myself offering an incentive. An *exclusive*. A collection of photographs. I hadn't seen it but I knew it existed because father had told me about it. He'd taken it into his safe keeping. All of Tom's photos, especially the ones pertaining to Murrayfield and the stadium's evolution. I was pitching this, pitching this hard, to the night editor of the *Scotsman*. It would be a great article, I said. It would enable them to do justice to Tom.

"Yes," he agreed with laconic enthusiasm, "I see."

He asked me to bring the photographs in the next morning so he could have a look at them.

I had to remind him that I was in London. But, I added, it was entirely possible that my father could give them to him some time tomorrow. Would that work? How should we arrange it?

So, the next day Father agreed to take the photographs in to the newspaper offices – though what with one thing and another, it wasn't until late in the afternoon that he was able to get there. The Scotsman building on its prominence above Waverley station. He was happy to do it.

The photographs were in a carrier bag. Most of the pictures were in an old crocodile skin album but there were quite a few loose prints in there too. There was no covering letter or anything – I mean, dad didn't have time.

I'd told the night editor the whole story. What Tom had done at Murrayfield. How he and a team of men had concreted the terracing one summer. His improvement of the drainage and the quality of the playing surface. His techniques for combating frost. The straw. The braziers belching a smoky warmth, as they are made to belch a smoky warmth in the most delicate of frost-fearing orchards. That word, *salamander*, in all its glorious resonance. His ploughing up of the pitch to lay the undersoil heating, the much-celebrated electric blanket, cable by cable. How it was one of the first such schemes in Britain.

I'd told my story. Father, I suppose, was delivering the corroborating evidence. The arrangement was that either he (the night editor) or his assistant would come up to reception and take charge of the pictures and, I suppose, make initial contact with father. And then they could take it from there.

But it didn't work out that way. Father went up to the girl there behind the reception desk and said he'd come to hand over some photographs to so-and-so (I can't remember his name now, though it's probably in an old diary somewhere, and I'm pretty sure father got it down right) and she phoned through and there was much um-ing a ah-ing. Then she told him that so-and-so had just finished a shift of nights and she wasn't sure when he was next due in. He didn't actually have a secretary. So father explained what the situation was and what the photographs were for and she told him that she would see that they got to the right person.

And so father left the carrier bag with her. It was a Safeway's bag, the flimsy, rustly sort with red-topped green livery on the side. It disappeared almost immediately.

Meanwhile, I was walking in ever widening circles. It was an odd sort of a day – overcast but muggy again, as it had often been throughout the summer. Something feverish in the mugginess too – it wasn't cold exactly, even if you were wearing just a t-shirt, but you suspected there was something at large, something in the air that might make you suddenly shiver.

Me and my camera. I took some pictures. Randomly, I suppose. Shopfronts, street scenes, weed-choked gardens, ragged edges of urban decay.

And then I had this great idea. I'd walk down Shoreditch Park way and take some pictures of whatever was still left of Gainsborough Studios.

And the thing of course is that just as I have some discarded news agency pictures of Madeleine Carroll, someone somewhere has a discarded newspaper archive picture of an infant sitting on the lap of a man driving a tractor. The man is in his late 50s and sports a small, neatly clipped moustache. The infant is half happy, half scared. There's a little knot of labourers in the background. Some are looking at the man on the tractor and some are looking at the camera. These labourers are all smiling, smiling mightily.

Someone finds this photograph in among some odds and ends in a junk shop and keeps it because there is something odd about it. Something unsettling, something that makes you stop and think. You'll lay it aside, unable to work out why it seems to exercise a strange power over you – and are therefore distrustful of it for that very reason. But you'll return to it again.

Its unsettling quality is maybe something to do with the fact that you associate tractors with agricultural settings. But this one is clearly in a built-up location. Those blurred steps rising inexorably behind, filling the picture's whole background. Could this be in some sort of stadium? And what's the infant doing there? Was everyone just fooling about? Or was this some sort of special occasion?

And also it's hard to pin down exactly when the scene is set. It seems positively ancient, partly due to the condition of the photograph, which is all faded and crinkled with blistered fold marks and in any case you don't get black and white prints these days. It's also partly down to the clothes worn by the participants, the labourers especially – there's something very unmodern about their cut. We're talking collarless shirts and high-waisted moleskins with a bit of old cord or a tie for a belt.

And yet, on the other hand, the tractor looks in fairly decent nick and it's not exactly a comedy tractor either. It's not exactly a steam traction engine. It almost looks modern. Modern era. Its shape is not unfamiliar – it's within evolutionary range of the here and now. It feels confident about itself and its place in history in the same sort of way that a Mini motor car does.

So you look at this picture and try to lay it aside but find yourself picking it

up to have another look because something is niggling at you. It makes you think. It makes you think in just the same sort of way that I often wonder what Madeleine Carroll is smirking about in the picture taken on the liner quay. Is it a private joke? Has her husband just said something he knows will make her giggle and embarrass her in front of the cameramen? Or is she remembering something from earlier this morning or last night? Maybe it's simpler than that. Maybe the strongest thing her look conveys is the fact that she's proud of her husband. He's just said something that is both witty and assertive. A reporter on the quayside has just asked a probing question and he's put him down in a hugely entertaining manner.

Of course, maybe it's none of these. Maybe the photographer merely looks ridiculous and Madeleine and Henri are both giggling about it but trying to restrain themselves because they're essentially trying to be polite.

***

I can't remember what time of year it was. Not for sure. But I can remember that I was seriously broke – behind-with-the-mortgage broke – which almost certainly puts it between Easter and Christmas of the year in question. I had my heavy grey suit on. The tweedy herringbone one from Hackett that I once thought was stylishly retro without being fogeyish. So I suppose the odds were that it was late autumn.

That morning, the morning of Tom's funeral, we all looked pinched in our suits – as if we all had shocking hangovers, which we almost certainly didn't. But there was too much aftershave in the air and we looked over-groomed and pale and not really of this world. We were strained. Strung out. There was a stuttering nervousness at large. A coldness that had nothing to do with physical temperature. A headachy coldness.

We'd driven over to their flat (was it still "theirs" now that Tom had died or was it now just Mary's?) because we were to be in the leading car of the cortege with Mary. We arrived there in plenty of time, so we had to stand around in the front room while Mary got ready. And we did literally stand around awkwardly as if we weren't family and had in fact just met and it would be rude or presumptuous for one of us to sit down.

And then father pulled a sheaf of papers from his jacket pocket. I thought at first they were banknotes but they were not. The little bundle was comprised of about half a dozen A5 sheets folded in half. He carefully, almost ponderously unfolded these papers and as he held the sheets out to me I sensed that his fingers were trembling slightly.

"Maybe," he said, "you could cast your practised eye over this."

I hesitated. I sensed a slight sarcasm here but I was used to that: it meant nothing, it was no more than nervous reflex on his part – a basically defensive need to assert himself in some way. But anyway, this sarcasm wasn't the cause of my hesitation. The truth was I just wanted to avoid anything that required focus. My head did not feel at all right. In any case, this was bound to be something trivial, a matter so spectacularly irrelevant that it would seem surreal. One way or another it was going to do my head in.

"What?" I challenged. "Now?"

He nodded grimly.

So I took the sheets and began reading. It took me ages and I didn't take in half of it. Words wouldn't precipitate their meaning or come together into sentences. But I was able to work out it was a speech. A hard hitting speech. A piece of invective. An attack on certain office holders of the Scottish Rugby Union, no less, for treating uncle Tom shabbily. For not recognising the worth of his extraordinary service, for failing to appreciate his qualities, for not giving him his due. Above all, for not extending him common courtesies when, following his retirement, he called to ask for the simplest of favours.

For acting shamefully. Meanly. Perniciously.

I recoiled.

"Is this for the crematorium?"

He looked even more grim, as if sick to his stomach with my stupidity.

"For after."

I glanced down at the top sheet once more. My first thought was that this was somehow unseemly. That it would leave a bad taste, that it would spoil uncle Tom's funeral for him, that it would leave ugly memories. (Anything to avoid a *scene*.) My second thought was that he had misspelled whisky. Whiskey. The Irish way.

I handed him back the papers.

"Well? What do you think?"

I shook my head once, puffed my cheeks, raised my eyebrows. "Are you sure?" I asked.

"It needs saying," he said. He sounded gruff, determined, set. A proud old bugger. And I supposed in that instant it irked me that I could never be any of those things. I recognised I just didn't have it in me – and in that realisation I felt small.

"At the hotel?"

"Yes," he said, replacing the papers in his breast pocket alongside his wallet. After the service at the crematorium chapel, people were being asked to a hotel on Inverleith Row where we'd booked one of the function rooms. Aunt Mary was in no fit state to provide the expected snacks, offer drinks and generally play host. So the hotel it was to be.

I could see it now. The extended family and friends, such of them that were left, a few ex-Internationals and a smattering of blazers. Committee men. Self-important men. Bronzed egos on granite plinths. The sorts of men that father's crowd had mocked in the stories and gossip they swapped out on the golf course. I could see them. And I could see father coughing loudly and then tinkling a teaspoon off the side of a wine glass to demand everyone's attention. I could see him stepping forward to excoriate them, to lift the flesh off their bones, those pompous little men in their blazers.

I could already feel a frisson running through the room as people began to realise just what it was he was saying. The cringeing embarrassment on some faces, the redness of humiliation turning to anger on others. Would this be accepted in silence? Or would father be cried down? Would abject members of the family, anxious to avoid any unpleasantness, plead with him to desist? Would they rise up to convince him that he was acting ungraciously?

These and other morbid thoughts made the whole funeral service doubly hard to take – and funerals really freak me at the best of times. I tremble – shake almost uncontrollably sometimes in fact – when I sense the coffin shudder and begin to move, to trundle forward towards the flames, from under its canvas sheet. And this is not a measure of how much I love or loved the deceased. It's just a horror. I don't know of what. But it's an extremely powerful horror. It engulfs me. It breaks my soul into a thousand pieces.

We couldn't get Tom's minister from the old days. From when he was an Elder of the Kirk. He'd died. In fact, they couldn't get a minister who'd known him at all, which became obvious when the address began. It was given by the new minister from the church where Tom had been an Elder. It made me sick to hear him chuntering on superciliously as if he knew Tom better than anyone and yet not managing to get even the simplest of facts right. It was thoroughly loathsome.

And then I was standing beside mother, shaking people's hands as they exited the chapel – a dazed Mary had been taken to sit in the big black undertaker's limousine. Then we set off for the hotel.

And as usual it was all a bit undignified – the limousine gliding past the hotel and stopping way up the street so we had to hurry back in disarray to make sure we were first there because other cars were already pulling up. And then there was some confusion as to which function room we were supposed to be in and we all had to hang about in the hall while they found the manageress. It wasn't a very big hallway. And more people were arriving by the minute.

Eventually someone came to see to us and we were led upstairs. Not every-one. Just me and mother. We went ahead to make sure everything was as adver-tised before anyone else came up. It was a smallish first floor room with windows giving out in the general direction of the Botanical Gardens. In fact you could see the very topmost sections of one of those new marquee-inspired structures they'd not long finished constructing. Pillars and spars and struts of that white plastic-coated tubular steel. It made me think (was this appropriate?) of the new(ish) stand at Lords.

When things got underway, I did the dutiful bit for a while, getting drinks and handing round plates of snacks. And then I went over and stood at the open window looking out. Not because I was being chronically wistful or choking with melancholy or anything like that. I just fancied some fresh air. But in doing so, I allowed myself to become trapped – because almost immediately I heard someone clearing their throat and I turned and to my horror there was this old guy standing right behind me wearing a blazer. He was not very tall, stocky in fact, grey, hair thinning, late 60s at the very least but somehow, for a blazer, not very imposing: he was looking at me benevolently, curiously, and somehow hesitantly before he stepped forward and joined me at the window.

He told me his name.

And all I could think about was the blazer, which obviously meant he was SRU – and I knew, I just knew, it was to be my fate to be standing beside him when father began his speech.

So I shuffled and mouthed air, which he obviously took for a symptom of overpowering grief because he continued, in an even gentler voice, to say that he assumed I was related.

Yes, I told him. His nephew. That's to say, great nephew.

And so this guy in the blazer started to go on about how Tom had always talked of us, me and my brother, and how he felt he sort of knew us a little bit. Every so often, as a little aside, he'd say how touching the service had been and what a creditable job the minister had done.

I hardly knew what to say to that. He had me sort of hypnotised. I couldn't get rid of him. He was talking at one stage about bowls and then about the Union Canal for some reason and then about bowls again. To me, though, he was an unexploded bomb; and all I could think about was getting away from him in time – yet every time he sensed me fidgeting, he upped the volume and renewed his determination to monopolise me.

And then it began to dawn on me. This wasn't an SRU blazer. I looked more closely at the badge. The Balgreen Bowls Club. He was not very tall. Barrel-chested. Grey hair, a tough, leathery, wrinkled face. Weather beaten. There was something dreadfully humdrum and uninspiring about him. He was talking about geraniums now. And how Tom was – had been – such a green-fingered gardener.

And the strange thing was that even though his barely modulated monotone made my heart sink, he was also making me ashamed of myself, especially as I began to feel the full force of the fact that he'd undoubtedly come here on his own – and he'd been rewarded for all his attempts at making conversation by a coolness that must have seemed like contemptible arrogance.

"Tom was a good bowls player too, wasn't he?" I said.

"Nay bad," he said. And then, after reflecting for good while, he seemed to concur with himself. "Aye. Nay bad at all."

And then I realised that people were already leaving. If father didn't watch out, he'd miss his chance. I tried and failed to catch his eye across the room.

"I'm sorry, you'll have to excuse me," I said to the bowls committee man.

Father was deep in conversation with a distant member of the family who I vaguely recognised – and when I edged my way into their space, he was much more distracted by my presence than father was. In fact, as father continued holding forth without missing a beat, it was almost as if he was deliberately ignoring me. So it must have seemed rude, to this distant relative at least, when I butted in.

"I thought you were going to say a few words?"

He glanced at me. Were his jowls colouring up with the whisky or was that a black look? Whatever. He looked sick to his heart once more; and when he answered, his words were rasped at me out of the corner of his mouth.

"None of them turned up. Not a one of them."

"What!"

"One of them was at the chapel. He slipped in late and sat at the back then slipped out again before the end. Ian Thompson saw him."

A brief appetite for violence surged through me.

But what do you do? Do you just tut and walk away? Is that enough?

I just tutted and walked away.

"What was that?" I could hear my distant relative asking father in one of those anxiously confused voices.

I can't say for sure why I didn't make it that far. To Shoreditch Park, I mean. I can't say for sure how the plan changed; or why; or even whether there was any sense of a plan any more. I can't say for sure, either, whether I realized this was turning into a farewell tour. I mean genuinely – as it turned out. I just know that at some stage I stopped heading south and began cutting an arc to the east.

Now and then I took pictures, almost at random.

Somewhere out towards Hackney Downs, I almost got into a scrap. I'd just detoured to take a picture of a dilapidated and rusty old railway bridge I'd spotted down a narrow side street and was walking back towards the main road when a couple of guys came running after me, calling, "Hey, hey, hey," and I walked on, pretending I hadn't heard them. But eventually they caught up with me and cornered me. They were both in their late 20s, a black guy and an Asian guy. The black guy was wearing a red silk shirt decorated with elaborate prints – tigers' heads, martial arts designs. He looked volatile. Volatile and spooked.

They asked why I'd just taken a picture of their car.

I denied I'd taken a picture of their car. I mean this was ridiculous, I thought – I hadn't even been aware of them or their car.

So they asked again.

And I lost it, I really lost it. I had a pettish, hissy fit, telling them it was a free country and I'd take a picture of anything I bloody well wanted to take a picture of and I'd been taking lots of pictures that day and I was going to take lots more. And all the time I could hear how pathetic I was being but I was also scared and the fear drove me on, though I was sure they were going to attack me (and it wouldn't take much to lay me out, I'd probably buckle from sheer terror itself) and they'd take the camera and all the time I felt how bitterly ironic it was that I'd just had the camera repaired.

But in the end it didn't happen. The Asian guy pulled the red shirted guy away – and though he was reluctant to go, giving me a meaningful couple of backward looks over his shoulder, he went in the end. I could tell they both thought me absolutely beneath contempt.

But anyway, throughout the day of Tom's funeral, my mind kept drifting back to that scene at his 80th birthday party. How could it not? Each time my mind wandered there, I cringed. And that in turn made me wish for the earth to open up.

Me saying to him, We'll remember your party now.

And he of course had heard it as: *We'll remember your parting now.*

That's the point. That's the sodding point.

The pathetic thing is that I was still speculating on whether anyone else had really heard the exchange, as if this calculation could save me. Did it matter that the one person who knew about it, truly knew about it, was now dead? And yet I was caught in a double bind. Or a treble bind. It made my head spin. The point was that Tom, because in all probability he had misheard or misinterpreted me, was not truly a witness to the scene in which he had participated. But that in turn was irrelevant because what I wanted more than anything was forgiveness and I couldn't seek forgiveness (presumed forgiveness, imagined forgiveness) because there was nothing to forgive. I did not say what he thought I said. I did not wish him dead that day, all those years ago, at the party to celebrate his 80th birthday. Neither in thought nor in deed. Not guilty.

The thing is, I'm not sure I worry about the fact that (apparently) he thought it even remotely possible I could have said such a thing. Because actually (and this is the sophistical bit) I'm not sure he really did think that. In fact I'm pretty sure that he was as embarrassed about the whole thing as I was. He was drunk, we were all drunk. Death might have been very much on his mind. Not that he was ill or anything – but it was after all his 80th birthday. And one morbid thought might have adhered to another and a response that he'd rather not have made might just have slipped out.

Or maybe (and this is not a possibility I consider very often or, for that matter, even like considering) he succumbed to the temptation of making a bad taste joke. Something akin to a pun – a joke-by-deliberate-misunderstanding.

I just wished that none of it had happened, that's all. Even if (in a manner of speaking) it did not happen. And it's true (whatever it says about me as a person): I really do wish I knew who else was aware of the whole exchange, brief as it was. Lots of people around the table knew that something had happened. They could see my great shame and embarrassment; and they could also see the mischievous savour in Tom's expression, a savour that had something in it of defiance, a defiance that burned hotly until the twinkle in his eye and the flush in his cheek faded to sheepishness.

So, obviously lots of people sensed the temperature change down our end of the table. But I'm not sure anyone else really heard, not with any real clarity.

"Who says I'm going anywhere?"

That's what he said.

Who says I'm going anywhere?

So, yes, one way or another, I found myself at Manor House in the early evening, at the tail end of the rush hour. There were still crowds massed at the bus stops at the top of the tube station steps. They were drained, everybody was drained, by this ambiguously cooler-than-body-heat day, the coolth of white spirit evaporating off the back of your hand. An anaemic day, fractionally thinner than blood. The sky was overcast, the light uncertain.

I stood at the far side of the railings round the tube station steps, at the junction's true corner, not really sure what to do with myself. That's where it came to me, the ridiculousness of all of this. The self-obsessiveness involved. The selfishness. The sheer preciousness. The self-deception. The vanity. I suppose that's the concept I'm struggling towards. Vanity.

So I took one more picture and went home.

Where everything was as it should be – except that Charlie was still up when normally by that time she'd have been in bed. Beth was cheerful. Hugely cheerful in fact.

"Here's daddy," she announced over and over to Charlie as I came in.

And it was true. I had to acknowledge that. Here I was.

I took Charlie off up to her bed and read her her favourite story, The Tiger Who Came to Tea; and oddly even that seemed fresh though I'd read it a hundred thousand times to her before.

And when I came downstairs again Beth said there was no need to cook, we could send out for a takeaway to be delivered. And we were both somehow light hearted and nothing more of any consequence was said the whole rest of that evening and I did not go up to my office and I did not study the Carroll photographs with an expectation that they might at any moment speak to me.

We were both cheerful and lighthearted the day after too. In the morning at least. Then in the afternoon Beth went out came back with Charlie from the child-minder's. As usual she sat her in front of the TV with a video on while she got her tea ready. The thing was, she couldn't find the Fun Song Factory video that she'd got it into her head Charlie wanted desperately to watch; so she went and rummaged back to the deepest recesses of the video shelf. Where she found The 39 Steps.

I was in the kitchen when she entered, holding the video case up for inspection and frowning. "Didn't we give this to your father for his birthday?" she asked.

I reckoned, on balance, this wasn't the right time to be smart-arsed, so I said, "No, don't you remember?"

She frowned again. Clearly she wasn't going to remember – but the truth was that *she* was the one who'd told me it wasn't the greatest present idea ever.

I thought it best not to make a thing of that, though.

"What did we give him in the end?"

"That food sort of hamper sort of thing."

"Did we?" she asked robustly, as if I was downright lying.

"Yes. Don't you remember me telling you what happened? How mother took me aside just after we'd given it to him and said that father doesn't drink champagne these days because it's too gassy. Oh, yes, and he was ill the last time he'd had truffles. And as for the cheese, well he generally prefers something less strong. Which left the gentleman's relish – and he wasn't at all sure about that."

"Oh," she said. "Oh." We were both still aware that the cheerfulness between us was forced and that our truce could hardly be described as fragile because in all reality there was no real truce. No formally ratified, multilaterally recognised truce. She considered the video case anew. "Weren't you writing an article about this or something?"

I smiled. "Or something," I said.

"Oh," she said again, putting the video down on the oilcloth on the kitchen table.

But I didn't want it to rest there. I smiled again.

"It's ironic, I suppose, in a way."

"Ironic?" She was beginning to busy herself getting Charlie's tea together.

Yes, ironic. I mean about father's present. My horrible knack of getting it wrong. The Nilsson single I once gave him? Looking for it on the toast rack that afternoon when I got home from school. That morning, father had been shaving when I gave him his card and his present. I went into the bathroom before leaving for school (steam, the smell of soap) and he turned from the mirror with his impossibly pure white foaming beard and told me to put them (the card and the present) on the bed in the bedroom, he'd look at them before he went to work.

The toast rack with its singles that wouldn't stay put. The toast rack on the sideboard by the wooden biscuit barrel (just larger than the barrel that a St Bernard would wear round its neck) with its shattered ceramic lining, shards of the stuff mixing with the other detritus down in the bottom of the barrel. Intricate metallic things. Keys, clips, safety pins. The odd pre-decimalisation coin. And a cabriole-contoured inset block (this a knuckle of wood, small enough to be enclosed in your fist, sculpted and varnished on its once-showing surfaces, a now-redundant glaze of hardened glue across its flush faces) that had fallen off from one of the dining chairs.

Stuff like that.

You'd put on a single and you'd stand at the sideboard, listening to it. It was a high sideboard. You could quite comfortably slouch against it, your elbows spread wide, your chin on its surface. And if you slouched there, nose almost against the stereo, you'd inhale its distinctive fragrance. The warm epoxy smell of naked, not-yet-dust-cocooned circuit boards, a volatile, almost glue-like smell from the casing's plastic mouldings, and the more rawly hot smell of electric motors and gently cooking coils.

And maybe (distractedly, dreamily, still concentrating on the music) you'd take the metal lid off the biscuit barrel and (distractedly, dreamily) look at the detritus in there.

My nose in the biscuit barrel, still thinking nothing of the fact that Without You hadn't yet joined the other singles on the toast rack.

Then, days later, the horrible truth. The fact that he'd binned it. This was astounding. This was dumbfounding. This was ENORMOUS. The mechanism, the psychology, the train of events, the cause-and-effect of this... all were of absolutely no interest to me at this point. I was just utterly amazed that anyone could throw away a record. A new record. A record that in all probability had not been played. How could anyone do that? Records were precious. Records were sacred.

He must, I began eventually to reason, have been very angry. The balance of his mind must have been seriously disturbed. But why had he said nothing to me about this? Perhaps it was more about disappointment, a classic case of More In Sadness Than In Anger. I could imagine him, slipping out after dark with the record (the bin was outside, under the kitchen window) and consigning all the hopes and expectations he had for me to a sad interment.

Hang on though. Wasn't that sort of childish on his part? Not saying anything? Sort of sulking? And doing something pathetically destructive and wasteful? This, after all, was a RECORD. You don't just bin records, I mean you just don't do it: even my little brother whose value system was as yet still relatively unformed and whose actions therefore were sometimes slightly less than predictable, knew better than to bin a record.

A week later, I gave father another present. That piggy bank we'd been making at art. You get a big blob of clay then cut it in half with a cheese wire, then hollow out each half. Stick the two halves together again and add smaller blobs for head, ears, feet, curly tail and so on. Cut the money slot. Paint it, glaze it, fire it.

Mine looked uncannily like a big blob with lots of other smaller blobs attached. It had started off bright yellow but that had already faded to a pale muddy mustard. I blamed (still do, actually) the art teacher for incompetence during the firing process. His name was Mr MacMillan, should you ever run into him.

And as for the film, the celluloid itself, the original object of my quest – the phone call wasn't quite the end of it. That phone call from the phone box in Shropshire. A rural phone box, I imagined, one of the classic old red sort, with flowering weeds growing up from the cracks around its base. At the edge of a village. More a hamlet than a village. When you come out of the phone box maybe you can smell damp earth and hear a stream gurgling nearby.

No, that wasn't quite the end of it. That phone call. Not quite. Days, weeks later, there was another letter from him. Or at least I must assume it was from him. It was in mauve coloured pencil again. And, like the last time, he'd used a sheet of lined A4 torn from a pad, but this time he'd turned it sideways and written, in somewhat shaky block capitals:

35MM PRINTS OF THIS VINTAGE WILL HAVE BEEN MADE ON NITRATE STOCK AND ARE UNUSABLE

I don't know if this is true. I'm not sure I have any intention of finding out.

So, yes, we needed to talk. Absolutely we needed to talk. I mean, yes, of course. And we did, eventually. Absolutely we did. I can't remember who was babysitting this time – it certainly wasn't my parents – but in most other respects it was like that time earlier in the year, when the summer was still young, and we'd strolled down to Church Street for an evening out.

Except that there was no Hasid drama this time – though I had an incredibly strong attack of déjà vu as we passed that particular house. "Do you remember?" I asked, stopping at the end of the path of chipped tiles that led to its front door. "That last time we went to the pub. There was a guy here who asked me to put the light out in his children's bedroom."

"Come on," she said, tolerably impatient. "I could do with a drink."

So we sat in the pub. We sat in a window bay of The Rose, with its faux Dickensian whorled windowpanes. We each sat behind a glass of beer. And it was strained at first, being out like this, in the community, in society at large and with just each other for company. We'd have to talk, we'd have to entertain each other.

It was she who broke the silence. "About the other day," she began.

"I know," I said. "I know. It couldn't be helped. It was one of those things."

But she shaped to begin again, so I followed on with: "You know what I did that afternoon?" And of course she didn't know, so I told her. "I wandered about a bit. And then I took a photograph."

"You took a photograph."

"Yes."

But the thing was, having got that far, I couldn't find a way to go on. And when I said nothing more, she set herself to steer this back, as she saw it, on course. So I stumbled on. "No," I said. "Hear me out. I want you to understand. Where I've been. Why I've been like I've been."

And at that point, almost miraculously, I remembered the way I'd explained it to Robbie all those weeks ago. "I sort of got stuck in the 30s," I said.

"The 1930s?"

"Yes."

She weighed this; the conversation missed a beat. And then: "That article you were doing."

"Yeah. Sort of," I said. "Or no. I don't know. Anyway, I went in search of something. I don't know what. But anyway, that afternoon, when we had that row. That afternoon, what I'm trying to say, I found it."

She was beginning to look disappointed. She was beginning to suspect we were back in Carroll country again. So I took a picture from my breast pocket. A standard postcard-sized print. I'd had it back from processing just that morning. I laid it carefully on the table in front of her.

She frowned, looked at it, frowned once more. Except that the second frown had a hint of a smile behind it. "I don't understand," she said.

Well, I mean, what was there to understand?

The picture showed a wall. Actually it was just a section of a wall. An inscription. A chink of masonry with lettering chiselled into it. The font, the design and everything was classy and the craftsmanship was first rate. It was up there, way about head height. It said:

Rebuilt
1931

That's all. A picture of one bit of an outside wall of a pub. The Manor House pub. Not that you can actually tell that – unless you stand at the Manor House bus stop regularly and have a photographic memory or something.

I went in search of the 1930s and all I got was a lousy picture of a pub wall. But she was laughing now. "You sad bastard," she said.

I don't know if the laughter was forced – mine as well as hers – but it's true, it was there. It happened. It existed. Then it was gone. She gazed out into nowhere in particular and for a minute or so her mind wandered. She looked slightly melancholy.

We had reached the heart of the matter. The heart of the matter was that Charlie might never walk. That was what it came down to. We might as well admit it. No-one had actually told us this officially, in the form of a definitive medical prognosis – but the reality (we were beginning to understand) was that a definitive medical prognosis was something we would never be given. Ever. It just wasn't the sort of things doctors ever did if they could help it. Somehow, without discussing this, we had more of less simultaneously worked this one out. More than that – we'd both moved to the conclusion that a part of the waiting was therefore over. We had, almost miraculously, cut through that particular knot. We had decided, jointly and severally, that Phase One was in fact now over.

In Phase One we had been waiting for a decision. A ruling, a judgement. And while we awaited that ruling, there was one thing we could take strength from – nothing, as yet, had been ruled out. No-one had actually said she wouldn't ever walk. And actually, maybe we deluded ourselves into thinking that the longer we went without a ruling either way, the better it actually was. The no news is good news principle. And in Phase One we seemed instinctively to feel that to entertain thoughts of the worst possible case (however fleetingly and provisionally) was to embrace the darker edges of pessimism. We had been desperately optimistic, unbendingly optimistic, zealously optimistic. Because to be anything else, surely, would be to tempt fate. It would also somehow be faithless. We equated our love of our child with a faith that she could she attain some basic abilities to help herself.

We saw that now. Now it was time to face facts. We had to assume, for instance, that the condition of her legs was not going to improve miraculously. We had to acknowledge the fact that, actually, she could not yet even sit up unaided. Or move a hand as high as her mouth. Furthermore, we had to realise that though they wouldn't ever admit this, the whole rest of the world had already started making certain assumptions about Charlie. It didn't mean we necessarily shared all of those assumptions – far from it – and it certainly didn't mean we had lost faith or had decided to collude now in an act of betrayal.

But for weeks now I had been outlining various scenarios in my head, working through the implications – and not just the material ones, the ones about wheelchairs and stairs, rooms sizes and layouts, corridor widths, access and transport issues. No not just the logistical sort of stuff like that. More the mind stuff. The story I would have to tell to myself of myself. My daughter is as she is. I am as I am.

And we were going to have to move from our nice house in a nice part of a city from which (supposedly) we derived a large part of our identity.

I told her I had been thinking about all of this for weeks. I thought about it non-stop when we were on holiday.

"Why didn't you say something?" She seemed sort of angry now.

I shrugged.

"We can't do this thing on our own. Either of us."

"I know," I said.

"I mean it," she said.

"We'll probably have to find a bungalow somewhere. Probably outside of London. There aren't too many bungalows in London. And I was thinking. You know that village we sometimes stop at on the way to my parents. You know. The one where we saw that white horse that time?"

She frowned. "Was it white?" she wondered.

"Yes," I said.

So, yes, absolutely, in that pub that night we made a start. A new beginning if you like. If that means anything. We talked. We revealed to each other and to ourselves the new reality of our inner souls. We were like alcoholics in a group therapy session. So actually it was rather neat that it all took place in a pub, really. The waiting wasn't done, perhaps, but it certainly seemed, that evening, as if some of it was now over. And maybe she read my mind because she said: "Do you remember that morning when she was having her operation?"

***

That morning, six months after she was born, when they took her away to saw off the top of her head.

When the sutures weld together prematurely in a baby's head, they have to be unwelded. But it's not merely a simple matter of opening it up and prising the sections of the skull apart again. They open up the scalp (the incision runs from ear to ear, up over the top, along the headphones line) and then they cut away a good part of the skull. They take it off like you'd remove the top of your boiled egg in the morning. The skull grows back again really rapidly, they reassured us. It is a long operation and a bloody one too – with children under a year old, a huge percentage of their blood has to be replaced. All throughout surgery they're putting blood in one end and it's draining straight out the other.

She was on a drip for what seemed like weeks afterwards too.

They spend an awful lot of time explaining just how dangerous this operation can be. They spell it out, chapter and verse. Diagrams and photographs available on request. The success rates are excellent, yes, but it doesn't pay to be under any illusions. Especially as there was a small chance that Charlie could react adversely to the anaesthetic they proposed to use. This was no picnic, no breeze, no doddle. Oh no.

She went in at nine. I suppose it's a cliché to say that you go numb. Numb and yet not so numb. We both felt frazzled, as if we had not slept in a couple of nights. The corners of our eyes pricked. There was an emptiness (an emptiness quite distinct from an actual hunger) in our stomachs. And we had time to kill so we went to a sandwich bar round the corner.

Beth had escorted Charlie off the ward, walking beside the bed as they transported it down the corridor; and she had gone into theatre with her and had been holding her hand as the anaesthetic kicked in. And the nurse, the nice nurse, our nurse, had of course led her weeping from the operating theatre as they prepared to begin. Nine o'clock bright and breezy, surgeons beginning the day briskly, as bank managers did once upon a time.

And we gathered up our stuff and walked numbly to the shop around the corner and I had coffee and a toasted sausage sandwich with brown sauce. I can't remember what Beth had but obviously it all tasted like ashes. And we knew that the operation would be three hours and it would be best not to come back until the three hours were up because, the nice nurse, our nurse, told us, the worst place to wait is on the ward.

So when we had finished our breakfast we walked and eventually we found ourselves at the British Museum. I'm sure we must have talked. We must have said stuff to each other during those hours, but in my memory it plays silently.

We went upstairs. Up many flights of stairs. And eventually we stood uncomprehendingly before glass display cases containing examples of the earliest known examples of writing, cuneiform writing on clay tablets from Babylonian times. We stood there for ages for some reason.

I think actually that if we talked, it was done in whispers. Unnatural whispers, the whispers of mentally disturbed patients on a day outing, whispers that are too loud, whispers that draw too much attention to themselves, no matter how hushed they are.

And it felt strangely cold in the British Museum. As if, even though we were inside, we were actually outside. Or as if someone had carelessly left a window open. A big window. We kept an eye out for it as we wound our way through the building, up stairs, down corridors, across densely littered chambers. We kept our eyes peeled for it, this open window. (Outside, we were aware, it was December.)

Of course we left the museum early. Well before time. We told each other in those oddly affecting whispers that we would take a couple of turns around the block and that maybe we would find somewhere to have another cup of coffee but both of us knew this was a lie or rather a deceit, a self deceit rendered twice over, once for her benefit and once for mine. And so we set out from the museum and without another word, without even a feint to right or left, not even a pretence that we were ostensibly in fact now looking for a place to have another coffee, and we headed back to the hospital, our pace quickening as we sensed it drawing near.

As the hospital building loomed and we entered it under its long-drawn-out perspex canopy, more of a covered walkway than a canopy, Beth stretched ahead of me. And as I reached the ward, she was already coming out again as if ejected by a revolving door, not that it had a revolving door, and she was shouting, "It's over, it's over," and I knew from the joy on her face that her words meant not that Charlie had died but that the operation was over. The nice nurse, the nurse who was our nurse, had been in theatre as an observer because although she had been a children's nurse for a good while and had even been a Red Cross worker out in the former Yugoslavia during the period of the civil wars, she had never worked on this sort of surgical ward. So as part of her training, she had to understand what they did, so she had been present throughout

the whole operation and it had been a success and there were tears in her eyes too. It was still almost an hour, though, before she, Charlie, came out of theatre and we were able to see her.

Beth went to fetch her and walked alongside her bed as they pushed it back to the ward. She held Charlie's hand and Charlie moaned softly as she began to come out of the anaesthetic.

For a brief period that morning, the waiting was over. For an hour or so, probably a whole afternoon. At that point, it was over. When she came out of theatre that time. We flipped a coin and she didn't die, which is the main thing. Pretty much the whole thing really. And maybe also it's true to say that what we've felt since has been a milder form of waiting because there is nothing more intense than true Life and Death waiting.

Afterwards she was placed on the intensive care ward for head injuries because of course she did have severe head injuries, it's just that the surgeon had given them to her. The comatose girl in the bed opposite had been in a car crash. Relatives clustered round the bed and took turns at holding her seemingly lifeless hand.

But Charlie was conscious, more or less. In a way, I suppose, she looked heroic. Immensely robust, funnily enough. The nurses would remind us of the irony of the situation in a jolly way that never remotely felt like black humour. "She's gone ten rounds with Mr Maunsell," they'd say, nodding in recognition of Charlie's head, which was badly bruised and had blown up like a balloon to twice its normal size. Her eyes were sunken within the swelling and maybe you wouldn't have known where they were at all if it wasn't for the fact that her dominant features were now a couple of real shiners. "They tend to come off second best," the nurses said, as if reflecting on one of the unfathomable oddities of the universe. "In the short term."

Mr Maunsell was the surgeon. The consultant. When they're consultants they're no longer referred to as Doctor so-and-so. They revert to Mister. Except it's not exactly plain Mister, you can tell that from the way the nurses all say it.

When you moved her, repositioning her on the bed to make her (so you imagined, so you told yourself) more comfortable, she rattled. She rattled because there were so many things attached to her. Life support stuff. Wires and tubes and clips and valves and probes and sensors. She was a spaceman, a scrap yard octopus, an embryo dalek. This cat's cradle, it all clacked together like dull jewellery when she was moved. Or actually, golf clubs – the sound was closer to the sound the iron heads of golf clubs make, clacking together as you shoulder the bag.

The thickest tube was a tube that fed right into the wound, right beneath the skin at the back of her head, beneath the sutures and clamps and stitching. It was there as a drain because still the blood seeped out of her. It kept seeping for a couple of days. And of course she was surrounded by towers of electronic equipment on trolleys – like the hi-fi and record storage trolley (black tubular steel, black shelving, very MFI) I had one time towards the end of the vinyl era. Charlie was right at the heart of mission control and we prayed that the world was safe in her hands.

"The referee had to step in. Sometimes I wonder whether it's much of a contest at all." That's what they said. The nurses. And it was funny. We laughed because we very much wanted to laugh, it was good to laugh, it was joyous to laugh and to be seen to be laughing, because Charlie had survived ten rounds with Mr Maunsell (a tidy mover, fast hands, dangerous when trapped against the ropes) and every minute she'd get stronger as her blood thickened.

And perhaps for a while we weren't *waiting for* her to become better, we weren't waiting on any outcome whatsoever, we were *working with* her to get her better. She was a fighter – she responded really well, even through the times when she was throwing up and was doing so almost impassively, with innocent detachment. We were no longer passive, that was the thing; and so for a while the waiting because a wholly different sort of waiting, hardly waiting at all.

This'll sound trite, I know, but the thing is that when they were opening up Charlie's head, they were also opening up mine too. They were lifting its lid.

Like it was hinged somewhere near the back. The occiput I think it is called. They opened it up and all sorts of things popped out. Some of them sprang up like jack-in-the-boxes and others fluttered out like butterflies, delicate and all trippy in rainbow colours. Some stuff seeped out too. It oozed out like treacle.

Sometimes it felt like a relief, as if there'd been pressure there. Other times it made my whole being feel raw and exposed. But it happened. It's there as a fact. It's simple and straightforward.

Which you can't say about the waiting thing. The waiting thing is difficult. The waiting thing is somehow beyond facts. Sometimes I even get this vague understanding that we are always waiting, or that waiting is always with us. Like some strands of it come to an end, yet there are always other strands and this thing is like a thick rope braided together out of many, many fibres, almost too many to count.

Eventually, Beth said: "Drink up. I feel like going back now."

And we both sort of woke up then. We stirred ourselves. "I know this will sound really banal," I said, "but when they opened up her head they also opened up mine."

"Yes," she said.

"Yes?"

There was deadpan mischief in her eyes.

"Yes it does sound really banal," she said.

I'd be lying, though, if I didn't admit that once or twice I contemplated pestering Heiskell. Carroll's fourth husband. Presumably he was still alive. The ex-publisher, one of Manhattan's Great and Good. Bet he has a huge house with wooded grounds on Long Island. Yes, I contemplating taking it on. Taking Carroll's story at least a couple of steps nearer a conclusion. Four failed marriages, the last one ending when she was 59 years old. Her only child conceived in her late 40s. And then that child dying three years before she died.

Heiskell is the lead. I could go to New York if necessary. We interview him. We ask him about the likely existence of memorabilia relating to The 39 Steps.

This was the story.

Yes. I admit it. I toyed with the notion of writing a really sycophantic letter to him. But then I'd only go and spoil it all by adding a ps. As in, *ps. You don't happen to have the handcuffs she used in The 39 Steps?*

I'm not sure that Robbie ever really forgave me. We never really talked about it, even that last time he rang.

No small talk, he just asks: "You got a number for Julian?"

And I go: "What? Who?"

"You know, your mate Julian. You know. We all met up that time in that pizza restaurant in Islington."

I thought for a moment. I was going to say something. I'm pretty sure I was going to say something. But in the end I didn't. Anyway, he was off again, burbling.

"I feel really bad about it. I lost his number and then I was out of the country for a couple of weeks and then I got back and then we were hectic and then what with one thing and another he kind of dropped off the agenda. But we're all systems go again hopefully."

I was thinking. Robbie was impatient.

"Er, hello? You still there?"

"Er, yes," I said. "Yes I am."

I gave him a number.

And then I thought some more.

So I called him back

"Actually Robbie, it's not Julian."

"What do you mean?"

"Jules' name. It's not Julian. It's Julius."

"Does it matter?"

"I would have thought so Robbie, wouldn't you? It is his name after all."

Robbie gave a little snort of laughter, as if to say, with a heavily sardonic sneer, *If you say so.*

The thing is, I was 39 when Charlie born. She is now three. Her birthday was in the middle of May. Father's is at the end of May. The birthday I gave father the Nilsson single for was his 43rd. That's the awesome thing, that's the thing I keep coming back to – he was older than I am now.

I didn't write to Mr Heiskell in the end. I did see something interesting in the paper that weekend though. Saddling Mahmoud. It was in one of the colour sections of one of the big Sunday broadsheets (and actually, it was just the sort of article that Jules could have done: it had just his sort of tone), a piece about a typical week in the life of Sotheby's auction house. Or houses. There was a

Saddling Mahmoud for The Derby 1936

9P

section about Sotheby's New York as well as London. The week in question was the first week in June, Derby week; and one of the highlights in New York was the sale of a painting by the finest British painter of horses in the 20ᵗʰ Century, a man who in the middle of the century was being disparaged as merely a "sporting painter" but

whose reputation had recovered sufficiently for him to become one of the most expensive British artists at auction. His name is Alfred Munnings. Sir Alfred. He's no longer alive, having died in 1959 at the age of 80.

Anyway, one of his paintings came under the hammer on 1 June. It was entitled, Saddling Mahmoud for the Derby, 1936. And there it is in the magazine. There are the two stable lads attending to the horse. And there's your actual Charlie Smirke chatting to the Aga Khan. It sold for $3.4 million.

The article points out that it was one of four paintings used by the Royal Mail in the design of stamps commemorating the bi-centenary of the Derby in 1979. It was used for the lowest priced stamp of the four, the 9p one.

She says: "And where does he fit into all of this?"

"Who?"

"Uncle Tom."

"Why, what do you mean?"

"You've been talking about him almost non-stop."

"Have I?"

"Yes."

"Really?"

"Yes."

"I suppose. I suppose I thought in some ways I was making connections. Tracing stuff back."

"Connections?"

"But. But maybe that wasn't it at all. Maybe that's never it. Maybe. Maybe the truth is I was just laying something to rest."

"Oh."

"Yes, maybe that's it."

Obviously it's true you can't choose the things you remember. With regard to uncle Tom's funeral day it was the terrier. A yapping little rat. At the hotel – the one on Inverleith Row after the crematorium – it followed the manageress everywhere. Or perhaps, come to think of it, not quite everywhere.

When me and mother got into the function room ahead of the rest, to check it out, the first thing we noticed was the way the chairs were laid out. Down the far end, towards the window, they were lined up in two rows facing out from the wall as if to accommodate a small but select audience to a lecture or a presentation or something. So that was the first thing we tackled – we immediately began shifting the chairs into more sociable formations.

That's when I saw it.

"Mother."

No answer.

"I think you'd better have a look at this."

I don't know why I thought this. She'd seen one before.

Under one of the chairs was this great steaming turd. Actually that doesn't do justice to it at all. It was a great steaming mound, freshly deposited, soft and very smelly. Mother left the room at speed, spitting venom. Her lips were pale. This, I remembered vaguely, was a danger signal.

She came back with the manageress. Roll of kitchen towel under her arm, plastic bucket in hand, terrier still in tow, this manageress seemed slightly querulous, obviously resentful that she was being harassed in this way. We were quite clearly snobbish folk hell bent on making a big fuss about nothing. There was a strained silence. Then mother sent me to stand guard outside the room with instructions that no-one, but no-one, was to enter.

As I took my stance there (best at ease like a nightclub bouncer, I thought, fists clenched at my groin), I could hear words being exchanged within the room. Not so much the words themselves. Just the clipped rise and fall of voices in a highish register. By now there were guests pushing further and further up the staircase towards the landing. Those who could see me standing there were torn between giving a brief, smiling nod in my direction and actually trying to talk to me. But I let no-one catch my eye – and though there was lots of chatter on the lower reaches of the staircase, the few who had been pushed up towards the top eventually took it upon themselves to form a respectful, almost reverential queue.

And yet, the longer this went on, the more awkward I felt. Sweat started trickling down my temples. I couldn't bear the pressure of not meeting anyone's eye. So I suppose I cracked. Slowly, very carefully, like Burglar Bill, I squeezed the handle, eased the door open and popped my head round. The manageress, who'd obviously only just got down to it (what the fuck had she been doing all this time?), was using the kitchen towel to scoop the bulk of the dogshit (and it was almost as big as the dog itself) off the carpet. Mother was busying herself at the other end of the room as if blithely unaware of the other woman's (not to mention the dog's) existence. Let's face it, she didn't even acknowledge me.

I withdrew and took up my stance again. It was a mistake, I know. Popping my head round the door, I mean. It had merely raised the stakes, giving added impetus to the undercurrent of tension out there on the stair: there was noticeably less chatter now. Which in turn made the sweat run ever more profusely. Which in turn forced me to open up the door, preternaturally sensitive to the creaking of hinges, a second time. And a third.

The second time I looked, the manageress woman had only just got down to scrubbing away at the stain with a rag. The third time, and was I pleased to see this, she was done and I was able to hold the door wide for her.

Inside, mother was opening a window.

By now the stair was thick with mourners.

The smell lingered most of the time we were there.

We'll remember your party now. There were tremendous parties in the SRU bar after all the officials had left. Heuchter Cheuchter music. Jimmy Shand and his dance band.

We'll remember your parting now.

At the end of the film a man dies. Mr Memory. He's gunned down on the stage during a performance. The hero and the heroine, standing side by side in the wings, surreptitiously reach for each other and, without taking their eyes off him, hold hands.

***

They, Mary and Tom, had a bottle made into a lamp base; and it was more intricate than most bottles-made-into-lamps because inside there was a tiny ballerina, two inches tall at most but rendered in exquisite detail, wearing a fuchsia pink ballet dress and with pumps on her feet. She stood up on her points on a little podium with a clockwork mechanism inside. It was elegantly constructed – the shaft of the key accessed the mechanism through a neat little hole punched cleanly through the side of the bottle. You turned the key and the ballerina danced. That's what I remember. Really remember. And also, Tom had built a home-made Chinese chequers board. The pegs, adequate but not quite uniform, were stained different colours. But there was a silver set. The silver paint was thicker, cruder than the paints used for the other colours. You never knew if you wanted to play with the silver set or not.

His bandy legs.

His dulled eye.

His cricket trophies.

The 1930s. The decade is a bungalow. That's the point. The real point.

Some time that autumn we headed out to my parents again and, just like before, we left the motorway about halfway and wound our way over the wooded hill. The trees were still rich in leaf, though they were well on the turn by then. The tree tunnel was somehow less awesome than it had been in the early summer, less like a cathedral nave.

Somehow we missed our way over the other side of the hill and for some reason I hadn't brought the maps. So we didn't make it to Nutwood again. We missed it – or maybe it missed us. We ended up at the horrible pub, the one in the pub guide. It was a great shame really because we wanted to check out the village again and find out if it really was our destiny.

Lunch in the pub garden was okay – though halfway through we had to gather everything together, balancing plates and glasses and a buggy and a small child, and find a table inside because it suddenly got really cold. The woman who doled out the food came round to see we were settled again and made a little bit of a fuss of Charlie and at one point later on I played naughty by giving her, Charlie, a tiny sip of my beer, which she really liked because she started making her opened-mouthed *ah, ah, ah* sound which is her signal for more.

Beth was a bit cross at that. She said we'd be arrested and Charlie would be taken away from us by Social Services and then I'd be sorry. But then a couple of seconds later she was giggling or rather trying to stop herself from giggling.

"What?"

"Every time I think of it, it makes me laugh."

"What?"

"You going out to find the 1930s and coming back with a picture of the pub at Manor House." We were both laughing now, me more in sympathetic

wonderment than because my funny bone had been tickled, particularly. And Charlie was looking at us in wonderment too, not at all sure what this laughter was about and whether it included her and whether she should join in. "It wasn't," Beth added, "even a picture of the whole pub, just a bit of the wall."

"Well… the inscription," I said.

We paid. We headed back to the car. And it became a bit of an undignified scramble to get Charlie out of her buggy and into her car seat and the buggy into the boot because a sharp little squall of a storm had come sweeping in just as we stepped out of the pub.

When we'd got in and battened down all the hatches we sat there for a couple of minutes letting drips drop from our hair, getting some tingling heat back to the surface of our skins and listening to bands of rain lashing the bonnet and the windows of the car.

"That last time we went to your parents."

"Yes?"

"It was your father's birthday, wasn't it?"

"Yeah."

"Are you sure we didn't give him that video?" she asked, frowning. "The 39 Steps?"

I was speechless.

Needless to say, we never found our way to Nutwood again.

I can't believe, looking back, that at one stage I actually contemplated taking Charlie with me on the train to Edinburgh. I can just see it. Getting off a train  at Waverley Station. I'd have carried Charlie in my arms and I'd have counted 39 steps up from the station towards the street and I'd have reached the 39th step and I'd have become struck there. Absolutely stuck. And that... well, that would have been it. End of story. End of.

All those months ago, the consultant, the one who was paged down to the recovery room after Charlie was born, the one whose first question or almost first question to us was whether we were related. That consultant. Well, in the days that followed, he said one thing to us that we didn't really take on board at the time.

He said to us, in response to a blizzard of stupid questions about Charlie's condition: *You have to understand. This is going to be a marathon for you.*

Oh, of course we nodded and made the right noises, as if he was saying the most obvious thing in the world – and the truth is we felt sort of offended, as if he were insulting our combined intelligence. But actually we didn't really understand at all. What we thought he was saying was, *There will be a painful battle ahead, a very long and very draining battle, and you will either triumph or fall.* Something like that.

But he wasn't saying that at all. He was saying something else. Now, I realised that maybe we were only just starting to get it. Get the point. And obviously it might be painful – but also maybe there were all sorts of things that I really wouldn't mind leaving behind. Now and again, I imagined what I would say if someone asked me about Colin – though it wasn't very likely, because I rarely saw anyone who knew or had known Colin. No-one from that era.

But if it happened, maybe I'd say something like: "Colin? Crikey, I haven't seen Colin in years. We sort of drifted apart soon after we moved to London."

Unless he called, of course. Colin, I mean. If Colin called, we'd chat, maybe meet up. I'm sure we could both pretend.

But it happens, of course it does. People drift apart. Lose contact. And yes, when I called Jules later that autumn, it was in the confident expectation that he too had moved on and had left no forwarding address. These days it's easier than ever for people to melt into the night. They're freelance, so you can't trace them through their place of work. They move on, they change their email provider, they ditch the old mobile number and in a blink they're gone. And maybe it was just as well that he'd moved on because if he'd picked up, I was going to tell him about the *Ashamed of Your English?* clippings I'd been sending him. I was going to tell him that it was me all along and that it was a joke, actually, and that he should just get a life and damned well see the funny side.

But it all went wrong.

"Er, um, ah, hello," he said.

"Jules?" I said.

"Yeah," he said.

"Jules." It was a long shot, I knew that. "Remember that idea I had? That article about coats…"